No Tricks,
Just Treats

No Tricks, Just Treats

Tijan

J. Daniels

Helena Hunting

Tara Sivec

St. Martin's Paperbacks

This is a work of fiction. All of the characters, organizations, and events portrayed in this novel are either products of the author's imagination or are used fictitiously.

Published in the United States by St. Martin's Paperbacks, an imprint of St. Martin's Publishing Group.

Previously published as *Eye Candy*.

NO TRICKS, JUST TREATS

For information, address St. Martin's Publishing Group, 120 Broadway, New York, NY 10271.

www.stmartins.com

ISBN: 978-1-250-21960-2

Our books may be purchased in bulk for promotional, educational, or business use. Please contact your local bookseller or the Macmillan Corporate and Premium Sales Department at 1-800-221-7945, ext. 5442, or by email at MacmillanSpecialMarkets@macmillan.com.

Printed in the United States of America

Swerve edition / September 2017
St. Martin's Paperbacks edition / October 2019

10 9 8 7 6 5 4 3 2 1

Contents

Fallen Crest Nightmare

Tijan

One

The pumpkin had a penis. I was sure of it.

I angled my head to the right, and yep—there was definitely a thick root growing out of the pumpkin's bottom. I angled my head to the left—still there. I wasn't sure about touching it, but then again, it was a *pumpkin*. I was pretty sure no swimming seeds were going to explode from the thick root, so I used my toe to tip it onto its back, and—*eureka*.

The root grew out, and pointed upward.

"What are you doing?"

I jumped. Heather had come out of nowhere, and I rounded on her. "Announce your presence before you just start speaking. You could give someone a heart attack."

Heather, one of my best female friends in Fallen Crest since high school, lifted an eyebrow. Her hand went to her slim hip. She gave me an "are you serious" look, but only pursed her lips and shrugged. "There a spider or something on that thing?"

In some ways, we were opposites. Heather had dirty-blond hair, a deep-throated and sultry-sounding voice, and heavily made-up eyes, while I had black hair and dark eyes, and I was pretty sure my voice sounded normal. What we did have in common was our slender build. We were both thin, though Heather had a few more pounds than me.

"Look at it." I used my toe to point at the root. "Does that look like what I think it does?"

She snorted, then turned to check out the rest of the pumpkins in the field. "It looks well-endowed. Give it to Logan. He'll be giggling like a schoolboy who got his first dirty magazine." She thought about it. "A schoolboy who doesn't have a self-conscious bone in his body."

I grunted. Her assessment of my stepbrother was dead on. Logan had a girlfriend now, one that was his perfect fit, but before that, he'd been the biggest manwhore since he was in high school.

Logan and I were in our last year at Cain University. Heather had finished school last year at a local college, but was up visiting this weekend. It was Halloween. It was party time! Granted, Logan tended to embrace it more than the rest of us, but this weekend was going to be one big Halloween party. We were starting with a girls' night tonight, and that meant no Logan—no guys at all. There'd be pumpkin carving, costumes, and drinks: lots and lots of drinks. Logan's girlfriend Taylor was joining, and so were two of my friends from the cross-country team. It was our night, and we were *even* going to gossip. See—we were girly. Gossiping wasn't our usual thing to do, but we were embracing our ovaries this weekend. I was fairly certain Logan and whoever he had in tow would try and scare us, and Heather would throw a wine bottle at them. That was my guess, but I wasn't really thinking about today or tonight. I was salivating over tomorrow.

Mason was coming to town.

Yes—him. My soulmate. Logan's brother. My other half. At the mere thought of him, I was already throbbing between my legs. Goddamn, I loved him. He'd been by my side since I moved into his and Logan's house my junior year in high school. My mom had cheated on my dad with their dad, and there was this whole family drama that ensued. So to say I wasn't happy would've been an understatement. I went a little mental that year, running for hours on end, throwing fireworks into my dad's car, realizing how much I hated my mom. I hadn't been the happiest at the thought of living with Mason and Logan Kade, either. I'd pegged them as wealthy and privileged pricks, since they were treated like gods in Fallen Crest. Guys either wanted to be their friends, wanted to be them, or hated them with a passion. The girls—well, I'm sure that's obvious. Mason was gorgeous. Tall, broad shoulders, slim waist, a body that was sculpted to perfection . . . and it wasn't even from trying. It was just from him being mouth-wateringly gorgeous, and from training for football.

They kind of adopted me as their family, and I became Mason's lover. I was his in every sense of the word, and Logan became just as protective of me. For a few years, it was the three of us against the world. There were others, like Mason's best friend Nate Monson, and then Heather, but it was always the three of us. And to an extent, it still was. No one could touch what we had, and tomorrow we were all going to be together once again.

Mason was in Los Angeles for a football game. He

was playing tonight, and then he'd travel to Cain on Friday. We'd have a full weekend together.

I almost groaned. It'd been two weeks since I had last seen him, and I wanted him here now, but . . . one more day. I kept telling myself that, trying not to count the hours on the clock. One more day. Actually, half a day. Maybe I could get super drunk tonight and that'd make the time go faster? No. Even as I half-entertained the thought, I knew I couldn't.

There'd be booze, Heather, Taylor, Courtney, Grace, and me. Plus pumpkins and carving tools, and I knew Logan would show up somehow. It wasn't a recipe to get blitzed out of my mind. I'd need to stay alert tonight.

"Sam!"

I looked back, realizing that Heather had moved on without me. "Yeah?"

She waved to the wheelbarrow she was holding, filled with pumpkins. "I got enough of these things for tonight and the party tomorrow. Come on, let's head out."

We had been tasked with collecting them not just for carving tonight, but also for a party that Logan was throwing on Friday night. He was partially doing it in Mason's honor, but also because it was Halloween and it was our last year of college. Logan was finding any excuse to throw a party this year. If I sneezed and the snot came out gold, he would throw a party to celebrate it.

I shook my head, making my way down the row to where Heather was paying for all the pumpkins. The penis one was on top.

"Really?" I looked at it. The thick root was sticking straight up. It had been pointing toward the air before, but now it was curved back against the pumpkin.

She grinned. "He's happy to see you. I wanted to make you feel special."

"A pumpkin has a boner for me. Special doesn't describe how I feel." But I was grinning too.

After the clerk handed her the receipt, we made our way back to her truck. Heather had offered to drive. My little Corolla had bit the dust that summer, and Mason had been letting me drive his black Escalade. He'd gotten a brand-new one as a present from his manager, and he was driving that in Massachusetts, where he was playing for the New England Patriots. For the weekend, he'd left his new one back there, and I'd cleaned his old one this week for him.

He kept asking how it was doing. I wasn't the only one he was missing.

She set down the wheelbarrow, then opened the truck's bed.

I grabbed that thick root and used it to put the pumpkin into the back of the truck. Moving to grab the next one, I asked, "What's the plan tonight?"

Heather was helping, grabbing for her second one too. "Logan's party is at the other house, right?"

I nodded. "He's renting it. He didn't want to do damage to ours."

"Okay. So, yes. We drop the pumpkins we want at your house, then drop the rest off at the one he's renting. I figure we can keep six for us. Five girls. Maybe an extra for Logan to carve tomorrow, or tonight if he crashes girls' night." She shrugged. "Or hell, we can just have one on hand for him to smash if he wants."

That was good thinking.

"Is Channing coming up tomorrow night?" I grabbed for my eighth pumpkin. We were halfway done.

She grabbed two at a time, placing them gently in the truck. She grunted from the effort, then repeated the process. "Yeah. He's coming up, but more to see Mason than me."

She bit off her sentence, and I frowned. I reached for another two, but I was a wimp. She was grunting from grabbing the bigger pumpkins. I grabbed two small ones. "That bad? Something going on with you two?"

Mason, Logan, and I had grown up in Fallen Crest, a small town on the northern coast of California. Heather still lived in Fallen Crest, which was a full three-hour drive from Cain University. In high school she'd always managed her father's bar and grill, Manny's, and now she was running it full-time. Her boyfriend, or on-and-off-again boyfriend, Channing, lived there too. Well, he lived close by in Roussou, Fallen Crest's rival, a neighboring town that was further inland.

Fallen Crest was filled with middle- to upper-class families, with a huge proportion of millionaires and billionaires. Roussou was mostly blue-collar families, and for some reason, the people from that town were rough and tough. Mason and Logan had tangled with some of them on more than one occasion, and most times the end result was spilled blood—if they were lucky. I suppressed a shiver. There'd been a couple of times I felt like I'd gotten out of Roussou with my life barely intact. But Channing ran his own bar in the town, and he'd become friendly with Mason and Logan because of my friendship with Heather.

He was the sunrise-and-sunset type of love for her, which, seeing that she still hadn't answered my questions, spoke volumes.

We had three pumpkins left, and I stilled. "I'm sorry."

She swallowed, looking pained, and shrugged a shoulder. "It's . . . whatever." She grabbed the last three and tossed them roughly onto the pile. As she took the wheelbarrow away, I ran a hand over the three pumpkins. All were still intact, but I cast a worried glance at my friend.

She was the toughest girl I knew. She rarely showed when she was angry, and my stomach sank.

This wasn't good. Not at all.

She bypassed me, her long legs keeping a brisk pace. "Come on. The quicker we get to drinking, the better."

I hopped in the passenger seat, threw my seat belt on, and sat back. She peeled out of the parking lot, and I had a feeling tonight was going to be worse than I had imagined.

Two

Heather was just as brisk when we pulled up to Logan's party house. He and his friends were turning it into a haunted house. Word had already spread around campus, and I knew half the school would be attending. It was going to be huge. A Logan Kade party, plus the fact that Mason Kade was going to be there, meant only a social recluse would want to miss out.

I wasn't going to let Mason out of my sight the whole time he was here. He'd moved to Massachusetts in June. It was now the end of October. I'd spent most of the summer there, but cross-country had taken every weekend from me. I flew out there on random overnight trips, but it wasn't enough. It never was. I didn't care if Logan was hoping for some brotherly bonding time, or if the guys wanted to do something just for the guys. It wasn't happening.

"Yo!"

Logan came out of the front door, down the steps, and over to the truck. His hair was messy, but he ran a hand through it, shaking it out, and I knew he'd left it that way on purpose. It suited him. His dark eyes were almost gleaming from whatever he'd been planning, but the look waned when Heather ignored his greeting and started unloading the pumpkins on the front lawn.

He slowed to a stop, his eyes finding mine with an unspoken question in them.

I shrugged. I knew what was wrong with Heather, but I didn't have to say anything. Logan was smart. He'd figure it out as soon as he saw Channing tomorrow night, if not before. With Heather in this mood, and knowing Logan was generally an in-your-face kind of guy, I was more worried the two would get into a fight tonight. I saw all the tequila she had stored in the back seat for later.

"Hey." I gestured to the house. "It looks great already. Good spot for a haunted house party."

He glanced back, shoving his hands into his pockets. "I thought so too." I heard the pride in his voice. "Saw this place driving around one night, and got a realtor to look into it. The owners were thinking of renovating it, but I twisted their arm." He grinned at me. "Everything's sound, so no one will be falling through the floors or anything."

I considered the three-story house. It was old. So much of the white paint was scraped off that it looked like it had been intended to be a black house, and the front walkway was so cracked, only a few of the slabs were still there. The rest was grass that had grown out and over the remaining rocks. As long as it was safe, I guessed I didn't care. "No cockroaches?"

He shook his head. "They had it inspected. No mold either."

Heather stopped for a second and looked at the house too. "Just spiders . . . and a few rats, I'm sure." Her gaze swept to Logan at the last word and she lingered a moment before turning back for more pumpkins.

Logan's eyes narrowed. His mouth firmed in a line. "What's your problem? I haven't done shit to you." His hands came out, and he crossed his arms over his chest.

She paused, reaching back into the truck's bed, and her eyes jumped to mine. I saw regret before she grumbled out, "Nothing." Her hand closed around the pumpkin and it was soon placed in the pile with the others.

Logan opened his mouth. I knew he wasn't going to say anything nice, so I jumped forward. "Hey," I suggested to Heather, "you can take a break. We'll finish the rest."

Her eyes darkened, but I saw the relief in them even though her shoulders remained rigid. "Thank you. I think I will." She ignored Logan, digging into her pockets as she headed for the sidewalk by the road.

Logan watched her go, his jaw clenching for a moment. "What's her problem?" His eyes swung back to mine, dark and angry. "She just took a shot at me, and I haven't done anything to earn it." He lightened his tone, a crooked grin showing. "Now, if I've done something against her, then have at it. I'd apologize for being a dick."

I waved him off, leaning in for the rest of the pumpkins. "Don't worry. I don't think it was actually meant toward you."

His eyes were studying me, and a second later, he nodded. "Got it." He walked over to where Heather had been standing and took four pumpkins at once. "Her and Channing must be fighting?" He didn't wait for an answer, but took the pumpkins to the front porch and disappeared inside. A second later he hollered, "PUMPKINS ARE OUTSIDE! COME AND HELP BRING 'EM IN!"

A line of guys came out. No one questioned him. No one barked back. No one even looked like they considered not doing what he ordered. They all just came out, one by one, picked up a pumpkin from the pile in the yard, and carried them inside. I had the last two in my arms, but one of the guys moved to grab them from me. He paused when he realized he would be grabbing where he shouldn't, and flashed an apologetic grin. "Sorry. I'll take them in, if that's okay."

I nodded slowly and held them out one at a time. He scooped them up, and soon all the pumpkins were gone. Remembering our own for the night, I whirled around. Three guys were reaching for the last pile and I held my hand out. "Stop! Leave six of them for us. Those are for us."

"Oh." All of them paused, then one counted the remaining pumpkins, and pointed to the two already being held. "Just put those two back. Leave the four in the truck."

Logan had come back to stand next to me, and he waited till everyone went inside. Heather was sitting on the curb, the smoke from her cigarette wafting in the air. She was resting her hand next to her, her cigarette pointing upward, until she took a drag from it.

"She looks ready to rip into anyone with genitals."

I gave him a look.

He corrected himself. "Anyone with a dick and balls."

I nodded. "Sounds about right." I clapped him on the arm. "Looks like you've got it all taken care of. It's girls' night tonight. We're at our house. That means you're not."

"Oh yeah." He snorted, raking a hand through his hair again. "I'm staying at a friend's."

I understood his dilemma. Taylor would sleep at our house, where they usually stayed, but she didn't live full-time with us. She might as well have, because she slept there almost every night, but her place of residence was still technically her father's. Unlike the rest of us, who had moved here for school, Taylor had moved back to Cain after a gruesome end to two years at her first college. Her father was one of the football coaches for Cain University, a D1-league school, and he was a big deal. Known for being wild and yelling at the games, her dad got the nickname Coach Broozer, but he was just "Bruce" or "Taylor's dad" to the rest of us.

I smirked. "I figured you'd sneak in tonight at some point."

"Nope." He grinned. "It's a girls' house tonight. I'm respecting it. The guys and I are going to watch Mason's game tonight anyways. We thought about driving down, but we'll see him tomorrow. It's not like we don't go to any of his games."

I knew what he meant. I hadn't been able to see that many because of my training, but I just had one more year and then I could see all the games I wanted. But that was me, not Logan. He'd been to a bunch of Mason's games, and this weekend was all about the Halloween festivities.

I remarked, "Maybe I'll see if I can put it on in the background tonight."

"Either way, you guys will have fun." He turned back to studying Heather again. "Looks like she'll need some female friends tonight."

"Channing's coming tomorrow night."

"I know."

I frowned at his wry tone. "You know something I don't?"

"Nope."

My frown deepened. His response was quick—too quick—and he moved a little so he wasn't facing me anymore. "Out with it," I said. "Now."

"Sam."

"Now."

He sighed, rolling his eyes. "You're a pain in the ass."

"I'm your stepsister, and future sister-in-law, so you have to tell me. Family loyalty."

He snorted. "That's what we're calling it?"

I knew what he meant. Mason, Logan, and me. It was the three of us, always and forever. I softened my tone. "Come on. Tell me."

"Like you were going to tell me, right?" But I heard the surrender in his voice. He was going to spill the details. "Channing called Mason last night, and Mason called me. He wanted to know if Heather was coming to the party tomorrow night, wasn't sure that he'd come if she was."

"What?" I was fighting not to let my jaw drop. Channing and Heather fought, but this sounded like it was on a whole other level.

"He broke it off with her, something about his sister."

I went back to frowning. Heather had mentioned his sister, and some problems with her last year. "I thought all of that was done."

"Who knows. Neither of them really confide in us, right?" He was eyeing me, and I moved my head in acknowledgment. It wasn't that Heather didn't trust me, it was just that neither of us really talked about our issues. If something happened, we dealt with it. If we had to cry, we did. If we needed to get drunk to take our mind off things, we did that too. If we needed to go dancing to help keep things at bay, it was known to happen. Heather had been there for me during a bad time last year, and if she needed to talk, she knew I'd be there for her too. We fought for each other, but we just weren't the type of friends to sit and spill our guts—not unless we really needed to do it or it'd literally rip us apart.

Heather had lit a second cigarette, but I knew what we needed to do tonight.

"Okay," I said to Logan. "If you had plans to scare us tonight, don't." My eyes were on Heather as I kept talking. "This might turn out to be a Ninja Sam night or a Dancing Sam night."

I heard him chuckle. "Those nights are fun. The reasoning behind them, not so much, but the actual drunken Sam moments . . ." He grinned. "Priceless."

"Heather! It's time for us to take off." Heather finished up her cigarette and joined us. I added, winking at Logan, "It's tequila night tonight."

"God, yes," Heather groaned, resting against the truck next to us. She lifted her head up, her chin jutting out toward Logan. "Sorry about being a bitch earlier. I'm sure you know why."

He shrugged. "It'll work out, you know that."

She grunted. "Not sure about that. Not this time." She pulled out her keys and went to the driver's side. "Ready, Sam?"

"Ready." I flashed my stepbrother a grin before going to the passenger door. "See you tomorrow."

His words were low. "Call if you need anything."

I knew his meaning. Heather was part of our family. We took care of each other. I nodded to him and climbed into the truck, and a second later we were off again.

Tequila night was about to commence.

Three

I pulled out the first bottle and placed it on the table. We already had the rest of the ingredients in the middle.

Courtney, Grace, Taylor, and Heather all stood around the table. Courtney and Grace's eyes widened at the sight of the full bottle, then trailed to the bag and the rest of the booze in there. A wary look came over Taylor's face, but Heather was focused on the bottle and nothing else.

"We are drinking this tonight." I was channeling Logan. The best motivational-speech voice I could summon came out, low and suggestive. "We are going to do this bottle proud."

Courtney and Grace nodded.

"Yes." Grace licked her lips. "Proud. So proud."

Courtney was nodding right along with her.

Taylor swallowed, then sighed. "Okay. This is what Logan warned me about, huh." But she wasn't asking. She already knew.

I said, "We are going to pay homage to the tequila gods tonight. We are going to kneel at their altar, lick their balls, stroke their members." My hand rubbed up and down the bottle's neck.

Courtney and Grace shared a look, cringing, but faced me again. Their shoulders rolled back and Courtney clapped her hands. "Let's do this!"

Grace let out a war whoop. "Yeah!"

Taylor took a breath and held it.

I raised the bottle up, then lifted it high. "May we make you proud tonight!" Then I opened it up, licked some salt, took a shot, and bit down on a lime wedge. As I felt the burn, Heather took the bottle from me and tipped her head back. She did the same, taking more than a couple shots. When she was done, the bottle was passed around again.

The salt was licked.

The tequila was downed.

The limes were bit into.

I grabbed the stereo remote and soon "Party Till We Die" by Timmy Trumpet filled the air. The bottle had gotten around to Taylor by now, and I was on deck. Courtney and Grace were both cringing and coughing, but they were waiting, just like me and Heather. After my second shot, when it was going around a second time, Heather took her double dose and passed the bottle, then leaned over to me. "Thank you."

I nodded. She didn't need to say anything else. She wanted to forget whatever shit was going on, and that was my mission. We were going to get shit-faced. When Grace was handing the bottle off to Taylor, I said, "Another two times around. We need to finish the bottle, and then we can move on to mixed drinks."

Courtney stuck her tongue out, shaking her head as

Taylor took the tequila from her. "I thought tonight was about wine and gossip, and weren't we going to do something Halloween-ish too?"

I shrugged. The pumpkins were still on the porch. "That's the second round of events. Costumes and then heading out and dancing."

Taylor moaned, finishing her shot, and slid the bottle across the table toward me. "Tell me this is the only round. Please."

I beamed at her, snatching up the bottle. "Nope. Mixed drinks." Then I tried to do a Heather and inhale two full shots at once. *Goddamn!* That burned. I couldn't hold in my own moan, but Heather took the bottle.

She drank.

And drank.

And continued drinking.

The rest of the girls went from being surprised to understanding.

"Oh." I heard a quiet murmur from Grace.

"No." Heather pointed at each of them. "I don't want your fucking pity."

Taylor asked, softly, "What do you want from us?"

"This." Heather took another shot, and even I was wincing. I was pretty sure we were already beyond what was a healthy amount to drink. She finished and blindly shoved the bottle in Courtney's direction. "I don't want to talk about it. I don't want lectures, or speeches, or inspirational pep talks. I want to get fuck-faced enough where I actually might get fucked on my face tonight."

Grace grimaced, blinking rapidly at the same time. "That sounds painful, confusing, and strangely erotic at the same time." She gave me the last of what was left in the bottle. "I think I'm turned on."

There wasn't much left, and before I could down it,

Heather took it. She finished it, then put the bottle in the middle of the table. "Phase one"—a silent burp came out—"complete." Her eyes were raw and the wall that hid her emotions was gone. I just saw the pain there as she whispered, "Next. Please."

My arms lifted as if to hug her, but she saw them and her eyes hardened. "No."

That one word kept me from reaching for her, and I lifted both to indicate the kitchen. I felt like I was an air traffic controller with that move. "Aaaaand everyone shuffle to the right. Long Island iced teas." I sang the drink's name and instantly they all relaxed into smiles. Everyone loved a Long Island iced tea. How could they not?

We probably didn't need them, but who cared. I wanted us to figure out costumes before the shots hit our minds. If not, we might end up clubbing in just underwear and bras, thinking we were Underwear Wonder Woman or something. I didn't want to worry about our pictures ending up in a sleazy tabloid. I was Mason Kade's girlfriend. I never knew where or when someone might try and sell a photo of me.

"Okay." I set out all the ingredients. "Everyone make your own drink, and then explore the house to find a Halloween costume."

"We're going dancing after this?" Taylor asked.

I nodded. "Did your other friends want to come?"

"Jason might. He might go somewhere else, but he can drive us there, if we need a driver."

I'd planned on an Uber, but I was okay with that, at least this early in the night. "Sounds good. We can cab it home."

Heather stepped outside, leaning against the wall, and reached in her pocket for her cigarettes.

Taylor said, "Logan told me."

Nope. I wasn't going to be that friend who talked about another friend the second they stepped away. I had earlier with Logan, but that was different. Taylor wasn't like that either, so she wasn't gossiping to be hurtful, but this could hurt Heather. If it'd been me, I would've felt there'd been enough talk by now. Talking wasn't even necessary at this point.

I said, "I need to make my own drink too."

"Yeah." Taylor flashed me a grin. "Me too."

We both reached for our glasses when Courtney and Grace stopped laughing. They had moved into the living room with their iced teas in hand. "Hey, Sam," Courtney said.

"Yeah?" I said.

She gestured upstairs. "Any rooms that's off limits for us? For the costumes?"

"Uh . . ." I exchanged a look with Taylor.

"Go to Nate's. Definitely go to Nate's room."

Mason and his best friend Nate had lived with Logan and me last year. The two graduated, but their rooms and their things were still here. It was like a second or third home for both of them. I knew they'd be back often enough for visits, so it didn't make sense to clean everything out. So most of Nate's things had been left behind in his room.

They started giggling again, then Courtney coughed, trying for a stern face. "And where is that room?"

The tequila had officially arrived.

"The first bedroom. There's a guest room, then a bathroom. The door that opens to another set of stairs is Logan's. Don't go in there."

"Thank you." Courtney waved as they headed up.

Taylor dropped her voice, even though no one was in the room. "I'm not sure what Logan left out on the bed from last night. He got, ahem, creative."

I finished my tea and shook my head. "I don't need to hear about Logan's creativity." I was trying to hold back a laugh.

She didn't hold hers back. "I'm going to grab something quick to wear. I'll help those other two. Should we dress them in Nate's underwear? I think that's more the dilemma I'm torn about." She started for the stairs, but paused. "It's not like he'll see them being used. He's in Boston too."

The clock said seven thirty-three. "Nope. He should be in the Los Angeles stadium right about now. He's coming back with Mason tomorrow."

"That's right. I forgot about the game." She looked at the television. "We could've watched the game tonight."

"Nah." I just smiled. It was girls' night tonight.

She seemed to understand and her eyes darkened. "Hey, uh." She flicked a glance to where Heather was still standing outside. "I didn't mean to come off like I was gossiping before. Thanks for not participating. The words were out before I realized what I said."

"It's fine."

And it was. Taylor wasn't like that. Courtney and Grace were her friends too, since Taylor had joined the cross-country team the same time I did, but they were more my friends. I stayed when she had to quit because her nursing program became too demanding. Even though Taylor was from Cain, she didn't have a lot of friends. That was her choice. She could've had them. She was beautiful on the inside and out, with light brown hair, almost golden-blond in sunlight, and the darkest almond-colored eyes. Logan was head over heels for her, but if she'd been a catty, gossipy kind of girl, he wouldn't have given her the time of day. I finished pouring my drink as Taylor went upstairs, then poked my head outside.

"Wanna help me look for something cute and sexy, but also comfortable enough where I won't want to get rid of it when the booze hits me?" I asked Heather. She was sitting, but now she was starting to look fuzzy to me. "Too late."

The booze had just knocked down my front door.

She sighed, leaning back and crossing her legs at the ankles. "Are they all talking about me?"

"Not one word."

I stepped out and sat down to rest next to her.

Heather held up her drink and I clinked mine against it. "Salute."

She raised hers up before taking a long drink. "I'm already fucked up."

I patted her leg. "That's okay. I am too." Or I was getting there. "Taylor's friend is going to drive us to the club."

"Do me a favor?" She put her cigarette out, then locked those so-sad eyes on mine again.

"Anything."

"Don't let me go home with some random tonight. Okay?"

"Not a problem. Consider me your lesbian bitch tonight."

She frowned. "Pretty sure that'd make me *your* lesbian bitch."

"Really?" I shrugged. "Either way, you're mine tonight. No guy or girl better even look your way."

She grinned. "Are you going to be Butch Sam tonight?"

"Oh yeah. I am all . . ." My mind was coming up blank. I gave up. "I have no idea what the jokes are."

We stood and moved to go inside, then headed to the basement.

I put all the costumes from last year down there. If the others couldn't find anything, I'd tell them about the storage room. I was selfish. I wanted to get there first. "You might not want to say that out loud around her. She looked at you this summer and said her favorite food was fish."

I didn't think she meant the food.

Four

Courtney was dressed as a sexy teacher. We were all giving her grief, since teaching was her major, but she shrugged us off. She said, "Think of it as me practicing what not to wear. I have to be the buttoned-up, prim-and-proper version next year. I want to be inappropriate tonight."

Grace was a colorful princess-fish. I had no clue where she'd found the tulle, but . . . okay.

I was impressed. The clothes looked like costumes bought from a store.

Taylor lifted her hand in a Vanna White motion. She wore a black corseted dress with her hair pulled up into a tight bun. A piece of a wig was on the front of her face; she was a bearded lady.

She clasped her hands together in front of her. "I like roller coasters. I couldn't figure out how to be that, so this was the next best thing."

Heather grunted. "You're one hot bearded lady."

"Really?" She perked up.

"Totally." Heather was leaning an elbow on my shoulder.

Then all of the attention was focused on us. I elbowed her in the side. "Oh, yeah." She straightened, her arm falling back against her side. She was holding her drink in the same hand she used now to motion toward both of us. "I figured we'd go opposite what we are in our real lives—"

I frowned. She hadn't said that when she'd suggested the costumes.

She kept going. "I'm an angel." She lifted the wings that we'd fastened behind her. They were made of white tulle, but I knew this tulle came from the costume closet. I might have to go on a mission to find the pink, sparkly tulle that Grace was wearing. I wondered if there was any left. I could do crafts with it . . . or ask someone who did crafts to make something pretty with it.

Heather was saying, pointing to me, ". . . darkness here. Sam's all light and beautiful, so she's going the dark hooker route."

I had on black fishnets, a black leather dress, and the same tulle as Heather's, but mine was black. We'd tried to cover it with black glitter we found in another container. The glue wasn't sticking, and half the glitter was on the floor. I made a mental note to clean when I got up tomorrow.

The girls weren't sure how to react, and I held my hands out. "I had no idea she intended us to be 'opposite' what we are." I turned to Heather. "Hearing that I'm all 'light' is news to me. You met me in high school."

"You're happy now." She saluted me with her glass.

"Trust me. The costumes fit our opposites." She finished the rest of her Long Island iced tea.

I raised an eyebrow, though I shouldn't have been surprised. Heather looked ready to bulldoze her way through a liquor store.

She was still standing. We all were, but I was starting to waver. I glanced over, and, yep. Taylor was holding on to the wall. Grace was holding on to Courtney, and Courtney was gritting her teeth, focusing on the spot behind me.

It was time to dance. We needed to start sobering up, just a little.

Here we were. We walked into that nightclub like we owned it. The bouncers opened the door, and we strode right past them. The wind kicked up and it was like a fan blowing for us, like we were walking on a runway. The angel, the dark hooker, the bearded lady, the sexy fish, and the teacher. All eyes were on us—and then Grace tripped and fell.

"Oomph!"

"Oh my gosh." Courtney stopped to help her up. She tried. Her heel slipped, and she landed right next to Grace, her elbow decking her in the face. "AH!"

I wasn't even trying to help. No way. Tequila and my heels: not a good mix, I'd learned, thanks to Courtney.

Heather and Taylor turned around. They were skilled at slinky Halloween costumes with heels. Both of them got the girls up, and no one flashed anybody.

"Are your friends okay?"

A guy materialized beside me, dressed as Batman. He

was asking about them, but his eyes were roaming all over me. He licked his lips. "Want a drink?"

Before I could reply, Heather was there. She positioned herself so her back was to him and, in one smooth move, edged him out so he wasn't even able to see me anymore. She remarked coolly over her shoulder, "Turn the heat down. This is Kade's woman."

"What?" He craned his neck around, his eyes narrowing at me, and that's when I saw the fear creep in. "Shit." He ran a hand over his head. "You're Samantha Strattan." And, as if the whole thing was a nightmare that wouldn't go away, he ignored Heather's body language and came right back into the circle. He stuck his hand out. "I'm Steve. Man. That pass Mason caught tonight." He whistled in appreciation. "It was fucking fantastic. My mouth was on the floor. I didn't think he could do it. All my buddies were like this." He pantomimed screaming, and shook his arms in the air. "Seriously. One of the best plays I've ever seen. That shit's going to be replayed on ESPN for weeks."

Heather fixed him with a glare. "Dude. Really?"

"What?" He blinked a few times in confusion.

"You just hit on her, now you're hitting on her man?"

He frowned. "I'm not hit—" He thought better of that, shaking his head. "Whatever. You don't understand. It's football. I'm a man. Mason Kade is legendary."

"Mason Kade tends to go nuts when it comes to his woman."

I tugged at the leather strap on my shoulder. That was kind of a sensitive topic. Last year we'd hit a rough bump. We got over it, but it still made me grimace to hear it. I coughed, linked my elbow with Heather's, and flashed the guy a smile. "I'll pass on your comments to Mason.

Thank you." I tugged my bodyguard with me. "But we need drinks."

His eyes lit up. "I can get you drinks." And he was raising his hand, calling for a waitress.

"No, no." I tugged his arm down, still trying to be polite, but I could feel Heather bristling for a fight behind me. "Thank you. Again. We're good. Independent women and all. We can get our own drinks."

I began pushing Heather forward.

The guy reached out behind me. "Are you sure? I can give you my Twitter handle. Better yet"—his voice rose as he yelled to be heard over the club's music—"I'll tweet at Mason. I'll let him know I'm watching out for his girl, making sure no one messes with you tonight."

Mason would hate that.

My smile froze in place, but I waved one last time. "Sounds good. Thank you. I'm sure he'll retweet you." I muttered under my breath, "And then he'll want to block you in person."

Taylor was waving from the bar. Courtney and Grace were beside her, huddled together like they were warding off a chill. I stepped around another group in costume and heard one of them say, "Hey. Isn't that Mason Kade's girlfriend?"

An excited buzz rose, and I cringed. Ignoring them, I pulled Heather with me into a small opening by Taylor and moved quickly to the bar's edge.

Taylor had overheard. "Do you want to leave?"

No, but . . . I glanced over my shoulder. That whole group was staring right at me. I looked past them and saw Steve talking with another group and pointing toward me. The tequila was starting to wane in my system.

I let out a sigh. "We probably should."

Mason's celebrity status was always big. I was used to it in high school—he and Logan ran their school—but he became more famous when he started playing for Cain University, and even more so when he decided to finish his degree. Teams had been anxious to sign him, but no one knew how he'd actually play once he got into the NFL. That uncertainty disappeared after the first game he started. He'd run in three touchdowns, and had continued to dominate most games since.

His status was ridiculous now. I tried to ignore it, keeping my head down and doing my thing, but some nights—like tonight—I couldn't ignore it. It wasn't that I didn't want to deal with it. It was just that . . . it was . . . he was my Mason, not theirs. The small modicum of privacy and normalcy we'd had before was gone now.

"I'm on it." Taylor waved the bartender away when he brought over a bunch of drinks. "We're leaving."

"No." Courtney pulled out some cash and tossed it on the counter. "He already poured them. Let's drink these quick, then have Jason take us somewhere else."

A new plan was hatched.

We downed our drinks and left, and were waiting on the curb for Taylor's friend Jason to come back. He'd opted not to join us inside, but he was coming back. She checked her phone after ten minutes, then sent off a text asking if he was close. A couple minutes passed without a response.

She looked at me. "He always responds. His phone is hooked up to his car." She texted him again.

There'd been a line outside already, but after we came out, more and more people followed us. A few who wanted to smoke, then their friends, then *their* friends. I heard the conversations pick up, and glanced over my shoulder.

Yep. Good ol' Steve was out there too, pretending to smoke. His eyes were on me, and when he saw me look, he lifted his hand in a wave. "Hey! You guys taking off?"

A growl erupted from Heather. She rounded on him. "For fuck's sake."

"Wai—" Too late. I reached for her, but she was already marching over to him.

Everyone tensed. Heather was formidable, even when she was laid-back and easy-breezy. She usually had a drawl ready, matched with a sultry and sexy grin. Nothing really ruffled her feathers. This Heather wasn't normal, and even I gulped to see her walk over to him. I felt like I'd gotten a glimpse of a black widow moving in for the kill.

Courtney's hand touched my arm. I looked over—her eyes were glued to Heather's back, and she gulped too. She was pale.

Grace's hands were clasped in front of her, pulled up to her chest. Her eyes were wide. She bit down on her lip.

I didn't look at Taylor. I already knew she was worried.

"Hey!" Heather snapped at him.

He had been watching me, but jerked his gaze to her. His spine straightened and his shoulders rolled back. His group of friends parted for her and she strolled in, stopping right in front of him. Her hands found her hips and she struck a defiant pose. "What is your problem?"

"Wh—huh?"

"You think she wants to deal with you?"

He seemed to actually think about it.

"You think she enjoys when meatheads like you hit on her, then find out who her boyfriend is, and turn into clingy stalker fans? And I heard that shit you said to her. You're going to tweet at her boyfriend and let him know you're watching out for her? Are you kidding me?

Mason Kade might be a football god to you, but get a reality check. He's a lethal machine, who turned his body into a weapon to bulldoze past running backs, linemen, and bigger assholes on the football field than you. Imagine facing him and telling him that you're *watching* the woman he loves, and really think how that might go over."

As she talked, his eyes got bigger and bigger. His face was close to Heather's by the time she finished. He looked like a ghost.

Heather wasn't done, though. "It's obvious that we're leaving, and here you are." She waved a hand around. "Coming out here too. Following her, like that clingy stalker fan you became. Then you wave to her? Like you're friends? Fucking get over yourself."

Taylor leaned close to me. "She's a female Logan." She readjusted her dress. "I think I'm a little turned on. Is that wrong?"

I shook my head. "Share the story with Logan. He'll love it."

Our ride pulled up in front of us. Jason leaned over from the driver's side to open the passenger door and shove it ajar. "Sorry. I wasn't expecting your text so soon. Too much fun, huh?"

"Thank God," Taylor groaned and climbed in.

Courtney opened the back door and started to climb into the back seat. Grace hurried around to the other side. I reached for the door, but looked over my shoulder. Heather was still in Steve-O's face, her cigarette lit and waving in the air.

Jason looked over Taylor's seat to me. "Looks like you have a situation. Want me to play interference?"

Did he have to use a football metaphor? But I nodded.

Jason was quick-witted and snarky. He could defuse the situation in half the time it would take me. And in a flash, he did. He wasn't a big guy. He was five ten and lean, and he was out his door and around the SUV in his pink polo, the collar turned out with gold on the inside, and white jeans that were molded to his skinny frame. Steve didn't even see him coming.

Jason was there. He dipped down, put an arm through Heather's legs, tucked his shoulders against her back, and looped his other arm around her waist. He picked her up, throwing her over his shoulder, and winked at the guys. "Have a nice night, folks. Only drink and drive if you're the only one on the street."

He carried Heather to the vehicle and deposited her in the seat next to mine. The door was shut. He was in his driver's seat before Heather comprehended what happened. Then she started laughing. Taylor cracked a grin. Courtney and Grace dissolved into the same giggles they'd had at the house, and I—I met Jason's gaze in the rearview mirror as he started to pull away from the curb. "Thanks for that."

He grinned back. "No problem."

We were moving past the crowd. Everyone was happy, even Heather, and I started to relax.

Then I looked to the right.

Standing there, facing us, was someone dressed from head to toe in a black robe. The face was gone. A white mask stared back at me, one that reminded me of the movie *Scream.*

There was no reason for my reaction, but my stomach dipped low.

A sick shiver wound down my spine.

That person was evil.

I knew it. I could feel it, and I couldn't breathe for a moment.

I also knew, without a doubt, that we'd see that person again.

My blood went cold.

Five

Jason took us to Pete's Pub, where Taylor used to work. She'd put in a good word for Nate, and we'd visited him throughout the past year, enough to know the regulars on a first-name basis. When we walked in, I was already starting to relax. I knew I wasn't going in there as Mason Kade's girlfriend. I was Sam to them.

Some of the staff and a few of the regulars waved to us, but I knew that when we took our booth in the corner, we'd be left alone. If we chose to be social, it was our decision. The bouncers would keep an extra eye out. They always did when Taylor was here, anyways.

The tequila, mixed with the Long Island iced tea, kept my body warm and floaty. The alcohol's effect had waned a little at the previous place, but my last drink was slamming into my body again. I was gone. I was in the clouds now.

Dark hooker: airborne.

The world looked all nice and cozy from my point of view.

I smiled, knowing it was droopy and messy, but I didn't care. I leaned into Heather's shoulder. "I love you, you know that."

The corner of her mouth curved down. "I went batshit at that guy. I don't know what's wrong with me."

"You have a man problem!" Courtney yelled from the other side of our booth. Her hand lifted and plopped on the table. A bowl of peanuts upended and rolled over, falling into her lap. She had no clue. "You're hurting, and you're drunk, and that's never a good recipe."

Heather grunted. "Works just fine for me."

"No. I know." She held her hand out in front of her, but paused. "I don't know what I was saying."

Taylor grabbed one of the peanuts on the table, opened it, and popped the shelled nut in her mouth. She said around it, "Man problems. Drinking."

"Yes." Courtney was off again. "You should talk about what happened. That might help all of us understand." She gestured around the table. "It'd be good therapy too. We've all been there." She burped and continued blinking, giving Heather an expectant look.

"The love of my life dumped me because his sister was arrested."

Courtney screwed her face up; the blank look came back. "I've lost the ability to compute that. Your fiancé was arrested?"

Grace snorted. Her shoulders started shaking with soft laughter.

Taylor frowned at Courtney.

Heather didn't react at all, merely drawling back, "His sister was arrested. And he's not my fiancé."

"Got it." Courtney slapped her hand back down. "You were arrested and his sister took back the ring."

Heather was reaching for a peanut, but paused. "No. What are you talking about—rings, and fiancés, and shit? No one's engaged here."

"Wait." Courtney's hand was back in the air. "Your sister was arrested and he dumped you because of that." She frowned to herself, pulling her hand back to her lap. "Oh man. Is he in love with your sister?"

"Unless my brother's had a sex change, and his sexual orientation switched too, then that's not even possible."

Courtney sucked in one of her cheeks, chewing on the inside of it. "I think I'm drunk."

Taylor spit out her drink, or the little sip she'd taken. It landed on the table . . . at least I thought it did. I was looking for it as she said, "That's the first logical thing you've said since we got here."

I was mesmerized by the glass in Taylor's hand, then saw we all had one in front of us. When had we gotten drinks here? I pointed at mine. "Who ordered these?"

"No." Heather propped her elbows on the table, leaning forward. "My problem is that my ex is amazing at fucking—"

Grace hiccuped. "Is that actually a problem?"

Heather kept going. "He's got a body like, like fucking Brad Pitt in *Fight Club*, and a face that could be a model's. I mean, he's gorgeous. He's beyond gorgeous, and he's a stand-up guy. The problem is that he's too stand-up. He's a bad boy and he can be a dick, so he's not boring or anything, but he's raising his sister, and she's not making his life easy right now. She got arrested for some really bad shit, and he thinks he needs to devote more time to her." She hiccuped too, jerking back in her seat. Then she went on, as if no hiccup had happened. "And that's my problem. He broke up with me and the reason makes me want him even more."

"It makes you love him more?"

Heather shook her head at Taylor. "No. My love meter is all the way over. It can't go any further. But damn, I want to fuck him, like right now." She let out a sigh.

"No, really"—I pointed at my drink—"who ordered these?"

Courtney bobbed her head up and down. "That is a problem. Wow. I wish I could find a guy like that. All you bitches," her finger waved at us again, "got all of them. I hate you guys sometimes."

Grace melted into the wall. Her eyes were closing and drool fell from her mouth.

I crossed my arms over my chest and leaned all the way back in my seat. "I'm not drinking this until I know where they came from."

Taylor grabbed my drink and took a sip, then put it back as she spoke to Heather. "You should call him. Right now." She waved a hand at the glass, saying to me, "It's fine. I'm not dead."

Nope. I was waiting a full five minutes. She could die. People ended up roofied like this.

"I can't call him. I'm drunk as fuck right now."

"No." Courtney's hand was once again in the air. "This is the best time to call. You'll be honest now. And he can say things to you that maybe he normally wouldn't if you were sober. You know, the walls aren't up now."

I couldn't handle it anymore. I smacked Courtney's hand down. "Stop it. That's making me paranoid."

Taylor choked on her drink again.

I held my breath. I was right! We were drugged. Were the drugs already kicking in?!

She sputtered out, her head going back and forth, "Courtney's not making you paranoid. The tequila is."

"Tequila usually makes me want to get naked," Grace announced to us.

We all paused. Our heads swiveled to her, and then she let out a deep yawn and rested back against the wall.

Heather gestured to her. "She's out for the night." She picked up her drink and motioned to me. "I don't think we're going to party like rock stars tonight."

I shrugged. "As long as you're okay, I don't care."

"Aww." Courtney stuck out her bottom lip. "You guys are so sweet together. I remember when I first met you, Heather. You scared the shit out of me."

"Yeah." Taylor was nodding. "You and I didn't hit it off either."

Heather lifted up a shoulder. "That's how I am. You either like me right away or you don't. You get what you see with me."

I scowled. For some reason, Courtney's last statement pissed me off. I wasn't sure why.

Taylor inclined her head to me. "What about you, Sam? How'd you react to Heather when you first met her?"

I tried to remember. A drunken fog was hindering my memories.

Heather chuckled, low and smooth. "She looked at me like I was her first drop of water she'd seen in the desert. I was the answer to your prayers. Admit it, Strattan. You had a lady boner for me when you stopped at Manny's all those years ago."

Had I? Then I laughed. I had been running to avoid my mom while Mason and Logan were out somewhere. I nodded. "You're right. I think you saved me in some ways."

"No, I didn't." Her shoulder nudged mine. "I gave you a job. That's all."

"You gave me friendship." I had Mason. I had Logan. I had no female friends. "I needed that."

A moment of silence hung over the table, and Heather turned to look at me. We'd talked about that time of my life, but I didn't think I'd ever said it as bluntly as I just had. Tears came to Heather's eyes and all the drunken anger, whatever was there, faded. She blinked back those tears. "Aww, Sam." She hugged me to her, burying her head in my shoulder and neck. I felt the wetness against my skin. "I think it was mutual. I needed someone too."

Taylor was blinking back her own tears. "You both scared me when I met you. I mean"—her hand reached for another peanut, and she gestured to me—"You're *Sam*. Logan loves you, like, *loves* you, in the 'he'd step in front of a bus for you' way. And it's not just him. Holy shit. The first time I saw Mason, when he looked at you and he didn't think anyone was watching . . ." She closed her eyes and shivered. "It gave me all the tingles, all over. It's the stuff that books are written for. It's till-the-end-of-days kind of shit."

"You and Logan have that."

"Oh, I know." A proud smile tugged at her lips. "But the first time I met you, you were big in my head. You were legendary stuff, until that summer when we started to really get to know each other. And you too." She indicated Heather, lifting her glass for a drink. "I was jealous of you. I knew you and Logan had a special friendship, and I was threatened, just a bit. I'm not anymore, but yeah. And now I love both of you so much." A tear slipped down her cheek. "Good friends are great to have. That's for damn sure."

Courtney sniffled. Her entire face was covered in tears, and her eyeliner was smudged. Black streaks had formed under her eyes. "I can't." She waved at us. "I can't even. This is the best night of my life."

Grace let out a snore.

Six

We drank. We danced. We laughed. Grace slept.

As far as Halloween-eve nights went, it was one of the best I'd had so far. I was going to be a dark hooker every year from now on. It was the end of the night, and we were waiting for a ride again. Jason had joined us for a few drinks, then left for a party, and Taylor said that that meant he was out for the count. Taylor offered a driver, and I had suspicions of who that driver would be, but I didn't care anymore. Heather had laughed for most the night. My job was done. She could experience heartache later. For now, she was good.

"You ladies have a ride coming?" One of the bouncers came over, knocking on our table.

They were letting us wait inside, instead of kicking us out to wait on the curb like everyone else. I was glad, because Grace was still snoring. My eyelids were drooping too, and if that ride didn't come soon, I'd have to be carried out.

"Tay-tay said we did," Heather said, sounding tired.

He chuckled, asking, "Your man?"

I didn't hear an answer, so I assumed it was a nod.

I tried to open my eyes. "Is girls' night officially over?"

"I think so, yeah."

"Okay." Heather said so, and so it was good. I went back to sleeping.

A hand shook me awake. "Sam?"

"Hmm?"

I felt sluggish. My body felt weighed down, even my eyes. I didn't want to look at whoever it was.

"Hey. Our ride is here. We have to go."

"No." I snuggled closer to Mason's hard chest. It felt more rigid than normal. "I'm good here."

A man laughed, in a soothing voice. "I'll carry her. It's no problem."

"You sure?"

"Oh yeah. She's family. It's no problem."

Wait. That didn't make sense. I tried lifting my head—my neck screamed in pain. It was stiff, but I looked. Yes, that was Logan. I recognized the voice, but who was he talking to? He was bending down over my side of the booth. No one else was there, but that voice—who was that? I looked as Logan pulled me over and scooped an arm under me.

"Hey." I frowned, but looped an arm around his shoulders.

He lifted me up, cradling me against his chest.

I tried to look. "Who was that?"

"Who?"

"That person you were talking to." The bar was empty. All the chairs were turned over on the tables. The only light on was by the door, and a staff member was holding it open for us. But . . . Logan had been talking to someone. The staff person was too far away for it to be them.

"I wasn't talking to anyone, Sam."

No. He had been. I knew he had been.

"You're drunk and tired, and by the time we get home, I'm pretty sure Mason will be there."

Mason—a thrill went through me. I started to wake up a little bit more, and as he went through the door, he had to turn sideways. I looked over to where I'd been sitting, and . . . there! I saw the swish of a black robe. Someone was there! I started to sit up, but Logan protested. His hand came to my head. "No. Don't sit up. You'll crack your head."

"Over there." I craned my neck to see, but we were through the door.

I couldn't see anymore, but there had been someone. Why didn't Logan remember talking to him? That didn't make sense. I yawned, unable to fight it, and my eyelids kept drooping. Logan deposited me next to Heather, who was already curled into a ball on the seat. Taylor tried to give me a smile from the front, but she was too tired too. She closed her eyes, and I could already hear Courtney and Grace snoring in the back.

"Logan." I stopped him as he was stepping back, reaching to close my door.

"What?"

"You were talking to someone in there. Who?"

He shook his head again, a slight frown marring his face. "I wasn't, Sam. I thanked the staff guy for holding the door for me, but that was it. There was no one else."

"But . . ." There had been. "A black robe. Or something black."

A chilling image of the black robe and white mask from the first nightclub flashed in my head. No. I wouldn't let myself imagine that it was him. That made even less sense. "Mason's coming tonight?"

He nodded. "He doesn't have that meeting tomorrow in LA that he thought he had."

Mason.

He was coming home.

He'd be there, or would be soon after we got there.

The black robe had nothing on Mason.

I fell back asleep, dreaming of my soulmate. It was his hands that woke me, that picked me up from the SUV. I recognized those hands. I'd recognize them if I was dead to the world, but I opened my eyes and gave him the biggest, stupidest smile of the whole night, and there'd been a bunch to compete against.

"Hey."

There he was, looking back down at me. I reached up to touch him and he caught my fingers in his mouth. He grinned, his tongue sweeping out to lick them before he released me. "Hey yourself."

I tucked my head further against his chest, content to gaze up at him. "I got really drunk tonight."

"Sounds like you had a good night."

"I heard you had a good night too."

"Not as good as your night." He went in the house, then down the hallway to our room. I felt like I was still dreaming. I was in a haze, and slowly he lowered me to the bed. He helped me get under the covers. "I could get undressed."

He shook his head. "Trust me. I'll be doing that in a moment."

He stripped off his shirt, his muscles shifting and bulging as he tossed it to the side, and came to bed only in his sweatpants. They dipped low on his hips, right underneath the V from his muscles, and I was already itching to push them the rest of the way off.

The bed dipped under his weight, and I rolled onto my back. Grinning, I looped my hands around his head as he knelt over me. I was cursing the bedcovers between us, and the rest of the space between my body and his. I ran my hands down his arms, feeling how strong they were. "I love you."

He smiled back down at me, his eyes darkening, softening. "I love you too."

It'd been three weeks since I had seen him last. Three weeks since I'd had enough time in my running schedule to fly out and see him. Three weeks since I'd touched him, tasted him, felt his body next to mine.

I kicked at the covers, pulling them down. Then I was right there, in my dark hooker getup. My breasts were straining against my dress. I knew my nipples were hard. The throbbing was there, and it was building as his eyes roamed up and down, lingering on my breasts.

He murmured, "A witch?"

"A hooker. I was the darkness to Heather's light."

He chuckled but bent down, and I closed my eyes. I felt his lips on my neck, and oh dear God, he could suckle like no one else. I squirmed, wanting those lips farther down. I wanted them on my breasts, on my stomach, between me and then in me. But I wanted them on my lips too, and I let out a soft breath as he moved up, grazing my neck, my jaw, and then lingering just above my lips.

"You're killing me." I was panting.

"Maybe that's the intent?"

I opened my eyes. That didn't sound like Mason? And

then it wasn't—the white mask was hovering over me. The man in the black robe was there, and he had a knife in his hands.

I screamed and kicked out.

"Sam? SAM!"

I tried to kick free and get off the bed, but he slammed me back down. "SAM! Stop!"

Wait . . . that voice . . . My head whipped back to his, and my body sagged in relief. It *was* Mason. "Oh thank God," I sobbed, wrapping my arms around his neck. He rested on me, letting his full weight down gently, and then shifted to the side. He pulled me back against him, and he held me. A hand smoothed down my hair. "What's wrong? What just happened there?"

I shook my head. I tasted the salt from my tears. "I've been seeing this guy. He's in a black robe and he's wearing a mask. He's evil, Mason." I trembled. "Evil. I don't know what's going on with me."

His hand shook as he asked, "Did someone drug you?"

I didn't know. I tipped my head back, looking at him. "If they did, it would've been that first drink at the club. That was when I saw him first."

He ran another hand down my hair, tucking some stray strands behind my ear. His thumb brushed over my cheek lovingly. "You should get checked out. Do you want to go to the hospital?"

"No." I clasped my arms around him, hugging him. "I want to stay here with you. I'm sure it'll leave my system by tomorrow."

"You sure? What about the others? Were they drugged too?"

No one had said anything about a robed guy. They'd all acted normal, just drunk. "I'm sure it's nothing."

"Sam." Concern weighed heavy in his eyes.

I shook my head again. "No. I'm really okay. Or I will be." I pushed myself up, covering his lips with mine. I tugged him back down until he was lying halfway on top of me again. "This is what I need. This is all that I need."

His body shook again, but one of his hands ran down my side and then pushed up under my shirt. It rested over my ribs, his thumb grazing the underside of my breast. He lifted his head. "You sure?"

"Yes." I gave him a look, then hooked my leg around his. I pulled him down at the same time I pushed up against him. We both moaned from the contact. He was right there. I could feel how hard he was, and he was aching to be inside me just as much as I wanted him. "I just want you. Only you." I ran my hand down the side of his face, my finger caressing the side of his mouth, and then I kissed him. My lips covered his, and I felt him surrender. He'd come home, and we fit together again. Just like always.

Before long, he was sliding inside of me, and I gasped, arching my back. This was how it always was supposed to be. Then he paused, pulled out, and began to thrust back in again. I locked my legs around him and moved my hips with his.

Seven

Everyone was hungover the next morning.

I woke around nine, washed up a little, pulled on pajama pants and a sweatshirt, then trudged out to the kitchen. Mason wasn't far behind, wearing just his sweatpants that dipped deliciously low on his hips. I made coffee as he started up the stove. Bread was in the toaster when Taylor and Logan joined. They took their coffee with smiles of thanks, then sat behind the kitchen table. They moved to the farthest seats. When the toast was ready, Mason put it on a plate and added it to the table. Butter, knives, and a handful of empty plates went next.

Without a word spoken, Logan started buttering the toast. He passed the finished pieces to Taylor, and by that time Courtney and Grace had joined us. They paused, their eyes wide and lingering on Mason, before gulping and averting their gaze. They sat, and Taylor gave them the first pieces of toast.

I gave them coffee too, then started another pot.

Mason began making bacon and eggs. I couldn't move away from him, not even if I tried to force myself. After fidgeting while the coffee was brewing, I ended up leaning against the counter and resting my head against his upper arm. It bulged under my touch. My hand rubbed down his back, ending and curling in on his sweatpants. It was my anchor, and I loved the feel of it.

Mason dropped a soft kiss to the top of my head, then went back to cooking. When the eggs and bacon were done, he placed them on a plate, and they went onto the table along with everything else. He came back and continued cooking, and I resumed resting my head against his upper arm.

Courtney and Grace took their turn. They scooped up the food and plated it, passing the plates back to Logan and Taylor, who were nibbling on their own pieces of toast now.

Heather shuffled in, yawning big, and she waved a hand to everyone. One of her eyes was still closed. She passed me by, going to sit next to Taylor. I held out a cup of coffee. She took it on the way there, not pausing a second, and took her seat.

Courtney put a piece of bacon on a plate. Grace stopped eating hers, and put an egg on the plate. Logan added two pieces of toast, and Taylor slid the plate right in front of Heather. She smiled, her eyes sweeping over everyone in the room.

Nate was the last. He paused in the doorway, a hand rubbing at his stomach, and he grinned at everyone. He frowned at Mason, noting his shirtless state, and shook his head. Logan snorted from the table, but that was the only response. Nate came over to hug me, then dropped down in the closest seat to Logan.

Mason added more food to the table.

I finished the last pot of coffee, pouring two new mugs for Mason and myself.

Logan, smirking, pulled off his shirt and tossed it across to Mason. It was caught and it was pulled on, and now the shirtless one was Logan. Nate stopped, his eyes skirting between the brothers, and shrugged. He pulled his own shirt off, winking at Courtney, before hunching back over his plate.

When Mason and I sat, our food was already waiting for us.

Everyone ate and thirty minutes passed. Not one word was spoken. I held Mason's hand under the table the entire time.

Best. Breakfast. Ever.

Two hours later

I was sitting on the curb, a pumpkin on the street between my feet, a large carving knife in my right hand. Heather was next to me, holding the same thing. I brought my knife down, embedding it deep into the gourd, and I cut away the stem. Yanking it up, I cleaned off the first of the pumpkin's guts.

Heather grunted, her hand covered in pumpkin goo. "Why did we get stuck doing the damned pumpkins?"

I went back to hacking at the thing. "Courtney and Grace went to their apartment, and the guys are going to finish decorating that haunted house for tonight. I don't know where Taylor is." A second thrust, and I had the first eye out. I paused. "Should I hollow it out first, then cut the face?"

Heather stopped, half her pumpkin's insides on the street between us. She considered it, then shrugged. "Makes sense, but is there a wrong way to gut a pumpkin?"

"If we gut ourselves first?"

"Touché." She pointed her carving knife at me. "Got any homicidal tendencies I should know about?"

I grinned. "I was a dark hooker last night."

"You were the angel of darkness. Different thing."

"You're right. That would've meant homicidal tendencies." I set down the knife and plunged my hand in. "No tendencies that I can think of, although . . ." I paused.

"What?"

"I think someone slipped something into my drink at the nightclub."

"What?!" She sat up. "Did you tell Mason?"

I nodded. "Yeah, but I was fine. I downplayed it a bit."

"Oh." She frowned. "Did you have any side effects from it?"

"I was hallucinating. Kept thinking I saw some guy in a black robe and mask."

"Mask? Like a *Scream* type of mask?"

"Kinda. The face wasn't pronounced. There were no eyes, nose, or mouth. It was just white."

"That's freaky as fuck."

I nodded. "Not arguing with that." I scooped out another handful of seeds and guts. "Am I weird in feeling like this is cathartic?"

She snorted. Her hand went back in and came out,

covered in the same orange insides. "I'm imagining this is Channing." She paused again. "Maybe I'm the one with the homicidal tendencies?"

I grinned. "You do seem to be enjoying that."

She shrugged, her hand plunging back inside. We stopped talking after that. The pumpkins were cleaned out. We set them aside to start on two more pumpkins. Once they were all done, we hosed down the street and carried them inside. We were close to finishing the faces for two of the pumpkins when a stampede of feet came up from the basement.

The guys popped out, arms full of costumes.

"What are you doing?" I asked.

Logan asked at the same time, his eyes on the pumpkins, "What are *you* doing?"

Heather pointed at the one in front of her. "This is self-explanatory." She waved the knife at them. "Your turn."

"Oh." Logan looked down at the costumes in his hands. He said to me, "We gotta take a bunch of these to the haunted house. We left most of the girly ones for you guys. Are you two doing the same costumes as last night?"

Heather and I shared a look. We hadn't discussed it. Heather shrugged, going back to cutting out a tooth. "We'll figure it out."

Logan paused, watching me. "This is okay, right?"

I didn't know why it wouldn't be. "Yeah. We'll figure something out with whatever we have here. It's no problem."

"Okay." He started outside, leaving the door open. Nate flicked two fingers up in a salute, ducking out behind him.

Mason was last, and he came over to me first. "Hey."

He dropped a light kiss to my lips. "I'll see you later tonight?" He glanced to Heather before kissing me again. "You'll be okay?"

Heather let out a sigh, put her knife down, and muttered, "I need a cigarette."

"Was that me?" Mason asked once she was gone.

"Channing broke up with her."

He lifted his head up two inches. "Are you serious?"

"And he's coming tonight to see you."

"Fuck." He looked to where Heather had slipped out the back door. Her back was leaning against the patio doors, the cigarette already lit. "That's harsh."

"Hence why we were so drunk last night."

His eyes darkened. *Remember our own rough patch.* I'd gotten drunk a couple of those nights, but I knew he'd gone on a bigger binge than me. I felt him starting to pull away and caught the front of his shirt. "I love you."

His eyebrows dipped together. "I love you." His lips tried to show me too. When we were done, a few heavy-breathing seconds later, he cursed under his breath. "What are the chances we can send Heather in my place?"

I grinned against his lips. "So she can decorate with Logan?"

He nodded, grinning right back. "The two will yell at each other the whole time."

"Pretty much." I frowned and looked around him. "Where's Taylor? Did she leave after breakfast?"

Mason shrugged. "I don't know. Logan never said anything. I assumed she was with you."

I shook my head, my stomach twisting. I stepped back, but my clean hand was still on his chest. It felt right, leaving it there, like he was anchoring me. I glanced around again, but I knew she wouldn't have magically appeared in the last few seconds.

"I'll call her." I nodded at the pumpkins. "We're going to set these out with tealights before we leave tonight."

He rubbed his hand up and down my arm. "What are you guys doing today? We'll be at the house the whole time. Logan's gone all out with this party."

I shrugged. We did have all day. I didn't have classes on Fridays, and Heather was up for the whole weekend. We weren't the type to do the salon. Saloon, yes. Salon, no. "I don't know. We'll figure something out." I pressed myself up, bringing my lips fully against his again. Logan would be yelling any second. "Have fun. I'll see you tonight."

I could almost count it down.

Three.

Two.

And on 'one,' I pointed to the door at the exact instant Logan shouted.

Mason laughed, and pressed one last kiss to my forehead. "Okay. Love you. Be safe. Have fun. And if you start drinking early, call. I'll be sober, I'll come and pick you up."

I flashed him a grin. "Bye, and all of that to you too, except the last part."

He laughed, going out the door, and right as it closed, I yelled, "I won't be sober tonight."

"Looking forward to it!" he yelled back, his words muffled through the wood.

I knocked on the patio glass, and Heather turned. She nodded, putting her cigarette out. "Your perfect soulmate left?"

There was no bite to her words, but I frowned. "You and Channing will be fine. You know that, right? Your breakups are never permanent."

She picked up her knife again, pulling the last pumpkin

in front of her. The knife was raised and poised, and she said, "I don't know about this time." And she brought it down with a vehemence she hadn't had earlier.

I went back to cutting mine, but looked over my shoulder one last time.

Where'd Taylor go?

Eight

"All right." Heather stepped out from the bathroom. We'd gone slutty last night, so we were going funny tonight. Bypassing whatever costumes were left downstairs, we spent the afternoon downtown. What we went home with had us both in stitches.

I was holding back my laughter again. I clamped my mouth closed and nodded. "Mmmm hmmm."

She was dressed in a white onesie, the opening around her face lined with pink hair. She reached up to grab a sparkling, pastel-colored rainbow horn. Heather's face was dead serious. "Is my horn in the right spot?"

Another laugh bubbled up. I stifled it, swallowing it back down. "Looks good."

She lifted up her hand and motioned in a circle. "Okay. Turn around. I'll check your ass."

Her voice hitched.

I bit down on my lip. No laughing. Not yet. I turned. I

was dressed in the same white onesie. There was an opening for my face, but it was only lined with white cloth. My hands were normal—they weren't supposed to have attention focused on them—and my feet ended in two large black hooves. Heather's arms had the matching two front hooves, but the back of my costume was where the action was.

A long white tail extended from my costume, pink hair at the tip, and underneath the tail was another small hole. A contraption hung from it on the inside, with a cord running from it down my arm, to a button resting on the inside of my palm.

We turned to face the correct way. Heather was in front of me. I was behind her. She was the head. I was the ass.

She said, "Ready?"

My finger moved to the button. In the same monotone, I replied, "Ready."

"Push it."

She had a similar contraption on her costume, and we pushed our buttons together. A loud horsey *neigh* came from a small speaker attached near her face, nestled in her pink mane, and at the same time, the tail on my costume lifted and a burst of glitter exploded in the air.

We were a glitter-farting unicorn. Together.

I dissolved in laughter. Heather was right next to me. We both ended up on the floor, like we'd been all afternoon once we found the costume.

She sat up and panted, "Best damned costume ever!"

I nodded. I couldn't talk. I was still laughing.

"Okay." She tried to stop laughing. Her laughter was coming out as half-hiccups now. She grabbed for my arm. "Let's get up. One drink, then we go?"

I glanced at the clock. We'd spent half the afternoon

putting the costume together while answering the door for trick-or-treaters, but it was long past time for any more. The costume was done and the party had started a couple of hours ago. It was time to go. "Yeah. I'll call Mason to pick us up."

Heather pumped her fist in the air. "Score. That means another two drinks."

My stomach rolled over. The hangover was still with me, but this was Halloween and Heather time. I was down for anything.

She mixed two Long Island iced teas for us, and I tucked my phone away after Mason replied. "He's leaving now."

She held one up for me. I took it, and she saluted me with hers. "To friendship." Her eyes met mine.

A look passed between us, and I felt myself choking up. Then I pushed my button and glitter exploded in the air. My lip twitched and I raised my glass up. "Best friendship ever."

After swallowing, she rested her glass on the counter. "For real, though. Thanks for this weekend. I needed it."

"You're probably going to get back together with Channing tonight."

She shook her head, her eyes downcast. "No. Sex, maybe. Getting back together, no." She closed her eyes a moment.

Breaking up sucked, even if it was the right thing to do. I'd been there. It hadn't been long for Mason and me, but I remembered that time. I'd felt like I was dying. Literally. Heather had picked me up off the floor. I didn't think I was doing the same for her now, but I was trying.

"One day at a time. You might not have faith, but I do. I know this breakup isn't permanent. He's going to be begging you to come back in no time."

Nothing else made sense. Heather and Channing loved each other. They were almost as inseparable as Mason and me, and more so in some ways. They'd been best friends since third grade, and the relationship had never waned after she'd transferred to Fallen Crest in junior high.

"Here's hoping, but God." She groaned. "He's already there. He texted me an hour ago."

I patted her hand. "Let me know when you need to bail tonight, if you do. We could do a code word. You just say 'llama,' and I'll know what you're talking about. We'll leave. We'll do whatever you want. I'm your sidechick tonight."

She snorted on her drink, spitting some of it out.

Mason pulled up into the driveway five minutes later, and we headed out. He only shook his head at our costume, but I saw a faint grin there. He was amused. I could tell.

I was pulling the door shut behind me when Heather frowned over her shoulder. "Did you ever call Taylor? Weren't you wondering where she was before?"

"Oh." I'd forgotten. "Yeah."

Heather climbed into the back seat of Mason's Escalade. I remained on the doorstep, pulling my phone out and dialing Taylor's phone. I reached for the door handle again. I was going to close it, when I heard a ringing from upstairs.

I stopped, pulling the phone from my ear.

Rrrrring! Rrrr—

It stopped.

I rang her number again and held my breath, listening.

It was ringing on my end, but I didn't hear anything from inside this time.

I stepped back into the living room. "Taylor? Are you up there?"

"Strattan!" Heather hollered from the vehicle. "My buzz is fading."

I pressed my lips together. I thought I had heard her phone, but that didn't make sense. If she was here, she'd be in Logan's loft on the third floor. I wouldn't be able to hear her phone all the way up there. No. I was just hearing things. That's all it was.

I texted her:

Where are you? Call me.

Then I put the phone in my pocket and locked the door behind me.

Nine

The house was insane.

People were lined up out on the front sidewalk, waiting to get in. There were tombstones on the lawn, with mechanical ghosts popping up from behind and screaming before going back down. As we pulled up, some girls who had just joined the line screamed and fell down after the first ghost. If I hadn't been buzzed, I would've too.

Heather scrambled out. "That's awesome."

I raised my eyebrows at Mason as I climbed out. He was dropping us off, then parking somewhere else, and, knowing Mason, he'd be jumping over some backyard fences in a shortcut to the party.

He shrugged. "Don't act like you don't know him. He's your brother too."

"He was yours first."

I shut the door and saw Heather's raised eyebrows.

"What?" I moved around her. "Yes. I went there."

"Not your best retort." She started beside me.

A few people grumbled when they realized we were cutting, but my glare shut them up. No way was I waiting in line for Logan's party. The three guys who were trying to keep some order started to hold up their hands to stop us. "Really?" I clipped out, and we were shown inside. They opened the doors and stepped aside.

The inside was just as impressive.

It was dark inside, with a single lit-up path leading down a hallway. The first room was covered in goo. I tried telling myself it was probably just pudding, but it felt disgusting. We went down the path and hands shot out from somewhere to grab our ankles. I screamed, then kicked out. A muffled curse came next, but I wasn't grabbed again.

That didn't last long.

We had to go past another set of rooms. I heard screaming, so I was ready ahead of time, but when we got there, there was no preparing. The lights on the path turned off, and we had to stand still. I grabbed on to Heather, and she held me back. Neither of us spoke. We both knew we had to just endure this.

Then suddenly a light flashed, and a body hurled toward us.

"AHH!" I screamed. I couldn't hold this one in either, and I jumped on top of Heather.

"Oomph." She caught me, but looked up. "Are you serious?"

"Carry me. Be my Mason."

"Fuck that." She tossed me off. "You got legs. Use 'em."

What she was saying made sense, but my knees weren't accepting it. They were knocking together and I was about to drop to the floor. I grabbed on to her, holding myself upright. "I'm going to kill Logan."

"Me too." But she held on to me and we moved forward, like two grannies looking for their dropped dentures somewhere.

The third room wasn't bad. We walked on crushed eggshells. Not a lovely feel, and they didn't sound the best either. The fourth section was a hallway. This one had zombies, and yes, they chased us. I punched one. I wasn't discriminating. Anything that came at us was getting hit. I'd never signed a disclaimer.

"I'm suddenly realizing why your knight in shining armor didn't come with us," Heather cursed, her hand clenched around my costume. "That fucker bypassed this for the real party."

We could hear bass music somewhere. I was assuming the basement, but we had to get there. I sighed. "Why didn't I think of wearing our night-vision goggles to this thing?"

Heather stopped. I ran into her.

As I bounced back, she whirled on me. "You have night-vision goggles?!"

"Logan's . . ." And yep, I was cursing myself again. He probably had them with him. He was probably wearing them. He was probably right behind us.

Acting on a theory, I punched the air behind me.

Nothing.

"What are you doing?"

I turned back, lifting my shoulder up. "Had a hunch. Didn't pan out."

She grunted, and we were told by a loud booming voice, "PROCEED, UNDERLINGS."

I jumped again, flicking my middle finger up. "Fuck you."

Heather snorted in laughter, but we edged forward again, practically wrapped around each other. She laughed, muffling it by pressing her mouth into my shoulder. "We're really embodying our costume. Two ends of a horse's ass."

"Shut up." But I was laughing. "And it's a farting unicorn costume."

"Is there really a difference?"

"Pastel colors and glitter? We could glitter these assholes later."

"I'm down for that." She raised her voice as we bypassed one more room, and someone lunged for us with a bloodied chainsaw. "We're going to fart glitter on you! Back OFF, CHAINSAW ASSHOLE!"

The guy did, holding his hands up. The chainsaw was attached to him by a strap. "Hey. Just doing what I was told."

"We're friends of Logan's. We want the shortcut to the basement."

He grinned, his face a grotesque green and bloody red. "Like we haven't heard that before."

"Hey!" I was in his face, shaking my finger. Heather was right behind me. "I'm Logan's stepsister." I wasn't above dropping names in this situation. "I fuck Mason Kade."

Heather's head popped out. "And I have a weird sisterly friendship with Logan." She paused. "I don't fuck Mason Kade. I don't even really talk to him. Full disclosure."

He held his hands up. "It's hard to recognize you with the whole . . ." he gestured to our costume. My black hair was covered by the white costume. "You know."

"Where's the basement?"

He pointed further down. "You're almost there. When

the line cuts right, go left. There's a back door to the basement there."

"Traitor!" someone called from behind us.

Heather glanced back. "You want us to fart glitter on you too? We'll come back and find you. It *will* happen, trust me."

The voice came back. "If the door sticks, just pull a little harder."

A second person said, "What a wuss. It's fucking glitter. Seriously?"

The first one retorted, "That shit doesn't shower off of you. You'll be wearing it for two weeks. Real turn-on when you're trying to get your dick sucked later."

Heather yelled back, "Okay. Thank you. We don't need to hear about your future date aspirations." Her hand tightened on my arm. "Let's go."

The line went right. We did as instructed, finding a doorknob, and when the door swung open to reveal pure darkness, I said, "Hold on." I felt the wall around us until I felt a light switch, and flicked the light on. Voila. Stairs appeared before us. We hurried in, shutting the door, but we left the light on. I was guessing we'd been told the back way into the basement party. There should have been more lighting.

"This place is freaky as fuck."

I nodded. "Good on Logan's part, huh?"

We got to the end. I was looking for another way out, but there was nothing. We'd stepped into a cement room. I couldn't even see bookshelves, or under a wall or anything. It was three cement walls around us, and I looked behind the stairs—nothing there.

Chills went down my spine. "Heather . . ."

"That asshole set us up."

I started to push her back to the stairs. "We should go upstai—"

The light went out, plunging us into darkness.

"AH!"

"AH!"

We both started screaming, and we didn't stop.

"WHAT THE FUCK DO WE DO?"

I sagged against the wall. I didn't know, but I stopped screaming. My voice was already starting to hurt.

"Phones. We have phones."

"You're right." I could hear the relief in her voice, and felt her reaching for her pocket—then she froze. "Fuck."

"Fuck?" I was feeling for mine too. Nothing. Both of my pockets . . . I didn't have pockets. Neither of us had pockets.

"We gave them to Mason in the car."

I hadn't wanted to run the risk of losing mine, so I'd handed it over. Heather had followed suit.

I finished her train of thought. "Because our costume doesn't have pockets."

We both paused, then said together, "Shit!"

Okay. Fine. We could improvise. I began feeling the wall. "We need to go back up. Just follow this back to the stairs and we'll go u—"

Something clicked.

It wasn't the lock.

But it sounded like it was.

And it sounded like it came from the top of the stairs.

I wasn't going to let myself think that way. No one would lock us in.

Heather's voice hitched up. "What was that?"

"Um." My mind was scrambling in the same rhythm

as my heartbeat. It wanted to pound its way out of my chest. "I . . ." had no idea.

It most definitely was the door upstairs. The chainsaw asshole had done this. He was probably following orders, just like he said. Logan might've said, "Hey, if two chicks try to cut the line, send them to the other basement." Then that guy might have been like, "Sure, no problem." And he had. He'd lied to us, instead of helping us.

I'd make Mason hold him down so I could stick our glitter up his real asshole.

And none of these thoughts were making me feel better. I felt ready to puke, if anything.

Heather was shaking behind me. I grunted. "Aren't you always the tough one in our duo? You're the unicorn's brains."

"Give me a bar brawl, and I'm there. Give me 'locked up in a dingy serial-killer basement'? Fuck no. It's all you. This is your expertise. You grew up with the psychopath." She patted my arm. "Get to it, prodigal psychopath. Lead us out of here." Fear put edges in her tone. She whimpered. "Please."

I groaned. She wasn't helping me. "I'm not a prodigal psychopath. My mom *was* a psychopath, I'll give you that." I started edging forward. The steps would appear again. "But I'm not a prodigal anything. If anything, I'm a running prodigy."

She snorted. "Or a prodigy at screwing Mason Kade." Her voice went up a notch. She mimicked me, "'I fuck Mason Kade.'"

I laughed with her, some of the tension easing now. "Shut up." I edged further ahead, using my hand to feel the wall. We came to the end and I felt the bottom of it with my foot. When I felt the stairs, I sighed in relief. "It was supposed to strike terror in that guy."

"Yeah. Didn't happen."

"Here." I took her hand and guided her around me, showing her where the handrail for the stairs was. "Feel that? Just hold it tight, and we can go back up the stairs."

"What if that sound was him locking us in?"

"Then . . ." I was hoping that wasn't the case. "We'll break that bitch down."

She groaned, falling in line behind me as we started up the stairs. "Why don't I have a good feeling about this?"

My hand held on tighter to the railing and I muttered under my breath, "Welcome to my life." But we were going up and we were getting out of here, whether or not that door opened.

I was ready to raise holy hell.

Ten

The door was locked.

That pissed me off. Even as I reached for it, tried to turn it, and it didn't budge—I wasn't scared. I was livid.

"Is that—it that locked?"

I ignored Heather and pounded on the door. "LET US THE FUCK OUT!" One second. "NOW!" When the door didn't immediately open, I didn't wait.

Holy hell, here I come. I was about to raise some.

I started banging on the door nonstop. There were no pauses between my fists and my yells. There were no windows down there, or doors, or secret walls. We were locked in a coffin. Okay, it might've been a pantry, but it was a coffin to me.

"LET US THE FUCK OUT! RIGHT NOW! I'M NOT GOING TO STOP!"

I banged the hell out of that door. I didn't stop until I heard a sob from behind me. "Heather?"

"I am scared shitless right now."

That was enough. My rage and terror switched to re-sourcefulness. This was a door. Doors weren't cemented in, unlike the walls below. They had to be added, and . . . I felt along the end of it, finding the frame. That meant they had to be screwed in. No. I had to pull the pins out of the hinges.

"Okay. Heather." I was going to get this door off, even if my fingers got all cut up and busted. I needed my feet to run, not my hands. "Do me a favor, okay?"

"I'm not leaving you."

"I know. I know, but I'm going to undo these screws, so I might need your help." I waited. Another pause.

Then, "What do you need me to do?"

"Hold me up, so that I don't fall. Just brace yourself on a step and dig in. If I start falling, hold on to the rail with everything you've got."

"That doesn't sound like a good plan."

"I know, but I'm improvising here."

"I'm going to murder Logan when we get out of here."

"That's good. Murder. Keep envisioning that."

"I'm going to take that carving knife we used on those pumpkins and I'm going—"

She kept going, but I tuned her out. I had to focus on the hinge pins, and they were in there tight. I cringed, already feeling my skin tear, but I didn't cry out. That'd alarm Heather. I couldn't have her scared any more than she was. That wasn't going to help, so I kept going. The pain was ignored. I felt warm wetness dripping down my hands and knew it was blood. I could smell it, but I hoped Heather didn't.

When I got one undone, the door sagged, just a tiny bit. It gave me more momentum and I had to stretch for the second hinge pin. The last was in the middle. I wanted to keep it for last, to help steady the door. Once that was done, I didn't know what was going to happen. I had a few theories, though. My stomach was twisting up at all of them.

Success. I felt the hinge pin fall free.

The blood was dripping down my arm. I ignored it.

"Okay." I took a breath.

It was dark. I knew Heather was there, but it was easy to let my imagination run free. It was just as easy to imagine someone behind us, someone sneaking up the stairs, someone that wasn't supposed to be there, someone who hadn't been there before.

I shut that down, real fucking quick.

We were almost free. I wasn't going to let fear stall us now.

"Heather," I said, reaching for the last and final screw. My fingers were almost numb. They were twisted in there so tight.

"Yes?"

She had been sitting on the stairs, but stood now.

I began to twist and I felt the door becoming more and more loose. "This door is heavy. We're at an angle. We're beneath it—"

"When you're done, it's going to fall."

She was steady. Her voice sounded calm.

I stopped unscrewing, just for a moment. "You're not scared?"

Another snort in disgust. "Fuck yes I am, but you're not giving up. I won't either. You're doing all the work. It's the least I can do to help you how I can."

Here was the old Heather, so sure of herself, so strong and confident. Relief surged through me, letting me breathe a bit more oxygen. I felt my lungs fill up. "Okay.

Yeah. That's what is going to happen. When I'm done, this door is going to go. It might even go before that." And it would plunge down on anyone that was sneaking up to scare the shit out of us, or kill us. Whichever came first. I knew it was a figment of my imagination. No one was there, but still . . . I could've sworn I heard a third set of breathing.

My ears were playing tricks on me, just like they had with Taylor's phone.

I stopped; the screw was almost out. I could pull it out in a few heartbeats. "You ready?"

She grabbed on to my arm, and I heard her tighten her hold on the handrail. "Ready."

I didn't get the chance to pull the screw out, or have it fall. The door gave way first. It fell, knocking against my shoulder, but it swung to the other wall. The screw held fast for just a moment, which stopped the door from taking us out; then suddenly, there was a harsh sound of metal being torn and a loud thud, and *BOOM!*

The door hinge had torn off, and the door dropped. It hit the stairs once, then flipped and landed on the floor.

I had a stinging shoulder and numb fingers as my reward. Stepping out, I ran smack dab into a chest.

Hands grabbed my arms. "What the fuck?!"

I almost cried out. It was Mason. He'd found us.

I was sitting on a bathroom counter with Mason standing between my legs. He was bandaging my fingers, while I held an ice pack to my shoulder. Heather sat on the toilet with the seat down. A blanket was draped over her shoulders, and she was resting her elbows on her knees. When Mason found us, or when I ran into him, he took a page from my book. He started raising holy hell too.

The entire haunted house tour was paused. Lights were switched on, and Logan ran to find us.

We were bundled up and swept into a bathroom, and that was where we were now.

"I swear to God, Sam. I didn't do this." Logan sent someone to the store to grab a first-aid kit. He'd begun pacing while he waited for them, and once it was brought up, he'd been pacing back and forth in the bathroom ever since.

I glared around him. He went past where Mason's back obstructed my view and I moved my head. I wanted to maintain constant glaring status. I loved Logan. He was family, but I was beyond livid.

I snapped, "Bullshit."

"I didn't." His hand hadn't moved from the top of his hair. He was pulling at it. "I mean it. I told the guys to show you to the basement as soon as you got here. I didn't even know about that room. The door—" He stopped.

When they flicked the lights on, a large hole stood before us, but when we looked down, I felt new chills. The door looked exactly like the rest of the kitchen's walls. It was a secret door, secret room. The whole thing was camouflaged, and if I'd been in the kitchen during daylight, I would've walked right past it like Logan was saying he had.

I had no idea how we'd found it, but we had.

I believed him, of course I did, but I was scared and I was mad, and I wanted someone to blame. Logan was throwing the party, so he got the brunt of it.

I wasn't alone in the glaring. Mason was doing his share, and Heather hadn't stopped. She was almost camouflaged under the white blanket someone found for her. Some of her pink mane was sticking out.

"That guy did it, then. He told us to go down there."

"What guy?"

"The one with the chainsaw."

Heather added, "Chainsaw asshole. That guy."

Logan didn't say anything. He stared at me, then Heather, then Mason.

My stomach dropped again. I was getting tired of this sick feeling.

But. I had to ask.

"What?"

He exchanged another look with Mason before his eyes found mine.

He said, "There is no chainsaw guy."

Eleven

"Logan!" Heather came out of her seat. It was like she had lifted off. She literally came out of the seat at him. Her eyes were irate. "Don't you dare joke like that! There was a chainsaw guy. Another guy talked to him. We aren't crazy."

He started to shake his head, dead serious, then stopped, and a smirk showed. "I'm kidding. Of course there was a chainsaw guy, but he told you the wrong door. We really didn't know about that room. The real basement door was just past it." He leaned back against the doorframe and crossed his arms over his chest. "I have no idea how you guys even found that door."

"The doorknob."

He swung his gaze my way. "I know, but no one else saw that knob. I swear, Sam. I don't think it was there before." He held his hands up, palms toward me. "No one, and I mean not one person, saw a doorknob there before tonight. Swear to God."

That didn't make anything better. A wave of helplessness crushed down on me. I rested my forehead against Mason's chest. He finished bandaging my hands, but once he was done, he smoothed a hand down my back. "You in pain?"

He said that so softly. It almost broke me.

I swallowed the pain, I swallowed the defeat, and looked up. "I'm fine, but I'm kinda not in the partying mood now."

He nodded. His hand was still on my back as he twisted around to Logan. "I'm going to take them back to the house."

Heather let her head fall back. "Thank goodness. I'm so down for that."

Logan nodded, his hand scratching the back of his neck. He was giving me an odd look.

"What?"

His eyes skimmed over my costume, then Heather's. "Uh. Do I ask what you guys are?"

I snorted. "Not the time for that."

"Okay." He nodded, then his hand dropped from his neck. "Oh. Hey. Where's Taylor?"

My body's temperature dropped two degrees. My blood was ice-cold again. "What do you mean?" I felt a lump form in my throat and keep growing. I knew. I so knew what he was going to say, and I had known it from the beginning.

Something happened to Taylor.

He spoke, and a buzz started in my ears. His words sounded like they were coming from a distance. "She said she was with you guys today. She didn't come to the party tonight?"

I saw Heather gasp. I didn't hear it.

Her mouth dropped open. Her eyes shot to mine, and

the small amount of color she'd gotten back drained once
again from her face.

Something had happened to Taylor.

The alarms were blaring in my head, but I coughed,
forced that fucking lump away, and managed, "Uh. I'll
give her a call once we get home."

We couldn't panic.

Not yet.

I had to get back to the house. I'd heard that ringtone.
I'd rip the fucking house apart if need be. And if she
wasn't there, if she hadn't just fallen asleep, or decided to
use Nate's room for some reason—or maybe she'd gotten
locked in the closet, who the hell knew?—I wanted to get
there and look first, and then I'd start raising holy hell all
over again.

Mason felt my body tense, and shifted back to get a
better view of my face. What he saw made a wall slam
down over his features. He glanced from me to his brother,
and his jaw clenched. His hand pressed harder on my
back, but he controlled his voice. It came out like he was
annoyed, but not too worried. "What's the fastest way out
of here?"

Logan paused in the doorway. His eyebrows pulled
together.

Mason's smile was strained. "So we don't have to go
through the whole haunted house part of it."

"Oh." Logan's eyebrows smoothed back out. He gestured to the bedroom that our bathroom was attached to.
"I'll show you guys the back way."

The short trek took forever. Every second that I had to
pretend to be calm stripped a year from my life. I was
almost shaking with the effort by the time Logan opened
that last door and I saw the night air. I shot past him, but

I couldn't race for the street. I didn't know where Mason had parked.

It was another few seconds that seemed like lifetimes before Logan waved us off and shut the door behind him again.

Mason didn't waste time. "What happened?"

I gritted my teeth. "Where's your Escalade?"

He pointed toward the back of the house. "I got a spot in the alley behind the house."

That was enough. I tore out of there. I was the one who'd gotten hurt, so everyone else needed to keep up with me. I wasn't slowing down.

Mason ran ahead of me and had the vehicle unlocked and the engine started by the time I hopped in. Heather was a few beats behind, and once he took off and our seat belts were on, I said, "She didn't answer her phone. All. Day. She didn't answer." I began searching the console. "Where's my phone?" He didn't show me fast enough, and my voice rose, "Where's my PHONE?"

"Here. Here." He pulled my and Heather's phones out of his pocket.

I checked again. There were my calls for Taylor. I hit dial again. I had to try once more.

Nothing. It went straight to voicemail.

Panic rose up, like vomit.

I pushed it down, but my stomach wouldn't stop clenching.

I choked out, "I called her when we left, and I heard the phone ring in the house." *Please be okay.* "It stopped, and I called her again. It went through on my end, but I didn't hear it again."

What if . . . Terror sliced through me. Did I really want to follow through on that thought?

What if . . .

The phone had been ringing. The phone was there. She was there. She had been there. It had been ringing—then stopped. It didn't ring again.

She would've called out.

She would've called me back, texted me back. She would've said something.

The phone was turned off.

Someone else was there.

Someone else turned it off.

I started shaking. I didn't even know I was until Heather grabbed my arm, reaching around the seat's divider from behind. She scooted to the edge of her seat and leaned forward, her cheek resting against where my shoulder was by my seat. Her hand gripped my arm. "We'll find her."

She's gone by now.

I couldn't say that, though. I couldn't even shake my head. I knew. I knew!

She was gone.

Mason pulled into the driveway. He stopped, and I threw my door open. I ran. My feet pounded on the sidewalk, going to the door. My heart was lodged in my throat. It was too scared to keep beating.

The door was locked.

I hit it, then bounced back.

Not even reacting, I dug for my keys.

My pocket—there were still no pockets. Fuck it. Fine. I grabbed under the step for the extra key. I fit the key into the lock.

My hands were shaking now.

The key fell.

I grabbed it again, and shoved it in. The lock moved, and I was inside.

That sound had come from upstairs.

"SAM!"

Mason raced behind me. He probably didn't want me going without him, or wanted me to stay behind, to let him look. I didn't care.

Taylor.

She was all that mattered.

She needed me. Only me.

It didn't make sense, but I knew it. I felt it. I almost thirsted for it.

My feet were a dull sound, stampeding up the stairs, like I wasn't hearing them, like I wasn't even there anymore. I was beyond, already searching the doors, looking for Taylor.

I threw open Nate's door.

Nothing.

His bed was empty.

I tore open the closet—the clothes he'd left behind fell off a hanger. Nothing. I could see every inch of the closet. There was nowhere to hide.

She wasn't there.

His bathroom next. No. The shower door was transparent; I could see inside, and it was empty.

On to the next room. I was leaving Nate's when Mason shot past me. He tore into the extra bathroom there—but it was the same. Empty. We didn't even have a curtain hanging over the tub in there. No one used it. The drawers were too small. A body couldn't be folded up in them.

I glimpsed someone standing behind me, paused at the top of the stairs, and I whirled around. A scream stuck in

my throat. It was Heather. *Keep going, Sam. I need you.*
A voice spoke to me in my head. It was soft, low, soothing.

It wasn't mine. It was Taylor's.

Mason opened the hallway closet, but no. Again, no.
Always no. It would always be no.

The last door was to Logan's loft. He locked it sometimes, if we had people over, or if there was a big party
going on. That was the only time he locked it. We all had
locks on our doors so our stuff wouldn't get stolen.

I yanked at the door handle. The door didn't move.

Someone gasped. It might've been me. I didn't care. I
whirled around, already feeling Mason behind me, and I
stepped aside.

He rammed into the door and it crashed open. It tore
from the hinges—a second door, lost. That thought was
in the back of my mind, and a part of me, the part that
was in the back of my mind, that was too afraid to come
forward, started giggling at that. It was funny to her. It
wasn't to me. I was acting on pure blind rage at this
moment.

Mason went first, barking at me to stay back.

No. If she was up there, I was too. If he was going
there, I would too. I was with both of them. I wasn't staying behind. But I knew—just at the sight of how Mason's
shoulders sagged—she wasn't there.

There was one last spot. Mason stopped in the middle
of the room. I veered around him. Logan and Taylor used
a bathroom that was attached to the far side of the room.

I crashed through the door. She was going to be there. I
had visions of her in the bathtub, her throat slashed. Blood
dripping down her body, coating it even, and those eyes . . .
I shuddered. They'd be glazed over and lifeless.

Nothing.

I stopped in shock.

Absolutely nothing.

The bathtub was spotless. Two towels were folded on the side. A bar of soap next to them. It looked like a hotel. The shower was spotless as well.

Wait . . . what? I had known. It was in my bones. I'd known I would find her here.

I stepped back, stepping into Mason, whose hands came to my shoulders. I shook my head. "I thought she'd be there."

His fingers tightened. He started to say something, when a blood-curdling scream ripped from beneath us.

Mason and I both tore out of there. I could outrun him in long-distance runs, but not sprinting. He dominated—it's what he did for a living—but not that day, and not in that house. I ducked around him, pushing forward with a burst of speed I'd never used.

I raced down the loft's small set of stairs, through the second-floor hallway—Heather was gone. I noted that in the back of my mind, but I kept going. That scream was beneath us. I barely touched the stairs.

Beneath us.

I kept repeating that in my head.

Beneath us on the first floor.

The hallway led to my room with Mason. There was a guest bathroom. Storage closets. Then our room.

No, that voice in my head said. She wasn't giggling anymore. She wasn't soothing. She just sounded sad. She added, *The basement, Sam.*

The basement door was open. I touched down on the stairs, leaping my way down—and there was Heather. She was backed up against the wall, her eyes glued to the bathroom, her hands cupped over her mouth, but she kept screaming. I didn't think she'd ever stop. Not anymore.

And I knew.

I faltered now, coming to the open door. I reached for the handle to brace myself.

I looked in—that voice in my head said, *Right spot, wrong bathroom*—and there she was.

She was just like how I knew she would be. Taylor was slumped in the tub, her head propped against the wall, eyes wide open to look at us, like she'd been looking at her killer.

I couldn't—another gut-wrenching scream. This one wasn't from Heather. It was me, and that voice, that person who was in the back of my mind, pulled away from me.

It wasn't safe to be in my body right now.

I crumpled to the floor, still screaming.

And I pulled away.

I passed Mason, who sprinted behind me, his hand automatically reaching to comfort me, but also to steady himself.

I was floating backward.

Away from them.

Up the stairs.

Through the house.

Out the front door.

Past Mason's Escalade.

All the way down the street.

And then I heard that voice in my head again, but it wasn't Taylor's and it wasn't mine anymore. It wasn't sad, or soothing, or laughing. It was someone else's.

He said, *Come to me, Samantha.*

Twelve

Taylor was dead.

I couldn't make sense out of that or comprehend it. I don't think I wanted to. No, she wasn't. She was alive. She lied to Logan when she said she was with us because . . . I searched for reasons. Because she wanted to surprise him? Because she wanted to shop for a secret gift for him? Because—any reason, except the real one. Then she'd be alive. Then she'd be breathing and sitting next to me. She wouldn't be covered in a blanket, and I wouldn't be sitting in a neighbor's living room, having a detective ask me questions that I couldn't understand either.

I became a robot. That's the only way I could keep going.

Mason was wringing his hands together. He was in the kitchen, just behind me. Heather was in a bedroom somewhere. They'd separated us and got a different detective to ask each of us what I was assuming were the same questions.

I told them what I knew.

Why hadn't I gone and searched for her if I thought I'd heard her phone? They'd asked me that four times now. Every time felt like another knife plunged into my stomach. I could physically feel it, and they would stop, adjust their grip on it, and yank it all the way through me. I would split in half.

But every time they asked, I said the same thing.

I wish I had.

God, I wished I had.

I was probably crying. They didn't care. I didn't care. My hands were wet, so I assumed it was from that, but maybe I should have stopped assuming things. I had assumed Taylor wasn't upstairs.

I'd been wrong.

What else had I assumed that was wrong?

A bubble worked past the two halves of my body, where they kept putting their knife in, and found its way in my throat, then up and over the lump that I had to stop trying to shove down. It came out, and when I heard what that bubble was, I was cringing again.

Hysterical laughter that bordered on mania.

I was a lunatic. And once the first bubble escaped, more kept coming. I couldn't stop them.

The two detectives standing over me shared a look. I saw the sudden suspicion in their gazes. I mean, it had been there already, but it went to a whole other level now that they heard me laughing. I was having a gay old time. I was going on a rollercoaster. I was at an amusement park—the laughter stopped then.

Taylor and Logan fell in love on an abandoned roller coaster.

Yes.

The tears came again. A heavy wave each time, and they were cascading down my face.

How did I get here? How did Taylor end up dead? Who did this? Why hadn't I looked upstairs?

I whispered, "This is all my fault."

The cops were talking to each other. Their heads snapped to mine. One bent down, resting his hands on his knees. He was peering down at me, almost on my level, but not. Just above. He still had to maintain his intimidating height. He couldn't do that if I started thinking he was on my level, that he was kind to me, that he cared about me.

He asked, "What did you say?"

I looked up, not giving one damn what they thought of me. I was Taylor. She was dead. So was I. "This is my fault."

The second detective moved quickly. He made a gesture behind his back. A uniformed policeman brought one of the kitchen chairs over, and he sat on it. He softened his tone, but I knew it was a farce. All of this was a facade. He asked, as if he *did* actually care, "What do you mean when you say it's your fault?"

"I heard her phone. If I looked, she might be alive." She would be alive.

"No, Sam."

Mason overheard me, and he left the kitchen. Four police got in his way, but he pushed against them. His eyes were only on me. He was holding an ice pack to his arm, like he'd been hurt. I frowned. When had he gotten hurt?

He shook his head. "This isn't your fault. You could've been killed too. You have no idea."

"But you were here." I clung to his eyes. They were the only part of him I could hold on to at that moment. "You were in the car. Heather was too. If I'd gone in, you would've come looking for me."

"And whoever did this could've gutted you."

I flinched at that word—gut. But it was used correctly. She had been gutted. We all saw.

"Don't blame yourself, Sam. Please don't." He was whispering. He was so agonized over what I was feeling.

Another reason among so many others why I loved him.

But he was wrong. I whispered, my throat burning, "I could've saved her." I knew I was right. I could've, and I hadn't.

All of this was my fault.

It wasn't long, but it seemed to take forever for the authorities to show up when they did. We didn't call them. One of the neighbors dialed 911 because of the screaming. We were still there, all still in our same positions when they came inside. Guns were drawn, then holstered when they saw there was no threat.

Time blurred after that.

I was led away, brought upstairs, and taken outside. I registered the feel of the air, and that I was crossing the street, then going into another home. Someone else lived there. I felt the aliveness of it. It was warm and loving, giving. It was what our house would never be again. At some point, I was shivering or trembling. Or, I don't know. A blanket was draped over me at some point, but I don't think it was because I was cold. They sat me in this living room chair and I wasn't allowed to leave.

I could see outside, but I didn't want to. I was waiting now.

Cop cars were everywhere, lighting up the street. An ambulance came. I didn't know why. No one was hurt— wait, no. Mason had an ice pack, maybe he'd been the hurt one. Or maybe that was how they transported her body? That made more sense. They'd have to take her to get examined, because this was a crime. The morgue wouldn't come to take her for a funeral.

She'd been murdered.

Our house was a crime scene.

We'd have to go to a hotel? I glanced up. The detectives were so suspicious of me. Would they even allow that? Maybe I'd sit in a cell? The thought of it almost warmed me. That made sense. I wasn't going to sleep anyways. I didn't think I'd sleep for the rest of my life. I could go there, be close to them for questioning, and I'd wait until they gave me answers. Who had done this? Why? Those were the most pressing ones.

I heard the screech of tires.

I'd been waiting for this, and I looked outside again.

Mason looked over—he'd been waiting as well.

A yellow Escalade careened to a stop. The door was thrust open and Logan launched himself out of the vehicle. I was sure the keys were still in there. The engine probably hadn't been turned off.

I tensed.

Waiting.

Then—there it was. Another blood-curdling scream from inside the house.

I closed my eyes, knowing who the owner was, and held my breath. If he got in there, they wouldn't let him get far.

"TAYLOR!"

I looked. I didn't want to, but I did. There was an agony that stripped all the way down to my soul. The sound would be in my nightmares, along with Taylor's body, and when I opened my eyes, I stood.

The cops buzzed around me, alarmed by my sudden movement. Mason was moving too, but we weren't going anywhere.

Logan was dragged outside, with five cops holding him back. Another two were in front of them, like a backup wall if he got loose. He wasn't who I was watching, though.

They were bringing *her* out.

Her body was on a stretcher, covered by a white sheet. Some of the blood had soaked through. I took another step toward the window. I raised my hand, touching the glass. This was her last farewell.

"Sam." Mason's arms wrapped around me. His chin lowered to rest on my shoulder, and we watched as a member of our family was taken away.

We wouldn't be whole again.

There was now someone gone, and she couldn't come back.

Thirteen

We were released, or that was the word the cops used. We weren't allowed to go back into the house. We had to give them a list of what we needed to stay at a hotel. After they looked through our phones, we got those back.

Channing came moments later, and he hadn't left Heather's side since she came back out from wherever the cops had taken her.

The ride to the hotel was the quietest, longest, and worst ride of my life. I'd remember it forever: the moment when we pulled away from the house, away from the flashing red and blue lights. I looked back and it was like I was seeing it in slow motion. Channing drove Heather, Mason, and me. Nate drove Logan.

I couldn't deal with it. Any of it.

Once we got to the hotel, a hot shower didn't help. I kept seeing her. The screams were ricocheting in my head. Heather's scream. Logan's. Mine. They all melded together and became Taylor's voice.

I shook my head; I was curled up in a hotel robe on the bed. I'd finished my shower, but left the light off. Felt appropriate.

Channing and Heather got their own room, but Nate, Logan, Mason, and I all got a suite together. We had a main living area with our own bedrooms. Our bedroom door was open, just a small inch, and I could hear Mason's voice. I didn't know who he was talking to. I guessed Logan, because Logan wasn't responding. No one was responding.

God.

I choked back a sob, burying my head in the robe's sleeve.

How had this happened? It wasn't supposed to, at least not to her.

I didn't know how to handle this grief.

Hating my mother. The knowledge that your father isn't really your father. Losing friends. That grief was mine. I was an expert at handling that, but this—really losing someone—I was floundering.

Big fat tears were rolling down my face, but I didn't move. What the hell would I do? What now? And Logan—I couldn't face him. He thought she had been with me. That made her my responsibility. He was my family, the third member of our fearsome threesome, and I'd done this to him. It was like I'd gutted him and left him to bleed out.

"Sam?"

I looked up. I didn't sit up from the bed. I remained in my curled fetal position, but I merely moved my head back so I could see who stood in the door.

Channing glanced over his shoulder, then back. His hesitation was obvious. "Uh." His hand curled around the doorframe. "Mason said I could just come over and knock." His eyes fell to my robe. "I can come back, if you want."

"No." I was dressed underneath. It didn't matter. I sat up now, pulling my knees close to me. "What's up? How's Heather?"

"That's why I came in. She . . ." Another pause. He looked down. "She's not doing that well. I was wondering . . ." His hand went to the top of his head. It rested there before falling back down. "I shouldn't be asking this of you. You were closer to the gi—her. Never mind. Sorry."

"No. What?" I wanted something to do. I needed something to do.

He hesitated. He seemed torn, but asked, "Could you come over and just hug her or something? She's just crying. Her brothers are coming, but you were with her . . . I thought it might help."

I frowned. There wasn't a word to describe how drained I felt. "She doesn't want you there?"

"It's not that. I'm not leaving, but I hold her, and she doesn't react. I just wonder if I'm the person she wants right now."

"You are." I nodded. I said it with such certainty. "You are. No one else can replace you in her life. She needs you."

His eyebrows were pulled together, but relaxed at my words. He nodded, blinking back some wetness, and coughed. He cleared his throat. "Okay. Thank you." He frowned again. "Are you okay? I mean . . ." He looked over his shoulder again. "Mason seems busy with Logan, and you're in here alone. Are you sure you don't want to come to the room, so you're not alone?"

He and Heather were family. Logan and Mason were mine. I should be with mine.

I shook my head. "I'll be fine. I'm going to join them. I just needed a moment."

"Okay." His lip twitched up in something that might've been a smile, or a small grin. I didn't know what. Everything looked off to me now. Nothing was right.

He left, and I was alone again.

I could still hear Mason's murmurings, but still nothing from Logan.

Where was Nate?

But even as I thought it, I knew: he was probably with them. He was probably in the same room with them. Or maybe he was doing what I was doing—sitting. Being alone. Listening to them. Or maybe he was like Channing, not sure what to do. Feeling helpless. Trying to find out what to do, how to help, who else to maybe help.

I closed my eyes and lay back down, curling into a small ball. I wanted to be as small as possible. I wanted to disappear, if that was possible.

I waited.

I didn't disappear. I couldn't.

Lying here wasn't helping. My insides were still in shreds. I just didn't want to think about why. It would make me go insane.

I stood, going to the door. I wanted Mason, but I couldn't be selfish and demand him. Logan was hurting the most. He needed his brother. Did Logan need me too? I was like his sister. I was his sister.

I was Taylor's killer too. She died because I didn't save her.

Maybe I should go and comfort Heather? Anything to tear me away from where I was.

I started to leave, then remembered to grab the key card on the table by the door.

"Where are you going?" Mason was behind me.

I couldn't look in his eyes. If I did, I'd collapse. I looked away. "I'm going to check on Heather."

"Oh. Okay."

I swallowed, but I still didn't look up. "How is he?"

"Hurting, Sam. He could use you."

"He has you."

"He needs both of us."

No. My heart squeezed together. He didn't need the person who would always remind him of her. But Mason wouldn't understand that. He wasn't thinking about it, not really. I didn't have the heart to explain it to him.

I shoved my hands in my robe's pockets, my shoulders hunched down, my head still hanging low. "I'll be back," I whispered. "I promise."

Before he could say anything else, I reached behind me, opened the door, and slipped out.

I rushed to Heather's room, but only because it was away from that suite.

I knocked on their door. "Heather? Channing?"

I waited. No response. I knocked again. "Hello?" No response.

I tried the door.

It opened, and I stepped inside, just one foot.

The room was cold.

The lights were off.

A breeze swept through the room, giving me the shivers.

"Heather?" I raised my voice. Were they in the bathroom? My stomach sank to my feet. Would everyone be in the bathroom now? Was this the beginning of a perverted joke? But I crossed the room. The hairs on the back of my neck stood on end. I ignored the pit in my stomach, and I knocked on the bathroom door.

There was no response.

I knocked again, then checked. The door was unlocked.

I held my breath and pushed it open.

Nothing.

I didn't even feel the warmth that lingered when someone had just taken a shower. I turned back around. There
was nothing in the room. There was no reason for me to
believe they'd even been in here.

Did I have the wrong room?

That was it. Had to be it. I started for the hallway again,
then heard a dash of footsteps in the hallway. Someone ran
past where I was.

I darted forward. Who was that? I got to the hallway, it
took two seconds, but they were gone. The tan-and-black
floral pattern on the floor stretched up and down the hallway. No one was there. I started forward.

I heard a soft click to my left, ahead of me.

A door closed.

My head snapped around again. No. The sound was
away from the suite.

I kept going.

I didn't have shoes on. I wasn't dressed to leave the
hallway, never mind the hotel. I'd have to go back if I
didn't find anyone. Still. I pressed on. I didn't even know
what I would find, or if I would find anything, but I kept
going.

I got to the end.

Nothing. No one.

I was sick of this.

I let out a breath of air and started back for the room.
I'd go back and call the front desk. I'd have them ring me
to Heather's correct room.

Another soft click.

I knew I'd heard it this time. My head whipped back around, but still nothing in the hallway. Not even the sound of the ice machine.

The hairs on my neck were standing up. Then again, I don't think they had ever relaxed.

I pressed a hand to my stomach, like that would calm me. It did nothing. I knew it wouldn't, but I had to try. I was walking back to the room. I hadn't realized how far I'd gone. I had four doors to go. Three. Two. I was at Heather's room again.

"Sam?"

I cried out, rounding and falling to the floor. My heart leapt out of my chest.

It was Heather. She stood right behind me, clutching an ice bucket.

I pressed a hand to my chest, making sure everything was still intact there, that nothing had exploded. "You scared the shit out of me."

"Me?" She pointed to me with the bucket. "What are you doing? You're being all creepy and sneaking down the hallway. I followed you from the stairs."

"The stairs?"

"Yeah. I went down there to get ice. Ours is out of order on this floor."

"Did you take the elevator?"

"No. Why would I? It's just one floor."

So *that* had been the door click. "My heart is still racing." I got up, but still held my hand over my heart.

But what about the second door click? The thought nagged me. I would've seen her. I was looking up and down the hallway. And come to think of it, where was the exit sign? I didn't see it. "Where are the stairs?"

She motioned to the door I'd just passed. I widened my eyes. It looked just like another bedroom.

Wait. That didn't make sense either.

I shook my head.

None of this was making sense. Those hairs—they were standing straight up, ramrod straight. There was no slouching. They were at full attention. I asked, "How'd you know that was the stairs?"

"Channing told me."

"What?"

"He said that they switched the signs around, something about not letting media up here, and that this is the door I needed to use for my smoke breaks."

"Where is Channing?"

She frowned. "He said he went to talk to you. I went to get ice after that."

"Oh." I could relax again. "He probably went to look for you like I just did."

"Yeah. Maybe." She shrugged, and went to the room. I followed her, but stood in the doorway. She looked fine, unlike what Channing had claimed. I asked, "Are you doing okay?"

She half-laughed at me. "Are you serious? I should be the one asking you, not the other way around."

"Oh."

There was no reason for me to stay here. I looked over my shoulder at the suite door. Maybe I should go and see how Logan was doing? Maybe he actually did need me? I let out another sigh. I just wished I knew what I should do.

"But how are you doing?" Heather put the ice down, then reached for her cigarettes. She folded them into her pocket and pulled on a sweatshirt.

"I—uh." I looked back at the ground. I didn't want to

think about her. Then I wouldn't even be able to stand. "I think I want to process it later."

"Okay." She held up her cigarettes. "I have to get out of here. I need a smoke. You want one? You look like you could actually use one, but don't get addicted." She grinned, the smile not reaching her eyes. "I've heard they're bad for you. She used to tell me that. Ta—" She stopped, clasping her eyes tightly shut. She bit down on her lip and her head hung low. "Oh God."

All the feelings came rushing in. I started to slide down to the floor. I could feel the sobs coming. I wrapped my arms around myself, warding everything off. I did not want to fall apart.

Heather rushed to me. She slid an arm around me and helped me stand. "I'm sorry, Sam." She tucked a strand of my hair behind my ear. "I'm so sorry."

I couldn't talk.

We stood there, her arms around me, my own arms around me, and I took a moment. Just one. I had to keep going after that, and after a few moments passed, I nodded. I stood straight again. Heather pulled away, still frowning. "You better?"

I flashed her a grin, knowing it was broken. I didn't care about that. I couldn't. "Enough."

"Okay."

We stepped back into the hallway. I went toward the suite. She went to the weird stairway door. She opened it and put one foot inside, pulling her cigarettes out again. "You sure you don't want one? Not trying to push bad shit on you, but." The little light she had in her eyes dimmed. "You know."

I shook my head. "Thank you, but no."

"Okay."

"Hey." I stopped her.

She looked back up.

I gestured to my door. "Find Channing and come in when you get back."

She started to nod. She started to say, "I will—" when a gloved hand appeared around her head. Her eyes bulged out. Her mouth opened to scream, but the hand covered her mouth.

I had one second of warning before the knife was brought to her throat, and in a nanosecond—her throat was slashed.

"NO!"

Blood spewed from her throat, and her body slumped to the ground. I froze.

Her eyes, like Taylor's, had been alive. They had been alarmed. They had been frightened. And then, like Taylor's, they'd become lifeless.

And I couldn't look away.

Fourteen

The suite door crashed open, and Mason rushed out. "SAM!"

She was . . . I couldn't look away, and I fell to my knees. It was like Taylor all over again. Mason came to stand behind me. "Shit." He knelt by me. "Sam."

There was no comprehension.

"Sam." His hand touched my shoulder. "Who did this?"

"Who—" I looked up. There'd been a gloved hand. There was nothing again, just like the other time. "I—" That word gurgled out of me. "I don't know."

They could've killed me. The fight or flight hadn't kicked in for me. I screamed and then froze.

"Wha—oh my God!" Logan rushed from the suite.

Mason yelled past us, "Nate! Stay there!"

"But—"

"STAY!"

I looked up. I didn't want Logan here either. He shouldn't have to see Heather like this too. "No." I began shaking my head, standing, holding my hands out. "Logan, don't be here. Go back inside."

His eyes were glued to her; then he pulled them with an effort to my face, and down to my hands. He didn't look away. A vein bulged out on the side of his neck. "Sam." A breathless whisper. He started to reach for my hands. "Is that yours?"

What? I looked at my hands. They were covered in blood, but—I looked back at Heather's body. I hadn't touched her.

Had I?

This blood—I lifted my hands higher to see. Then I looked at myself. I wasn't cut. It wasn't my blood.

"She touched her." Mason blocked Logan and me from seeing Heather. He stood between me and her. His hands came to my shoulders. They were firm. Authoritative. "Go back inside, both of you."

"Who is it? I can't see." Nate spoke from behind us. Mason was blocking him too.

"Fuck that." Logan frowned. He wasn't trying to look at Heather around his brother. If anything, he backed away a step. "What are you going to do?"

"Someone killed her in front of Sam. I'm going to look for him."

"What?" Logan and I spoke as one. I rounded on my boyfriend. "No, you're not."

"Sam." He gentled his tone. "I have to search for whoever did this. They could've hurt you too."

They could've done worse than that. But neither of us said those words out loud. We were both thinking it, and I saw the plea in his eyes. He wanted me to let him go, let him look. I shook my head. No way. I reached for him. "You go, I go."

Logan cursed and stepped up to us. He avoided looking at Heather. "We all go." That vein popped out again. He looked down at the ground. "Does Channing know?"

Nate asked from the door, "What's going on?"

He was ignored. Mason looked at me.

I shook my head in response to Logan's question.

Logan swore again. "We need to tell him, and we need to call the cops."

"I'll find Channing." Mason pointed back to the suite. "Get in there. Deadbolt the door, and call the police."

"Mase."

Mason had started to go. Logan stopped him, uttering that one word.

Mason looked back.

Logan shook his head. "You're not going anywhere without us. We *all* go inside and call the cops."

Nate cleared his throat. "Yes. Come back in here."

I asked, "And if Channing comes back and finds her like this?"

"I don't care. For all we know, he's the one who did it."

I frowned.

Logan avoided looking at me too, but added to what Mason had said. "We don't know who did it, Sam. You have to be cautious. With everyone."

Not them. They had been behind me in the suite. Not them.

Mason muttered a curse under his breath, running his hand over his face. "Fine." He grabbed my elbow and began walking me back. He used his other hand to push Logan forward too. "We all go in. We need the cops called five minutes ago."

We deadbolted the door. Nate went to the couch. Mason went to the phone, and Logan stood and stared at me.

"Mason said you saw someone last night?"

I nodded to him. "A guy in a black robe and white mask."

"Like *Scream*?"

"There were no facial features in the white mask. It was just a white mask."

"No place for eyes, nose, mouth?" Logan narrowed his eyes.

I shook my head.

"How do they breathe?"

Mason put the phone back down. He'd overheard. "Maybe the material is breathable and thin enough for them to see through?"

Logan gave him a skeptical look, his lips thinning. "You don't know that."

"Neither do you, and what's your issue? You got a tone. You blame Sam for this?"

Logan didn't answer, but his gaze came back to me. It was unflinching. Hardened. His jaw clenched again.

"Bullshit," Mason threw right back, standing between us. He turned to face off against his brother. His back was to me. "For all we know, this is *about* her. Maybe she's the one he's obsessed with? Maybe he's saving her for last?"

"And how would you know all this?" Logan's voice was so biting. "You seem to have put a lot of thought into this already."

Mason tensed. "Walk away, Logan. Before you say something that'll affect our family."

"Shit." It was so soft, so lethal. "Something already has."

But he walked away, and I moved into Mason, resting

my forehead against his back. We stayed like that for I don't know how long, but I didn't want to move.

The cops came, and everything was repeated.

Enduring the cops was a nightmare in and of itself, but I answered the questions. We were moved to another hotel. The crime scene was too close to where we were staying. They wanted to search the hotel anyways. Once everything died down, I just sat there.

They never found Channing. They were supposed to tell us the moment they did.

It was Taylor.

We were trying to get our bearings.

Then it was Heather.

"Sam?"

It was three in the morning, but no one was sleeping. Mason and Nate had both gone to check on Logan, but I wasn't in the room with them. I didn't want to go in there, not yet. I looked over now. Mason was closing Logan's door behind him, crossing to where I was sitting. I was smack dab in the living room, facing the hotel door. The lights were off except for the soft glow from two lamps in the corners. I would've thought it was a romantic setting, if I didn't know the reason we were there.

"Hey," I murmured back.

His hand came to my shoulder, sliding to the back of my neck. I closed my eyes, relaxing into his touch. I sought solace there, but only for a second. I couldn't any longer than that. There were things to do, emotions to ignore, and a killer to handle. I was shoving down all the normal emotions a person might have after having two friends murdered in such a quick amount of time.

I was stewing.

I was letting my anger churn inside of me. It was giving me fuel to keep going, and that was all I had at that moment.

Mason stepped closer and I rested my head against his stomach. He asked, sliding his fingers up through my hair, "How are you?"

I shook my head. I didn't want to talk at that moment. I reached up and held on to his arm, keeping him anchored to me, and he moved in even closer.

No, that wasn't right before, to think I only had my anger left. I still had Mason and Logan.

Mason was comforting me, content to let me not talk. I was drawing in strength just by being near him. He was reaffirming what I needed to do.

I looked back at that door.

I was waiting. That's what I was doing.

And as if the killer could see me, could know what I was doing, a snarl came to my lips. *Come and get me, you asshole.*

And as if I could hear him too, he murmured in my head, *I'll be right there.*

Fifteen

"Samantha."

I woke, my heart pounding, and bolted upright in bed. When had I gone to bed? But I looked around. Mason was sleeping next to me, his eyes closed, his chest lifting up and down at a steady pace. I ran a hand through my hair, feeling the exhaustion pulling at me. It wanted me to lie back down and let it take over, but no. I heard my name. That's what woke me up.

I moved to the edge of the bed, and started to stand up, when *he* showed up in the doorway.

I could only stare at first.

There was no scream. No gasp. Just the view of a man in a black robe with white all over his face. There were no eyes. No mouth. It was like he wasn't even a person.

I froze.

Ice-cold fear ran down my spine and chilled my entire body.

Run, Sam!
Tell Mason!
Wake Mason!
Get Mason to safety! Get yourself to safety!

All of those thoughts raced through my mind, but I couldn't do a goddamn thing. I could only gape at him, and he stepped into the room, showing a knife in his hand now.

A choked gurgle came out of me, and I felt Mason move in the bed. "Sam?" he murmured, the same exhaustion I'd felt seconds ago evident in his voice. "What's going on?" He ran a hand down my arm.

I was shaking.

That's what woke him up.

I was making the entire bed tremble beneath us. He felt the quaking tremors in my arm and sat up.

"Sam—" The words died in his throat. He saw him too. Unlike me, Mason didn't freeze, but almost levitated out of the bed. He lunged for him, but the guy was gone. Mason fled the room, and I heard the door slamming shut seconds later. I still couldn't move.

He'd been here.

He was standing over us.

He could've killed us. One plunge, one swipe at the right angle, and Mason would be bleeding out on the floor right now.

Now I felt the bed shaking. It was like an earthquake.

"Sam?" Logan appeared in the doorway, pale and wide-eyed. He braced himself, resting both hands on the door-frame. "What's going on?"

"Ma—"

Finally! Words came out of my throat, but Mason returned, saying, "The killer was here."

"What?!" Logan's mouth dropped, his hand fisted into his hair. "He was here?"

"He got away." Mason shouldered past him and stood over me, his eyes narrowed. "You okay?"

I bounced my head up and down. That's all I could manage. The fear still had a paralyzing hold on me.

He waited for my answer, then closed his eyes and drew in a deep breath. "Fuck." He sank onto the bed beside me, catching his head in his hands. "Fuck! He was here!"

"We have to move."

"No." Mason stopped Logan, reaching for the phone. "We have to call the cops."

"What for? The fucker's not getting caught. He keeps showing up." Logan clipped his head from side to side. "No way. We take care of him ourselves."

"What are you saying?" Mason asked.

"That we take care of the fucker ourselves. We set a trap. Catch him, then call the cops."

Mason didn't reply, not at first. He stared at his brother. The two were embroiled in some form of stare-off, but I knew Mason was contemplating Logan's idea. Logan was waiting.

Call for help, to those who hadn't helped us so far, or do the deed ourselves.

Fear like I'd never felt before pooled at the bottom of my spine, but I already knew what we were going to do. It was what we always did. We fought.

And a moment later, Mason said what I knew he'd say. "Let's catch the fucker."

Logan dipped his head in a nod this time. "Good." He pounded the door frame. "I'll wake Nate up. We should—"

Mason finished for him. "—move locations. I've already got an idea."

I waited to see if Logan would look at me before he left. He didn't. This killer was here because of me, I was sure of it, and he'd murdered Taylor, and then Heather. We never had found out anything about Channing. The killer could've taken him out too, but I was feeling the weight of both of my friends' deaths. It was like they were with us in that room, they were beside me, breathing down my neck.

It was my responsibility to avenge them.

"What's wrong?"

Mason had been watching me, and his hand came down to rest on my knee.

My insides were twisting together. I felt the need to purge myself, throw everything up, but I just stuffed the urge down. "Nothing."

"Sam."

"No. I mean it. I'm fine." I wanted to get this asshole. I wanted to take the knife and plunge it into his heart.

"You're pushing me away. Don't do that."

"Why not?" I couldn't hold back the bitterness. "You might stay alive that way."

"Come on."

"No, I mean it." My voice rose in volume. "You want to catch this killer? Let me go. He'll follow me. You can follow him, or better yet, just tell the cops. They'll follow me." But not before I killed him. He'd appeared to me tonight. I saw his hand before he killed Heather. He was showing himself to me more and more. I felt like there were unspoken rules. He could have a knife. I wasn't supposed to have anything, but screw that. I'd take a gun. He'd show himself and this time, instead of freezing, I'd just raise that gun and pull the trigger.

I could do it.

Sickening waves of disgust rolled down my back.

I could do it. I could kill someone, especially someone who was killing my friends.

Not Mason. Not Logan.

He would *not* get them too.

"We're not using you as bait." Mason stood and began to change clothes, pulling on dark sweatpants and a black shirt. It fit snugly, molding to his physique. He called to Logan, "You ready?" He began stuffing clothes in his bag. "Sam, get up. We have to get going."

I nodded, sliding off the bed. "Sure." Even my voice sounded normal, but I wasn't normal. This was not happening how they wanted, and my mind was racing. Could I go with them, wait till they were somewhere safe, and then go on my own? As I was contemplating it, I already knew it wouldn't work. We might go somewhere I couldn't leave on my own, or worse, the killer would follow, and instead of leaving them, he'd kill them first.

I had to go now.

That was resounding in my head.

Now, Samantha. Now.

I dressed as Mason grabbed the little we'd left in the room. I could hear Logan doing the same. I was sure Nate was too.

I put my sneakers on, and stood at the door.

This felt wrong—no, it didn't. That wasn't what I was feeling. It was ice-cold fear, spine-chilling, but this was right. I had to finish this.

I'd run.

That's what I'd do. It was what I did best.

I'd run, and I'd force the killer to run too. I could best him or her at that. I bested almost everyone I knew, but I needed a gun. As Mason and Logan were moving around me, a tentative plan began to formulate in my mind.

I need a reason to leave.

I looked around the room, but there was nothing I 'needed' to get badly enough that they wouldn't think twice before letting me leave the room. I didn't smoke. Wait—I felt my pockets and looked around. My phone was gone.

Where'd my phone go? I couldn't remember where I'd put it last. "I gotta find my phone."

"What?" But Mason ducked into the bathroom.

NOW!

Logan was in his room too, and Nate's door was still closed. It was now or never. Hurrying to the door—my phone was on the counter. I snagged it and slipped out of the room. Once that door was closed, I picked up my pace, speed-walking away from it, and when I didn't think they'd be alarmed by the sounds of my footsteps, I took off.

Sprinting to the end of the hallway, I crashed through the door and fled down the stairs.

The killer was around. He was watching. He would know.

I pushed through the exit door, and after that, nothing held me back.

The hotel was in front of the woods, and I knew those woods well. A few running paths wound through them, connecting to two parks. I headed for those paths, tearing past the first trees. I didn't let up, going the fastest I'd ever gone. This asshole could try and catch me.

No car.

No bus.

Nothing. Not even a Segway could work on these paths.

Dirtbikes, maybe, but even those would be hit-or-miss. This fucker had to go on his feet. It'd be the only way he could follow me, and I didn't let up until I came to the first park.

I needed that weapon. I couldn't sit and wait for him without one. If I did, I would lose. It was my only chance to fight back.

I looked around, my breathing shallow, my heart pounding. Cold sweat trailed down my back.

Gun, gun, gun. Where would one be?

I needed one.

A car—nope.

A little Toyota like mine. No.

I looked at the people in the park.

A pair of mothers pushing strollers—no.

No.

No.

NO! I wasn't seeing anyone who might have a gun.

The pressure was building. I needed to find something. A house? Could I break into a place? A gun store? I almost started laughing. I'd get arrested. The killer could kill me off when we were cellmates.

I was going to die.

I wouldn't be able to defend myself—wait. A truck pulled into a parking spot and a guy and a girl got out. Yes. He had Texas license plates. I began heading for the truck. They walked farther down the hill. The guy turned back once, and I flattened myself against a tree. If his suspicions were raised, yes, yes yes. As I watched, he turned back. His girlfriend was going to a farther section of the park. If he followed her, he wouldn't be able to see his truck.

Maybe there'd be an alarm.

If I broke his window, I'd have to grab the gun and get out before he could follow me too, or send the cops to where I was hiding.

Shit. This was getting complicated.

Okay. I relaxed a little bit. The guy kept going forward, following behind his girlfriend.

I moved closer to his truck. A gun rack hung off the back of his truck. Chances were good he'd have some type of weapon in there.

I stood on my tiptoes, cupped my hands around my eyes, and tried to see inside his truck. Nothing. Some beef jerky, a scented decoration hanging from the rearview mirror . . . but wait! I began to look in the back, but a black bulge between the two seats caught my eye. I zoomed back, and yes. I thought it was a gun. I was pretty sure.

Hold up. Was I really sure? I had to be sure.

My phone was buzzing. Mason and Logan were probably calling.

Yes. I had to go. Even now, the killer could be on me.

I drew a deep breath, grabbed a rock and lifted it. I was ready to throw it against the window, but I glanced at the driver's side door. It was unlocked. No way. I couldn't be that lucky.

The passenger side door was locked. His wasn't.

This guy—I sent up a prayer and ran to his side, opened the door, and reached forward. My hand wrapped around the black shape and I pulled out a handgun.

God.

My hand was shaking.

Bullets? Was it even loaded?

I pushed on the chamber, pulling it out, and yes. Three bullets were in there. I put the chamber back and breathed out slowly to steady my nerves. Logan had insisted on going to the gun range a few times. I'd thought he was nuts, but I went later with Mason a few more times. He'd helped me learn how to shoot. I just needed to remember his words.

I swallowed a lump in my throat. It was time.

It really was just me now.

Making sure the safety was on, I held the gun in a tight grip and began running again. I went deeper into the woods. The forest could extend for miles and miles; I didn't care. The farther away from civilization, the better.

I ran for two miles.

When I stopped, I was far in the woods.

It was then, and only then, that I stopped and bent over to gasp for breath.

My phone had been continuously buzzing. I pulled it out, seeing twenty-eight missed calls from Mason and almost the same number from Logan. Forty text messages filled my inbox.

Please, forgive me, I thought as I turned my phone off. Then I sat.

It was just me and the forest.

We were waiting for him.

I heard the first footstep crunch over the gravel.

Everything in me was primed for action. I was sitting at the base of a tree, twelve feet off the path. I was already dressed in dark clothing from before, but I tucked my sneakers under my legs. They were neon yellow and they were my weakness, or one of them.

Another footstep.

He was being so quiet, slinking along, but I kept my breathing even. Years of marathon training were helping me out now. I couldn't see him, not yet, but a third footstep wasn't too far away.

I was searching the path's shadows for him. He'd have to stick out. He should have the mask.

I was waiting.

I was looking.

A fourth footstep. Gravel crunched beneath it again.

It was like he wasn't there, but I knew he was. He had to be. That's what made sense, if he followed me instead of them.

A flash of light, moving.

He was on his phone, and that's when I saw him. It was him. I couldn't see him that well, but it was him. I knew it. He was in all black. I couldn't see the mask, but it was him. I felt it. He was standing right in front of me on the path, punching numbers on his phone, and then he waited.

God.

I bit down on my lip, closing my eyes for one agonizing moment.

A dial tone rang, then my voice sounded from his phone. "This is Samantha, leave your—Logan, I was recordin— BEEP!"

The killer was calling me.

I sat there, stunned.

I'd turned my phone off, but he would've found me in two seconds if I hadn't. Fucking hell. He knew my number. I . . . A ton of bricks landed on me.

The killer knew me.

I knew the killer.

"SAM!"

No!

I froze again.

No, no, no.

That was Logan.

"SAM!"

He was coming down the path. I turned—the killer vanished.

Who was he? Who could he be? I kept trying to think, but then Logan was coming fast. He was almost to us.

If I said something, I would be exposed.

If I didn't, he could be dead.

I held my breath, waiting. I didn't know what to do.

"SAM! Where are you?"

But he didn't stop. He soared right past where I was sitting.

I almost sagged from relief, but I heard a rustling sound. A black shape began to grow in size until he was standing up. The killer had stepped back out onto the path from where he'd been hidden.

My teeth sank through my lip, breaking skin. Something warm and liquid seeped out, but I wasn't paying attention.

The killer turned to follow Logan.

He was going after him.

I wanted to yell, scream, stop him.

Calm, Samantha. Think.

If I revealed myself now, he would kill me here. He could go after Logan anyways.

Where was Mason? If Logan was running down this path, was Mason on a different path? Did Logan say he would cover the running paths and Mason would search somewhere else?

My time for sitting was dwindling, and fast.

The killer was farther away.

I had to go now.

I didn't feel my legs. Everything was becoming numb, but I reminded myself to be quiet. He couldn't hear me. If he looked back, he'd see me. My shoes were my weakness. I needed to make sure he had no reason to look back.

Silently, I stood and stepped out onto the path. I crept forward, spying the killer's black shape in the darkness around us. When he moved, I moved. I tried to time every step to his.

I gripped the gun tightly against my leg.

If he looked, I'd shoot him—or try—but I didn't want to risk the shot from where I was. I had to make sure I got him. I had to draw closer.

I sent up another prayer above for help.

Where was Mason?

"SAM!"

That was Logan, but farther away. It was quieter.

Keep going, Logan. Just keep going. Don't turn back.

As if hearing my thoughts, the killer slowed.

So did I.

A silent gasp left me, and I didn't dare move. Not. One. Inch.

I could hear Logan running farther and farther away, but this guy wasn't moving. He cocked his head up, like a panther listening for new prey. If he turned around—I was gone.

I had no choice. I couldn't keep trying to sneak closer to him. It was now or never.

I raised the gun, and I waited.

If he turned . . .

He did.

He turned halfway toward me, then stopped.

Shit!

My heart was pressed into my chest cavity. It was trying to work its way out of me. I could barely hear anything anymore. My heartbeat was deafening in my ears.

Then he . . .

I waited.

My finger was on the safety. I'd have to remove it, then quickly shoot him.

He'd hear the safety. I *had* to wait. I couldn't unlock it yet.

One.

Two.

Three—he began to turn all the way.

Another half second and he'd see me.

But then someone ran ahead of us. Whoever he was, or she, they were moving fast. There was another path that ran across ours. I hadn't known it was there, but this person was going fast.

Fuck. Mason? Could it be?

He hadn't been yelling my name, but that wasn't Mason's way. He'd be silent, stalking, and dangerous. He would run like this.

Suddenly, they zipped past us.

The killer whipped back to the front, where he'd been facing before, and he brought the knife up, like he'd have to defend himself. He looked where the person ran, pausing, then he ran after them.

I couldn't move.

Good God.

I lowered the gun, my arm visibly shaking. My knees were knocking against each other.

I had just missed my chance, but I hadn't known for sure if I would've gotten him.

My legs were like jelly. I literally couldn't make them move.

"Samantha!"

I turned around. Logan was behind me now? What?

It clicked at the same time that he hit me.

If I turned around—if I heard Logan behind me—so could he—and there he was.

He took me out, tackling me to the ground.

The breath was knocked out of me, his heavy weight anchoring me for a moment before I realized what he was doing.

"NO!" I screamed.

He was keeping me in place as he was reaching for the gun still in my hand.

Shit.

"No, you fucker!"

I had to fight for that gun, or I was dead.

The knife too—I looked for it. He was holding it in his hand. I twisted my arm between us, and tried knocking the knife out of his hand with my elbow. He was distracted for a moment, pausing to see what I was doing. The gun or the knife? He decided for me.

He tossed the knife to the side and rolled, his shoulder jamming into my throat as he began tugging the gun from my hand.

It was now a fight for that, and I cried out, feeling him clawing at my wrist and hand. He was tearing my skin apart, literally pulling it off in a desperate way. He was trying to get under the gun, to get a better hold on it.

"Motherfucker!" someone grunted, right above us.

I looked up, but they tucked their shoulder down and slammed into the killer. He was tackled onto the ground, caught and lifted off me in one motion.

I scrambled up, or tried. I was bleeding, I could feel it, from my arm, my hand, my face. I could even smell it.

"Mason!"

I looked up and Logan was airborne over me. He launched himself into the wrestling foray—that was Mason fighting the killer.

No, no, no. The knife.

They were where it was. The killer knew it. Mason didn't.

It was two to one. I sat there, dazed, before I could think of what to do to help.

I still had the gun in my hand.

I began to raise it, saying, "Stop . . ."

It came out a croak. He had hit my throat, and I tried again. A second hoarse whisper. I coughed, feeling blood spitting up my throat, and I yelled, "Stop!"

This one worked.

They did, freezing in place.

Logan twisted around, his eyes wide. "Sam. The gun."

I had it pointed at him, and I gasped, correcting myself. I over-corrected. It pointed at Mason.

The killer had a second, and he dove for the knife.

"Mason! Get ba—"

Too late.

The killer grabbed the knife and brought it up, slicing the back of Mason's knees.

"NO!"

But I felt it too.

The knife cut Mason, and it cut me too. I could feel it behind my knee, and I crumpled, still holding the gun, or trying to. It was beginning to fall from my hand. "No." Another croak. This couldn't happen.

I couldn't lose everyone. I couldn't lose my family.

"NO!"

The killer wasn't done. He brought his knife back, at the same time Logan ripped out "NO!" and jumped at him. The killer rotated swiftly, the knife sticking straight out. Logan impaled himself on it.

No, no, no.

I was whimpering those words.

A gurgled gasp came from Logan. He began spasming, his back and entire body twitching, and somehow he worked his way farther onto the knife.

Like with Mason, I felt the knife in me. It was like I was impaled on it, and my body was shaking and trembling. I was sinking farther onto the knife, past the part where I could come out of this at all.

I was dying.

If I felt I was dying, that meant Logan was dying.

No.

Ignoring all the pain, I raised the gun.

If I was dying, so was he.

He twisted back to me, weaponless, and it was my turn.

I undid the safety, my finger went to the trigger, and I pulled it.

The bullet slammed into him—

Gasping, I surged upright.

Everything was bright. It was too bright, and oh my God. The pain. It was everywhere. It was seeping from me, and I whimpered, my mouth muffled. I closed my eyes, wishing that brightness away. I wanted to go back where I was. I didn't want to be here.

It hurt.

My insides were being pulled out, one scoop at a time. I could feel them, feel how they were raw and exposed, how they protested individually.

I couldn't—please God. Take me away. Take me back. I'd take those woods again, not this.

Tears slipped down my face and they felt like scalding burns.

"Tsk, tsk, tsk, Samantha. Wakey, wakey."

No, no, no.

I want to go back to where I was. Please.

"No, no."

I could hear his enjoyment. It was sick and twisted. He was enjoying this, whoever he was. I didn't recognize his voice.

"Come on. Wake up." More of a clipped tone now. He snapped his fingers, nudging me with a knife that had something wet, something warm on it.

My stomach rolled over.

I knew what was on that knife, but I didn't want to think about it. I didn't want to comprehend it.

"Come on!" He knelt in front of me.

He poked me—and I screamed, bucking under his touch.

I opened my eyes, and he pulled back a bloodied finger. It was mine, not his. My blood.

I began writhing around on the floor. I wasn't consciously doing it, but I couldn't stop myself. I was flailing all over, like a fish on a hook.

"Come on. Stop that." He kicked my side. "You were just doing that before too. Don't know why. I didn't cut your tendons or anything. Stop it. We're about to move on to the second stage."

A breath.

A second one.

A third.

I was able to stop, on my stomach now, with my head turned toward him.

He wore large black boots, but regular jeans, and a blue shirt. I angled my hand back, blinking against how bright it was. Blasts of sheer pain exploded in my head.

"Come on, come on." He tapped his knife against the side of my skull. "You've been out of it since I got you. I don't like to wait this long for some fun, and the best part is coming."

God.

I opened my eyes wider to see better.

I was on a bathroom floor.

There was no killer in a black robe or white mask.

The white wasn't him, it was the light behind him. The black had been the shadow of him as he bent over me. It had all blended together, and the pain—I gazed down.

I was covered in blood.

I was dressed in jeans and a shirt, but I didn't remember putting them on.

Was it all a dream? A lie?

"Yeah. Yeah." He knelt in front of me, the same knife from my hallucination in his hand. I couldn't see his face. I could only see the knife. His face was blurred, and he was waving it back and forth. It was covered in almost-black blood. "Are you starting to get it? You've been whimpering and saying all sorts of weird shit. I finally had to muzzle you because I couldn't get any sleep myself. Your friends aren't dead. None of them are." He grinned. I saw the whiteness of his teeth, how his lips pulled back, but I couldn't see him.

He was still a blur to me.

Everything else was in stark detail.

He let out a deep sigh. "You're not going to get it. I can see that. I don't have time to wait another day. I've got a job to get back to, but we'll have to finish this now. Okay, Samantha. No, I've not touched your friends. Heather, Taylor, whoever else you were saying. Channing? Nate? Logan? You were especially concerned about Mason, and Logan. He only got a knife wound in your dream. That babbling was entertaining at times. He got sliced, right? I heard that right? Sometimes it was hard, deciphering what you were mumbling. You weren't the clearest. That was all in your head." He tapped the knife against my temple again. "Your friends are fine. They aren't the ones dying."

I was.

I was dying.

And I couldn't move. I was still on the bathroom floor. I tried to move my hands, but they were twisted behind me, soaked and covered in blood. I could even feel it between my fingers. I was even beginning to recognize the texture and weight of blood.

A mangled cry ripped from my throat.

I didn't want to die, but I couldn't move. My legs were tied together too. He was half-kneeling over them now.

"You ready?" He sounded disappointed. "I thought you'd be a better fighter than that. You spent the whole time trapped in your head, but okay. I have a date. Gotta get another girl, so here you go." He brought the knife up, his mouth twisting into an ugly smile. "See you on the other side."

He brought the knife to my throat.

Sixteen

I sat upright in bed, and déjà vu settled over me.

My third time in a row of suddenly waking. This time there were no woods, there was no bathroom. I was in bed—*my* bed.

I heard deep breathing next to me, and looked.

Mason was curled toward me, his hand on my thigh. He'd been holding me.

My heartbeat was stampeding inside of me, but I felt myself over.

No knife wounds.

No blood, just sweat.

I could move my hands around. I could move my legs.

I looked over Mason. He was peaceful, and he rolled to his back, his hand leaving my leg. The bed cover slipped down his chest, and I could see all his muscles were intact. He hadn't been stabbed.

"Sam?" He opened one eye, squinting up at me. "What are you doing?"

"What day is it?"

"It's Friday."

"You came home last night." I was breathless. The relief brought tears to my eyes.

He opened both eyes now and lifted his head up. "Are you okay?"

"You carried me from the bar, right?"

"Yeah. You drank too much. You were out of it." He reached up and cupped the side of my face. "Heather said the girls' night was a lot, but are you sure you're okay?"

I patted myself down again, just once more, and flicked those tears away. "I had a nightmare."

"A nightmare?" He curved an arm around my waist again, bringing me down to him. "I'm sorry."

I started to melt back to his side, but a nagging feeling wouldn't settle. I had to know. I had to make sure.

Reaching over, I grabbed my phone and texted Taylor, Heather, and Logan all the same text. Are you okay?

Mason's hand rested just under my breast. I could feel him starting to fall asleep again, but I wouldn't be able to go to sleep again, not until I knew.

I only had to wait a few seconds before the replies starting filtering in.

Taylor: Yeah. Why? Are you?

I pressed a hand over my chest and could breathe easier already. One down. One was fine.

Then Heather: Channing and I just had fight sex, so not really. What's going on?

A second one. She was alive. Feeling tears in my eyes, I texted back, Nothing. Have sex again, then again. Keep having sex until you guys forget what you're fighting about.

She replied again, but it was late. Whatever she had to say, I was more relieved that she was fine. She and Channing would be fine too. They always circled back to each other.

I was waiting for Logan still, and as if on command, my phone buzzed from his reply.

#logansdickisinsidehiswoman
#thisisanautomatedtextreply
#pleasereplyduringnormalwakinghours
#justkiddinghisdickwillbeinsideheragain
;) All serious, you okay? You texted Taylor too.

I groaned out loud, feeling the boulder that'd been sitting on my stomach disappear. They were all fine.

"Sam?" Mason woke from my noise. His hand moved, and he tightened his hold on my breast. "Another nightmare?"

"No." I laughed, more from relief than anything else. "I'm good. I'm fantastic actually."

"Yeah?" He lifted his head, his eyes peering at me.

I grinned at him, but sent a quick text to Logan. Nightmare. Better now. Send my apologies to Logan's dick. Then I tossed my phone on the floor and settled back, feeling Mason moving over me. I looped my arms around his neck. "I am. I could be better, you know?"

"Really?" He grinned, leaning down to nuzzle my neck.

Everything was fine. Everyone was fine.

With that last thought, I turned, seeking Mason's mouth with mine. Now it was my turn to be fine, and as his mouth met mine, I knew I would be.

Later, much later, after we were both sated, I saw my phone blinking from the floor.

Rolling over, I grabbed it and began to turn it over, but then something caught my eye, and I looked.

A pile of clothes were on the floor.

Mason must've left them, but I saw what was on top. There were no holes or openings for the eyes, nose, or mouth.

I whipped back.

Mason had fallen asleep after we had sex, but he wasn't asleep anymore. He was looking right at me, like he knew what I found.

It was all a dream.

Right . . .

So Much More

J. Daniels

Ben

"Happy Halloween, Daddy!"

I wince when Nolan—my six-year-old—pounces on top of me, his bony knees digging into my sides and his elbows jamming between my ribs.

"Halloween's tomorrow," I say, peeking an eye open.

Dressed in his Captain America costume, minus the mask, Nolan presses against my chest and sits up tall. "No, it isn't. Mommy said it was today. She showed me on the calendar." Worry pinches his eyebrows together. "It's today. I know it is."

I smile and bend my arm up underneath my head.

"Daddy, are you fibbing?" Nolan leans closer to me and studies my face. "You're fibbing, aren't you?"

I squeeze his side until he giggles.

"I knew it! I *knew* today was Halloween!"

"Are you excited to go trick-or-treating?" I ask.

"Oh yeah!" He pumps his fist into the air. "And to go to the party tonight! I'm gonna get so much candy. Mommy said I can have whatever Chasey can't eat, so that's gonna be a lot. I'm gonna be set for life, I think."

I glance at the empty side of the bed and sit up, yawning and scrubbing my hands down my face. "Where is Mommy?"

"She's in the bathroom with Chasey trying to get him to pee." Nolan shakes his head. "I don't think he's ever gonna stop using diapers, Dad. He's just not getting it like we did."

Laughing, I rustle his dark hair. "He's only two. Give him time. He'll get there."

"I don't know . . . Mommy said he's stubborn like you."

"Oh yeah?"

"Yep. I heard her. She said it."

Mm. Stubborn, huh? I'll show her stubborn.

"Daddy! Daddy!" Chase yells, running into the bedroom wearing his pajamas.

"Nobody is ready except me," Nolan grumbles.

"We have, like, eight hours, Nolan. Relax."

"That's not a lot of time."

I lean over and pull Chase up onto the bed when he struggles to climb up by himself. "Did you go potty, little man?" I ask against his cheek.

"No potty!"

Nolan sighs. "See? I told ya."

"Captain 'Merica!" Chase bends sideways and reaches for his big brother. I let him go, and the two of them giggle and tumble over together onto the bed.

I smile watching them.

They look alike and they don't. It's the dimples that tie them together. And the big gray eyes they both share.

Other than that, Nolan looks more like me, and Chase resembles Mia. He has her full lips and milk-chocolate-brown hair. He acts like Mia too. Chase gets quiet when he thinks, where Nolan will tell you every thought that's going through his head as he's thinking it. There isn't anything he won't share with you.

"I gotta poop."

I laugh under my breath, watching Nolan scramble off the bed and run out of the bedroom.

Chase giggles around the thumb stuck in his mouth and looks over at me. "Poop," he mumbles.

"Yeah. He's going potty like a big boy. Are you gonna go potty?"

"*No* potty!"

I grab his ankle and pull him closer to me, biting his belly until he squeals in delight.

"*Mom!*" Nolan hollers down the hallway. "I gotta get in there! Hurry up!"

Mia says something I can't make out, and then Nolan is running back into the bedroom with the top part of his costume hanging around his waist, mumbling something about Mia taking forever. He darts into the master bathroom and slams the door shut.

The hallway bathroom is the kids' bathroom. They use it. We don't, unless we absolutely have to. Anyone with little boys knows what goes on in their bathrooms. It's like a war zone in there. Nolan's been potty-trained for years, and he still gets distracted when doing his business. If he hears the slightest noise outside that door, he's turning around mid-stream to check it out and pissing all over the place.

So why is Mia using it right now? That doesn't make sense.

I stand from the bed and tug on my sweatpants, staying

shirtless for now, then I pick up Chase. "Come on, little man. Let's go get Mommy."

He wraps his hand around my neck and watches me closely as I carry him out into the hallway, blinking those big, round eyes at me while he continues sucking on his thumb. He giggles when I slowly lean in.

Goddamn, I got the cutest kids.

"Mia?" I knock on the bathroom door. "You better not be cleaning in there. You know I'll do that."

Mia does everything else. I think it's only fair I handle the piss accidents.

The door unlocks and swings open, and before I have the chance to say anything else, question what Mia was doing in there, or simply take another breath, she's grabbing my face with both hands, pulling me down, and kissing the shit out of me.

I no longer give one fuck about what she was doing in that bathroom.

Mia shoves her tongue inside my mouth and moans when she feels mine. I grip her soft waist through the shirt of mine she's wearing, and tilt my head when she tilts hers. I tug her against me, groaning. She tastes like coffee and that sweet vanilla creamer she uses. So . . . fucking . . . good. And I'd keep kissing her. I would—it doesn't even bother me that Chase is watching this happen. I'm sure he's seen it plenty of times before. My boys should be immune to the PDA that goes on in this house. Besides, we're clothed. Mostly. Mia isn't wearing pants, but she's covered. But she seems to get enough and drags her teeth across my bottom lip before finally dropping her arms and pulling away.

"Happy Halloween," she says softly, grinning from ear to ear and looking like a damn temptress doing it.

I adjust my dick. "Jesus. It's starting off good, that's for sure."

Mia giggles and looks at Chase when he reaches for her. "Hi, baby boy," she coos, kissing his hands. "My little stubborn man. Are you ready to go trick-or-treating and get some candy?"

"*I'm* ready!" Nolan hollers, walking toward us. "We don't need to wait until it's dark outside. I'm pretty sure people are ready for us now."

"We're eating breakfast first, Nolan. No candy before breakfast," Mia says.

"And we'll go when it's dark outside," I tell him. "A lot of people wait to buy candy until the last minute. If you go too early, you'll get what they have laying around, like apples and canned food."

Nolan scrunches up his face. "Like those beans Mommy makes? They really give those out?"

"Yep."

"Gross. Forget it. We'll wait."

"Baby," Mia plucks Chase out of my arms, kisses his cheek, and then sets him on his feet. "Go with Nolan. You boys go ahead downstairs and play. Daddy and I will be down in a second."

I give Mia a look. *Quickie?*

She blushes, her fingers pressing to her lips, and shakes her head no.

Damn.

Nolan grabs Chase's hand and tugs him along. "Come on, Chasey. Let's go make some pancakes."

"Nolan, do we need to have another talk about messing with the stove?" I ask.

My son is in a hurry to be a man. He's always doing shit he shouldn't be doing yet.

"I was just kidding!" he yells. "I'm not gonna cook anything."

Arms drawing across my chest, I shake my head and watch my boys disappear down the stairs.

Just kidding my ass.

I know my son. He's one unsupervised meal away from burning the house down.

"Ben."

I turn back to Mia and watch her slowly back away so she's standing inside the bathroom again. She crooks her finger at me.

"Come here."

I cock an eyebrow.

She bites her lip.

Fuck. Yes.

I move quickly, grabbing her waist and pressing her up against the sink. She moans when I lick her neck. Her fingertips dig into my shoulders.

"*Ben.*" She's breathless.

"Mm?"

Mia gasps when I bite the soft skin above her collarbone. I squeeze her ass until she's standing on her toes and tipping into me, her hip rubbing against my hard cock.

I groan. "*Fuck,* Mia . . ."

We fucked twice last night, but you wouldn't know it. This need—this overwhelming desire to taste and touch and fuck this woman—never goes away. Never lessens in the slightest. It's always there. A plea whispering in my ear. An itch underneath my skin. I need her.

I need this. *Us.* Always.

She reaches behind her back, and when I hear objects moving I think Mia's clearing a space and giving us room to do this fast and now, right now, and I swear to God, I'm not going to last, but then she's bringing her hand between us and whispering in my ear, "Look," as she presses something hard against my chest.

I lean back enough to see what she's trying to show me. I look at the object in her hand.

I blink.

I look.

I blink again . . .

What the fuck?

"Mia?"

Her soft laugh lifts my head. She has tears in her eyes and she's nodding and telling me, "Yes," like she knows what I'm going to ask her.

And I do. I need to ask. I need to hear her say it . . .

"You're pregnant?"

"Yes."

"Are you . . . holy fuck, are you sure? Really?" I take the test from her and look at it again, studying the two pink lines in the tiny window. I bring it closer to my face.

Why the fuck can't they make this shit any bigger?

"Ben," Mia giggles, grabbing my face with both hands and forcing me to look at her. "I'm sure. Two lines means I'm pregnant. I'm very pregnant. Look."

She twists sideways and allows me to see the counter behind her. There's another test lying there next to the sink.

"You took two?" I ask, setting the test in my hand down next to the other and studying them both now.

Four lines. Plain as day. Right there.

Fuck.

Holy fuck, this is happening.

"I wanted to be sure," Mia answers, her hand wrapping softly around my arm. "I have more. I've been hiding them in here so you wouldn't know I've been taking them. They're in a bag underneath the sink."

"What?"

She shrugs when I meet her eyes. "I wanted to surprise you. And I didn't want you worrying if they weren't positive. You know how you get, Ben."

I straighten fully and give her a look, making her smile. "How long have you been taking tests?"

"Not long. Three months. No . . ." She tilts her head. "Four. I've been taking them for four months."

"Four months?"

What the fuck? How did I not know?

I knew Mia stopped taking her birth control five months ago, the weekend of Reed's wedding. We decided then we wanted more kids. And even though it's not something we talk about every second, it's constantly on my mind.

It's there, in the back of my head, every time we're together.

Did it work? Is this it?

How did I not know she was in here worrying all alone about this for the past four months? Where the fuck have I been?

"Ben." Her hands cup my face again, lifting it.

I look at her, at the one person I would do anything for, no questions.

It wasn't always like this between us. But it's strange—I can't remember all those years I spent hating her when we were kids. It's like she was never my sister Tessa's annoying best friend. She was always my Mia, the way she is now.

My mind goes quiet when her thumb tenderly strokes my cheek.

She's like a drug. Just Mia's touch alone can still me.

She calms me down and eases my mind, even when I don't necessarily want her to. Like now. I want her to know how I feel about her being alone in this the past four months, but I don't. I can't. I stare deep into her eyes and ask in a hoarse voice, "Yeah?" When I'm really saying, "Anything. I'll give you *anything*."

"Hey," she whispers, her thumbs sweeping over my cheeks. "Talk to me. Are you happy?"

I blink. "Yeah. Fuck yeah, I'm happy. Are you kidding?" I grip her waist and pull her closer, feeling her body relax. "Sorry. I'm just thinking about you being in here by yourself taking these. I don't like it."

"Babe . . ."

"Were you sad? Disappointed?"

She shrugs. "I don't know. I guess I was a little disappointed when the tests would come out negative." She links her hands behind my neck. "But I knew we'd get pregnant again eventually. I wasn't worried."

"Doesn't matter."

Her brow furrows. "What doesn't matter?"

"You were disappointed, Mia. You were in here alone feeling that. I should've known about it. You don't go through anything without me. Nothing. Not even this."

"But I wanted to surprise you."

I dip my head and get closer to her, explaining, "I would've been surprised standing here staring at that test with you every time you took it. And when it was negative, I would've held you the second you felt *anything*. I didn't get to do that."

Mia stares up at me, eyes soft and tear-filled. "*Fuck.* Sorry." She shakes her head, blinking fast. "I'm sorry."

"Fuck?" I chuckle, running my nose along hers. "Yeah? You wanna?"

She bumps her fist against my chest, sniffling, her tears falling past her cheeks. "I messed it up."

"No, you didn't. Hey." I get her eyes again. "We're having a baby. How could you mess that up?"

"We're having a baby," she echoes, smiling up at me as her worry leaves her. "I'm so happy, Ben."

"Me too, angel."

"Do you want to tell the boys with me? I know it's like, really early. I'm probably only a month along, but I really want to tell them. I think Nolan will be excited."

I smile, picturing his face.

"Yeah, we can tell them. In a minute though." I drop down to one knee and lift her shirt to expose her stomach.

She gasps watching me. Mia loved when I did this when she was pregnant with Chase.

I press my lips to her skin, whispering, "Hey," and "We can't wait to meet you." I close my eyes. I can't stop kissing her.

Mia pushes her fingers through my hair. She doesn't rush me. She gives me this, knowing I need it, knowing *me,* and only suggests we get downstairs before Nolan gets tired of waiting after I stand and pull her into my arms.

"I love you," I say into her hair.

"I love you more."

"Not possible."

She tilts her head back, gives me a long, adoring look, and softly kisses me. "Let me love you more today," she requests against my lips. "Just today, Ben. Let me have that. Please?"

I look down at her and brush my thumb along her cheek. "Just today," I tell her, knowing she needs this. Knowing Mia.

I can give her a day.

She smiles and kisses me once more. "I know you're excited and probably want to tell everyone the second we get to McGill's tonight, but let me talk to your sister first, okay? I want her to find out before the group does."

Tonight is the Halloween party Beth, Reed's wife, is throwing together. She works at McGill's Pub, a bar we all frequent, which is owned by her aunt and uncle. We're all meeting up there later after trick-or-treating. It should be a good time. I know Nolan's excited about it.

"You can't call my sister now?" I ask, thinking we can handle this ahead of time so I don't have to keep my mouth shut when we get there.

Mia's right. I want to tell everyone, and I don't want to wait.

"No. I want to tell her face-to-face. It's important," Mia explains. "I know she'll be happy for us, but with her and Luke having difficulties getting pregnant . . . I don't know. I just feel like she should find out before anyone else, you know? I'm just thinking about her, that's all."

I know how hard things have been on Tessa. And I get Mia's reasoning. That's her girl. She'd do anything for my sister.

I would too.

So, I agree to this while thinking of a way I can help ease her mind. "Yeah. All right."

"Promise me you won't announce it the second we walk in the door."

I smile. I can't help it.

She narrows her eyes. *"Ben . . ."*

"I'm excited, Mia. I might not be able to control myself."

"Well, I suggest you do, or no funny business later with me in my costume."

I cock an eyebrow. "Funny business?" I chuckle. "You mean fucking?"

"Yes."

"Are you gonna put on that hot-as-fuck angel getup you bought and deny me, baby? That's just cruel."

Her cheeks warm instantly.

Yeah fucking right. We both know I'm getting some later.

"I can try," she says, sounding determined. She smiles and gives me another kiss before stepping out of my arms and moving around me. "Let me go put on some pants, then we'll go downstairs and tell the boys."

"I'd prefer you didn't."

She gives me a cheeky look over her shoulder on her way out of the bathroom.

And . . . cue erection.

Yep. Like fucking clockwork with her.

Jesus.

We find the boys in the kitchen after Mia pulls on a pair of sweats.

They're sitting at the table—Chase on his knees as he pushes his toy truck back and forth and Nolan across from him, his drawing pad opened and colored pencils nearby.

I watch him flip to a blank page, and I know he's getting ready to draw another picture for that girl he's absolutely fucking crazy for. I know it before he even taps out the pink colored pencil to use.

He's in love. Full-blown, out-of-his-mind in love already at six years old. And if this was any other kid, I'd laugh, knowing they didn't mean it.

Six-year-olds don't feel love like this. Little kids don't meet one time and feel what adults feel. It isn't possible.

But this is my son. And I know he loves that little girl

as much as I love Mia. Crazy, but it's true. He hasn't been this obsessed with something since the first time he saw a knight on TV.

Mia kisses the top of Chase's head and looks across the table at Nolan. "What are you drawing, baby?"

"I don't know yet. I'm still deciding." Nolan lifts his head and looks at me. "Daddy?"

"Yeah, buddy?"

"I'm gonna marry Ryan."

Mia gasps and grabs hold of my hand as something warm spreads underneath my ribs. "I know you are," I tell him, smiling proudly.

"I really am. I mean it. She says she's my friend, but I just love her so much. Do you think she loves me too?"

"Ben," Mia whispers.

I don't need to look at my wife to tell she's crying again. I know she is. Every sweet word out of Nolan's mouth gets to her. So I keep my eyes on my oldest, and answer, "I'm sure she does."

He smiles then, the dimples caving in his cheeks, and nods once. "Yeah, me too. I think she loves me. Mommy, guess what she's being for Halloween?"

"What, baby?"

"A princess!" Nolan's eyes brighten as he sits up, leaning his elbows on his drawing pad. "That's so perfect, right? I didn't even tell her to be that! She's so cool. She just *knows*."

When Nolan gets back to his drawing, Mia drops her head on my arm and squeezes my hand. "I love the way he loves. He's just like you," she says, quiet enough for only me to hear.

I kiss the top of her head. "You ready to tell them?"

"Yes."

I pull out the chair closest to me and guide Mia to sit

down, then I pick up Chase and stand with him beside her.

"Nolan, come here."

Nolan puts his colored pencil down, slides out of his seat, and stands in front of Mia. "Yes?"

She grabs his hands and holds them in her lap. "Daddy and I have something very important to tell you."

His eyebrows shoot up. "Are we taking another trip to *Chicago*?"

I shake my head, smiling.

One-track mind—getting to see his girl.

He is definitely my son.

"No, not right now, baby," Mia says, holding his cheeks. "I love your heart, Nolan. Do you know that?"

"Yes. You say that *all* the time."

"Good. Because I don't want you forgetting. And I don't ever want you to stop loving the way you do. It's really special."

"Well, I don't know any other way, so . . ."

Mia whimpers and pulls Nolan against her chest, crushing him into a hug. His muffled protest doesn't stop her.

I look to Chase and shake my head. "We do have news, little man. Not sure you're going to hear it today, but we do have news."

"Oh, Ben. I can't help it. Did you hear what he said?" Mia looks up at me with big, fat tears rolling down her cheeks. She wipes at her face, then eases Nolan back with her hands on his shoulders. "Okay. Okay. I'm ready to tell you the news."

Nolan blinks, looks up at me, and then back at Mia.

"We're having a baby, Nolan," she shares. "You're going to get another little brother or sister. Isn't that exciting?"

"Do I get to pick?" he asks.

"Do you . . . get to pick what, sweetheart?" Mia cups his cheek.

"If I get a brother or a sister, because I want another brother." Nolan looks between Mia and me. "I think sisters are cool and everything, but Ryan has two sisters and I want us to match. So, I'm gonna need another brother. If I get a sister, we won't match."

"Buddy, we don't really have control over that," I tell him.

"Just do what you gotta do, Dad."

I laugh.

"Baby, whatever is in my belly right now, that's it," Mia tries to explain to him. "We can't change it. I might have your little sister growing in there."

"She's growing in there right now?" His eyes light up.

Mia nods. "Yes. He or she. They're really tiny right now."

"Can I feel them like I did when Chasey was in there?"

"Not yet. But as soon as you can, I'll let you know, okay?"

Nolan nods and looks up at me. He smiles. "Cool. This is the best Halloween ever, and I haven't even gotten any candy yet."

Smiling, I crouch down beside Mia. I put my hand on her belly, and grin when Nolan puts his hand on top of mine. Chase reaches out too, and Mia takes his hand and rests it next to Nolan's.

"Chasey, say baby," Nolan prompts.

"Baby," Chase repeats, the word getting muffled around the thumb in his mouth.

Mia smiles at me with tears in her eyes again.

"Angel."

She leans forward, meeting me halfway, and we kiss until Nolan whines and tells us to stop.

"Okay. Now, who wants some special Halloween pancakes?" Mia asks.

"Me!" Nolan yells.

"Me!" Chase echoes. "Pamcakes! Pamcakes!"

Reed

Staring up at the ceiling, I toss one end of the rope I'm holding over the exposed beam above me and catch it when it drops through.

The bar is quiet. McGill's typically doesn't close on Saturdays, but with Danny and Hattie, Beth's uncle and aunt, being out of town most of the day, they decided to keep things locked up so Beth wouldn't be running things alone.

I appreciated that. I didn't want her stressing out or worrying she wasn't handling things. And it worked out with the Halloween party tonight. We've had time to get everything ready.

"I don't know about this," I say, giving the two ends of the rope a tug. "I get making this place look creepy for the party, but what about Nolan and Chase? Isn't it kind of fucked up having nooses hanging from the ceiling with kids herc? It's morbid, right? What if Nolan is like *'Uncle*

Weed, what's that for?' What am I supposed to say? No. Yeah, no, we're not doing this." I pull the rope off the beam. "The spiderwebs and ghosts we got up are enough. I'm not traumatizing kids and then getting my ass beat when I *do* traumatize them."

Ben wouldn't hesitate. He'd kill me. I know he would. It doesn't matter how long we've been friends or how much my death might upset people—mainly the girls in the group.

I can't imagine Luke shedding a tear over my demise.

Beth doesn't respond, not even with a reassuring, "You're being silly. Ben would never kill you," and when I turn around to look for her, expecting an empty bar behind me to explain her silence, I see her standing in the same spot she was in a minute ago.

Behind the counter, rag in one hand and an apple she's wiping off in preparation for tonight in the other. Bobbing for apples is one of the games she's putting together for the kids. I didn't think it was necessary to clean off the apples since they're going in a big bucket of water anyway, but Beth thought it was important, and while I've been decorating, she's been wiping pesticides off fruit.

Up until this point, she's moved through the process rather quickly. Now, though, with her eyes fixated on the rope in my hand, she seems to be slowing down. Or maybe she just found the world's dirtiest apple. I don't know, but if she doesn't move on soon, she's going to take the skin right off that thing.

"Sweetheart."

Beth's eyes snap up, and her hand holding the rag stills. "Mm?"

She's fresh-faced, no makeup on yet, has her hair pulled back in a messy pony with several pieces falling out by her ears, and looks one bend away from busting out of the

Nirvana shirt she's wearing. The material is stretched tight across her belly.

I smile at her.

My wife is sexy as fuck pregnant.

"What are you doing, Mrs. Tennyson?" I ask.

Beth smiles then, and *fuck,* what that smile does to me.

That's her Reed smile. She calls it that, so it's not weird that I call it that. And fuck anyone who says it's weird.

I get that smile. Not them. Never them. So *fuck off.* I'll call it what I want.

"Cleaning off the apples for the party," she answers with a sweet tilt of her head.

I chuckle. "I think that one you got there's good. You can probably move on."

Beth blinks, looks down at her hands, and then quickly drops the apple into the large tin bucket on the bar. She huffs out a breath.

"You all right?" I cross the room and stop in front of her, folding the rope and setting it down between us on the bar top. I keep my hands wrapped around either end. "Beth . . ."

Lips parted, cheeks flushed, eyes wide and glassy, she stares at the rope.

I can hear her breaths leaving her. Ragged. Wanting.

Hungry.

"Uh . . ."

"I miss getting tied up," she shares, lifting her chin to look at me.

My eyes widen.

She clears her throat, pausing for a breath. "Not that the sex we're having now isn't amazing, because it is," she continues. "But it's not *you,* Reed. You tie me up and you spank me and you do really dirty things, freaky things, *awesome things,* and you're not doing them anymore.

We're having *Beth is pregnant* sex. And I miss *Beth is just as much of a freak as I am* sex. Because I am. I mean, you know, with *you* I am. And watching you with that rope is driving me crazy. Because I know what you can do with that rope, Reed. I know exactly what you can do with it. And I want that. So, yes, I agree with you. Hanging nooses from the ceiling is a bad idea. But you tying me up with that right now is *not* a bad idea. It's a great one. It's an idea that needs to happen before I explode." Her shoulders sag. She places her hand on her swollen belly and nods once. "There. I said it."

Eyebrow cocked, I look from her face to the rope in front of me and back up again.

Jesus. That shit almost sounded rehearsed.

"You been wanting to say that to me?" I ask, needing to know if it was.

"Yes."

"For a while?"

"Yes." She drags her teeth across her bottom lip. "I know you're worried, but I checked with my doctor and she said we're fine. A lot of pregnant women spot in the beginning. It had nothing to do with you restraining me the way you did that night. She said it didn't."

What the . . . "You told your doctor about the way we fuck?"

"I needed to make sure it wasn't what caused the bleeding. And it wasn't."

I run my hand down my face, a heavy breath leaving me.

Jesus Christ. I suspended Beth from the ceiling that night and took her ass while she rode a dildo. Now the entire Obstetrics department at St. Joseph's Hospital is probably aware. News like that travels.

I'm sure my name will be mentioned in textbooks now.

Reed Tennyson—the man who took his kink too far. Don't do what he did.

I exhale slowly. "Beth—"

"I miss you."

Her whispered confession lowers my hand and presses a heavy weight on my chest.

"I know you need that stuff," she continues, her shoulder lifting with a jerk. "I know you love doing it. And . . . well, I need it too."

"I need *you*," I correct her, needing this to stick since she's obviously questioning it. "I don't need to tie you up to get off, Beth. I feel like I've made that point pretty damn clear. You smile at me and I'm like . . . fucking *there*, just from that. You know how you get to me. I've told you. It doesn't take much."

"I know. But it's not the same."

"Sweetheart . . ."

"Reed, *please*."

"What if I hurt the baby?" I throw my fear out into the open between us. "What if I go too far with it and something happens? The last time we played, you started bleeding, Beth. I can't . . ." I shake my head as that same worry forms a knot inside my stomach. "I can't stop picturing that. It scared the fuck out of me. I didn't know what the hell was happening. I thought I was losing you both."

The sound of Beth calling out from the bathroom—I can still hear it. The panic in her voice. The fear. I can still see the tears in her eyes. I can't do it.

"I can't," I tell her.

She pulls her lips between her teeth and looks away, blushing in her embarrassment for bringing this to my attention. For wanting it, maybe.

I frown.

She's disappointed now.

Fuck though. Not as much as I am.

My wife needs something and I can't give it to her.

My hands grow tighter and tighter around the rope as I take in a deep breath, thinking, weighing the consequences. I play devil's advocate with myself.

I could do this with Beth and everything could be fine. That incident was a one-time thing. It wasn't even related to what we did. Listen to the doctor. Doctors know everything.

Or . . .

Fuck that doctor. She doesn't know shit. I was too rough with my wife and nearly cost us our baby. The best thing to do is wait the five months we have left. What's wrong with regular, standard-issue sex? With *Beth*? Nothing. That shit's fantastic.

But she's right. I do love the *really dirty things* we used to do. The *freaky things. Awesome things.* God, do I love it. She's so right.

The act of sex isn't the only thing that gets me off. It's the lead-up with Beth. The prolonged, almost agonizing wait. The way she looks with her hands above her head or behind her back. Her skin—wrapped in rope. Glistening with sweat and red from my mouth. How she quivers and drenches my hand the second I touch her. The begging. The *begging.* How we're both shaking and panting when I finally . . . *finally* take.

Okay, so maybe we don't go all in.

Fifty percent kink. Fifty percent normal fucking. That might work.

"Maybe we just don't involve any dildos," Beth murmurs, her eyes slowly meeting mine again.

I laugh under my breath, feeling lighter, like she somehow plucked the worry right out of me. And when I open my mouth to tell her "Okay," or "Maybe, we can try it," she cuts me off.

"It isn't me, right?"

My brow furrows. "What?"

Hands resting on her belly, Beth looks down at herself. "I know this gets in the way a little," she says. "I already look so different. My face is rounder and *God,* my butt—"

"Don't even finish that thought, 'cause that's fucking crazy," I interrupt, lifting her head. "Your ass could be the size of this room, and I'd still want to do you at all times. You being pregnant, Beth? I am *into that.* I am into that in a big fucking way."

"Really?"

"*Yes.* Are you kidding?"

She blinks, and I can see on her face how much doubt she's holding on to.

I could tell Beth anything right now. I could say how unbelievably attracted I am to her, looking the way she does. I could tell her she's never looked more beautiful to me, and it wouldn't matter. She wouldn't hear it.

I look down at the rope again and run my thumb over the harsh fibers. *"Fuck,"* I groan, pushing it aside. "I can't use that. It'll hurt you."

Her shoulders pull back. "What?" she whispers, voice racing with excitement.

"That isn't like the rope I use and I don't have any with me, so . . . I mean, if you want to do this *now,* I'm gonna have to use something else. Or we can wait until tonight when we get home, which I think is the better idea. Hattie or whoever could walk in and catch us. I can't imagine explaining to anyone why I have you tied up on the bar. Or what that would do to business here."

McGill's Pub would close. I would be to blame for it.

That's nice. I'm sure Danny would really warm up to me after that.

"There's always the storage room."

My brow lifts at her suggestion.

Beth wets her lips and steps closer, reaching for the rope. "Hattie and Danny won't be back until later after the party starts. And nobody else is coming in. The door is locked. But just to be on the safe side, we could use the storage room. It's private."

"And what are you doing with that?" I ask, tipping my chin at the rope as she clutches it against her belly. "I told you. It's too rough."

"You're wearing a belt, right?"

"Yes."

"I have an idea."

"Do you?" I smirk, bringing my arms across my chest and standing tall. "A kinky one?"

"I think so."

"That's fucking hot. Care to share, Beth Davis from McGill's?"

Her eyes narrow as she fights a smile. "That's not my name anymore."

"I know. It's just a habit."

"Have you changed it in your phone yet?"

I nod my head, grinning. "No."

"Reed," she giggles.

"What? It makes me happy when I see it."

"Oh, and seeing *Beth Tennyson from McGill's* wouldn't make you happy?"

"That would make me lose my mind."

"Then change it."

"I will. I just like remembering you and your dick deprivation. Oh, how far you've come, sweetheart."

She throws her head back and laughs, hand to her chest.

I like to tease my wife about her little autocorrect mishaps. Telling me she didn't get dick very often instead of *sick* very often right after we first met isn't something I'm ever likely to forget about.

"Seriously though, Beth, if we do this, I need to be careful. Okay? For me and my own sanity. Nothing too wild."

"Careful," she repeats through a smile.

"Yes."

"That can be hot." Her voice drops lower and melts, moving like a warm touch up my spine and making my skin tingle. I feel it everywhere.

Everywhere.

Dick hardening in my slacks, I watch Beth move down the bar. Her eyes meeting mine over her shoulder, drawing me in . . . in.

"Is that a *we're doing this now, so move your ass* look?"

"Come with me, Mr. Tennyson."

My chest heaves.

Right. Fucking *right*.

We're doing this now.

The storage room is just off the kitchen, nestled in the back corner of the pub beside the giant, walk-in refrigerator.

I've never been back here when it's been this quiet. I can hear every sound as I follow close behind her—the smack of Beth's boots against the wood floor. Her heavy breathing. The thundering beat of my heart.

Beth walks through the kitchen and steps inside the room, flicking on the light overhead. I follow in behind her and look around the small space.

I've been in here before. Once, to help Danny lift something. Crates of canned food and supplies are stacked against the wall and scattered along the floor. There's a metal table in the middle of the room, which I know is used for sorting. Aside from that, there's really nothing else in here. And there's definitely not much room. But it's secluded. It's got a locking door.

Very private.

I close the door behind me and lock it, drawing Beth's attention before she stops beside the table and turns around.

"So, I was thinking you could use your belt to bind my wrists together, and then tie the rope to the belt?"

I follow her eyes to the exposed beams above her head.

God bless Danny for keeping shit rustic in here. I fucking love that guy.

"You want your hands above your head?" I ask, stalking closer, my fingers working at my belt. I whip it off.

Beth sucks in a breath. "Yes," she whispers, tipping her chin up to look at me when I stop an inch away. "God, yes, please."

I smirk. "Begging already, sweetheart? I haven't even touched you yet."

"It isn't going to take much."

"Really?" I run my finger down the side of her neck to the dip between her collarbones, feeling the wild hammering of her pulse and the labored swallow she seems to manage.

"*Really* really."

"Mm." I take the rope out of her hand and place it on the table with my belt, leaning in to press my lips to her ear. "Get undressed."

Beth nods once, immediately reaching for the hem of her shirt. Her fingers tremble.

"Nervous?" I ask, stepping back to watch.

"No. Worked up."

"Yeah?"

"Reed, you have no idea. I'm like, the horniest woman ever."

"Lucky me."

Her shirt hits the floor. Her bra is next.

Panting, she locks eyes with me and wets her lips, and that's when I finally look at all of her.

I stare at her swollen tits, so full and heavy, and the bump she has.

Being as tiny as she is, Beth started showing early. It seemed to happen overnight. She woke up two months ago and boom. There it was. It shocked us both. Beth seemed a little uneasy at first. But me? I was fucking giddy over it. I still am. I love looking at her. *God,* I love it. Her body is fucking unreal all the time, but like this? With her nipples a shade darker and permanently hard, just aching for my mouth. The curve of her hips. Her ass, peach-shaped and tasting as ripe as one—I would fucking know. I eat it enough. *Jesus.* It's torture looking at her and not touching. But I do look.

Seconds tick by, and it gets to her as much as it's getting to me. The waiting. The watching I'm doing. Shyness dips her head.

"Do you see how hard I am, Beth?" I ask, shoving my jeans and boxers down.

Head still lowered, she looks at me from beneath her lashes. At my dick, and my hand moving over it. Stroking. I squeeze the tip and moan.

"*Fuck,* I don't think I've ever been this hard before," I rasp. "It hurts, Beth. My dick . . . *God.* Do you see it? Do you see how much I want you?"

"*Reed.*"

She only says my name, but she's begging me.

To move. To do something. Anything.

I grab my belt.

I don't need to tell Beth how to position her hands. She knows, and she never hesitates. She never did. Even in the beginning, the first time I did this with her, she was always so willing. So trusting.

That drove me fucking wild. It still does.

Linking her fingers together, she extends her arms out in front of her, offering them to me.

"You were made for me. Do you know that?"

Her cheeks burn hot.

I loop the leather around her wrists, pull the strap through the buckle, and tug hard, tightening it.

She gasps at the pressure.

"Okay?"

"Yes," she says, nodding, wetting her lips. "I'm okay. I'm okay."

"Fuck, I love you." I kiss her, fast and hard, and grab the rope.

She giggles. "Wait. What about my pants?"

"We'll get to that. First things first . . ." I secure a knot around the belt where the backs of Beth's wrists are touching and test it, yanking on the end and giving her arms a light jerk. "Wouldn't want you to get free," I tease.

She blushes and bites her lip.

"Ready?"

"Hurry."

"So bossy, Mrs. Tennyson. Don't forget who's tied up here." I toss the rope over the thick, wooden beam and pull until Beth's arms are fully extended above her head. Her back is arched, her lips parted, breaths leaving her like she's being chased. If I were to pull any more, she'd go up on her toes, which is typically where I like her to be, *but* . . .

"Careful," I remind her, when her eyes question why I'm not putting any more tension on the rope.

She nods once and watches me tie the end of the rope to one of the table legs.

The table is heavy. Solid metal. The only way she's lifting it and putting slack on the rope is if she starts swinging from it. And that won't be happening.

I'm a dirty fucker, but even I have limits.

"Now, about those pants." I move behind her and run my hands down her sides, pressing my lips to the skin beneath her ear as my fingers tease the button of her jeans. "Mm. Do you feel that?" I ask, my cock rubbing her hip. "I think I'll leave mine on and fuck you like this— just my dick out. What do you think? Are you gonna get it nice and wet for me if I do that?" I smile when all she can do is nod, her breathing so ragged she can't form words anymore. I unfasten the button and slowly drag the zipper down. "But where should I fuck you . . . that is the question. I'll leave this up to you. Where do you ache most, sweetheart? Here?" I push my hand into her panties and thrust two fingers inside her.

"Oh, fuck," she gasps, her back arching away and her arms shaking. "Oh . . . oh, God."

"No need to be formal when I'm finger-fucking you, Beth. I'll answer to Reed." I chuckle darkly, biting her neck. "Now, option two. I'm going to need to slide these pants down so I can get to that sweet little hole. Are you okay with that?"

"Yes."

"So, you're saying you *want me* in your ass . . ."

She drops her head forward and whimpers. "You know I do."

"I do. I just like hearing you say it." I pull my fingers out and drag them over her clit until she shudders. "Say it, Beth. Or I'll stay right here and do *this* for hours."

I'm bluffing. I'm too hard not to fuck her until we both can't walk, and I think she knows that, until . . .

"Yes!" she cries out, craning her neck to glare at me. "I want you in my ass, okay? I want you everywhere, Reed. God, just . . . hurry up and do it already. I'm dying. Get in my ass."

I smile, keeping my laughter silent, and kiss her cheek. "You might want to watch the volume. I'm pretty sure our daughter can hear you."

Beth blinks, eyes going as round as saucers, her lips pinching together into a tight thin line.

"Horniest woman on the planet. You weren't lying," I tease.

"Well . . . you asked for it."

I lose the smile and bring my fingers to my mouth, letting her watch me suck them. "You're perfect," I say. *Fuck, the way she tastes.* "Absolutely fucking perfect. I don't deserve you."

"Yes, you do."

"I'm glad you think so. Not that I'd let you back out of this now even if you tried. But I would feel bad leaving a pregnant woman tied up in a storage room."

She giggles sweetly, and we share a kiss that's too tender for this moment, but we let it happen anyway. And even though our lips are soft and there's barely any tongue, we're both still panting when I pull away, because it's *us,* and we know what's coming.

We share a look—desire. Beth wets her lips. I squeeze the base of my dick until I groan, grip the sides of her jeans and yank them down to her thighs. Her panties follow. Then, moving to stand beside her, I cup her pussy with one hand and slide my other between her cheeks.

I'm not smiling anymore. Neither is she.

I dip a finger into her pussy until it's wet enough to press against her ass and do just that, slipping past that impossibly tight ring of muscle to the place where she grips me. I move my digit in and out. Her mouth falls open and her eyes roll closed.

"Reed," she gasps, wiggling against my hands, taking me deeper.

Two fingers in her pussy. One in her ass. I drop my head beside hers and bite her jaw.

"You squeeze me so fucking tight," I say, licking my way to her mouth. *"Fuck, Beth."*

"More," she begs.

I don't ask where, because I *know* where. I know Beth. I know us.

I wet a second finger, push two in her ass, and add a third in her pussy. I fuck her steadily, rubbing my cock against her and moaning into her mouth.

"Fuck," I breathe, pumping my hips and sliding along her skin. I stare at myself, at the swollen head dripping. "God, Beth, I could come like this."

She's so soft and warm, and *wet.* So fucking wet.

"Oh . . . oh, God." Beth sags against me and rolls up onto her toes. "Let me come. Let me come," she begs, knowing I'd typically stop now so I could feel her go off around my cock, but fuck, she doesn't need to beg. Not now. Not like this.

I can't stop.

"Yeah, do it," I tell her, holding the fingers in her ass still and just fucking her pussy now. "Come. Come all over me, and I'll lick it up after."

"Oh *shit*." Her back arches. "Reed. Oh . . . oh, God, yes. Yes!"

By some miracle, I'm able to slow the thrusting of my hips as she clamps down on my fingers, and lazily rub myself on her stomach. Beth moans through her orgasm, turning her head so I can take her mouth. I suck on her tongue, her body trembling and those sweet pulses dying out until she's sighing and sated.

"God," she pants against my mouth. "That was—"

"Nothing yet."

I slip my fingers out of her and put a good amount of slack on the rope, then I press against her back and squeeze her breast with the hand she just drenched. "Bend over so I can eat. I'm fucking starving," I growl against her ear, biting the lobe.

"O-okay." Beth drops her elbows on the table and leans forward, sticking her ass out.

Standing behind her, I remove her boots and peel her jeans off so she can widen her legs. I drop to my knees and hold her open with one hand, stroking my cock with the other as I stare.

"Fuck, look at you." I lean in and swipe my tongue between her legs, licking her cunt. She gasps and sits back, pushing more of herself into my mouth, and I groan. "You taste fucking unreal, you know that? So sweet. Like honey."

"Reed."

I lick up to her ass and wiggle my tongue inside her.

"Oh *yes*," she moans.

I chuckle. "Dirty girl. Always want me right here, don't you?" I slap her ass. She yelps, and I keep eating, moving my tongue all over her. Dipping in and out. Circling. "I'm not stopping until I get it all. Every last drop, Beth."

"Shit." Again, her thighs begin to shake, and she rolls up unto her toes and pants my name, over and over.

I pull back and stare. "Fuck. Are you coming again?"

Beth doesn't answer. She can't. She's moaning and cursing because she *is*.

And there is no fucking way I'm not feeling that around my cock this time.

"Hold on. *Fuck*. Just hold on for me." I stand and twist her around so we're facing each other. Her eyes are wide. Her head flops on my shoulder.

"I can't. I can't stop," she pants, elbows bent above her head. "Reed, *hurry*."

I lift her up and set her on the edge of the table, grab the base of my dick, and sink in.

Wet. Tight. Perfect.

Fuck.

"Beth," I gasp, just the first inch inside. "Good God, holy *fuck*."

"Fuck me. *Please!*"

I guide her legs around my waist and reach around her to pull the rope free from the table. She stretches out on her back, arms still bound, which she keeps above her head. And when I watch her lips form that word again, *hurry,* with her eyes rolling closed, I squeeze her tits and thrust in.

"Yeah. Fuck yeah. Just like that," I pant, bucking into her wildly.

"Reed." Her body locks up, her pussy jerking my dick as her orgasm rips through her. "Yes! Oh, God. Don't stop."

"I can't," I tell her. I bend down and suck her nipple into my mouth, moaning against her slick skin. "Ah, fuck. Fuck! Touch me. Fucking *touch me,* Beth. Please."

Beth's fingers slide into my hair and tug until my eyes water.

"Ah, yeah, God. Fuck yeah." Blood rushes in my ears. My orgasm races down my spine and tingles in my balls. "Close," I grunt. Growling into her cleavage, I fuck her deep, keeping myself from getting too rough with her, and I think I have it—that discipline it takes to keep from getting too lost, too wild in this moment, but then I feel her nails dig into my scalp, and it's over. I can't.

And doctor's blessing and all, so why not?

I lean away just enough to watch her, keeping her hands in my hair, and fuck her mad, crashing my hips against the back of her thighs. The table beneath us drags along the floor, screeching over our grunts and heavy breaths. Beth's heels dig into my back. Sweat drips from my brow onto her tits, and I lick it up. My vision blurs. *Right there. Right there.* I suck and suck on her skin until she demands I bite her. And when my teeth sink into the plump flesh around her nipple, I come with a growl.

"God . . . *damn,*" I murmur, breathless and body spent. I kiss the red sting away and lick up to her neck, moaning, "Beth. Beth. Beth."

Her name is my favorite sound.

She hums in content beneath me, stroking my hair. "Well done, Mr. Tennyson."

I smirk, lifting my head to meet her eyes. "I wasn't too . . . *me,* was I?"

It's still a fear, even though I have all the assurance I need. I know it'll always be something I worry about.

I couldn't live if I hurt her.

"You were perfect." She hits me with that smile, my smile, and sighs. "Everything. You were everything."

I look down at her flushed cheeks, her messy hair falling out of her pony, and her lips—wet and ready. I bend and take them in a kiss that matches my dependency for this woman. Heavy. Pulse-pounding. And all-consuming. Even in the moments after, when my limbs can barely hold me up and I couldn't feel more connected to Beth, it's still there. That desperation. I'm hopeless against it. I'm hopeless against *her*.

In this bar, I've always been. From that very first kiss.

"I believe we have a party to get ready for," I murmur, kissing her softly now.

"Mm. Just a few more minutes of this."

"A few more minutes, and I'll be hard again."

"I know."

I lean away, eyebrow cocked. "Good Lord, Beth. I just made you come how many times?"

She bites at her lip, fighting a smile. "I don't know. Three?"

"Are you still horny?"

"It kind of doesn't go away," she reveals. "But, I mean, it's not *me*. I read something about pregnant women being like this. It isn't weird or anything."

I chuckle and press a soft kiss to her mouth. "Well, that settles that. We're having thirty kids now. One after the other. TLC will probably offer us a show."

"Reed," she giggles.

"I could stop working. Hell. *You* could stop working. We can just fuck all day and collect our checks."

"And eat," she says, beaming up at me and no doubt remembering the time I suggested we do those two things, and only those two things, for the rest of the day. "Actually, I am pretty hungry. Maybe we can break for a snack real quick, and then I can tie *you* up?" Her brows wiggle suggestively.

Tie me up?

Yeah fucking right.

"You would hate every second of that, and you know it," I say, knowing how my wife gets off better than she does.

"I'm not sure." She pinches her lips together, thinking. "I might like it."

"Beth." I give her a look.

"What? Reed Tennyson, from McGill's." She gives me a look back, which she loses almost immediately when a laugh tears from my throat.

"God, I can't wait to do this for the rest of my life with you," I say, kissing her smiling lips.

"You and me," she murmurs, her bound arms tightening around my neck.

I breathe deep, loving the way that sounds but loving even more that soon, it'll be changing to us—you, me, and *her*. Layla.

I close my eyes, happy, relaxed, my life so fucking good because of this woman.

The same one gently tugging on my hair and shyly requesting, "Um, Reed? About that snack . . ."

Luke

The line I'm standing in moves ahead a couple feet when another group is instructed to "Stay on the path. Don't divert, or you'll regret it!" by some kid dressed as the Grim Reaper.

He holds out his scythe and tries to look intimidating as thunder claps from stereo speakers mounted to nearby lampposts, and four teenage girls squeal and run past him, disappearing into the dark woods.

"I'm so scared! I might pee myself!" a young girl behind me shrieks.

"If anyone touches me, I'll die!" another cries before breaking into excited laughter.

Two kids holding lightsabers carry on a fight just off to the side while they wait their turns. They can't be any older than Nolan. And for yet another time tonight, I shake my head and wonder what the fuck I'm doing right now, because aside from their parents and whoever oversees the lighting and special effects at Weber's Haunted Woods, I am the oldest motherfucker here.

Halloween is a holiday for kids and women who want an excuse to dress up. I don't have any reason to be coming to shit like this anymore. I haven't been to one of these things since I was in middle school. And if it weren't for the voice that turns my head every fucking time I hear it, I wouldn't be standing here now.

"I'm not cutting in line. *Relax,* before your hair frizzes out any more."

Laughter shakes my chest as I turn sideways and watch Tessa.

She moves down the long line of people like she owns this fucking farm, walking with attitude the way she always does—hips swaying in those tight jeans, chin lifted, eyes bright and daring, looking sexy as hell with that smirk on her face she wears when she's either thinking about telling someone off or just got finished doing it.

Fucking love that look. Especially when it's being directed at me.

And it's directed at me a lot.

I shouldn't get off on riling Tessa up and getting a helluva lot of lip from her, but I do. And she gets off on giving it. That shit just works for us.

As Tessa moves closer, curiosity has me scanning the crowd, and I spot the woman who will absolutely think twice before she gets up in my wife's business again.

Scowl on her face and cheeks flushed in embarrassment, she quickly smooths her hands through her hair.

"The Porta-Potties are disgusting," Tessa shares, stopping beside me, her nose wrinkling in disgust as she wipes her hands off on her jeans. "Seriously. People are animals. Fucking aim already. It's gross. I basically had to bathe in hand sanitizer."

"You could've just held it," I offer, knowing anything I say right now aside from agreeing with her is a gamble.

That's a risk I gladly take though. *Give me that fucking look, babe.*

And she does.

Her eyes harden and narrow. Her mouth pulls tight.

I smile, my cock hardening in my jeans.

I can't help that shit. It's *her.*

"Shut up." Tessa laughs, knocking her fist against my chest. "You got it made, you know that? I swear to God, Luke, my life would be so much easier if I had a penis. I wouldn't even need to get out of line. I could just whip it out right here. Problem solved."

I glance around us, making sure no kids are standing close enough to hear the conversation we're having, because knowing Tessa, she didn't bother to look. Then, getting the go-ahead I need, I pull my arms across my chest and turn to face her again. "Can we not talk about a scenario involving you having a dick? 'Cause that's really fuckin' weird for me."

She tilts her head back, her mouth fighting a smile. "Why? 'Cause you'd still be interested and wouldn't know what to do about that?"

"Wouldn't be interested once I got your pants off, babe."

"Yeah you would. My dick would be huge."

The fuck?

Shoulders pulling back, I stand taller before blinking away and moving forward with the line, and I don't know what look I'm giving off now, but whatever it is has Tessa clutching at her stomach and nearly doubling over in half.

"Oh my God. You look freaked," she cackles.

"There's something wrong with you."

"Oh, stop it. I'm just kidding." She elbows my side, her

laughter dying out. "You look seriously stressed out, Luke."

"Wouldn't *you*?" I look down at her, glaring. "And don't act like you'd really want a dick. You would hate not having my mouth between your legs every fuckin' second of the day."

Her eyebrow lifts.

Mine furrows. "Not fuckin' happening. Ever."

Jesus Christ. She thinks I'd blow her.

Tessa giggles and leans her head on my arm. "Okay, okay. I wouldn't *really* want a dick. You're right."

"Usually am."

Her teeth sink into my bicep.

I reach around and slap her ass, hard, making her yelp before I wrap my arm around her shoulders and tug her close, preventing her from biting me again.

She sighs into my neck as the cool October air swirls around us.

"This is going to be so fun, right?" she asks, sounding happy, her hands sliding around my waist and linking by my hip.

I kiss the top of her head and pull her closer.

I can bitch to myself all I fucking want about being too old for this or feeling out of place here, but the truth is, there was nothing stopping me from making this happen for Tessa tonight.

I know how stressed she's been. I know the constant worrying and wondering she's been doing.

She tries to hide it from me, but I know my wife.

She's inside her head, freaking out all alone in there.

Starting a family is supposed to be exciting. Fun. The amount of fucking we've been doing alone should keep this next step in our lives enjoyable. And yeah, the sex we're having is un-fucking-real. Always is. But it's been five months since Tessa and I decided we were doing this, and even though no one's saying it out loud, I know we're both thinking the same thing.

What the fuck?

I figured we wouldn't have any issues with this. Why would we? We're still in our twenties. It's not like we waited until our forties to get this going. Not that I was expecting it to happen right away, overnight or anything crazy like that, but I sure as hell wasn't expecting it to take more than a couple months.

Even so, I'm not worried. I know it'll happen. And if I'm wrong and it doesn't, I'm still not worried.

But Tessa?

It's been the only thing on her mind.

So when she came up with the idea of hitting the haunted woods before we go to the party tonight, looking excited about it, with that smile on her face that I haven't seen enough in these past few months, I didn't hesitate.

Yes.

Anything.

Everything.

Whatever she wants.

That doesn't mean I won't suggest something else while we're here, though.

I really fucking hate shit like this.

Turning my head, I watch the group standing in the line next to us move forward when the tractor returns. "You sure you don't just wanna do the hayride? There's an actual *point* to that. We can finally get pumpkins."

And it doesn't take as long.

"The hayride isn't scary," she says, nuzzling closer. "I want to be scared, and I want you to protect me."

"Protect *you*? The people running this are gonna be the ones needing protection. You can hold your own, babe. In any situation. I just witnessed it."

Tessa looks up at me, smiling wide. "Yeah, you're right. They better be ready too. I've already made one person cry tonight."

I chuckle as we move forward together when the next group goes ahead, and then we're at the front of the line, and the kid dressed as the Grim Reaper gives us the same warning about staying on the path.

Tessa leans away, sliding my arm off her shoulders, and grips my forearm, her fingers digging in when the thunder claps through the speakers above us. She covers her mouth, giggling, and I can't help it. I smile then too because *fuck,* she was right. This *will* be fun. Look at her. How could I not have a good time when she's this excited about something?

The kid extends his scythe, giving us the go-ahead, and Tessa grabs my hand and tugs me forward.

"Woo! God, I haven't been through one of these things in *years,*" she says, breathing faster as the branches overhead darken the path. "Bring your worst, punks!"

I shake my head as her voice carries through the woods around us.

Eerie music begins to play as fog rolls out like a blanket from behind a tree stump. It covers our feet. We move slowly, leaves and twigs crunching and cracking beneath us. It takes a minute for my eyes to adjust to the darkness.

Aside from the lit torches stuck in the earth every ten feet or so, there isn't much light, and Tessa's grip on my hand grows tighter and tighter the farther we walk.

"Oh my God, look at that." She points at what's supposed to look like bodies wrapped in blood-stained sheets. There's a group of them stacked together on the ground near an overturned wagon.

I think I hear something—a moan or a word I can't make out. When we get closer, the body on the bottom of the pile begins to jerk and scream for help.

"Jesus," I grunt.

Tessa gasps and squeezes my hand.

"Isn't this supposed to be for kids?" I ask, brow furrowed as I watch the guy's legs smack against the dirt. "Nolan would freak out seeing this."

"Yeah, seriously. There were a lot of kids in that line." Looking over at me with wide eyes, she shrugs. "Maybe this is the scariest thing we see?"

A chainsaw starts in the distance, startling Tessa. She stops on the path as several women scream, and squeezes my hand to the point of pain when a young boy runs toward us with his mother close behind.

"What the fuck?" I squint through the fog.

When the boy gets closer, I can see how frightened he looks—like Chase when he has those night terrors.

Eyes wide with panic, mouth open and ready to scream, a steady stream of tears spilling down his face.

Jesus. This could scar him for life.

"Sweetheart, it's okay! It's not real!" the mother yells as the two of them run past us. "They aren't really burning people alive! I *promise*!"

Tessa and I share a look.

"Um, why don't we walk a little faster," she suggests, tugging on my hand. "Come on."

The path bends around a tree, and we move quicker now, Tessa not even bothering to look at the haunted displays around us. She clings to me with her arms squeezing my waist and her head smashed against my ribs, keeping her eyes focused ahead.

We pass a corpse on the ground with his intestines torn out of him. His guts are spilling out onto the dirt. When zombies emerge from behind a large rock to feed on the remains, looking real as *shit*—like a bunch of extras straight out of *The Walking Dead*—Tessa gasps and clutches my shirt with both hands.

"Luke," she whispers, her voice shaking as she watches them with unblinking eyes. The corpse starts to groan. His legs twitch and kick out. *"Luke."*

"Thought you wanted scary," I remind her.

"Yeah . . . not *this* scary. Do something."

"Do what? Arrest them?"

She nods frantically.

I chuckle and guide her around another bend to keep us moving.

I know she's scared now. And I don't mind getting this over with so we can get out of here and get to the party at McGill's.

That's more my style—hanging out with our friends in a well-lit environment. Alcohol to get my mind off this fucked-up shit.

I'm going straight for the liquor tonight.

We come up on a run-down house. It's pitch black inside the windows, but there's screaming coming from somewhere close by.

Kids screaming. How fucked up is that?

And it sounds real too, not some recording they're playing to freak everybody out.

Tessa's body goes rigid in my arms and her feet start to drag on the dirt. I look up to see what's got her reacting this way and freeze, every muscle in my body locking up.

On the porch, a man dressed like a baby rocks in a chair, drinking from a bottle filled with blood. His chin drips red.

"Jesus Christ. Are you shittin' me?" I glare at the guy when he lowers the bottle and grins, pushing blood between his teeth. My lip curls. "You got a problem?" I ask him, stepping closer.

"Luke." Tessa peels herself off my side and pulls on my hand. "Come on. He's creeping me out."

We keep moving. I feel my heart pound against my ribs as I watch the freak keep smiling at me over my shoulder.

He stands from the chair.

I stop walking then, and for a split second I think he's coming after us.

My shoulders pull back. I give him a look—*Do it, motherfucker.* I am so fucking ready to drop this weirdo, but he sits back down, laughing his ass off, and drinks more from his bottle.

Fuck. Maybe Tessa was right. I should just start arresting people. I bet this freak has a shitload of helpless victims locked in his basement. His outfit alone is probable cause enough for me.

What grown-ass man would volunteer to dress up like a baby?

"What?" Tessa asks at my back. "What is it?"

I turn away from the guy then and put my arm around her, leading her away before she sees what I'm seeing. "Nothing. Let's go."

The path narrows. We duck beneath branches and low-hanging cobwebs, following a sharp curve around a tree, and when something jumps out at us and scares Tessa so bad she nearly takes off running, I work on instinct and throw a punch, knocking the dumb prick to the ground.

"Luke! What are you doing?" Tessa yells, moving around me to see who I've just hit.

I hear groaning.

Lots of groaning.

The word *lawsuit* flashes in my mind.

Oh, fuck. This could be bad.

Breath holding in panic, I lower my fist and follow her eyes to the poor bastard on the ground.

Wearing a clown mask, the guy I just leveled holds his face as he rocks side to side on the dirt.

He's in pain. That's clear.

And I caused it.

Fuck. What the fuck am I doing? I need to relax.

"Shit. Sorry. Didn't mean to do that." I reach out, offering to help him up—he's not that big. He's gotta be in college.

Please be in college. If I just hit a minor . . .

"Oh my God. Are you okay?" Tessa reaches out then too. "Jesus. Are you hurt?" she asks.

"*God.* What the hell, man?" the guy moans, getting to his feet without taking either of our hands.

I exhale a relieved breath when I hear how deep his voice is.

Thank fuck. That could've been bad.

Another reason why I don't have any business coming to these things anymore—I'm too reactive. My ass is lucky if I get out of here tonight without anyone suing me.

The clown straightens out his mask so it's sitting right on his face. "You're on a haunted woods walk," he says, looking in my direction. "People are going to jump out at you, you know. It's part of the *experience.* You get what you paid for."

"Yeah, my bad." I run a hand over my buzzed hair, wincing. "You all right? You're not bleeding or anything, are you?"

"I'm *fine*," he bites out, sounding irritated as he brushes leaves off his pants.

Can't say I blame him for being pissed. I went full strength with that punch.

Don't know any other way.

"Jesus." The guy pokes at the side of his mask, pushing it into his cheek. "What's wrong with you? I bet I'll have a black eye tomorrow. My mom's gonna be pissed."

"It's that fuckin' baby back there, all right? It got me all freaked," I try to explain. "What the fuck is that? Kids are coming through here. Are you seriously trying to fuck 'em up for life?"

Tessa covers her mouth and giggles.

I glare at her. "You were scared too. *Rushing me along.* It's your fault I hit him."

"Oh, please." She rolls her eyes. "You were ready to deck that giant man-baby. That had nothing to do with me, Luke, so don't even."

"He was *grinning* at me. Like he wanted me to tuck him in or some shit and sing him a fuckin' lullaby. You saw him."

Bastard probably has people buried in his backyard too. I wouldn't doubt it for a second.

"Oh yeah. Chester likes to do that," the clown shares, drawing my attention. "*Really* freaks people out."

"*Chester?* As in *Chester the molester*?" I take a step closer and hook my thumb behind me in the general direction of freakville. "That fuck better not be a registered sex offender. I don't give a damn if it's Halloween or not. I will haul his ass out of here and shut this shit down. Where's Weber? Is he here?"

I'm sure that old man keeps files of everyone he hires for shit like this. Just saying I'm a cop can get me all the access I need.

You're going down, motherfucker.

"Luke, *relax*," Tessa chuckles, grabbing my arm. "He's just playing a part. I'm sure he's not some creepy perv."

I gape at her. *"Are you?* 'Cause I'm bettin' he's on a watch list. You saw him."

And with a name like that? There's no doubt in my mind now.

The government has all eyes on that fucker.

"Dude, you need to chill." The clown crosses his arms over his chest and stands tall. "That's not his real name, bro. He just goes by that when he's here. It's part of the act. His real name isn't pervy at all. It's Dave." He cocks his head. "Does that sound pervy to you, my man?"

My man?

"Dude. Bro. There's something wrong with him," I grunt. "I don't give a fuck if it's part of the act. Who the fuck smiles like that? It's weird."

Giant baby freak. The second he stood up, I should've leveled his ass. Why the fuck did I hesitate?

"Didn't you see the signs? Be ready for *anything.*" The clown shrugs. "We mean anything, brah. Just wait. You thought the baby was bad . . ."

Brah?

Is this kid serious?

I shake my head, advising, "Okay. Quit with the nicknames already. We aren't friends. Even if we were? You sound like a fuckin' douchebag. Just talk normal."

Tessa snickers.

"Free country, guy."

I close my eyes and breathe deep, searching for calm. *Don't do it. Don't do it. Hitting him again will bring you nothing but trouble.* Then, looking to Tessa, I suggest, "Can we just go? I've seen enough, and two more seconds of *this* conversation and I'm gonna get arrested. No joke."

My wife, who seems to be enjoying the hell out of herself right now, and who in no way looks scared anymore, tilts her head with a smile.

The clown laughs, causing the muscles in my shoulders to tense up. "Come on, amigo, don't be weak," he says. "Weber's is for kids. It's sad if you can't handle it."

I glare at the piece of shit and step closer until I'm up in his space, adrenaline coursing through me now. "You want to say that to me again?" I ask.

Fuck this prick. *Don't be weak?* I will gladly spend a night in jail if it means shutting him the fuck up. I'm not even sorry I hit him anymore.

Before the guy has the chance to repeat himself, Tessa quickly wraps her hands around my neck and kisses my cheek. "Come on. It can't get *that* much worse," she whispers. "Let's keep going."

I look at her. "You sure? You were pretty fuckin' scared."

"I'm sure. You'll protect me."

"You know, it's typically the guys making their girls push through this," the clown shares. "Funny how this is the other way around."

I slowly turn my head.

The clown jerks back like he's afraid I'm going to hit him. Then, thinking wisely for the first time in his life, I'm betting, he backs away from me, his hands raised defensively as he pleads, "Cool. Stay cool, bro," before spinning around and running off. He turns a corner, but his voice carries in the wind.

"Be ready for anything, sport! And don't say I didn't warn you!"

"Jesus Christ," I grumble, looking to the sky. "That kid is gonna get decked *a lot* in his life. Nobody should use that many fuckin' nicknames. It's not normal."

"I can't believe you punched him. You're such a dick." Tessa smiles up at me when I meet her eyes. "Aw." She touches the furrow in my brow, pressing closer, and wraps her arms around my neck. "I love you so much right now, babe. It's crazy."

"'Cause I punched him, or 'cause I'm hatin' every second of this?" I ask her.

"Both." She smiles again when I shake my head. "Really though, I know you didn't want to come here. *I know you.* You think these things are stupid . . ."

"You ask, babe. Whatever it is, I'm there. You know that."

"I know." She tilts her head up, inviting me for a kiss I take zero seconds to fucking get in on. "Thank you for bringing me."

"You're welcome."

"Now let's hurry up and get through this because I am *seriously* freaked out."

I lean back to glare at her. "I fuckin' knew it. You don't want to be here either, do you?"

She shrugs, smiling as she slips her arms off my shoulders. "It does seem a little too real, right?"

"You think?"

"It can't get that much worse though. Weber would be paying for everyone's therapy and lose the farm. It isn't like they made us sign any waivers when we bought our tickets. They're liable for any psychological damage."

I rub at my mouth, thinking on this.

Tessa has a point.

That clown could've been bluffing. The little prick would do something like that just to mess with me.

Paybacks are a bitch.

Doesn't explain the freaked-out kid, though . . .

Christ. Whatever. Pushing that memory out of my head,

I grab Tessa's hand and lead her down the path. "Let's just get this shit over with. I need a drink."

"Me too."

We move deeper into the woods. Around the next curve, we see three witches hanging from a tree. There's a mob standing there watching, pitchforks and torches raised, while they chant out "Cursed!" and "Begone, devil worshippers!" The fog grows thicker at our feet and rises to waist level.

We keep going, Tessa staying pressed against my side until she sees a graveyard and tombstones up ahead.

"Ooh. Let's go read what's on them," she suggests, pulling away from me to step off the path.

"Go for it."

I stuff my hands in my pockets and stay where I am.

When I hear a branch break, my head whips around and my muscles tighten. Eyes narrowed at the tree line, I stare into the darkness and watch for movement.

"Aw, these aren't scary. *Here lies Bea. A. Fraid.* Lame! Luke, come look. Some of these are kind of funny."

My phone vibrates in my pocket. I turn around and dig it out, saying, "Just read them to me," as I swipe my thumb across the screen.

I look at the message from Ben.

Mia's pregnant. We just found out today. She wanted to tell Tessa first, but I'm thinking hearing it from you might be better. Not sure how she's gonna react.

The sound of Tessa's soft laugh lifts my head, and the words pour out of my mouth before I have the chance to even think about what I'm saying, how I'm saying it, if I should be fucking saying it at all. They just come out.

Words that could kill her. I just say them.

"Mia's pregnant."

Tessa stands from the squatting position she was in and blinks at me. *"What?"* she asks, voice quiet.

My shoulders pull back.

That *what* isn't because she didn't hear me. I know she heard me.

That *what* is just another way of saying *what the fuck? Why them? Why not us?*

"Your brother just texted me," I tell her, stuffing my phone away without giving him a response. He knows what I'm dealing with. "They wanted you to know first. They just found out. Hey . . ."

Tessa starts shaking her head, her hand coming up to cover her mouth and her eyes lowering to the dirt. "I did it again," she murmurs. "I can't believe I did it again."

I move closer, staring hard at her face and trying to see her better. "You did *what* again?"

What is she talking about?

"I felt . . . I don't know, *angry.* I was angry at Mia. That's the first thing I felt, Luke." She looks at me then, and even though it's dark and the light is shadowing her face, I know she has tears in her eyes. "The same thing happened when Beth told us on girls' night that she was pregnant. I got pissed off. I got pissed off because she was pregnant and I wasn't. How could I feel that? That's so fucked up. And to Mia and Ben? God . . . what the fuck? *Seriously?* How could I feel that toward my best friend and my brother? What's wrong with me?"

"Babe—"

"What's wrong with me, Luke?" she repeats, her voice cracking. "I'm serious. There's something wrong with me. I know there is. *God* . . . this shouldn't be hard! Everyone else is getting pregnant. So why not us? I don't get it! Is it something I did? Is it something I'm *not* doing? I know five months isn't that long for some people, but *I'm not some people*. So *what*? What is it?" A sob catches in her throat. Her fists clench, shaking as she raises them next to her face.

Tessa looks ready to scream or cry or both.

I can't breathe. Seeing her like this—it fucking kills me.

I move, needing to get to her. Needing to touch her somehow. But just as I'm about to reach out and pull her into my arms, Tessa rounds the tombstone she's standing in front of to get back out onto the path and charges ahead.

"Let's just go," she says, staying just out of my reach, her feet hurrying her. "Let's just keep going and get the fuck out of here. I can't be here anymore. I can't—" Her voice cuts with a scream when a figure lunges out of the shadows, and Tessa reacts, no hesitation, throwing one helluva punch.

The figure hits the ground, groaning.

Lots of groaning.

Exactly the way he did the first time . . .

"Oh fuck," I mumble, eyes wide and locked on the guy who is absolutely going to fucking sue us. No doubt about that now.

"Dude! *Again?*" he bellows.

Hands raised, I watch the clown slowly get to his feet and adjust his mask. "Wasn't me. Swear to God. I was back there," I say, looking over at Tessa and expecting her to confirm my innocence. "Babe?"

Tessa has her hand covering her mouth and her head lowered, keeping her face out of view.

My gut tightens. I feel nauseous and ready to knock this idiot out again just to get some fucking privacy with my woman, until Tessa's soft, breathy laugh pushes out from between her fingers. Her shoulders begin to jerk.

I smile.

Running a hand over my hair, I start laughing then too. I can't help it.

"Oh. Nice. *Real nice.* You both are major assholes, you know that?" the clown asks. "Fuck you very much. My mom is going to *freak out* on me now. Two black eyes? We're getting family pictures tomorrow!"

Tessa leans into me, laughing harder now. She lowers her hand from her mouth to grip the Henley thermal I'm wearing.

I wrap my arms around her and bury my face in her hair, my entire body shaking against hers.

"I think it'd be best if you both just go."

Not a bad idea.

"Babe?" I lean away to see her face.

This is her call.

Briefly meeting my eyes, Tessa nods and then looks at the clown. "We're going. This place sucks balls," she tells him before spinning around so I can lead her back the way we came.

"*Sucks balls?* You both just can't handle it!"

"Go get some ice, junior!" I holler, causing Tessa to fall into a laughing fit again, her head hitting the side of my chest when I pull her closer and her arm circling my waist.

"Don't make fun of me, guy! That's so not cool!"

"Dumb fuckin' idiot. I told you that kid was gonna end up getting punched a lot in his life," I murmur against the top of Tessa's head as we follow the path. We pass a group of teenage girls who look two seconds away from turning around and following us out. "Didn't think it'd be my woman doing it though. That was fuckin' hot, babe."

Tessa remains quiet.

When I tilt my head down to look at her, I can see her

eyes are lost in focus on the dirt. She's not smiling anymore or laughing at what just happened.

She's back inside her head again. Worrying. Wondering. Most likely thinking the worst about herself in terms of reacting the way she did and the shit we're going through.

That's just it though—*we're* going through it. She's not alone. And it's my fault if she thinks she is. I should've made sure Tessa knew I was with her months ago when I first started seeing signs of concern. I should've brought it up, even if it did mean upsetting her even more.

When you pick at a wound, it bleeds. But we should've been talking about this.

Her question from minutes ago circles around in my head. I can still hear it. Only now, I'm wondering the same thing.

What the fuck is wrong with me?

"Babe."

Tessa's body stiffens at the sound of my voice. She blinks, sending a tear rolling down her cheek, and turns her face so it's buried against my side and I can't watch her break apart.

Regrets sits like a heavy weight pressing on my chest. It's unforgiving.

Maybe it should be.

I didn't say a fucking word to her, and I should've.

"Come here." I stop walking then and bend down, slide one arm underneath Tessa's knees, and pick her up so she's cradled against my front. "I love you. I love you so fuckin' much. Nothing's changing that," I tell her, needing her to know this in case she's questioning it.

Tessa sniffles and lets me carry her the rest of the way. She doesn't fight it. Her hand slides around my neck as she presses her face against the underside of my jaw. Her tears, wet and warm, soak into my skin.

"Shh," I whisper against her hair.

We pass the freak with the bottle. The zombies. The bodies wrapped and bleeding through the white sheets.

Nothing stops me. Nothing turns my head or pauses my steps. I'm focused on her and getting us out of here.

I don't give a shit about any of this.

We get to the parking lot and reach my truck in the far back corner.

I manage to open the passenger side door without putting her down and climb in, keeping Tessa in my arms and sitting her on my lap. There's no point separating and getting in on the driver's side. I'm not going anywhere and risking a wreck, knowing full well where my attention is going to stay. And we sure as hell are not having this conversation without my hands on her. I'd go fucking crazy and cause a wreck myself just so I could pull her into my arms.

I close the door and slide Tessa's legs closer to my hip so she's facing me more, her weight sitting on my knees and her back against the dash. The silence in the truck is heavy around us and thick in the air. I can't stand it.

And there's not a damn thing she needs to say right now. This is all me.

"Good or bad, if this works out or if it doesn't, tell me you know—I'm not going anywhere." I pause, meeting her eyes when she lifts them off my shirt.

She blinks.

I swallow the lump forming in my throat. "Tell me I've done my fuckin' job as your man, Tessa, and made sure you aren't doubting that. 'Cause if I haven't and that's what's got you stuck in your head thinkin' the worst the way you're doing right fuckin' now, the way I've watched you do the past five months, my life might as well end right here, 'cause I don't deserve shit. Not you. Not anything more than this. Nothing."

"Luke," she whispers, lips trembling as those damn tears well up in her eyes again.

"I'm a fuckin' asshole," I continue on. "I know what I am. I know what I've done and all the bad I got coming to me. I haven't exactly been a model son. More times than I can count, I've been a worthless friend. I'm basically a prick to everyone. And landing you? Fuck, that was . . . I don't know. Crazy fuckin' luck, or maybe the universe cutting me a break for once in my goddamned life. I've been shit on a lot, but that doesn't mean I'm worth dick. I know that. And the good you give me, babe? The good I feel every fuckin' day knowing I'm attached to you is more good than I ever fuckin' deserve to feel. I know it is. I'm not stupid. Honest to God, I basically walk around waiting for you to figure it out and question what the fuck you're even doing with me. So you gotta know, Tessa, if this is it? If we can't have a kid for whatever reason and it's just me and you for the rest of our lives? I'm good. Babe, I am so fuckin' good. I might not walk around grinning like a fuckin' idiot every second of the day like Reed does, or get that stupid, fuckin' dopey look on my face like Ben when he talks about Mia, but I'm right there. I'm just as fucked over you, and nothing's ever changing that. Kid or no kid. Ask me."

Tessa goes to wipe the tears from her cheeks but I do it for her, then keep my hands on either side of her face, pulling her in so our foreheads are touching.

"Ask me," I say again, watching her mouth twitch. "I don't need anything else. I swear to God, I don't."

"But you want kids," she whispers.

"I want *you*. Everything else is just bonus."

Tessa breathes deep, her hands sliding up my chest to my neck and holding there. "Mia thinks I'm stressing out too much, and that's why I haven't gotten pregnant yet."

"She might be right."

Makes sense. Not that I'm a fucking expert on it or anything, but I know what stress can do to a person. I know it can make you sick.

I watched it happen to my dad after my mom died.

"I don't know," Tessa says, moving her fingers back and forth on my neck. "I worry it isn't. And I can't get that worry out of my head. I want to give you this so bad, Luke, and I might not be able to. I don't know if I can handle that."

"So know I can handle it, and focus *only* on that," I say, watching the way her lips press together. "I'm serious. If you think I haven't thought about every fuckin' way this could play out, Tessa, you're wrong. I'm ready. If we can't do this on our own and end up seeking help from some doctor, and still, nothing? I can handle it. If we look into adopting and that shit doesn't pan out? Fine. I told you, I'll be good no matter what happens."

"Why wouldn't adopting pan out for us?" she asks, sounding confused as she leans back to see me better.

My brows raise. "Don't you gotta be interviewed for shit like that?"

"I don't know. I guess."

"Don't take this the wrong way, babe, but we're both assholes. It's why we fuckin' work. And I'm betting whoever is interviewing us is gonna figure that out real quick and shut that shit down, labeling us unsuitable or whatever the fuck. No way is anyone willingly giving us a kid once they meet us. I can't act nice. And you basically hate everyone."

A low, sweet laugh pushes past Tessa's lips.

I drop my head against the seat, smiling for the first time in what feels like days, my limbs lighter now and that weight shifting off my chest. "So yeah, worst-case scenario, like I said, I'm good," I tell her, dropping my hands to her hips. "Know that, and don't ever forget it. I will always be good with just this. Okay?"

Her shoulders drop on an exhale, and she nods her head. "Okay."

"Quit stressing."

"Quit thinking you don't deserve the world, Luke, because you do."

I cock my head.

She cocks hers, brows lifting in challenge.

"Christ. Is this gonna be an argument?" I ask.

"No. Not unless you agree. You deserve my good. You always will, even when you're being the world's biggest prick, which is like, most weekdays and every major holiday."

I close my eyes on a heavy exhale, feeling Tessa's lips press against mine.

"I want to give you that, Luke—all the good in the world. I want you to have it."

Hands gripping her ass, I slide her closer and nip at her lip. "I do. I got it all."

She growls, deep in her throat. "Quit being so fucking sweet. It confuses me."

Jerking back, I meet her eyes, and with a raised brow, question, "Is telling you my dick needs to find its way in your mouth right fuckin' now too sweet for you? 'Cause I can reword it."

She smiles, wetting her lips. Her hands slip under my thermal and tug at my belt. "Nope. Total asshole move right there."

"It's all I know."

"Lucky for you, it's all I like."

She slides off my lap and kneels on the floorboard between my knees.

I push my hands into her hair, head dropping back and mouth falling open when her hot tongue lashes against my skin.

"Fuck," I groan.

She swallows me whole.

"Lucky for me" is right.

CJ

Elbows resting on the bar, I stare at the bottle of tequila on the shelf in front of me as *Monster Mash* plays through the speakers overhead.

"Jesus. Is this song on repeat or something?" Reed asks Beth when she emerges from the kitchen. "This is like, the seventh time I've heard it in the past hour."

Beth stops in front of me and smiles, wearing her gumball machine costume.

It's basically just a white shirt with colored circles drawn in a cluster over her stomach. It's simple, especially considering the shit I see women wearing when I typically work Halloween night, but there's no doubt about what she's trying to pull off.

Looking to Reed when he stops at the stool next to where I'm standing and plants himself in it, Beth explains, "It was the only Halloween playlist I could find on Spotify. There aren't that many songs on it. In fact, there aren't a lot of Halloween songs in general. I was pretty limited."

"Just hand Reed a mic. That'll be terrifying enough," I joke.

Reed shoots me a glare. "I've been told my voice is fucking poetic. Don't hate, Tully. Oh, wait. I get it." He smirks then, slapping me on the shoulder. "You got a lot on your mind right now. On edge a little, are we? How are you not fucking drinking yet? Sweetheart, hook the man up."

I shake my head.

He runs his mouth way too fucking much. I gotta remember that next time I feel like sharing shit.

"What do you want? Beer?" Beth asks me.

"Tequila."

"Fuck yeah." Reed rubs his hands together. "Line 'em up! I'm getting hammered."

The door opens and catches my eye. I watch a group of people walk in, recognizing them from hanging around here now and again but not knowing them personally. So I don't linger.

"What's got you so fucking giddy?" I ask Reed, turning back around.

He opens his mouth to give me some obnoxious answer, I'm sure of it, but Danny's voice cuts him off.

"Why the hell was there rope hanging from the ceiling in the storage room?" he asks, stopping behind the bar and looking to Beth. "Did Hattie put that in there? I didn't see it yesterday."

"Ah, Christ," Reed grumbles under his breath.

"Um . . . I think that's always been there," Beth says, her eyes jumping from Danny to Reed and back again, voice an octave higher than it usually is. "Right? I'm sure I've seen it a million times. It's always there. You just miss it when you go in."

"I don't think so," Danny returns.

"Maybe a ghost put it there," Reed throws out, clearing his throat when Danny cuts him a look.

"Ooooh, yes!" Beth nearly drops the bottle of tequila when she jumps an inch off the ground. "I bet that's what happened! This place is probably haunted. I'm sure we'll be finding rope everywhere around here for *weeks*."

"Yeah?" Reed asks, looking to Beth with his brows raised, like he actually believes this shit, or at least hopes it's really happening.

What the fuck is going on?

Danny stares at Beth for another second before shaking his head. "Well, I left it there, for the *ghost* to get it." He cuts his eyes to Reed. "And I'm expecting it to be handled before my mind goes to places I'd really prefer it didn't. Am I being understood?"

"Loud and clear," Reed replies, getting to his feet. "I'll just save us all the trouble and get that taken care of. You can thank me with free drinks all night. I'd appreciate it."

Danny doesn't respond.

"Or not. That's cool. I brought my wallet."

Reed disappears around the corner while Danny serves the group of people who just walked in. They step up to the far end of the bar, and when Hattie makes her way over wearing her Greek goddess costume, she gives Danny a hug from behind and asks the group if they want anything from the kitchen.

I watch Beth line up four shot glasses in front of me.

"You getting in on this?" I tease, pointing at the row.

"Oh, yeah," she giggles. "And then I'm going outside and smoking a whole pack of cigarettes before I go off-roading in Reed's truck, *without* wearing my harness."

"Now, Beth. Is that smart? We all know your truck is a helluva lot nicer to drive than Reed's."

She tips her chin up, looking proud before focusing her attention on pouring the tequila.

"Stop flirting with my woman," Reed says, reclaiming his seat.

My brows shoot up when he sets the rope on the bar. "Should I even ask?"

"Probably not."

"Yo!" Tessa's voice turns my head, grabbing everyone else's attention in the process, I'm sure. Wearing a devil's costume equipped with a pitchfork and horns, she strolls over with Luke at her side. "Ooh. Are we doing shots, kids?"

"If there was ever a costume more fitting for someone," Reed comments.

"No shit," I add.

Tessa flips us both off, and leans her pitchfork against a stool. "Fuck. Off. Before I drag you both back to hell with me. I wear this every year."

"You could just punch 'em," Luke suggests, meeting my eyes and then explaining to the group, "She knocked out this kid at Weber's. Solid right hook."

"You *punched* someone?" Beth asks, eyes wide and trained on Tessa.

Tessa shrugs, picking up a shot glass. "Luke did it first."

"Nice," I mumble. "I'm guessing you're both banned from future attractions there."

"Oh, fuck that. We're never going back." Luke picks up a glass. "Bunch of freaks. You should've seen this man-baby. Creepy motherfucker. *Fuck.* I meant to get his real name before we left. I wanted to run him when I get back to work."

"He wasn't a pervert," Tessa says.

"You say that like you *know,*" he argues. "I'm telling you, babe. Watch. List. Bet money on it."

Tessa rolls her eyes, then gestures for Reed and myself to grab a shot. "Let's go. I'm getting shit-faced."

"Me too. Danny's onto me."

I slowly turn my head.

Reed shrugs.

I take his advice and don't ask questions. That's just shit I don't want to know about.

We all clink glasses and shoot the tequila. Tessa coughs. Reed slaps his chest. As Beth goes about pouring us another round, the room fills up more, people in costumes filing in. Some linger on the dance floor while others move to the bar and get served by Danny and Hattie. The booths start filling up.

My eyes wander to the door every other breath, it feels like. I'm watching for Riley.

I always am.

For the past five months, ever since I first laid eyes on Reed's sister, she's the only woman I look for.

Reed nudges me, glass raised. We all take our second shot.

"Where's your girl?" Luke asks me, minutes later.

"School. She'll be here." I push the glass in front of Beth. "One more."

She raises her brow. "You sure?"

I nod, rubbing at my mouth.

"We're here! We're here!" Nolan cries out over the music and commotion going on around us.

Ben and Mia are walking behind him, Ben looking like the happiest guy on the fucking planet, which is pretty typical for him. Mia though, something's off. She has tears in her eyes and a look of hesitation weighing heavy on her features. Her focus is glued on Tessa, no one else, who immediately sets her glass down and breaks free from the group.

She runs over, knocking people on the dance floor out of her way, and wraps her arms around Mia.

"What's going on?" Reed asks.

"Mia's pregnant."

All eyes move to Luke after he speaks.

Beth gasps and goes over to be with the girls.

"No shit?" I ask.

He nods, smiling.

His reaction is good to see. We all know how much Luke and Tessa have been struggling. I hear about it from Riley, so knowing they're on board with this makes it really fucking easy to feel happy for Ben and Mia.

"That's awesome," Reed says.

I jerk my head, agreeing, and reach behind the bar to grab another glass for Ben. I pour us all another round.

Nolan and Chase finally make their way through the crowd, running over wearing their superhero costumes. The pillowcases in their hands drag on the wooden floor.

"Look how much stuff we got! We hit the mother lode!" Nolan hoists his pillowcase in front of him, lifting it to waist level so everyone can see it. His eyes are big and bright as he looks at everyone through his mask that stops just above his nose. "Do you guys got some candy for us?"

"Don't you have enough?" I ask.

Nolan blinks. "No way. I'm just getting started."

"Here, Nolan. Come with me," Hattie says, waving him over to where she's standing behind the bar. "I have some candy for you."

"Sweet!" He takes off running.

"Uncle Wuke." Chase tugs on Luke's jeans, getting picked up.

I grab his pillowcase off the ground and set it up on the bar.

"What's up, bud?" Luke asks him.

Dressed as Superman, Chase yawns around the thumb in his mouth and drops his head on Luke's shoulder, looking a second away from passing out.

Luke rubs his back.

No fucking way is that guy not going to be a dad.

There's certain things that are meant to happen for certain people. One way or the other, it always works out.

Ben steps up beside me, grinning big, while the girls continue to hug and do this weird half-crying/half-laughing thing a few feet away.

"I hear congrats are in order," I say, offering out a hand for him to shake. "That's awesome, man. Really happy for you."

"Thanks." He exhales heavily, releasing my hand and then reaching out to take Reed's. "Couldn't let you have all the attention," he jokes.

Reed snorts. "Can't say I'm surprised in the *least*. My happiness means jack shit around here."

We all share a laugh.

I gesture at the glasses lined up and hand one out to Ben, and we all drink them down just as the girls walk back over.

"Awesome news," I tell Mia, giving her a quick hug, the wings of her angel costume scratching my arm.

"Thank you. We're so excited." Keeping hold of Tessa's hand, Mia leans her head on Ben's shoulder and smiles at Reed when he offers his congratulations.

"Let's get a table," Luke suggests. He's still holding Chase, who has his eyes closed now.

Tessa leans in and kisses them both.

I rub my hand down my face, liking the idea of sitting more than I did when I first got here. Three shots in me and I'm feeling pretty relaxed, but just as I turn to follow the group, Riley steps through the door.

And it's like the crowd wants me to see her. Needs me to see her.

They part like the fucking Red Sea, and if I were a religious man, I'd be thinking this has got to be some biblical shit right here, because without a doubt, that outfit she has on was touched by God.

Or made by the devil.

Probably a mix of both.

"Holyyy shit," Tessa snickers from her seat at the table. "Okay. Riley wins best outfit of the night. Hands down."

"Hey, I thought mine was pretty creative," Beth whines, but there's a playfulness to her voice. I'm sure she's smiling.

I just can't look at her right now to confirm that. I can't look anywhere else.

Letting my eyes roam up and down the length of Riley, I take her in.

Black police vest stopping at her ribs to show her stomach and unzipped to her cleavage, tight black pants—possibly leather, which I will confirm the second I get close enough to touch—thick black belt with cuffs and a night stick hanging off her hip, and leaning to the side, squinting . . . yep. That's my Nerf gun sticking out from behind her. I recognize the bright orange handle.

She's wearing dark aviators and a black uniform hat, and her long blond hair falls past her shoulders. Lips shiny and lifted, no doubt appreciating the look I'm giving her right now. And when Riley pulls out the night stick and starts walking toward me, twirling it in the air, hips swaying, I cock my head to the side and smirk, waiting for the show that I am one hundred percent participating in to start.

Ben whistles, the sharp noise cutting through the air and gaining some eyes. But mostly everyone except our group is minding their own business.

"Ma'am," I greet Riley when she stops in front of me, giving her cleavage some attention now that it's close up before admiring the patch on her vest.

It reads *Officer Booty*.

"Wow," I chuckle, looking to the ceiling. "God, I am so glad I committed all those crimes on the way over here. Lock me up now. I won't fight you, darlin'."

Holding in a smile, Riley jams her night stick against my chest. "Turn around, and don't call me that again. I am not your darlin'."

"Burn!" Reed hollers, earning laughs from the table.

Riley's cheeks turn red beneath her glasses.

"Are you sure?" I ask, leaning in and putting some pressure on the stick. "'Cause you look exactly like this girl I know. This real sweet little thing."

Her mouth twitches but she covers it quickly, pursing her lips together. Removing her glasses, she tucks them in her shirt and narrows her crystal blue eyes at me. "If you don't listen to orders, I'll cuff you now and drag you out of here."

"Well there goes my willingness to comply."

"Turn." Riley presses the stick firmer against my chest and crowds me. *"Around."* Her voice drops lower.

I feel that straight in my dick.

"Yes, ma'am," I say, winking before I put my back to her.

The girls clap and cheer Riley on behind us, who tries to keep her sweet giggle quiet so she can stay in character, but I hear it.

I meet her eyes over my shoulder, letting her know I'm enjoying this as much as she is.

"Hands flat on the bar." She kicks my legs apart and presses between my shoulder blades after setting her night stick next to the glasses we drained. "Do it. I have to search you."

My mouth twitches.

Now, there's an idea.

I press my hands on the worn wood and look down the bar, watching Nolan dunk his head in a large metal tub and retrieve an apple with his mouth. Hattie cheers him on.

"I have to tell you," I begin as Riley reaches underneath my arms to pat my chest. "I had three shots of tequila before you got here. Just want to be upfront so you know I'm not trying to hide anything." I moan when she moves down my stomach, her hands stilling at my belt.

Christ, this is probably not the best time to get hard.

"Did you really?" she asks, leaning around me.

She's stepping out of character now. This is real—the way she's looking at me. Those big blue flames burning me up the way they always do.

There she is.

I nod, keeping her eyes.

"Well," Riley furrows her brow and leans back around behind me. "That was very irresponsible of you. I suspect you were looking to drive yourself home?"

"Nah. I wouldn't do that."

She pats down the front of my thighs. "Why did you drink that much?"

"Nerves," I answer. "Just needed to take the edge off, ya know?"

"'Cause of all those crimes you committed?" she whispers at my shoulder as her hands press the pockets of my jeans. "Are you feeling guilty? Is that why your nerves are shot?"

"No."

"You should. Breaking a law, or several, isn't something we take lightly around here." The fingers of her right hand curl under, taking more of my pocket with them, and grip. "Ah ha," she says, sounding triumphant.

I blow out the breath I'm holding, grateful for the bar. My body sags into it as a thousand heartbeats fill my chest.

"Well well. What do we have—"

Riley's voice drops out when she pulls the small black box out of my pocket.

I take one last deep breath before I turn around, watching her study the thing she's holding like she doesn't have any idea what it is, or what's in it.

And that's definitely not the fucking case.

Every woman knows what's in that box.

"Wait! That's my cue." Reed shoots out of his chair and moves off to the side, phone raised and pointed at us.

I glare at him. "Really?"

He's fucking filming this?

If I wasn't already nervous enough . . .

"My mom insisted," he replies, smirking above his phone. "Whenever you're ready."

"Gee. Thanks."

"Oh my God," one of the girls whispers, sounding the most like Mia. "He's proposing."

"Told you. That's a winning outfit right there," Tessa says.

"Reed, make sure you zoom."

That suggestion comes from Beth.

"I'd like to take care of this *today,* if everyone's finished speaking up and ruining the moment." I sweep my gaze across the table, brows lifted in question. "We good? Anything else?"

"You might wanna kneel," some guy I don't even know suggests from the crowd.

I realize then all eyes are on us, on me and what I'm about to do. And looking to Riley, to her sweet face studying that box like it's the most precious thing she's ever held in her hands, the tears in her eyes, her head nodding like crazy, already answering the question I have yet to even ask, suddenly, I forget why the fuck I was nervous about this in the first place.

I'm doing this here in front of everyone for a reason.

I'm giving her this moment to look back on and remember who she shared it with, knowing the most important people to Riley are filling this room, and the ones that couldn't make it will apparently see a video.

This is how I've had it planned for the past three months. And that look on her face is why.

I can stand a little attention for that look. It's worth it.

"Do you wanna open it?" I ask her, my voice carrying like we're the only ones in the bar now that everyone's gone quiet. Even the music got turned down at some point. "I was gonna do it, do the whole *present it to you* thing, but if you—"

Riley quickly shoves the box against my chest and pulls back. "You can do it," she rushes out, hands knotting together and pressing against her stomach.

I chuckle, watching Riley give me the prettiest smile I think she's ever given me and cutely shrug her shoulders.

"I'd hate to ruin the moment," she teases.

"Certainly not." Clearing my throat, I drop to one knee and look up at her.

Tears start spilling down her face.

"CJ, what are you doing down there?" Nolan asks me.

I lower my head for a breath as collective chuckles fill the room, then looking down the bar, I spot Nolan hanging over the edge, head tilted down and face serious. His mask is off now and his hair is wild. Hattie's holding on to him so he doesn't fall onto the floor.

"Asking Ms. Riley to marry me," I annouce.

At those words, Riley whimpers.

"For *real*? That's really what you're doing?" Nolan questions before pushing up and looking toward the table. "Mom, I gotta do this for Ryan. This is what I'm talking about."

"For fuck's sake," I grunt, keeping my voice low, but Riley hears me and giggles.

I look up at her with pleading eyes.

"Oh, baby. Come here," Mia urges, sniffling, a steady stream of tears pouring down her face now too. "We'll talk about it later. Let CJ do his thing."

"Yes. Everyone *please*." Riley stomps her foot and shushes the crowd. "Let my man do his thing," she says, smiling at me and lifting her chin.

Shaking my head, grinning, already thinking this is the best fucking proposal in the books just going off her reaction alone, I pause, but only to make sure I don't get interrupted again, before I finally open the box and lift it for her to see.

Riley gasps, hand flying up to her mouth.

"I think you know how crazy I am about you," I begin, watching the best thing that's ever happened to me finally pry her eyes off the ring to look into my face. "I *don't think* you know how I'll go out of my mind if I can't spend every day of my life with you."

"Aww," Reed says.

I grit my teeth. "I'm regrettin' asking your permission."

"No, you're not."

Riley looks shocked. "You asked his permission?"

I nod. "His. Your parents'. I'm suddenly wondering if I need to take a moment and survey the room."

Riley bursts into laughter, along with the crowd gathered around us. "Please don't take another minute," she says. "Oh my God. I'll die if you don't ask me soon."

I smile at her, looking down briefly before meeting her eyes again. "We were always meant for this, darlin', and for everything that's coming after this. And there's a lot coming. I'm telling you—I want it all. Whatever it is. And I want it with you. Will you marry me?"

"Yes!" she shouts, as if she's been holding that one word in her entire life, just waiting on me so she can say it.

Clapping, cheering, and hollering, the crowd goes nuts around us as I slide the ring on her finger, letting the box fall to the floor. Standing, I pull Riley into my arms and lift her up, kissing her while my hands roam all that black leather.

"Jesus Christ. Please tell me this isn't a rental," I say against her smiling lips.

She giggles and kisses me. "It's all mine. Bought and paid for."

"Sweetest words I've ever heard, second to that yes you just gave me," I say.

Riley leans back and cups my face, staring into my eyes. "I love you."

"I love you, darlin'."

We share another slow, soft kiss before our friends come over to give well wishes, practically trampling us to do just that.

Riley shows off her ring to the girls, the group of them screaming, hugging, and crying. Arms around each other in their little squad—the one Riley couldn't wait to be a part of.

I can't stop looking at her. She's so fucking happy.

The guys congratulate me with slaps on the back and handshakes. Reed tells me he captured it all on his phone, even my tears.

Feeling too good to fucking care, I let that one slide and thank him for doing that for us.

I'm sure Riley will want to watch the video every chance she gets. I tell him to send it to us both, then, feeling a tap on my leg, I look down, finally pulling my eyes off Riley and giving Nolan the attention he's seeking.

I got my entire life to look at her. That's the only reason I do it.

"What's up, man?" I ask, smiling at his hair, wet and sticking up all wild. When he waves me closer, I bend down, grinning when I see what he's holding in his hand.

"Is it okay if I keep this?" he asks.

"Yeah, sure. What do I need it for?"

"Yes!" Nolan pumps his fist into the air, then peers around me, holding up the ring box. "Mommy, look what CJ said I can keep! Now I just need a ring and I'm set!" He rushes around me to show Mia, who walks over with the rest of the girls, smiling and wiping tears from her eyes.

"That's great, baby," she says, cupping his cheek before giving me a look of appreciation.

Nolan rushes off toward the apple-bobbing setup at the bar, squeezing in between people to get through.

Ben throws his arm around Mia's shoulders and kisses the top of her head. He's holding Chase now, who's still passed out. I'm surprised the commotion didn't wake him.

"This place just got even more awesome," Tessa says, stopping beside Luke. "You did good, Tully."

I lock eyes with Riley when she finally pulls her attention off her ring. "Yeah, I did."

She smiles, rushing at me, and wraps her arms around my neck, pulling me down for a kiss.

"So, when's the wedding going to be?" Beth asks, leaning back against Reed when he steps behind her and holds her swollen stomach.

I look down at Riley, brow raised. "Your call, darlin'."

She pulls her lips between her teeth, thinking for a second before informing the group, "Maybe this summer after I graduate? I don't want to wait too long. And I'd really love to do it at the beach." Riley peers up at me. "Would that be okay?"

"You wanna do it at Sparrow's Island?" I ask.

"Hey, that's our beach," Reed says.

I glare at him. "You don't *own* the beach."

"I didn't say we own it." He rests his chin on Beth's shoulder, smirking now. "We just . . . made a lot of memories there."

Beth turns bright red.

"So did we," I argue, watching Reed stiffen.

Fuck that.

I'm sure Reed and Beth did make a lot of memories at Sparrow's Island, considering that's where they spent their wedding/honeymoon, but that's where Riley and I began. We met for the first time officially that weekend. We fucked for the first time there too, and if that's where she wants to get married, Reed can take his memories and fuck right off with them. I'm getting that beach.

Riley tenses in my arms while Ben and Luke crack up laughing, watching Reed grow increasingly uncomfortable.

"You guys are funny," Mia says. "I'm pretty sure we all made a lot of memories there . . ."

All eyes widen and turn to Mia. She never says shit like that.

She shrugs, leaning into Ben and laughing. "I'm just saying. If that's all it takes—Ben and I own that beach too."

"Yeah, us too. We own *a lot* of that beach," Tessa adds, biting Luke's jaw.

"Fine," Reed grumbles, looking around the group. "But Beth and I own McGill's. We're the only ones allowed to make memories here. So no *couple* bathroom breaks, and stay the hell away from the storage room. We own the shit out of that after what went down in there earlier."

Danny stops behind Reed, glaring at the back of his head.

Everyone tries containing their laughter as Reed stays unaware.

"This is going to be good," Riley whispers, leaning back against me and drawing my arms around her tighter.

"You wanna see him get his ass beat?" I ask against her ear.

"If it means we get Sparrow's Island, then *yes*."

I chuckle and kiss her cheek.

Realizing something is up, Reed slowly turns his head, spots Danny and smiles wide. "Hey! You know, I was just coming to look for you." He releases Beth and puts his arm around Danny's shoulders, leading him away. "Let's talk about all those renovations you were wanting to do here, and how it's not gonna cost you a damn thing . . ."

Beth throws her head back and laughs, then everyone joins in.

I guess Tennyson Construction will be footing that bill.

"Come on. Let's order some food," Ben suggests, motioning toward the table they left that's still vacant.

I turn Riley in my arms when the group leaves us in the middle of the dance floor. "You happy?" I ask her.

Beaming, she looks from my face to her ring, letting go of my neck to study it. "You could've tied a string around my finger and I would've been happy," she says, gripping hold of me again and smiling up at me, her sinful body tucking closer. "It's beautiful. It's so beautiful, and I'm so happy, Cannon."

Cannon.

Fuck. What it does to me to hear her call me by my real name.

Growling, I let my hands travel lower, settling at the top of her ass. "Don't be calling me that here," I say. "Unless you wanna go find out what the fuck is so cool about the storage room."

Giggling and rolling up on her toes, she offers me her mouth, and I take it in a long, slow kiss, getting rock hard by the end of it.

"Where are we going?" Riley asks, startled, when instead of leading her toward the table and our friends, I pull her in the direction of the door, shoving people out of the way when they aren't moving fast enough on their own.

"My truck. Your brother didn't say shit about making memories in the parking lot."

Nolan

Two days later

I punch my finger against the screen of Mommy's phone, making sure I'm hitting the right numbers this time. I studied them good off the paper.

"Oops," I say when I hit one too many. I lift the phone to my ear, breathing faster and faster like I do when I'm running when I hear it start to ring.

My eyes open all the way up.

"Holy crap. This is it," I whisper.

I'm actually calling her.

"Hello?"

A man answers the phone. He sounds probably as old as my dad, so I know exactly who it is. I got this.

"Hi, Ryan's dad. This is Nolan." I sit on the edge of my bed, listening.

I don't hear anything except his breathing. He's breathing

a lot. Then I think he says something like "Handle this," but I don't know what that means.

I pick at the edge of my shoe.

"Nolan? Is that you, sweetie?"

This lady sounds just like my mom. I bet they're the same age and everything. I remember her from the wedding. She was really nice to me.

"Hi! Can I talk to Ryan, please?"

Daddy told me to make sure I asked nicely. He said it's good to get in with the parents.

I don't know what that means, but I'm making sure I do it.

A soft laugh tickles my ear. "Sure. Hold on one second, okay?"

"Okay."

I keep picking at the edge of my shoe.

"Baby, did you give Nolan our number?" Ryan's mommy whispers, but I can hear her real good. Then somebody's breathing again, but faster this time, just like I'm doing.

"Hi, Nolan."

I sit up straight and forget all about my shoe.

"Hi!" My stomach does this weird flip-flop, like when we ride the roller coasters at Six Flags. "Um, I got your number off the picture you sent me. That's like, the coolest thing I've ever gotten in the mail so far. Even better than when I get money from my Nana for my birthday."

She giggles in my ear. "Did you like the picture? I got yours today too. I put it on my wall above my bed."

Holy crap. I'm in her room.

"I loved it. It's just like the dragon tattoo I'm gonna get one day." My head wrinkles. "Did I tell you about that?"

I can't remember. I think I did.

I think I told her a bunch of times.

"Yep," she says.

"Good. Just making sure." I stand from the bed and walk around my room. "So, I needed to ask you something, Ryan. It's a really big deal for me."

"What is it?"

"I know we're just kids, and my dad says I don't need to worry about this yet, but I can't help it. I wanna marry you. And I gotta make sure you wanna marry *me*. If I don't know for sure, I'm gonna lose it."

I stop walking so I can listen really good, holding my breath as I look at a spot on the carpet.

I don't move a muscle.

"Okay," she says.

I lift my head. "Really? You'll do it? You want to?"

"Yep."

"That's great!" I run over to my bed and climb on. "That's great. Wow. Okay. I think I'll be able to sleep now."

She laughs again.

I really *really* like the way she does that.

"I gotta go. My daddy needs the phone," she says.

"That's cool. I can call you anytime I want now. That was such a good idea to send me your number, Ryan. Probably the best idea anyone has ever had."

"And I have your number now too. I can see it on the phone."

"So you can call me . . ."

"Yep."

"Will you?"

"Yep."

I smile. "That's great. I hope you do. Okay, so my dad always tells my mom he loves her before they hang up the phone. It's just . . . I don't know. It's just something people say."

I bend my knee up, getting ready to pick at my shoe

when she doesn't say anything, but I don't start picking at it, because she speaks just when I'm about to do it.

"My mommy does that too. She says it all the time. She won't get off the phone until she says it."

"Sometimes my mom says it first."

"My dad says it first a lot."

I chew on my lip. "Mm. Okay."

"Okay." She giggles again.

I smile really big. "I love you."

"I love you."

"Dylan."

That is definitely her dad talking to her mom. I know his voice by now.

"Bye, Nolan."

"Okay, see ya!"

I hang up the phone and spring from my bed, running out of my room with my arms raised in the air.

"She said yes!"

Getting Down

Helena Hunting

One
Party Time

Ruby

I try to sneak a peek at my reflection in the mirror during the brief pauses between strokes of eyeliner, but I'm sitting on the vanity so it's impossible to get a good look. "How much longer before I can see?"

Amalie Whitfield, my best friend for over a decade—we survived high school and then college in New York together—huffs an annoyed sigh and gives me the stink-eye. It's a hilarious expression on her makeup-caked face. She throws down the lip brush and pulls a tissue from the box. It's the third time she's had to do this. "Can you please stay still? I'm almost finished and I don't want to have to start over."

I grip the edge of the counter and press my lips together. "Staying still."

She dabs at the spot I messed up, and tilts her head to the side. "Pout for me."

I make pouty lips at her and follow it up with a wet kissy sound. Amie—which is what I like to call her since Amalie sounds a bit stuffy—rolls her eyes and goes back to painting my lips, while mirroring my expression. For the past ninety minutes she's been working on our makeup—like she used to do in college when we went out clubbing. She's amazing with makeup. It's a gift.

"We should've videoed this for your YouTube channel," I say through mostly still pursed lips. Back in college Amie started posting short tutorials as part of a research project for one of her marketing classes. What began as a way to bump up her grade turned into a hobby she actually managed to make money from. She even managed to raise something like seventy thousand for one series she did for cancer patients. My best friend is pretty incredible.

"I haven't done that in a long time. I doubt anyone watches those videos anymore. But maybe when I'm not quite so rusty I could do it again. It would be fun to put something up, just to see if anyone would still watch it."

Last time I checked, Amie had close to a million views on the video she uploaded six months ago. Right before she started dating her fiancé, Armstrong. She's a bit of a YouTube sensation, even if she pretends she isn't. Sometimes I miss this version of my best friend, the carefree fun one who puts on costumes in the middle of the day and does my makeup. She's so serious most of the time now.

I'm used to sitting while getting my makeup done, but this is a lot more intricate than what I wear for a performance. Today I brought home a pile of old costumes. I just happened to be around when my producer opened a trunk of donated costumes, none of which were helpful for performances on the stage, but all of which were perfect for Halloween. Halloween may be weeks away, but the second I walked in the door I started trying on costumes. And the moment Amie arrived, I made her do the same.

I love Halloween. It's my favorite holiday of the year, even though technically it's not a real holiday since no one gets the day off. I also love horror movies. I love being scared more than ever now that I have a super-hot boyfriend to watch those movies with. It didn't take long for him to learn to share that love. Especially when it means I'm cuddled up in his lap, using his neck as a place to hide my face when the movies get too scary. As a side note, the movies are never really that scary, I just like the way he smells. And more than half the time we never make it to the credits, since I use the scary part as an excuse to get all up on him. That often leads to kissing, and nakedness inevitably follows.

But back to Halloween. Beyond scary movies and morphing the condo into a haunted house—which I've already done thanks to several shopping expeditions to local Halloween specialty stores and a few consignment shops, all before October first—I love dressing up. Like love, love, *love* it. But then, I'm an actress, so playing pretend is kind of my thing. Even the bathroom Amie and I are currently occupying has been decorated. I've turned it into a haunted bathroom, with bats hanging from the ceiling and fun accessories containing creepy-crawly things lining the vanity. I've actually scared the crap out of myself a couple of times when I've had to pee in the middle of the night.

My phone buzzes on the vanity. I glance down and see that it's Bancroft, my boyfriend. It's his vanity I'm currently sitting on. Well, ours is probably more accurate. We've been dating since the spring and I moved into his condo two weeks ago. Our beginning was a bit unconventional. Not too long ago I was jobless and nearly homeless.

So when he presented an opportunity to be his pet sitter while he was out of town on business, he also offered me the spare room in his luxury penthouse condo. Of course I took it. Five weeks of pet sitting turned into five weeks of video chat flirting that turned into seriously hot sex when he got back, which turned into an actual relationship.

I reach for my phone, but Amie slaps my hand. "Don't move."

"Ow."

"I said don't move. That includes your lips."

"God you're bossy." It's so hard not to smile at her angry expression. Especially with the way she's dressed up. Amie's a gorgeous, ultra-fit, sandy-blond-haired, blue-eyed goddess. She has a sweet face, but under that pretty exterior is a whole lot of bite. Bite that I haven't seen much of since Armstrong came onto the scene.

She pinches my arm and I turn into a mannequin.

Less than a minute later I hear the door open and the sound of my name being called from down the hall. I'm not allowed to speak, so Amie answers for me, shouting, "We're in your bathroom."

The heavy tread of shoes—they're not Bancroft's, he always takes his off when he walks in the door—echoes down the hallway. Bancroft is not alone. He's with Amie's fiancé, who happens to be his cousin. I find him to be a pretentious asshole, but Amie seems to love him, so I keep those thoughts to myself most of the time. Unless I'm alone with Bancroft. Then we share our disdain for him openly.

Tonight they're staying for dinner. Later we can bitch about him and I can distract Bancroft from his scorn with a blowjob and he can return the favor.

"What're you ladies up t— Holy fuck." Bane's voice drops to gravel pitch.

Bancroft's massive, broad shoulders take up most of the doorway. Sweet lord he's gorgeous. Currently his luscious mouth is hanging open as he holds on to the jamb, as if his grip is the only thing keeping him where he is. His gaze bounces over Amie and lands on me, sweeping down and back up again.

"What's going on?" Armstrong asks from behind him. He can't see anything because Bancroft is impeding his view. Armstrong is shorter than Bane by a few inches. Although, to be fair, Bane is huge. I think he's at least six-three, and he weighs twice as much as I do. He's a wall of solid muscle and sexiness.

"That's a really good question," Bane mutters. His eyes drop to my red-toenailed bare feet, and move up, tongue dragging across his bottom lip as he takes me in.

Beyond the fact that I'm dressed the part of a villainous fairy with the makeup to match, I'm also sitting on the vanity with Amie standing between my legs. If I take off the makeup and the costume, it's a rather common position I find myself in with Bane. Except both of us are usually naked and he's often inside me. Or on his knees with his face between my legs. Based on the way he's looking at me right now, I might very well get to experience his adeptness in both departments later tonight. I look forward to ripping off his suit and treating him like a ride at an amusement park. Once Amie and Armstrong leave, of course.

One eyebrow quirks as he asks, "You two playing dress-up?"

I grin. I assume it must look incredibly evil considering the makeup I'm currently sporting but am not allowed to see yet. "We're practicing for Halloween."

His mouth tilts in a smirk. "Fuck yes you are."

Oh yeah. I'm getting so lucky later. I don't think I'm changing out of this costume, as difficult as it might be to sit in all night considering the massive wings attached to my back. I'll make it work. Bancroft is very well acquainted with my love of all things Halloween and horror.

"What's happening in there?" Armstrong elbows Bancroft in the ribs so he can poke his head in the door.

He edges inside the bathroom and his eyes go wide as they move over Amie. I suppose I can understand why. I've managed to get her into a pair of red satin booty shorts and a tight T-shirt. Her bra is very, very visible through the thin fabric. Her amazing legs are on display. Her hair is pulled up into two pigtails. If I wasn't one hundred percent sure she wasn't even close to Bancroft's type, I might be inclined to make her cover up. But he's not into leggy blondes. He's into somewhat petite brunettes. He also likes the sass, which I have an abundance of.

"What're you wearing?" Armstrong asks. He sounds very much like he's sucked on a helium balloon for shits and giggles.

Amie looks down at herself, as if she doesn't understand his concern. She does. Fully. We talked about how he wouldn't approve of this costume at all before they arrived. Which is the exact reason I suggested she continue to wear it.

I'm not actively trying to interfere in my best friend's relationship, but I'm not fully convinced he's the perfect fit for her, either. He's far too trust-fund-pickle-up-ass. I'm worried she's settling for the wrong reasons. The last boyfriend she had was a little too far on the wrong side of the law, so I'm concerned she's swung a bit too much in the other direction to compensate for the near prison record she incurred over it. My hope is that pushing his buttons will help improve what I'm beginning to suspect, based on recent conversations, might be a fairly lackluster sex life. Or, if I'm really lucky, it might make her see that he's not the best penis to spend the rest of her life riding.

"Doesn't she look amazing?" I ask with extra enthusiasm.

Armstrong ignores me. "You can't ever leave the house like that."

I glance from Armstrong to Amie and then to Bancroft. Seriously? Who says something like that? This isn't the dark ages.

"We were just playing around. Having some fun." Amie smoothes her hand self-consciously over her stomach. Her flat stomach. Amie could be a model and until she started dating this goon, she seemed relatively happy with the way she looks, but ever since the ring went on her finger, I've noticed she's far more cautious about what she eats, making flippant comments about staying in shape for the wedding.

"You need to cover up. You can't wear those shorts in front of Bane." Armstrong gestures behind him, at my boyfriend, who's giving me the eye. It's not the I-want-to-fuck-you eye anymore, now it's the can-I-murder-him eye.

I'd say yes, but then my best friend would be unhappy and dinner would be ruined.

"My bikini covers less than this," Amie retorts.

Three heads snap in her direction, mine included. This right here, this is the Amie I know. This is my best friend. The one who won't put up with other people's crap. The one who does what she wants, when she wants, regardless of what people think. Even her fiancé. Especially her fiancé. She might feel some regret later, but that's what I've always been here for—to help her manage that. To assist in making her feel less like she needs to atone for having fun. Armstrong is the biggest wet blanket ever. How he and Bane share DNA is a wonder.

When we were in high school I was the one people tended to look at when there was trouble brewing, but Amie was most often the instigator. I just followed along. She's sweetly beautiful, and it makes her look incredibly innocent, which she is not. She's always been a bit of a wild one. It's the reason I nicknamed her Anarchy Amie. To everyone else she's always been Amalie, prim and proper, sweet and sunny. I know all too well what she's really like—feisty, fun, and with a love for getting into trouble and a penchant for dating bad boys—at least she was, until she started dating Armstrong and settled right down. The stunts she used to pull in high school were epic, though. Once she spiked the football player's Gatorade with vodka to get back at the quarterback, who started rumors about her when she refused to go out with him.

"We should have some wine and order dinner!" I suggest brightly, hoping to cut some of the tension. I hold on to Amie's hips as I slip off the vanity. Armstrong looks scandalized as my boobs brush below hers. Bancroft looks like he wants to spank my ass. Among other things.

"But you're going to change first, right?" Armstrong asks.

"We need to take some pictures first. The lighting is better in the living room." I grab my phone and Amie's hand and flounce past the men, towing her behind me.

"I should really get changed," Amie mumbles in my ear once we're past them.

"You went to all this trouble to make us look awesome and you look hot as fuck. We need evidence." I haven't even had a chance to look at my own reflection. I pause in the hallway, where a decorative mirror, rimmed in spiders and fake skeleton bones, reflects my terrifying yet starkly pretty face back at me.

I'm not being intentionally egotistical. On a good day, with enough stage makeup, I'm decent to look at. Bancroft seems to think I'm gorgeous with zero makeup. I'm not going to fight him on that assessment since he's the one looking at me all the time, but I think some of it has to do with my incredible skill set in the bedroom and my ability to hoover his cock.

"Wow. This is amazing. Are you sure you don't want to switch to a career in stage makeup?" I get up close to my reflection, then take a step or two back. She's done an unreal job. I hover in the gray area between eerie and beautiful.

Armstrong and Bancroft follow us down the hall to the living room, where the bulk of my Halloween decorating has taken place. I've made a tape outline of a dead body in the center of the living room floor. A life-sized zombie girl stands disconcertingly in the corner, cobwebs span the windows and over the shelving, where fake potions and containers full of gum eyeballs and candy worms and gummy brains are strategically placed. Bane and Amie are used to it by now, but based on Armstrong's wide-eyed, distasteful expression, he's not a huge fan. Whatever.

I make us pose in front of the windows, and then against a wall with two skeletons who look like they have their arms around us. I make a point of draping myself over Amie every chance I get, mostly because it makes Armstrong look like he's going to have an aneurysm. I can tell Bancroft knows what I'm doing, because he offers to take pictures for us and then suggests poses that are far from PG.

By the time we're done with our impromptu photo shoot, Armstrong is already done with his first scotch and onto his second, fidgeting anxiously with his tie.

I cross over to the wine fridge and search for a nice bottle of red. There are actually two fridges, one for white so it's cold and one for red so it's room temperature, or whatever is ideal. Bancroft knows this better than me. Amie prefers red over white. I don't really care either way. Actually, I prefer prosecco over anything else, but it's not her favorite, and based on Armstrong's pinched, sour face, she needs the booze more than I do. "You know what we should do?"

"Change into real clothes?" Armstrong mutters into his scotch.

"We should throw a Halloween party. Wouldn't that be fun?" I look first to Amie and then to Bancroft, ignoring the party pooper in the corner.

Bane's not paying much attention to anything apart from my ass. The skirt I'm wearing is gauzy, and my black shorts are very visible through the transparent fabric.

"That's a great idea! Where should we host it?" Amie's enthusiasm matches mine.

"I was thinking here. There's lots of space."

That snaps Bancroft out of his ass-induced trance. "What about Francesca?"

"We'll keep her in your room. It'll be fine." Francesca is Bancroft's fugitive ferret. They're illegal in the state of New York, which makes my boyfriend a very sexy, animal-loving criminal.

"I don't know—" He's tapping on the counter, wearing his furrowed brow. Serious Bancroft makes me want to get naked. All versions of Bane make me want to get naked, but when he's all scowly and furrowed-brow it makes my lady parts want attention. I need to rein in my inner hornball, since we haven't even ordered dinner yet.

"Actually, a Halloween Ball would be a fantastic idea. Don't you agree, Bancroft?" Armstrong swirls his scotch in his glass.

"Uh? I guess?" Bancroft looks as stupefied by Armstrong's sudden interest in the conversation as the rest of us.

Armstrong agreeing to any kind of party, with any level of enthusiasm, is grounds for confusion. Planning parties is not his thing. The entire wedding has fallen on Amie's shoulders. Well, it did in the beginning. Until their mothers stepped in with their many opinions as to what would be best. Mostly it's Armstrong's mother with all the opinions.

Amie's family comes from new money and Armstrong's comes from old, which means there's a bit of snobbery over her status. Just because her family hasn't been rolling in piles of cash for the past three centuries doesn't mean she can't have a say in her own wedding preparations.

The mother contingent is making Amie a little crazy. Every time I bring up the wedding these days she seems to need a glass of wine followed by two hours of hot yoga.

"We need to throw some kind of charity event in addition to the year-end Christmas fundraiser. Father's indicated there's money we need to spend and this would be the perfect way to accomplish that, don't you think? It could be some kind of masquerade ball so you girls can get dressed up." He gestures to Amie and me. "Although this is certainly not appropriate. Anyway"—he sips his scotch—"we'll figure out a charity we want to support. Of course it needs to be something that will get us good press. What's relevant right now? I thought I read something recently about some kind of epidemic in one of those impoverished countries. We could raise relief money for that. Anything with babies or animals would make for excellent media coverage going into the holiday season."

It's always about press with Armstrong. Although I suppose since his family runs one of the biggest media corporations in the country, he's always going to be concerned with public perception and what will pull at people's heartstrings the most.

Bane leans on the counter, and while the tic in his left cheek indicates his annoyance, I can also see that he's contemplating it, likely for very different reasons. He's capable of looking at something from both a business and PR perspective without it being all about the public image. Bancroft's altruism is the reason I'm living in his condo with him right now.

Bancroft used to be a professional athlete before he started working for his father. The Mills family comes from a long line of hotel magnates.

I'm so focused on Bane that it seems I may have missed some of the conversation.

"Where do you think would be a good place to hold a Halloween Ball?" Amie asks.

I suppose if they're making it an event it can't be here, which is what I'd hoped for. If it was the small party I'd been planning in my head it would be one thing, but a ball means hundreds of guests. I slap the counter and startle Armstrong. "What about one of the New York hotels?"

Bancroft looks at me. There's lust in his sexy eyes. I'm not sure if it's the costume or my awesome idea that's making him so hot for me, but either way I plan to capitalize on that later. "The Concord."

"Oh my God, yes." I might moan the words. That hotel is stunning: the rooms lavish, the spa services unparalleled. I clear my throat in hopes of making my reaction less awkward. "The Inception Ballroom would be perfect, wouldn't it?"

"It would." He nods his agreement.

The Inception Ballroom is antiquated, with burgundy velvet drapes, black carpets, and gold accents. Very Dracula. The perfect location for a Halloween soirée.

"And we could stay the night."

"On the penthouse floor." Bancroft's grin is full of dirty promises. Those rooms are incredible. Full Jacuzzi tubs, showers that can fit a dozen people comfortably, king-size poster beds, a separate living room with a massive couch, endless amenities. I've never had a chance to stay there, because we live in New York, but this would be the perfect opportunity.

"I'll talk to my father tomorrow to make sure the funds are there, and you can talk to yours about the ballroom," Armstrong says to Bancroft.

"And we can plan the costumes and the theme!" I say enthusiastically. This is a little different than my original idea, but it could still be fun. As long as I get to dress up and we get to stay in one of the penthouse suites, I'm all for it.

Armstrong shifts his gaze from me to Amie and slaps at the bat hanging just above his head, which keeps brushing his hair when it swings back and forth. "I can give you full control over the project. You do well on the planning side of things."

"Um. Okay?" She looks taken aback.

I am too, because I think that was an actual compliment. "It has to be classy though, so the costumes can't be anything like this." And he just ruined it.

"Of course." Amie nods dumbly, but under her shocked, plastered-on smile is a glimmer of excitement and mischief.

"And I can help out, of course," I say.

Armstrong has absolutely no idea what party planning looks like when Amie has full control. We're going to have so much fun. The last time we planned a Halloween party we were in high school and her parents had gone away for a spa trip to Hawaii.

It didn't go quite as well as we'd anticipated, what with half of the school showing up. Three guys got into a fight over her that night. In their defense, they all thought she was dating them. Amie had a lot of boys wrapped around her finger in high school. Even in college, actually. She left a trail of broken hearts and pining boys behind her.

This party is going to have a killer budget. And maybe, just maybe, it'll have a couple of Amie's ex-boyfriends in attendance. I can think of one or two from a few years back who might be on the fringe of our social circle—and unlikely to have a criminal record, or at least one that has already been expunged. Either way, I don't think it will hurt Armstrong to know there have been others before him who fell all over themselves for the chance to date her. It might shake things up a little.

Bancroft's cell phone buzzes on the counter beside his

hand. One of his older brothers' names flashes across the screen. Bane frowns and pulls up the message.

At the same time, there's a knock at the door, followed by the sound of a code being punched in. "I hope you're not fucking!" Lexington calls out as he steps into the foyer.

Lexington, better known as Lex, is two years older than Bancroft.

"Damn," Lex says as he takes in the scene before him. His brow pulls down when he sees me and then shifts to Amie in her tiny red shorts and her see-through T-shirt. "If this is some kind of weird role-play shit, I want in."

Bancroft snorts. Sometimes when Lex and Bancroft get together the conversation degrades quickly. I still haven't quite figured him out, but I like him a lot, even though he seems a little guarded at times. He's a bit of a cynic and I've gotten the impression that he has a player reputation. Whether that's true or not, I'm unsure. Right now it looks like he'd love to play with my best friend. Too bad she's marrying his cousin in a few months.

"Production was getting rid of a bunch of old costumes so I made Amie try some on."

"In front of you?" The corner of Lex's mouth curves up as he looks Amie over.

She drops her head, hiding her blush and a smile.

Armstrong is suddenly all over Amie, which is very unusual. He's not openly affectionate most of the time. Unless he's goosing her or something. He wraps his arm around her waist and whispers something in her ear. Based on her expression, she doesn't appreciate his comment.

Bancroft grabs Lex by the back of the neck. "Don't flirt with my girlfriend unless you want your nose broken, brother." He's mostly kidding. Lex and I get along just fine. And I don't think I'm his type. But then again, I'm not one hundred percent on what his type actually is.

Lex elbows Bancroft in the side. "I'm not here to steal your woman." His gaze shifts to Armstrong, who's busy adjusting Amie's shirt. "I came for something else."

Two
Hanging

Amie

I'm trying to keep my eyes on my glass of wine, but I can feel Lex looking at Armstrong. Or maybe it's me. Which is understandable, considering I'm not wearing much of anything. Armstrong is annoyed. The way his fingers keep flexing on my side tell me this. His insistence that I change is hint number two. He's been annoyed since he walked into the bathroom.

I'm very familiar with Armstrong's annoyed face. His lips thin until they almost disappear. He's also on his second scotch. Or maybe it's his third. I kind of want to keep pushing his buttons to see if it will have the desired impact. Which is me coming back to his place tonight for some sex. It's Monday, though. He has squash in the morning, so I typically don't stay over on Mondays. Although in a few months that's going to change. When we get married I'll sleep beside him every night of my life. Hopefully once the stress of the wedding is over and we're occupying the same living space, we'll go back to having the same amount of sex we did when we first started dating.

I played it safe with Armstrong, knowing his family background. We went out six times before we had very sweet, very missionary sex. It was very reminiscent of my first time, although it lasted a little longer.

"You want to stay for a drink?" Bancroft asks Lexington.

"No, thanks. I don't want to crash your party. I just need the Beacon files and I'm off."

"What do you need those for?" Bancroft taps the counter as he regards his brother.

They definitely look related. They're both tall and broad. If Bancroft is Thor, Lexington is more like Captain America. Lex is a little narrower and maybe an inch or so shorter, but then Bancroft's previous career as a professional rugby player gave him the build of a superhero. Lex is similar, but in lieu of a head of curls, his dark hair is straight; a crisp part and product keep it tamed. The sides are neatly trimmed and short. He must've gotten a haircut recently. It was longer the last time I saw him. Beyond that he has perfectly straight teeth to go with his perfectly straight nose and his manicured nails—yes, I noticed those. And every time I've ever seen him he's been impeccably dressed.

Armstrong's hand slides down my hip and cups my ass cheek. His lips are next to my ear. "Sweetheart, you should really consider changing out of this. It's not appropriate for other men to see you dressed so provocatively."

I grit my teeth and say nothing, aware that there's some kind of tension between Armstrong and Lex. I have no idea what it's about, but every time Lex is at an event we're attending, Armstrong does everything he can to avoid him. Unfortunately, under these circumstances that's not possible. I'm not sure why they don't like each other.

Armstrong's worry over my state of dress seems irrelevant since Bancroft finds whatever files he's looking for right away. "Sorry for interrupting," Lex says, then gestures to Ruby. "This is badass, by the way."

He shifts his gaze to me and Armstrong, a slight smile tugging at the corner of his mouth. "It's always a pleasure to see you, Amalie, especially after you and Ruby have been playing dress-up."

Bancroft coughs and gives him the elbow.

The smile becomes almost a sneer and Lexington tips his chin at Armstrong. "Later, cousin. We should schedule a round of golf before they close the course for the year."

"We should," Armstrong says tightly.

"I look forward to beating your ass on the green."

Armstrong makes a displeased sound. "Unlikely. I think it's been proven time and time again that I always come out on top." He strokes my arm and when he reaches the hem of my shorts he drags his finger along my skin. I shiver.

What the hell is going on?

Lex's smile drops and his eyes narrow, his cheek ticking. "That's only because you play dirtier than me."

Bancroft clears his throat. "You need anything else, Lex?"

Lex flashes his brother a dark smile and raises the folder before slipping it under his arm. His hands are huge. It must be a Mills man trait. One I'm not sure why exactly I'm noticing. "I got what I came for."

As soon as Lex leaves, Armstrong goes back to being his usual self. I really don't understand what the issue is there, but Armstrong can be very competitive, about pretty much everything. I want to ask what that whole standoff was about, but I don't think I'm going to get any kind of answer that makes sense, and I don't want to put a negative spin on the evening, so I leave it alone.

Twenty minutes after Lex leaves, I change back into my normal clothes and wash all the makeup off my face. Ruby, on the other hand, stays in her fairy outfit and eats the Italian takeout delicately so as not to mess with her glitter lips. I don't want to be jealous of my best friend and her relationship, but sometimes I am.

I have a feeling the second we leave those two are going to get their freak on. And I doubt she's going to change out of her costume or wash her makeup off.

I know an awful lot about my best friend's sex life. In the past I would've been just as free with mine. Except ever since I've been with Armstrong there's not as much excitement to share. But then I guess that's to be expected since I'm settling down. No more Anarchy Amie on the prowl. Not like when we were in high school and college and I went a little wild.

That kind of reckless freethinking can't last forever. And discretion is far more important than hanging-from-the-rafters sex.

Although we did have a bit of that, back in the beginning. Once we had sex in a coatroom at a huge corporate function. That night I moved from date to girlfriend status. A few months later he took me on a trip to Paris and proposed under the Eiffel Tower with an orchestra playing behind him. It was incredibly romantic. We had a beautiful dinner and then we had sweet engagement sex. That's what sex with Armstrong is like: sweet and polite.

Over time I'm sure that will change, that I'll be able to persuade him to get a little dirty with me. And that he'll learn what's guaranteed to make me come. Sometimes I take a long time to orgasm with him, and he gets frustrated. Armstrong likes to be good at everything. So occasionally I fake it and take care of the situation later, after he's asleep. That's been happening more frequently as of late, but with the wedding coming up, we've both been under stress, so sex has taken a backseat.

At nine thirty Armstrong calls for the car. He's been touchier than usual tonight, so maybe if I play it right, I'll be able to stay at his place and get some relief for the tension that's been building since Friday.

I hug Ruby, who's still dressed in her costume. Her makeup is still nearly perfect. We make plans to have lunch later in the week before Armstrong ushers me out the door and into the elevator. The car is waiting for us when we arrive at lobby level.

We've been in the car for three minutes. I glance at Armstrong, then at the tinted divider. We're isolated from the driver. He can't see or hear us. We have at least twenty minutes in the car together, and that's a conservative estimate based on there not being any traffic. But this is New York. There's always traffic.

Armstrong is frowning while checking emails on his phone. I unbuckle my seat belt and slide closer.

He looks up. "That's unsafe. You should put your seat belt back on." Armstrong is very concerned with safety. He drives no more than five miles over the speed limit. Once I drove his car and he nearly had a heart attack. I wasn't going that fast.

I drag a fingernail down the side of his neck. "Ivan is a very safe driver. It's fine."

He eyes me. "What're you doing?"

"I was thinking, maybe I can come back to your place tonight instead of going home."

He appears confused. "But it's Monday. I have squash in the morning. It's why you don't stay over on Mondays."

I'm not sure whether to laugh or roll my eyes. "We could live on the edge. You could miss squash tomorrow."

"It's too late for me to cancel, and if you stay neither of us is going to get enough sleep."

Always so pragmatic about everything. I sink to the floor with the intention of giving him some incentive for a Monday sleepover.

"What're you doing?"

"What does it look like I'm doing?" I go for his belt.

He glances up at the divider that keeps us separate from the driver. "Amalie, we're in the car."

"I know." I give him my naughtiest grin and pull down the zipper. Slipping my hand in the fly I find him already semi-hard. It shouldn't take much to get him excited. I pop a couple of buttons on my blouse and push his boxers down.

He must've decided he's not so concerned about my safety anymore, because he spreads his legs wider and brushes my hair out of the way. I try to stay in the moment while I'm pleasuring my fiancé, but my mind starts to wander to the Halloween party we may be planning. In my head I start creating the guest list, reviewing cocktail options, deciding whether it will be a seated dinner or just appetizers. Soon enough I'm being given the complimentary warning that an orgasm is imminent.

Afterward, I crawl up his body, thinking maybe we'll make out for a bit en route to his place, but he turns his head and gives me his cheek when I go in for a kiss. I make my way over to his mouth, but he keeps turning away. "Oh, no, no. Not after you've—" He purses his lips and shakes his head.

"Not after I've what?"

"You need to brush your teeth first."

"What?"

"You have my cum in your mouth."

"I swallowed it." I stick out my tongue. "See. No cum."

He makes another face. This one is disapproving. "Amalie."

I straddle his lap and tug on his tie, bringing my lips to his ear. "Come on, Armstrong, I'm horny. I wanna fuck."

He puts his hands on my hips and makes another disapproving sound. Dammit. That wasn't the right thing to say. Armstrong isn't turned on by my potty mouth, as he calls it. I keep hoping if I say things like that he's going to turn me over his lap, flip up my skirt, and spank my naughty ass. I should know better. It's a turnoff and I've ruined any chance of getting a reciprocal orgasm.

I mutter an apology and flop down in the seat beside him, buttoning my blouse. I really need to find a way to loosen him up. In addition to the wedding preparation, he's been under a lot of stress at work with the changes happening at his family's media empire. They've been talking about a merger with a rival corporation. I shouldn't be upset about this, but after spending an entire evening watching Bancroft and Ruby make sex eyes at each other I'm seriously wound up and in need of some release. Not to mention how territorial Armstrong seemed to become when Lex showed up.

When Ivan pulls up in front of my apartment building several minutes later I don't ask about sleeping over again or invite Armstrong up, because he's already fallen asleep post-orgasm. At least I have the ability to take care of my own problem. God bless the sex toy industry and multiple orgasms.

Three
Naughty Girl

Ruby

"You know what I need right now?" Bancroft wraps his arm around my waist. He also tries to press his chest against my back, but I'm still wearing the fairy wings, so he can't get that close.

"Another glass of scotch?" I'm being snarky. Mostly. Even I opted for a second glass of wine at dinner and I'm not a big drinker.

"Now that Armstrong is gone I can manage without alcohol."

"What does it say about him as a person that no one can deal with him without drinking?"

"That he's an asshole."

"Who you happen to be related to," I point out.

"And who your best friend is going to marry. Can't you do something about that?" He fiddles with my wings, making them flap against my back. "You're a fairy, you should be able to make magic happen."

"What kind of magic do you think I'm capable of? I can't tell her not to marry Armstrong just because we don't want to hang out with him." I finish washing the last wineglass and set it in the drying rack.

"What does she even see in him? He's a pompous dick." That Bancroft talks this way about his cousin speaks to his absolute disdain. Bancroft doesn't often have nasty things to say about people without some serious provocation.

"Well I'm pretty certain his dick is not part of the allure, so I'm at as much of a loss as you are."

Bancroft rests his hip against the counter. "Wait a second. What do you know about Armstrong's dick?"

I peel off my rubber gloves with a shrug. "Amie said he's average in the penis department."

"You've talked about my cousin's dick?" Bancroft makes a face as if he's eaten something offensive.

"Just in the general sense of size." Prior to dating Armstrong, Amie and I used to share sex stories. I have the disconcerting feeling that he's not only average in size, he might also be very average in ability, based on the lack of details she provides these days. I've tried to temper my sharing so as not to appear as though I'm gloating.

Bancroft crosses his thick arms over his defined chest. It's been hours of glances and soft touches. Now that our friends are gone we're gearing up for playtime. I was extraordinarily careful while I ate dinner so as not to ruin my lipstick. It's deep purple-pink and sparkly. I think it will look quite hot in smeared marks across Bancroft's cock. It's a weird fascination I have. I really like to wear lipstick before I blow him. One of these days I'm going to get the glow-in-the-dark stuff and give him a ghost BJ.

"Have you talked to Amie about my cock?"

"Not in great detail, but she's aware that you're well above average." I assess the look on his face. I can tell he's trying not to smirk at the compliment. Bane knows he's well-endowed. His cock is like the rest of him, big and beautiful. I pull the plug from the drain and toss the dishcloth on the counter.

Before I can turn around again Bancroft starts fiddling with my wings as if he's trying to fold them out of his way. "How do these come off?"

"They're attached with snaps."

"Well, they need to go. They're obstructing my ability to rub my huge, hard cock against your ass," he complains.

I laugh and turn in his arms. "Wow. You do such a great job embellishing phrases such as 'above average.'"

"I was just helping with your descriptive word choices, 'above average' sounds boring."

"What exactly is your plan once you get the wings off?"

"Well, since I just spent the last four hours listening to my cousin tell me how awesome he is, I feel like me and my dick deserve to rub against something nice and warm."

I run my hands up his chest. "As nice and warm as the inside of my mouth?"

Bancroft's gaze drops to my glittery lips. "That would be an excellent place to start."

"I think so, too." I slip his belt free from the clasp. Bancroft braces his hands on the counter, eyes on my fingers, as I pop the button. The head of his erection strains against the elastic waist of his boxer briefs, which barely contain him.

I pull the band back and peek inside. I bite my lip—gently

so as not to mess with my glitter lips—and glance up at him, skimming the slit with my finger. A bead of wetness pools there. I lift my finger and bring it to my mouth, carefully sucking the tip. Bancroft groans when I slip it back out, a deep purple-pink ring and some glitter now decorating it.

"For fuck's sake, Ruby."

I slip my hand under his tie, fisting it to pull him down to meet my mouth. I bite his bottom lip, dragging my tongue across the smooth skin. At the same time I reach into his underwear and wrap my hands around his hot, hard cock.

Until Bancroft, I hadn't really been a huge fan of the blowjob. I mean, sure, if I was in a relationship I'd bite the BJ bullet because to get oral you have to give it. But Bancroft turns it into quite the event. And the lipstick thing adds a strangely erotic twist. Also, he loves them. And watching his face when I'm on my knees, or in a variety of other positions, is enough to keep me coming back for potential lockjaw.

As I pull back he wipes at my bottom lip, purple-pink and glitter staining his fingertip. "Should we get this off first?"

I shake my head.

He rubs his fingers together. "Isn't it going to stain? It seems to be on pretty good."

I drop to my knees. "That's what makeup remover is for."

We're right in front of the sink. My knees hit the padded mat he put there so he can hump me from behind when I'm doing dishes. It's supposed to be good for your back. The mat, not the humping.

I shimmy his pants and boxers over his hips until his erection juts out. Bancroft wraps his fist around it and

strokes a couple of times. I run my hands up under his
shirt, sighing as my fingers pass over the hard ridges. I
wait until he angles his erection down before I press a
tiny kiss to the tip, leaving glitter behind.

"Fuck, babe. You're killing me here."

I grin, because of course this is ultimately my plan: to
give him a killer blowjob that he will repay in kind with
some amazing oral of his own. And then he'll get inside
me and fuck as many orgasms out of me as he can. He often
treats sex like a rugby match—the more I come, the better
his mental running score.

I kiss all the way along his shaft, leaving lip prints.
He's quick to unbutton his cufflinks and loosen his tie
enough to get it over his head. The top button of his shirt
pings on the hardwood in his zeal, but then he's yanking
his shirt over his head and the thin white tee underneath
follows, revealing his glorious chest.

God, his body is magic. His abs ripple and flex as I
take him in my mouth.

"Motherfucker." He shoves his hands in my hair. Bane
is very good at controlling his dirty mouth unless we're
having sex. "You always look so good with my cock in
your mouth. Even with this fucked-up makeup on."

I try to smile, but my mouth is pretty full.

Bancroft's expression grows serious as I stop playing
around and start sucking in earnest. His hands stay in my
hair, guiding, stroking my cheek, telling me how much he
loves my pretty, sexy mouth.

He eases me off after he comes, his blissed-out expression quickly morphing as his eyebrow rises. He sweeps
his finger under my bottom lip, and then does it again, his
mouth turning down at the corner. He nabs a paper towel
and wets it under the tap. "Jesus. It looks like you blew a
unicorn."

I motion to his cock, then use the counter to pull myself up. "So does that mean it looks like you fucked a unicorn?"

"I feel like I need to retract the whole unicorn statement, because I really don't want that image in my head before we have sex." He wipes at my mouth, gently at first, then more vigorously. "This isn't coming off."

"I just need makeup remover. We can worry about it later." I grab his tie and try to get him to kiss me, but he turns his head.

"Oh, fuck no. You look hot and that blowjob was incredible, but that lipstick has got to go before anything else happens."

I roll my eyes. "You're really ruining the spontaneity of this, you know."

He gives me the eye and crosses his arms over his naked chest. It would be effective if his half-limp cock wasn't hanging out of his pants, covered in purple-pink lipstick smears and glitter.

"It wasn't a problem when my lips were wrapped around your cock," I point out.

Said cock twitches like he can hear us and would like to give some input. I gesture to his penis. "I think he agrees."

"I think you need to see what I'm talking about. It's pretty distracting right now, and when I'm inside you, like I plan to be very soon, I'd like to able to kiss you without feeling like I'm in some whacked-out sci-fi movie."

"Fairies are fantasy, not sci-fi."

Now it's Bancroft's turn to roll his eyes. He spins me around, tears my wings off, and pulls me back into his chest.

I know what's coming. He's going to take me to the bathroom so I can get this lipstick off. I'm pretty sure he's overreacting. Bancroft likes to show off just how strong he is and picking me up like I'm an oversized doll and toting me around is one of his favorite pastimes. Okay. That's untrue, sex is probably one of his favorite pastimes. But I actually quite enjoy throwing down the stubborn card just so he'll pull this move on me.

Except he doesn't wrap an arm around my waist and carry me away. Instead he cups me, fingers pressing against my clit through the unfortunate barrier of shorts and panties. He slides his hand farther back. Oh my God, what is he—and then he lifts me up. By my crotch.

"Seriously, Bane?" I cross my arms over my chest.

It does nothing to deter him. In fact, his left palm finds my right breast, presumably to make me more secure. And honestly, the way his palm presses against my clit is rather enticing. As a result, I don't struggle to walk my own ass to the bathroom.

He uses his shoulder to turn on the light. He's slow to set me down in front of the vanity, and even when my feet hit the floor, he doesn't move his hand away. Either one. Although the one between my legs shifts, and the pressure to my clit becomes more direct and purposeful.

"See the problem?" Bancroft's mouth is right beside my ear, lips brushing my cheek.

I've been so caught up in sensation, and the anticipation of what's coming, that I almost miss the issue. "Oh, wow." My eyes go comically wide, which with the current eye makeup makes me look rather demonic. Purple-pink lipstick and glitter are smeared all over my chin. It appears I'm a bit of a sloppy dick sucker.

While I get to work on the lipstick smear removal, Bancroft makes a show of getting naked behind me. He's about to start on clothing removal for me, but I clear my throat, looking pointedly at his black socks.

"I'll get to those when I'm not standing on a tile floor."

He hates cold feet almost as much as I loathe socks during sex.

"You should probably do the same to your unicorn horn." I toss a pad soaked in makeup remover at him and he stands beside me at the sink, rubbing it up and down his quickly hardening cock, swiping away glitter and the purple-pink lip prints and smears. After a minute of rubbing and three new cosmetic removal pads apiece it's better, but I still have all sorts of glitter stuck to my face, and there's a very distinct pink hue to my chin.

"Do you want me to take off the eye makeup, too?"

"No. Leave it." Bancroft yanks my panties and shorts down my legs.

"Because it'll take too long and you're impatient?"

"That and it's hot." He slips his finger between my legs and any snarky comment dies. "Come on, naughty fairy, I'm hungry and you've got exactly what I'm starving for."

Two days later I'm sitting in the lobby of the Concord hotel, waiting for Amie. I'm pretty much glitter-free, although I swear there's still a pink tint to my chin, and I haven't needed lipstick at all for the past couple of days.

Bancroft hasn't tried very hard to remove the remaining purple-pink streaks from his dick, proudly wearing the remnant of my lipstick smears. Not that anyone other than me is going to see it, but he seems to think it's rather funny.

Anyway, the purpose of lunch with Amie today is twofold: we must sample their appetizer selection for the Halloween soirée, and any excuse to hang out in the middle of the week is a good one.

It's already one in the afternoon, but I've only been

awake for little more than an hour. My performance schedule means I don't go to bed at regular hours and I sleep late. Amie, on the other hand, has likely been up for at least seven, if not eight hours. Since five forty-five, I've received at least fifteen text messages with thoughts on this party we've been given the go-ahead to plan. My fun Halloween get-together is turning into a huge deal. I hadn't fully considered the implications of what this would become if we were given access to things like the Inception Ballroom and Armstrong's apparently endless pocketbook.

Yesterday we were officially given the green light, which means Amie's already in full-on party planning mode. While the soirée—the official, pretentious label given to this event—is still weeks away, we honestly don't have a lot of time to get things organized. Typically these events take months of planning. Or so I'm being told by Amie, whose messages have grown increasingly frantic and detailed in the past two hours, but stopped suddenly just over an hour ago.

While I wait for her to arrive, I send messages to Bancroft. Well, not so much messages as emoticon vegetables illustrating what I plan to do to him when I get home from my performance tonight. Often I'm going to bed just as he's starting his day. It's been quite an adjustment for both of us. But Bancroft has learned how to appreciate being woken at five in the morning by my vagina alarm most days of the week.

I don't hear back from him right away, which means he's probably in a meeting. I check the time. It's after one. It's very unusual for Amie to be late for a lunch date. She's typically waiting for me.

Less than a minute later she comes bustling into the lobby. She's carrying her purse and a gym bag. Windblown hair frames her face, which is also atypical. Not her face—that's gorgeous—but her unkempt hair. Amie is usually very polished, and more so since she started dating Armstrong.

"I'm so sorry I'm late." She drops her gym bag and comes in for a hug.

"It's fine." I give her a squeeze. "Is everything okay?"

She releases me from her death grip and adjusts her skirt and blouse as she explains. "I thought I could fit in a yoga session and still be here on time, but two of the showers weren't working and there's this woman who always hogs the mirror after the lunch classes, which I don't understand since she doesn't even work up a sweat." She swoops down to reclaim her bag. Slinging it over her shoulder, she nearly takes out a woman carrying her Chihuahua in her purse. The tiny dog expresses its displeasure in yippy barks, scaring her owner and several people close by, including Amie, who skitters behind me.

"What's up with you? Did you do too many wheatgrass shooters this morning?"

"I've been up since two. I couldn't sleep last night. I think I may have overdone it on espresso shots this morning. I honestly thought the extra yoga session would help calm me down. Maybe I should've done cardio instead."

Amie is a big fan of yoga and running. She goes a minimum of four times a week. While it's great that she likes to stay active, I think she might be going overboard these days, although maybe it's her way of managing stress. When I'm stressed I wash a lot of dishes and eat a lot of takeout. Since moving in with Bancroft I've developed new stress management techniques that often include his penis. I've found it has a one hundred percent effectiveness rate in stress reduction. At least temporarily.

"Why couldn't you sleep?" Amie's always been an

early riser. She's one of those people who can get only four hours and still look fresh the next morning. If I get less than eight the bags under my eyes are so big I can fit the entire contents of my closet in them.

"Thinking about the party." She slips her arms through mine and we head for the restaurant where Bancroft has made us a reservation for lunch.

As we pass a mirrored wall Amie grimaces and pats her hair. "I'm going to have to do something about this before I go back to work this afternoon."

"You look great."

"I'm having dinner with Gwendolyn tonight. She wants to talk about the guest list for the wedding again. I'll definitely need to fix myself up before I see her."

"As long as it's not the kind of fix-up she seems to be fond of." Armstrong's mother's face doesn't typically move apart from her lips. It's a little unnerving how infrequently she blinks, to be honest.

"She suggested I go for a Botox treatment a month before the wedding."

I snort. "What could you possibly need Botoxed?"

"She says I make this face when I'm nervous and it's creating lines in my forehead. Armstrong said it's not a bad idea. I'm only twenty-five and I don't want wrinkles yet."

I really have to bite my tongue against the scathing comments just itching to fly. In all the years we've been friends, Amie has never been this concerned about her appearance. She works for one of New York's leading fashion magazines, and they perpetuate the "you're not good enough" ideal at every turn. Buy this cream, use this technique. Fix yourself. How to be prettier, sexier, a better wife, a better girlfriend, a better lover. I think she might be brainwashed.

Obviously her soon-to-be mother-in-law is exacerbating Amie's newly developed insecurities. In fact, I think this entire wedding is pushing her insecurities. Broaching the subject without upsetting her is impossible, though. I tried in the beginning, but soon learned it wasn't worth the stress it seemed to cause her.

"You don't have wrinkles, Amie."

"It's sort of preventative, isn't it?"

God. I really hate how uncertain she sounds. "If you mean it prevents you from having facial expressions, I guess. Besides, I've read some studies about that stuff. Apparently if you can't make the facial expression, you can't experience the emotion attached to it, which might explain why Gwendolyn is such an insufferable bi—"

Amie's nails dig into my arm. Hard. Hard enough to nearly cut the skin. I stop before I'm able to finish the sentence, assuming my mouth is the issue.

"Oh, sugar snap peas," Amie mutters under her breath.

Seriously. Even her dirty mouth has disappeared in the past six months. Along with almost everything fun about her. Okay. That's untrue. When it's just her and me it's fine. She's still fun to be around, but add her fiancé to the mix and it's like he sucks all the awesome out of the room, and her.

I follow her wide-eyed gaze. Speak of the insufferable bitch. Gwendolyn is sitting across from Meredith Mills—my boyfriend's mother. They're sisters. How Meredith and Gwendolyn can be related and so very, very different is beyond me.

Bancroft's mother—everyone calls her Mimi—is probably one of the sweetest women I've ever met. Is she concerned with unnecessary, ridiculous things like plastic surgery and highbrow gossip? Of course. But it's not her fault, that's the environment she was raised in. At least she's nice about it, and she can make fun of herself. Gwendolyn, on the other hand, believes she's one step down from royalty and that everyone should kiss her feet and offer to wipe her ass.

Before I can turn us around, Mimi raises her hand in a wave, beckoning us over. I survey the table at our approach. It appears they've already eaten. Thank God. I don't mind lunch with Mimi, but if I have to spend an entire lunch hour with the insufferable bitch I'll need alcohol to survive. Lots of it. Enough to make me dance on top of a bar. Topless.

Mimi pushes away from the table and daintily places her napkin beside her mostly empty plate. "Ruby! It's so lovely to see you!" She hugs me and Amie in greeting while Gwendolyn remains seated. Both Amie and I are forced to bend and air-kiss her since she refuses to get up.

Of course Gwendolyn has to make a comment about Amie's gym bag and her slightly disheveled appearance, while Mimi tells me how pretty I look.

"We're just finishing lunch, but come join us." Mimi doesn't even have to summon anyone. Two servers appear out of thin air with extra chairs and we're quickly seated. "I was hoping I'd see you today. Harrison informed me we'll be hosting a soirée here at the end of the month. It's such a fabulous idea. Have you decided on a theme?"

"We're just in the planning stages," I say quickly.

If there's one thing I know about Meredith Mills, it's that she loves a good party. Bancroft only introduced me to his family a little over two months ago, and in that time I've attended at least four dinner parties at the Mills mansion. Each time, Bancroft and I have snuck away for a quick screw in a different room. We were almost caught once. That was super fun.

"Well that's perfect, isn't it, Gwennie? We can help you plan!"

"Now isn't the best time. We have an appointment in fifteen minutes at the spa, remember, Mimi?" Gwennie checks her watch. I assume she's frowning, but it's hard to tell since only a slight lip twitch results.

"Oh right! Silly me. Well why don't we plan another lunch for later this week?"

"If we're planning a party we'll need more than an hour," Gwendolyn cuts in.

"That's true." Mimi taps her lip. "We should have dinner, then. Maybe next Monday since that would work best for you, right, dear?"

"Mondays are usually okay." I look to Amie, searchingly. Planning a party with Mimi will be fun, but I'm not sure if that'll be the case if Armstrong's mother is involved.

Amie checks her calendar. "Monday would definitely work."

"It's settled. Monday dinner at our place. We'll invite all the boys so Harrison doesn't get bored and try to interfere," Mimi says with a smile.

Awesome. Another evening spent in the company of Armstrong. I can't wait.

Four
Orgasmless

Amie

Mimi offers another round of hugs once we've set the time for dinner. Gwendolyn isn't pleased that they're going to be late for their appointment and Mimi reminds her that she owns the damn hotel, they can be late if they want.

As soon as we're alone, I wilt like a flower under a heat lamp.

"I wonder if they could inject her with a new personality the next time she goes in for a Botox touch-up," Ruby mutters once they're out of earshot.

I sip my Perrier and sigh. I've wondered the same thing on many occasions. "You know, I keep thinking she's going to warm up to me eventually, but it never seems to happen."

"I don't think she can warm up to anyone. How she

managed to procreate is truly a mystery." Ruby picks up the appetizer assortment menu the server has left for us.

We're trying a little of everything so we can narrow the menu down to something reasonable. Well, Ruby will try everything. I'm on a very strict eating regime because the wedding is coming.

"I don't want to think about what procreating looks like with her."

"I imagine it isn't much different than what she looks like most of the time, except she'd be naked." Ruby takes a sip of her mimosa. It looks delicious.

"Or maybe not. Maybe she just wears crotchless panties so Fredrick can get up in there without inconveniencing her," I whisper.

Ruby snort-giggles and smiles. "Oh my God. Can you even imagine?" She grows serious again. "I really don't get it, though. Everyone loves you."

Everyone except for Armstrong's mother, anyway. "Armstrong thinks she feels threatened because I'm taking him away from her, but I think she just doesn't like me. It seems like the harder I try, the worse she gets."

"So you've talked to him about it then?"

"I've tried. He doesn't seem to think it's a big deal, but we spend so much time with his family. I just want her to like me."

Since Armstrong has a very close relationship with his mother, I have an unreasonable level of perfection to live up to in her eyes. It's difficult to see Bancroft's mother with Ruby. It's clear she genuinely likes Ruby, and that Ruby likes her as well. In fact, his family acts as though the sun rises and sets for Ruby. I don't need Gwendolyn to worship me, I just want to have the kind of relationship with my mother-in-law that doesn't involve excessive anxiety. Unfortunately, I don't know how to make that happen.

Ruby pats my hand and smiles. "It's impossible not to like you, Amie. Maybe planning this party together will help."

"Maybe." I have my doubts.

"How's the wedding planning going, anyway?" Ruby asks. "You must be excited now that it's only a few months away."

I should be excited. Unfortunately, wedding plans fill me with dread these days. It's not that I have cold feet. Not more than is normal, anyway. It's that I've given up far more control over the wedding plans than I ever intended just to make things easier with Gwendolyn, and clearly it hasn't improved our relationship at all.

I decide to focus on the positive. "The dresses are supposed to arrive in a couple of weeks. If we're lucky we'll have a fitting before the Halloween soirée."

Although if that happens, I'm sure to be spending even more time with Armstrong's mother. She has an opinion on everything and since the reception is being held at one of the Millses' hotels she's been heavily involved in all aspects of the planning, which Armstrong seems to think is totally reasonable. Since my family lives out of state, my own mother hasn't been very involved.

"And you must be super excited for the honeymoon, right?" Ruby lowers her voice to a whisper so only I can hear her. "You'll finally be deflowered after all these years."

I snort indelicately. Ruby is very well aware that there is no flower to pluck where I'm concerned. I dated a lot in high school. And typically not the kind of boys I could or should bring home to meet my parents. I figured if I wasn't supposed to have sex it wouldn't feel so good. Speaking of, I could really use some soon.

"I hope once we're married things will pick back up in the in bedroom."

"What do you mean?" Ruby stops sipping her mimosa, which is already half gone.

I wave my hand around in the air as if my comment doesn't matter. "The stress of the wedding is making things . . . difficult."

Ruby frowns and gives me her full attention. "Does that mean you're not getting much action?"

I fiddle with my napkin so I don't have to look at her. Ruby and I have always been pretty open with each other about our sex lives. I've probably shared much more with her than she needs to know, but then, we've been friends for more than a decade.

She was the first person I told when I actually was deflowered back in my junior year of high school. Well, Ruby and I went to prep school. The boy I gave my virginity to was the son of my father's mechanic. Brent Harper was a serious bad boy and oh-so-good with his fingers. That translated very well fully naked. Unfortunately, that "bad boy" reputation was well earned. Last I heard he was in prison for embezzlement with no chance of parole. Ironically, he's not the only boyfriend I've had with a mug shot. The bad ones were always hard to resist.

"Hello! Amalie?" Ruby waves her hand in front of my face.

"What?"

"Are you low on action?"

"I don't know. Maybe I'm being too demanding. I mean, I know I have a healthy drive, probably a little too healthy sometimes. It's why I'm at the gym so much these days, but running and yoga really aren't a replacement for sex and orgasms." I realize I'm playing with my hair and fold my hands in my lap to cease the anxious behavior.

Ruby glances around the restaurant, maybe to make sure we have privacy. "When was the last time you had sex?"

"Umm . . ." I look up at the ceiling as I ponder the answer to this question. Beyond the blowjob I gave to Armstrong in the car on Monday, it's been a while. "Maybe a week ago?"

Ruby raises a brow. "Maybe?"

I consult the calendar in my phone, just to be certain of the accuracy. "Oh. Wow."

"Oh wow, what?"

The last day marked with an "O" was nearly two weeks ago. "It's been thirteen days."

"Since you've had sex?" Ruby asks, maybe just a bit too loud. Thankfully we're in a private corner of the restaurant. "Didn't you stay at his place on the weekend?"

"I did, but he'd had a busy week and fell asleep before I could jump him, and no. I was right about the sex being a week ago."

"Then what's been thirteen days?" Ruby's eyes go even wider and she grips the edge of the table. "Don't tell me your period is late."

I shake my head. "That's next week. It's been thirteen days since I've had an orgasm."

"Oh." Ruby sags with relief. And then her mouth drops open. "*Thirteen days*?"

I nod.

"That doesn't make sense if you had sex last week. How is that possible if you haven't had an orgasm? And how can you survive that long without having an orgasm?"

Maybe this wasn't the best place to bring this up.

The server stops by our table with an assortment of

appetizers and goes to the trouble of describing each and every one of them.

"Oh my God! These are adorable!" Some of them are adorable, others are a little creepy. They're all Halloween-themed. There are coffin-shaped tarts, the mushroom caps look a lot like eyeballs, which is a tad unappetizing, and there's something on the plate that looks unnervingly like a spider. We wait patiently while he talks. I can tell it's taking Ruby a great deal of restraint not to dig right in and try everything.

I think I've managed to get out of our discussion about my lack of orgasms, but as soon the server has disappeared, Ruby leans in and whispers, "Is your clit sucker broken or something?"

That's Ruby's affectionate term for my favorite personal pleasure device. In my opinion, there is no better way to get off. Apart from actual sex, obviously. "No. It's not broken."

"Is your clit broken, then?"

"It's not broken either."

"You need to explain this. Aren't you the one who said an orgasm a day keeps the mood swings at bay or something?"

This is totally my mantra. I've lived by it for years. Since I had my first orgasm, to be quite honest. I learned exactly what it took to get me off by the time I was seventeen. It was a fluke really, and I generally don't have trouble reaching orgasm. Well, lately with Armstrong it's been a bit of a problem, but I think it's psychosomatic on my part.

I can usually manage to get off in under three minutes under the right conditions. I don't need the typical ten to fifteen or sometimes more that seems to be the general average, at least not when I'm excited, and who isn't excited when there's the prospect of an orgasm?

"I'm trying something new," I mumble.

"Something new? Well it sure can't be good if you haven't had an orgasm in thirteen damn days." Ruby pops a mushroom cap in her mouth and moans. "We definitely need more of these. These go on the list." She dabs the corners of her mouth with a napkin.

"I think we may want to consider the appearance of some of these. We could save the horrorish themes for the drinks instead," I suggest. I pick up something that looks much like a stabbed heart. It tastes delicious. I think it's a stuffed pepper.

"So what's this new orgasmless torture you're trying out? This sounds worse than that burpee regime last month."

I choose one of the normal-looking appetizers, an endive and shrimp hors d'oeuvre, and nibble the end. "Well, I've been having some difficulty orgasming with Armstrong lately."

"Like he gets a finger cramp from all the rubbing? Just get out your clit sucker and you're golden. Better yet, make him be the clit sucker."

"He doesn't know about the CS."

Ruby blinks at me. "Wait a second. You haven't introduced him to your toy collection?"

I can feel my cheeks going pink. The honest answer to this is no, I haven't. I did try once, but he was not pleased when he saw the size of my vibrator, which surpasses him in both length and girth. "I stay at his place all the time and my collection is at my place."

"I can see how carting around your trunk of magic tricks would be a little cumbersome. Oh my God. Remember that time you forgot to take the batteries out of your g-spot lover?"

"Oh, I remember." The vibrator Ruby's referring to has

a rounded angled head to it that hits the g-spot. It's rather accurate in its curvature.

"I'm pretty sure that airport security guard fell in love with you that night. He wanted to give you the rubber glove treatment so bad." She wags her eyebrows.

"He was hot, wasn't he?"

"So hot. And those tattoos. My lord. Just delicious." She picks up a tomato tart and takes a small bite. "Almost as delicious as these. They go on the list, too. So back to your orgasm drought. I'm not getting why you haven't had one just because Armstrong is having difficulty getting you there."

"I think it's just the stress. I figured maybe if I wasn't helping myself out every day it would be easier for him to make it happen."

"But you haven't had sex in a week."

"No."

"Didn't you stay at his place on Monday?"

"I don't stay at his place on Mondays because he has squash on Tuesday morning and if I stay he won't get enough sleep."

Ruby sets down her fork and regards me for a few long seconds before she releases a long, slow breath. "Please don't be offended, but are you sure you really want to marry this guy?"

I know she's just trying to be a good friend, but when she says things like that, wearing that expression, it makes me wonder if my cold feet are more than just normal wedding jitters. Armstrong is a good choice; he's stable, solid, intelligent, organized, and goal oriented. He's everything my other boyfriends haven't been. And he's never been arrested, so that's a serious check mark in the plus category. Also, my parents approve wholeheartedly of my choice, another huge check mark. "We're just going through a phase. I'm making it sound worse than it is. We've both been busy. Planning a wedding is stressful, especially with Gwendolyn involved."

"If you say so. It's never too late to back out and find a new penis to sit on for the rest of your life."

The server returns with a new platter of appetizers, ending the conversation. But now I can't help but worry: What if it doesn't get better? What if things don't go back to the way they were before the engagement? The CS is amazing. It gets the job done every time, but I don't want it to be my primary source of orgasms for the remainder of my sex-having years.

Five
Dinner with the Mills Family

Amie

I've been to the Millses' mansion for dinner before. It's far more relaxed than dinners with Armstrong's family. Those are all very formal affairs, where we all sit primly and talk about business and the state of the world and what charity organizations will give the best promotional opportunities.

Mimi greets us with hugs and air-kisses. She tells me I look beautiful, gushing over what she calls my "stunning figure." Armstrong pats my ass when he thinks no one is watching and Gwendolyn comments on the amount of time I spend taking yoga.

Ruby's already here with Bane. I know because she messaged me ten minutes ago, asking where I was. She's not in the living room, and neither is Bane. The two of them better not be off screwing each other. They do that frequently at these dinner events. Just slip off for twenty minutes thinking no one will notice, and Ruby always comes back looking like the cat who ate the canary. Or has been eaten by her cat. Which is probably likely. According to her reports, Bane enjoys frequent dining at the vagina buffet.

I look around for Bane's brothers, expecting the entire family to be here, as seems to be typical whenever dinner is arranged. Bancroft's oldest brother, Griffin, is across the room, close talking with his fiancée, Imogen. I don't see Lexington. Maybe he's not coming. Not that it matters. Actually, it's probably better if he isn't here since his presence seems to put Armstrong in a bad mood.

"Oh! Yay! You're finally here!" Ruby leaps across the room. Her cheeks are rosy. I imagine this means she's been imbibing. "Come with me to the kitchen! We're making the coolest drinks! Well, I'm not making anything, but you need to see this."

"Don't let her drink the red shots," Bane calls after us, "I don't want to have to carry her to the car tonight!"

Ruby blows him a kiss as we pass.

The kitchen isn't bustling with people prepping food, because that happens in the chef's quarters. The Millses are beyond rich. They own one of the most luxurious hotel chains in the world. There's an industrial kitchen beyond the "normal kitchen," which is bigger than my entire apartment, probably twice over.

Everything is stainless steel and state-of-the-art. And in the middle of the massive, gorgeous kitchen, standing behind the island, is Lexington.

He's wearing a black dress shirt and a plaid tie. It's a very strange combination, oddly lumberjackish, but in a hipster kind of way. And it's impossible not to look at. It's also very difficult not to notice the tattoo peeking out of his rolled-up sleeve. Armstrong would never get a tattoo, but I think it has more to do with his fear of needles than his actual dislike of body art.

Ruby lets go of my arm and shrieks, bouncing her way across the kitchen over to where Lexington is busy making drinks. And not just any kind of drinks; Halloween-inspired ones.

He watches her with amusement, his gaze shifting briefly to me. And then it moves over me. Slowly. The right side of his mouth turns up and we make eye contact. It's short-lived. Which is good, because the way he's looking at me feels rather inappropriate. I look down, checking to make sure my dress isn't showing anything it's not supposed to. Nope. Everything is as it should be.

She hugs his arm and grins broadly. "Look at all the cool drinks Lexy made!"

He looks down at her with an arched eyebrow. "Uh, no." At her confusion he gives his head a shake. "We're not adding a y to the end of my name so you can feel better about having one at the end of yours."

Ruby's smile turns evil. "Isn't that what Brittany calls you?"

"Please do not bring her up. Especially around Mimi. Maybe just not ever, actually."

"Isn't that who Bancroft brought to my engagement party?" I ask, just so I can feel like part of the conversation, I suppose.

That brings Lexington's attention back to me. "Yeah. Apparently, that doesn't mean she's undateable in this family."

"I hear she likes lollipops, a lot," Ruby snickers.

Lex makes a face. "Yeah. Well, I'd like to keep my lollipop as far away from her as humanly possible. Are you going to try one of these or are they just for people to look at?"

Ruby points to one layered with yellow at the bottom, orange in the middle, and white at the top. "What's this?"

"Exactly what it looks like, candy corn." He hands Ruby the glass and she sniffs it before she takes a small sip.

"Oooh! This is amazing. Amie, you need to try something!" Ruby elbows Lex in the arm. "Give her something yummy."

"I've got lots of yummy things. Which one would you like?" he asks.

It takes me a moment to realize he's not being inappropriate. Why is my brain turning everything into something dirty? I gave myself an orgasm before Armstrong picked me up. I gave myself three, actually.

In the time since I revealed to Ruby my lack of Armstrong-given orgasms, I considered that maybe I've been overthinking things, and the lack of orgasms has nothing to do with Armstrong and everything to do with me. So I took the pressure off of both of us. Except my mind is still clearly hanging out in the gutter, and enjoying being there.

"How about a Vampire Kiss?" Lexington pushes a martini glass toward me.

"Um, sure?" The concoction is rimmed with something pink and a set of fake black vampire teeth is poised on the side. It's really rather creative. I take a small sip. It's also rather delicious.

"Amalie." Armstrong's arm wraps around my waist. "I've been looking all over for you. My mother wants to go over details with you and Ruby about the charity event. Something about picking a theme for costumes." He runs his nose up the side of my neck. "Lexington. I didn't expect you'd be here tonight."

"It's my family. Why wouldn't I be here?"

"I just thought you'd be away on business. Or out doing whatever it is you usually do. Sampling leftovers, that kind of thing." Armstrong plucks the glass from my hand and sniffs it. "What is this?"

"It's a Vampire Kiss. Lex made it."

"Shouldn't the bartender be doing that?" Armstrong takes a sip, then dumps the rest down the drain.

"I liked that!"

"It has too much sugar in it. Come, Amalie, we'll get you a glass of champagne." He keeps a firm grip on my waist and steers me in the direction of the sitting room.

I look over my shoulder, shooting an apologetic look at Lex, who's scratching his forehead with his middle finger. I really hope that's not directed at me. I mouth *help me* to Ruby before we round the corner and I'm forced to contend with Armstrong's horrible mother alone. Ruby better do her job and save me, since this entire thing was her idea in the first place.

Six

Boyfriend Auction

Ruby

"Why is he always such a dick?" I mutter.

"That's a rhetorical question, right?" Lex downs a shot and then a second one. "You've met my aunt. I'm sure the answer to that is quite clear."

"But Fredrick is a nice guy. Or at least he seems nice."

"Appearances can be rather deceiving, though, can't they?"

I don't have a chance to ask what that means because Bancroft pokes his head in the door. "I think you should come out here and help save your friend from being tortured."

I sigh, but take my candy corn cocktail with me to the sitting room where Amie is trapped between Bancroft's mother and Armstrong's mother.

"Ruby!" Mimi beckons me over. "We're debating the theme of the soirée. Help us decide!"

Bancroft gives my butt an affectionate squeeze. "I bet you're regretting this awesome idea right about now, aren't you?"

I bite my tongue and say nothing. My original plan was to host a small party in his condo. Our condo. Not a five-hundred-person event. I can handle the extravagance. My regrets stem from Gwendolyn's involvement and how much it's stressing Amie out. My idea for a zombie apocalypse theme gets shot down quickly. Apparently not everyone wants to dress up like the undead for Halloween. Go figure.

"What about a prince and princess theme?" Gwendolyn suggests.

"Oh! That's a great idea!" Amie claps her hands excitedly.

I try to hold back my snort of disbelief. One that indicates I do not agree with her enthusiastic response to this horrible idea. I don't for a second believe that Amie wants to dress up like a princess for Halloween. Why don't I buy her reaction? Because during our first year of college we managed to score fake IDs proclaiming we were of legal age to drink.

There was a Halloween party at a bar downtown and Amie, also having Daddy's credit card in her back pocket, decided we needed to dress up. And dress up we did. She went as a dominatrix, which really means she just went out and bought very expensive, very leathery lingerie. And a whip. I went as a zombie bride, before zombies were all the rage. Guess who got all the phone numbers that night. Not me.

Guess who also had to explain the thousand-dollar credit-card bill from a fetish store. Again, not me.

The following year she went as an angel. In lingerie. The year after that she went as a wood nymph. In lingerie. There's clearly a trend here. So while Amie pretends to be excited about dressing up in layers of tulle and satin, she's really thinking about what kind of garters she can pair with her newest corset. I have to wonder if Armstrong has ever experienced Amie in her garter glory and whether he's capable of appreciating it.

I try to wear lingerie with Bane, but he gets overzealous and often destroys it in the process of its removal. The other night when I was dressed as an evil fairy is a case in point. That costume is now in need of a few repairs. But God that sex was hot. I would like to have more of that. Preferably soon.

I tune back in to the conversation in time to hear Mimi suggest princesses throughout history. I have no desire to drown in a dress. I raise my hand, as if we're in school, then realize I don't need to be addressed before I speak. "That might be a little narrow. What if we made it famous couples throughout history."

Gwendolyn makes a face. "That's actually a very good idea." She sounds rather surprised that I could have one of those.

"That way we're not confined to royalty. We can choose any famous couple." Like Bonnie and Clyde. The more notorious the better. "They could even be fictional."

"Like Romeo and Juliet!" Mimi proclaims.

"Exactly." I think Romeo is a wishy-washy douche and Juliet ends up dying for nothing, but I love that Mimi is referencing Shakespeare when we're planning a Halloween party.

"This is just going to be so much fun!" Mimi gives me a side hug. "I'm so glad Amalie introduced you to my son.

If you have any other girlfriends with enough spunk to tame Lexington, I would love to meet them."

I laugh. Amie smiles as she watches us, but I can see the strain in her eyes. It makes me sad that her soon-to-be mother-in-law is such a cold fish.

Mimi's excitement is contagious, despite Gwendolyn's nearly constant poo-poo attitude toward almost every aspect of the soirée. It appears they've decided to inject themselves fully into planning the event. Which, in reality, isn't terrible. Both Amie and I have full-time jobs, and party planning has been theirs for years. Eventually we move to the dining room when we're called in for dinner, but the conversation continues to revolve around the Halloween party. It becomes more and more grand as the discussion continues.

I have no idea how they expect to pull this off in only three weeks, but it seems like it's spiraling out of control in terms of size and grandeur. I wonder if this is what planning the wedding has been like for Amie. If so, I can definitely understand why she's not more excited. And her excessive need for yoga. And her lack of orgasms. It makes me sad.

Lex, who's seated on the opposite side of the table, has been relatively quiet. Other than our bartending extravaganza in the kitchen, he made himself scarce until we sat for dinner. Although I've been busy with the soirée planning, so maybe he's been around the entire time and I just didn't notice.

Since we've sat down, Lex and Armstrong seem to be having a stare-down contest. Armstrong's arm has been slung across the back of Amie's chair possessively, like he feels the need to protect her. From what, I have no idea.

Meanwhile, Bancroft has been trying to get his hand up my skirt. It's distracting, but enjoyable.

Mimi is three glasses of wine in, and her voice grows louder with each sip. "I have another idea!" She waits until she has everyone's attention. "I think we should have a bachelor auction."

That gets a round of groans from her sons.

"What?" Mimi waves her hand around, giant diamonds flashing in the chandelier lighting. "It's a wonderful idea. We raised almost a quarter of a million dollars for charity last time."

"It was excellent publicity," Fredrick, Armstrong's father, agrees.

"Who's going to be up for auction? There's no one eligible at this table," Bancroft squeezes my thigh, his pinkie sliding under the hem of my dress for the five millionth time. My vagina is going to explode before we get home.

"Except for Lexington," Armstrong adds with a smirk. "How much did your date pay at the last one? Was it twenty or thirty thousand?"

Lex taps on the table. "It was fifty. What was it you got? Fifteen?"

That wipes the smirk off Armstrong's face and puts one on mine.

"It was twenty-five," he says irritably. "Who did you take out again? Wasn't it the Firestone girl? I hope she got her money's worth."

Lex's grin spreads slow across his face. "I believe she did. I think she called me, hmm, what was it again?" He taps his lip. "Very charitable. She said I was worth every last penny."

"Lexington!" Mimi chastises.

His expression morphs into wide-eyed innocence. "What? If a woman is going to donate fifty thousand dollars to charity on my behalf, I'm going to be an exceptionally attentive date."

"Especially if she's hot," Bane mutters, but not quietly enough. I elbow him in the side.

"Bancroft!" Mimi purses her lips and gives him a hard look.

I clasp my hands together and rest my chin on my knuckles. "If I wasn't already dating Bane I'd donate fifty thousand to charity for a date with you, Lex."

That dimpled grin makes another appearance. All the Mills boys have killer smiles. "Thanks, Ruby."

Bancroft's fingers tighten around my thigh. He leans in close and whispers in my ear. "Don't stroke his ego."

"It's too bad you can't be auctioned this year, Bane. You always fetch a pretty penny." Gwendolyn sighs and then turns a strangely disdainful grimace on Lex. "At least we have you. We'll just have to find a few more gentlemen to participate. What about that Williamson boy, he did well last year, didn't he—nothing like your boys, Mimi, but well enough."

What odd dinner conversation.

It's late by the time we leave and I've had several fun cocktails, compliments of Lex, so I'm feeling absolutely no pain. I'm also a wee bit unsteady on my feet. And horny. Dear God, I need to get laid. So bad.

I think my harmless little joke about a charity date with Lex is making Bancroft a little territorial. Although I'm not sure why. I live with Bancroft, it's not as if I'm going to jump brothers and beds. That's just . . . gross.

So now that I'm in the car with him, alone, I want to get my hands in his pants and I'd like his up my skirt.

I slide over so I'm right beside him and rub my boob on his bicep. "Put the divider up."

He stretches his arm across the back of the seat and

glances at me. His expression is remote, giving nothing away. In fact, he's completely flat. Huh.

He brushes my hair over my shoulder, fingertips skimming my throat. "Why do you want me to do that?"

"For privacy." Duh.

His voice deepens from the already-low baritone. "And why would we need privacy?"

I bite my lip and cross my legs, letting my skirt ride up. His gaze drops there and then shifts to the open partition. "Because I'd like to be inappropriate with you."

"Oh? Are you sure it's me you want to be inappropriate with?" His tone isn't playful, it's hard, annoyed.

I lean over him and hit the button, watching as our driver's gaze moves to the rearview mirror and then back to the road. He disappears behind the black glass. I narrow my eyes at Bane's tight jaw, then run my fingertip along it. He jerks away.

"Explain that reaction, please."

"You were flirting with Lex at dinner. In front of everyone."

"Pardon?"

"At dinner. You said you'd donate fifty thousand to charity to go out with him if you weren't with me."

I am sure my expression is incredulous. "Armstrong was being a dick. I was defending Lex."

Bancroft scoffs.

"What is that sound? What does that mean?"

Bancroft lifts his gaze from my cleavage. "He flirts with you."

"Lex? He doesn't flirt with me. He treats me like a sister or something. I wasn't being serious, and he was just being grateful since Armstrong is always a jerkoff," I reason.

"I don't like it."

Wow. I had no idea Bancroft could be so sensitive. Well, that's not entirely true. I just didn't realize it extended to Lex. "You know you're the only one I want."

He's still frowning. And now he's not looking at me.

"Bancroft?" I take his chin in my hand and make him look at me. "How can you not know that?"

"I just don't like how much he enjoys the attention. He gets enough from everyone else. He doesn't need it from you, too."

"So you're jealous?"

"I'm not jealous."

"You sound jealous."

"You're mine. Everyone knows you're mine. Lex knows you're mine, and he still flirts with you, and you played right into it tonight."

I raise an eyebrow. "How very un-twenty-first-century of you. What is this really about?"

He sighs and his head drops back on the seat. "You spent a lot of time with Lex tonight in the kitchen making all those drinks and then you were with Amie talking about this party thing, and you've been with Amie all week."

I shift around and straddle his lap. Now it makes sense. And I can actually see a pattern. Whenever we spend a lot of time with his family or with friends he becomes extra needy. As if sharing me with other people somehow makes me less his. And I suppose in a way that's accurate, because he can't have me all to himself like he normally does. "Aww, baby, are you feeling neglected?"

His brows knit together, but his hands go to my thighs and slide under the hem of my dress. "Maybe."

I drop a kiss on his lips. "Am I yours?"

His eyes are dark, heavy. "Yes."

"So maybe you should take me."

"Maybe I should." He unzips my jacket and pushes it over my shoulders. His fingers trail over my collarbone and along my throat. He walks his fingers up my chin and slips one into my mouth.

I suck and bite, easing forward so I can grind up on him.

That dark look on his face becomes downright lecherous. "You think I should fuck you right here? In this car?"

There's my dirty boy. I nod once.

"You sure you can be quiet? That's not soundproof glass." He tips his chin toward the divider.

"I can be quiet."

I suck in a breath of anticipation when he slips his hand back under my dress, searching for the edge of my underwear. Which he doesn't find. His lip curls. "Where'd your panties go?"

"They were damp after dinner, so I took them off."

"Naughty girl." He drags a knuckle along my slit. "You're ready for my cock right now, aren't you?"

I make a strangled sound as he lifts my skirt so he can watch two fingers disappear inside me. He drops the fabric and slaps my ass. "Shh. Remember how you said you could be quiet. You don't want to embarrass our driver, do you?"

"No." There's music playing up front, and it's unlikely that he will hear, but I don't want to make it awkward for him. He's a nice guy.

"That's right. You don't want him to know what's going on back here, do you?"

I give him another headshake and bite my lip when he curls his fingers to prevent any unwanted sounds from escaping.

"You know what you should do right now?" He circles my clit with his thumb.

It's incredibly difficult not to moan loudly. I manage one stuttered word. "N-no."

"You should get my dick out so you can ride it like you are my fingers."

I crush my mouth to his in a bid to quiet the desperate noise I'm about to make. I fumble with his belt buckle, yanking it free of the clasp. Bancroft is zero help since he has his hand between my legs and the rhythmic twist and curl of his fingers is incredibly, blissfully distracting.

Freeing his shirt, I struggle to undo the button. The zipper gets caught in the fabric, sticking while I tug roughly. At his low chuckle I nip at his lip. That gets me another slap on the ass.

I gasp. Bracing a hand on his chest, I push back enough so I can glare at him. It's not super effective since my eyes roll up a little at the angle change. "Stop that."

"Stop what? This?" He makes an attempt to withdraw his hand from between my legs, but I grab for his wrist. In all honesty, I'm not remotely strong enough to prevent him from stopping, but he grins up at me and curls his fingers again.

"Oh. You mean this?" He smacks my ass again.

I have to fight another moan.

He kneads one cheek with the hand that isn't between my legs. "Don't pretend you don't love it. I can *feel* how much you want me to do that again."

I try not to clench. I really do. But I brace for the hot sting and the warm flood of pleasure that follows and all my muscles contract. Bane knows exactly how to push my buttons. And one of my buttons is a sweet spanking.

"You better be on my cock when you come, babe." It sounds a bit like a threat.

I let go of his wrist and whine when his fingers

disappear. It forces me to refocus, though. I shove my hand down the front of his boxers and grip his erection. Bancroft has a magnificent cock. It's just as huge and gorgeous as the rest of him. The constant flash of lights as we pass under the street lamps and through busy New York traffic gives me a sporadic but sufficient view.

Bancroft grabs my hips and pulls me forward. I line us up and drop down. "Fuck yes," he groans.

I want to ridicule him for being loud and potentially embarrassing the driver, but he cups my ass and rocks me forward. I only need a few well-timed thrusts and I'm coming. I thread my hand through his hair, gripping it tight. My mouth drops open and I rasp his name, a soft, pitchy sound catching in my throat.

One corner of Bancroft's mouth turns up in a wicked sneer. "That's it babe, that's what I want, you squeezing my cock, looking at me like I'm your fucking God."

Have I mentioned that Bancroft is a cocky dirty talker when we're having sex? Especially the public kind. Car sex isn't super frequent, but we do have sex at his parents' house pretty much every single time we're there. Most of the time it's quick and dirty; the appetizer before the main course when we get home.

When I'm done coming, Bane reaches behind me and unzips my dress, pulling it roughly over my head. He ruins my bra when he can't get it off fast enough. Not that I care. I have lots at home.

Bane runs his hands down my sides, exhaling a hard breath. Grabbing my left breast with one hand and my right butt cheek with the other, he slides down the seat and uses the anchor points to lift and lower me while he pumps his hips and I start grinding.

"Look at you. You're goddamn glorious."

My reflection wavers in the tinted glass. I'm grateful

no one can see in, considering I'm completely naked and Bancroft is fully dressed. I don't know why it makes the sex hotter. As does the fact that we're sitting at a red light at an intersection and I'm bouncing away on his lap, heading for orgasm number two.

"Please tell me you're going to fuck me again when we get home," I groan.

He releases a breast and wraps his arm around my waist, pulling me close until my chest presses against his. "You bet your sweet ass I am. This is just a warm-up."

"I guess it's good you're working from home tomorrow, huh?" I ask breathlessly.

"Damn right."

Note to self: insecure Bane is insatiable.

Seven
Costumes Are Crazy

Amie

"We need to pick costumes for the Halloween soirée." We only have two and a half weeks left. That's not a lot of time. I might need a dress customized. Ruby has the skill set required to do it, but I'll need time to find the appropriate pieces to put together and she'll require time to work her magic.

Armstrong looks up from his newspaper. "Why can't it just be a masquerade? Why can't I just wear a tux and put on a mask and you get a new ball gown that matches my tie and we're done."

"Because it's not a masquerade party. It's a Halloween soirée and we need to come up with coordinating costumes because that's the theme. Your mother's the one who picked it," I point out. Although Mimi had a hand in making the decision, thankfully. Otherwise it would've ended up being extraordinarily boring.

Armstrong sets his paper down, possibly aware that I'm not going to let up until we make an actual decision. "Remind me what the theme is again."

"Famous couples."

"Why don't we go as royalty. That's simple. Then I can wear a tux and you can wear a ball gown and everyone wins because you're dressed in a costume." He smiles as if he's come up with the best idea in the world and picks his paper up again.

I round the table. Armstrong is in his typical bed wear: a white cotton T-shirt and a pair of cotton pajama pants. The shirt fits a little loosely instead of hugging his chest and arms. Although he has a lean build, so that's part of the reason.

His dark blond hair is a little longer, curling at the base of his neck and hanging across his forehead. I run my fingers through it, pushing it back.

The unexpected affection catches him off guard and he sets his paper down again, looking up at me. I take the opportunity for what it is and sit in his lap. Neither of us has to be at the office early. There's plenty of time for morning activities of the pleasurable variety. Draping an arm over his shoulder, I ask, "What royal couple would you like to go as?"

He settles a hand on my hip. "What about Kate and William?"

I finger the curls at the back of his neck. "Kate has dark hair and William is losing his."

"Hmm." His gaze dips down to the gape in my robe. I'm wearing a pale satin sheath. My nipples are very prominent. "What about Prince Charming and

Cinderella? That should be easy. Or Sleeping Beauty and Phillip."

It would be a little odd that Armstrong is so familiar with the names of the Disney princes and princesses if his aunts and uncles didn't have children who were significantly younger than he is.

"Or we could just go as Ken and Barbie." I mean it as a joke, obviously.

"Your breasts aren't large enough for you to pull off Barbie."

I'm about to push out of his lap, but he tightens his grip on my waist. "I didn't mean that in a negative way. Yours fit nicely in my hands." As if to prove his point he cups them. "If at any time you become unhappy with their size, we can always visit a cosmetic surgeon and have them augmented."

"You want me to get a boob job?" Never has he ever mentioned being unsatisfied with the size of my breasts.

"No. No. Not now. They're quite perky. I just mean down the line, if things should change and it's something you want." He pulls at the tie on my robe, pushing it over my shoulders. He traces the satin strap and brushes over my nipple through the thin fabric. "Yes. More than adequate, really." From Armstrong, that's a compliment.

I suck in a quick breath. Armstrong isn't really a morning sex kind of guy. It messes with his routine, which he's very particular about. But we have all this time. What's fifteen minutes? A quickie. Something to take the edge off. And maybe this time I'll come.

I push the strap over my shoulder, exposing the nipple. It tightens at the kiss of cool air. "Maybe we should get naked."

"Right now?"

I lift a shoulder and let it fall. "We have the time."

He nods slowly, absorbing this potential deviation from his morning ritual. "We do."

I go in for a kiss and he turns his head. "I have coffee breath."

"I like coffee." I kiss my way over his chin.

"We should shower first."

"Why bother when you're about to get me all dirty, anyway?"

"You know how I feel about . . . freshness."

If there's a way to kill a mood, it's referencing freshness. I used to find the pre-sex-shower ritual adorable. He'd be all wet and smelling fantastic. I'd join him in bed when I was done cleaning up. There would be a very sexy inspection. At least it used to be.

I heave a sigh, pull my strap back in place, and grab my robe from the floor.

"Are you going to shower?"

How can a man be so damn oblivious? "No, Armstrong, I'm not going to shower."

"I thought we were going to have sex."

"Apparently I'm not fresh enough."

"What about a blowjob?"

I whirl around. "Seriously?"

"I'm hard now." He gestures to his lap.

"I guess you'll have to figure out what to do with that then, because I'm going to be busy solving my own damn problems." I stalk down the hall to his bedroom and root through my overnight bag. It doesn't take me long to find what I'm looking for. My travel vibrator. This sweet baby has gotten me through a few unsatisfying nights in the past few months. Now it's going to take care of my morning problem, too, alone, in the bathroom.

I grab my earbuds and my phone and rush across the hall, through the spare bedroom, and into the private bathroom.

Locking the door, I turn on the fan and strip out of my sheath. The mirror reflects my pink cheeks and my heaving chest. My boobs are nice. They're not huge, but they're certainly not small. They're a very reasonable, ample C cup.

I slap my fake penis on the vanity along with my phone and earbuds and grab the edge of the counter, trying to calm down. I'm really worked up, and not just in a clit-throbbing kind of way. The ability to come may very well be a challenge based on my level of irritation. But I'm going to try. Forget the shower-before-sex rule. Is it too much to ask for a little spontaneity?

I turn on the shower, not because I'm planning to get fresh for Armstrong, but to drown out the sound of my vibrator and hopefully the sound of my orgasm. I slip my fingers between my legs. I'm barely even wet. Which makes sense, because I'm more angry than I am turned on. My clit is almost as angry as the rest of me.

Snatching my plastic dick from the vanity, I decide the showerhead is going to be my friend. Sliding the glass door open, I'm mindful not to be too rough, since shattering it won't help my situation, even if the destruction will make me feel good.

I am rough with the removable showerhead, though. Making sure the water isn't too hot, I lift it from its resting place and lower it between my thighs, adjusting the stream so it pulses against my clit. The warm, direct pressure makes my eyes roll up. It's almost like being licked, but better, more consistent.

Leaning against the tile I let the rhythmic pressure do its job. If I had my clit sucker this would be over in two minutes. My agitation is going to make this take longer, but that's fine, I have time. Plenty of it.

Reaching for my vibrator—waterproof of course—I turn it on and slide the thick, warm plastic inside me. I don't imagine that it's Armstrong fucking me, because I'm too pissed off at him for that to help me get where I need to go, which is the land of Orgasmia.

The vibrations inside, combined with the warm pulse against my clit, cause my knees to buckle. "Fuck. Yes." It echoes in the enclosed space, louder than I mean it to. But, God, it feels good. So good.

A knock at the bathroom door dulls the tingle spreading from the center of my body outward. "Amalie?"

I close my eyes tight and press the showerhead harder against my clit. Lowering myself to the floor of the tub I rock on the vibrator. And I moan.

"Darling? Are you crying?" Armstrong's voice rises at the end with panic. "I'm sorry—" The doorknob rattles. "Why is this locked?"

I bite my bottom lip, picturing the confused expression on his face. His hard-on tenting his pajama pants. It makes me smile and brings me closer to the orgasm I'm chasing down. I groan as sensation builds in waves, water pulsing over my clit, streaming down my legs, and the buzz of the vibrator makes a heavy, tinny sound against the tub.

"What is that? Is that the pipes? Darling, are you okay?" The door continues to rattle.

I'm so close. So, so close. And knowing he's on the other side of the door, unable to get to me, confused and unsatisfied, helps push me to the edge and hold me there. I move the showerhead a few millimeters to the right. "That's it. Fuck me."

I'm so engrossed in the pleasure that I fail to notice the

silence on the other side of the door. The orgasm hits me, clit throbbing, muscles contracting hard, waves of satisfaction sweeping through me, draining out my anger, replacing it with bliss. I chant the words *fuck* and *oh god* and *yes* over and over again.

A loud click is followed by an even louder bang as the door slams open. Armstrong stands at the threshold, one hand on the jamb, his expression morphing from panic to confusion to disbelief. "What're you doing?"

The reflection in the mirror across the room draws my gaze away from his. His toned back flexes as his arm lifts, fingers running hard through his hair. Armstrong is a very attractive man. His features are regal, his body is toned, though not heavily muscled. He's taken his shirt off, so I watch the sinew pull and tighten with his movements.

I look beyond him, to my own cloudy reflection. My expression is exactly the opposite of his, heavy lids and parted lips, satiety clear on my face. On my knees, legs spread with the showerhead still pressed firm against my pulsing clit. I drop it and turn off the faucet.

Rising up on my knees, I ease the vibrator out; the whirring grows louder, and then echoes through the room as I lose my grip and it drops into the tub, bumping its way across to the drain.

"Are you *masturbating*?" His incredulity is only offset by the lump in his pajama pants.

"Not anymore." I grab the bar and pull myself up. The bottom of the tub isn't very nice to my knees, which are a little on the wobbly side. But at least that took the edge off. I'm slightly less angry now.

"You were masturbating." He blinks several times. It's very strobe-like.

I don't know why he's so surprised. "Don't you masturbate?"

His brow pulls down, causing a crease to form between them. I wonder if he knows that happens and whether it will make him want the Botox injections his mother is so fond of.

He lowers his hand to his crotch and strokes his erection through the fabric. "Well, of course, on the days I don't see you, I take care of myself, when it's necessary."

I don't know what that means. He's in his twenties—late twenties, but still. I would think every day would necessitate a lone-love session to keep constant hard-ons from happening. But then I do have a higher drive than he does. Maybe he doesn't need to come every day like I do. I suppose I'll find out eventually if this is the case, once we're married and living in the same space. And then maybe he too will want to have sex every day.

"But you—" He flails a hand in my direction. "I'm right here and you locked the door."

I prop a fist on my hip, intent on making my annoyance clear. I don't think I'm very convincing what with my being naked and wet from the waist down. "You turned me down. I wasn't fresh enough, remember?"

"But you've showered now." His expression grows serious. "I want you to come for me like that. Like you just did."

"Guess you better get to work then." I hold my arms out, inviting him to take on the challenge.

His face registers shock first. Then determination. Here's an interesting thing about my fiancé. He cannot resist a challenge. I don't know what it is that drives him, but when he's taken to task over something, he likes to be the best at it. Which is part of the reason I initially faked a few orgasms. I think I suffered from orgasm performance anxiety, which drove his.

Also, sometimes the friction gets to be too much when the licking or rubbing becomes excessive. But I'm already primed. I've come once. The second time is always faster and easier. I might as well get something out of his current remorseful state.

He grabs me by the wrist and tugs me out of the bathroom, his strides purposeful as he brings me over to the bed. He quickly shoves all the pillows to the floor and turns down the sheets. The mattress sinks as I climb up and stretch out. Pajama pants drop to the floor. His erection bobs as he follows after me.

I keep my legs together. As intrigued as Armstrong might be by what he witnessed, he prefers demure to brazen. Warm, gentle fingers trail up my shins. When he reaches my knees he carefully pries them apart. I provide just a hint of resistance and he glances up. His tongue peeks out to wet his lip.

Armstrong is a gentle, considerate lover. Which is nice. It's lovely to be worshipped. But sometimes I'd like to be ravaged. Fucked. Sometimes I'd like to be pounded into the mattress, sweaty and sticky with afterglow.

Sex with Armstrong is sweet and tender. There's no profanity, no dirty talking, no ass slapping or hair pulling. When I whisper a quiet, accidental *fuck* his eyes lift with their telling disapproval. I censor my pleasure. I try to come. I really do. I get close, but it's taking too long and I'm too preoccupied with watching my language.

So I fake it. I try to mimic what happened in the shower, but the censored, PG version. I need to figure out how to make this better for both of us. This is what I want. Armstrong is what I want. We'll have a beautiful life together. He just needs to relax a little. It's just going to take time; either that, or I'll have to bury Anarchy Amie forever. And maybe I should, because all she ever gets into is trouble.

"Hold this for me." The words are garbled as Ruby hands me a pincushion. She has three pins poised between her lips. It makes me nervous. I imagine her inhaling them and accidentally swallowing one.

She plucks one from between her lips and threads it carefully through the fabric, then does the same on the other side. "Can you do me a big favor and not lose any weight between now and the Halloween party?"

She's well aware that this is not a promise I can make. We have two weeks to go, that's fourteen days of hot yoga. As the party gets closer and my soon-to-be mother-in-law's involvement in this event escalates, I become increasingly aware of how much more involved she's likely to become with the wedding as the date approaches. It's causing me stress. She's already overly involved. You'd think it was her getting married, not me. So I've been doubling up on hot yoga sessions and cardio. I've accidentally lost four pounds in the last week and a half. I've been adding protein to my morning smoothie to make up for it, but to no avail.

Ruby pats my butt. "You're going to look gorgeous."

I smile. "The dress is going to look gorgeous." The dress is stunning. How she's managed to make an old costume from the basement of a now-closed theater into something so incredible is beyond me. Ruby has a hidden talent. She can sew. I think if she hadn't been on the stage she might've been behind it, designing costumes. Her personality is too big to be confined, though.

My dress is huge, blue, and puffy. It's going to be

incredibly uncomfortable. But I'm used to uncomfortable clothes. I can deal with it for an evening. I would've preferred to go as a more interesting couple, like Harley Quinn and the Joker, but Armstrong would never agree to color his hair green, even temporarily, so I'm stuck being Cinderella.

"Have you decided what you want to be?"

"I think I've narrowed it down. Wonder Woman is a strong contender, but I need to try on the costume and see what you think. It might be a little too . . . revealing."

"Well now I really need to see it."

"When I'm finished with you."

"You can take a break from stabbing me to death with pins." I nudge her in the direction of the bed, where all the costumes are laid out.

Ruby doesn't seek privacy. We've seen each other naked probably more times than Armstrong and I have at this point. Which is a little disconcerting, but then Ruby and I have been friends for more than a decade and Armstrong and I have been together for less than a year.

She strips down to her underwear, which happens to be a lacy little thong in hot pink zebra print with little black bows at the hips. I miss wearing fun underwear. Armstrong thinks anything that isn't pale lace or satin is trashy. I turn back to my reflection and my high-coverage dress. I can't move much or I'll end up with more holes in my skin.

"Okay. Check it out." She jumps in front of me.

"Okay. Wow." Ruby has an unbelievable dancer's body. It's almost infuriating how toned and muscular and just fit she is, especially with all the junk she's constantly shoving in her mouth.

"Is that a good *wow,* or a bad *wow*?"

"Well, I suppose it depends. Your ass looks damn well fantastic, but I'm not sure Gwendolyn will survive seeing you in that. I'm also concerned that Bancroft will have zero blood flow anywhere in his body apart from his penis."

"It rides a little high in the back, doesn't it?" She checks out her own rear end in the mirror, wiggling it around a little.

"Just a wee bit." Half of her butt is on display. While it definitely would've been something she'd wear to a party back when we were in college, there will be far too many influential people for either of us to attempt something quite so risqué.

She frowns. "I guess this is more like a bathing suit than a costume."

"Or lingerie." I'm sort of being sarcastic. Sort of not. I remember the way Bancroft reacted when she was in the fairy outfit. He couldn't keep his hands off her the entire night.

"Oh my God! That's a fantastic idea. Bancroft will go crazy." She repositions me, still wearing the costume, and resumes the pinning. "I could do the same with the Harley Quinn costume if you want."

"Don't bother, it's not really Armstrong's thing." I purse my lips at my accidental sourness.

"Don't be silly. All men like lingerie. Even the Armstrongs of this world."

"What does that mean?" I try to look at her over my shoulder and a pin digs into my side. "Ow!"

"Stop moving and I won't stab you."

I suck my teeth but turn around and remain still so I don't bleed out before she even manages to alter the dress. "You didn't answer the question."

"What question?" she says distractedly.

"About the Armstrongs of this world."

"He's just a little uptight, right? Not much of an out-of-the-box guy from what I've seen. Traditional."

"Oh. Yeah. I guess." That was a nice way to put it. Those things are what drew me to him initially. He was just so different from the guys I normally dated.

"It's funny, isn't it? All these years you've spent dating the bad boy and here you end up with the quintessential Prince Charming."

There's something in the way she says this, as if there's more under the words, but then she twists my hair into a half-assed knot and gives me one of her genuine, mischief-filled smiles. "You really are going to be the most beautiful bride, you know that, right? You could probably wear a paper bag and you'd still be the most stunning woman in the room. And look at your rack." She squeezes my boob through the millions of layers of fabric and the built-in bra.

I bat her hand away and wince at the prick of a pin against my ribs. "Are you flirting with me?"

"Don't tell Bane. He's still not over the whole fairy-makeup you-between-my-legs scene he walked in on."

"They all have such dirty minds, don't they?"

"If we're lucky." I get another sly grin.

I sincerely hope I can bring out the dirty in Armstrong eventually. "So . . ." I shift gears again. "Since Wonder Woman is going in your private lingerie collection, what other options do you have over there?"

"I haven't sorted through it all yet, but I'm sure there will be something."

There's a princess outfit, Snow White to be exact. I spot a black mask on the bed. It reminds me of Batman. "Oh! I have an awesome idea!" I gesture toward the pile.

She glances over, and then gives me the eye. "I'm not going as Snow White. No one should be that clueless.

And she should've ended up with the Huntsman, not that d-bag prince."

"I wasn't going to suggest that. What if Bane goes as a character from Batman? What if he goes as Bane?"

"You mean the guy who wears that metal spider thing on his face?"

"It's not a metal spider."

She props a hand on her hip. "How will he even breathe? Or eat. Or talk. Or make out with me?"

"Okay. Good point." I tap my lip. "He could be Batman, though, couldn't he?"

"Who will I be? I don't want to wear some boring evening gown." She grimaces, realizing what I'm wearing. "Sorry. This isn't boring, though. It's going to be amazing once I'm done with it. Halloween is my favorite holiday. I just want to go as something fun."

"You could be Catwoman?"

Her eyes light up. "Oooh! That would totally work. And it wouldn't be hard to make it happen at all. I'm sure I have all the pieces here. I just have to put them together."

She finally finishes pinning me. "Let's get this off and then we can try on some of the other fun costumes."

As soon as I'm out of the dress—and no longer at risk of being pricked to death, which Ruby finds hysterical—she tosses a costume at me to try on. I've just finished squeezing myself into what I think is supposed to be some kind of sexy witch costume when Bancroft's voice booms down the hall, calling for my best friend.

He must've finished work early. I didn't expect to be here when he got home.

"In here!" She bites her lip, looking down at her costume and the mess on the bed.

"I have a ferret that needs to be played with!" Bane comes barging through the door.

I expect him to be holding Francesca, their pet ferret, who has been penned up in her cage because it's not safe for her with all the pins and stuff. But apparently Bane isn't referring to his pet. It's the one in his pants he'd like Ruby to play with. And I'm looking at it right now.

"Holy mother!" I bring my hand up to cover my eyes because I'm unable to look away. I think I might be having a hot flash. All I managed to get a glimpse of was the head, because Bancroft's enormous fist is covering the entire shaft. But that alone tells me an incredible amount about the size of that thing.

I feel bad that I immediately compare Armstrong's penis to what I've seen of Bancroft's.

Eight
Costume Design Flaws

Ruby

"Bane, put that away! You're scaring Amie!" I'm actually not sure if he's scaring her at all. She has her hand up in front of her face, but she's clearly peeking through her fingers.

I've shared the size of Bane's cock with her. I've mentioned my new religion: the Church of Bane Cock. I've written sonnets about how beautiful it is. Not really, but I've made up a couple of limericks. In my head. That I've shared with no one but the bathroom mirror.

Amie has also mentioned the averageness of her fiancé's penis. I wonder if it's possible that she's even exaggerated the averageness for the sake of his ego. And if so, I'm so very, very sad for her. Bane's cock is the kind of thing that inspires shrines. And lockjaw. Although at this point I'm fairly good at the unlocking part.

Bancroft's irritation is fused with disappointment and lust. "For fuck's sake." He turns around and tucks himself away, much to my dismay.

While he's doing this, Amie frantically searches through the costumes for her clothes, rambling about how she should be going. She practically slams into the wall trying to give Bane a wide berth as she exits the room.

"I'll just see myself out." She fumbles for the door handle and pulls it closed behind her.

Bane, red-faced, motions to the bedroom. "Why didn't you tell me Amie was still going to be here? What the hell is going on?"

"We lost track of time, I guess. We were trying on costumes." I think it's pretty clear what we've been up to.

Bane runs a hand through his hair, which messes it up. He has curls. Gorgeous, thick curls. The kind I fuck up when I grab his hair.

"We need to talk about this shit."

"I'll clean up the mess."

"Not the mess, Ruby." His gaze rakes over me.

It's then I realize I'm still wearing the Wonder Woman costume.

The knock at our bedroom door startles us both. "Okay. I'm leaving. Talk to you later, Ruby. Sorry about surprising you, Bane!"

We stare each other down as we listen to the patter of her heels grow fainter, followed by the beep when the door closes, signaling her departure. "If it's not the mess then what's the problem?" I climb onto the bed and sweep the costumes into a pile.

Bane is a very neat and tidy man. He dislikes disorder. I imagine this pile of costumes is stressing him out. "I'm going to ask you a question and I need you to answer it honestly."

I sit back on my heels. "Ookaaay." Man, he looks very serious.

"How many hours did you just spend in here getting naked with Amie?"

"What?"

"You said you were trying on costumes. I assume that means you were both without clothes on multiple occasions."

"What exactly are you asking?"

There's silence. His and mine. His chest rises and falls. It's distracting. So is the very obvious lump jacking up the front of his pants. "Should I be concerned?"

I gesture to his crotch. "Your dick doesn't look very concerned."

He glances down.

"In fact, your dick looks very excited. So maybe the question is, should *I* be concerned?"

He frowns, as if he's uncertain as to what I'm asking.

"Our potential mutual nakedness seems to be something you're rather fascinated by," I prompt.

His lips purse. Eyes narrow. Fingers flex. He stalks over to the bed, lifts me easily from the mattress and sets me on my feet. Then he circles me. Predatory. "What is this outfit?"

"I'm Wonder Woman." This is not an answer to my question.

He comes to a stop in front of me. Then he winds an arm around my waist, pulling me against him. His nose brushes along my jaw line and then sweeps down my throat. "The last two times I've come home when you and Amie have been hanging out you've been mostly naked in provocative situations."

"Do you think she's sexy?" It comes out sounding insecure instead of confrontational.

Bane picks up on that. He's smart. "Do I think Amie's sexy?"

At my lack of response he pulls me in closer. "Do you know where my attention went when I walked into this bedroom?"

I shake my head, not trusting my voice.

"You. In this fucking outfit. On our bed. That's what I saw. And do you know what I was worried about?"

I give my head another small shake as his hand slides down my back.

"I worried about all the Anarchy Amie stories you've told me."

"I don't get what that has to do with us playing dress-up."

"I guess my head went to all the worst possible places. You two are close. You're always together. Lately you've been together and naked. Or semi-naked."

Well this conversation is going very differently than it did in my head. Sometimes my worst-case-scenario radar messes with reality. Or is as far from reality as I can get. "Amie and I have been friends for ten years. We've been seeing each other naked since before either of us had boobs."

"Do you understand that it drives me insane that she sees you naked at all?"

"It's just Amie."

"But it's not just Amie, is it?"

"What?" Now I'm confused.

"Every night before you get up onstage you're in a dressing room with all these other people, in various stages of undress. And then you get up there and kiss another man, five nights a week."

"I'm acting and Michael is gay. And he has a boyfriend. He's about as interested in getting it on with me as

Amie is. Also, if he wasn't in a relationship, he'd be picturing you while he's kissing me. He probably still does, actually."

"I highly doubt I'm his type."

"You're exactly his type. His boyfriend looks a little bit like you." The only resemblance is that they're both tall, built men, but that's not really the point. Bancroft is typically a very confident man, but recently I've noticed these brief moments of insecurity. They're fleeting, but they exist. As if he needs reminding that I love only him. That the attention I get from everyone else when I'm on the stage is only related to my ability to depict a character, and that beyond that, his is the only attention I want.

"That's . . . interesting."

"He's not the only man to lust after you, I'm sure."

"The only person I'm concerned about lusting after me is you." His hand glides down to cup my ass. He's grabbing a solid handful of cheek since half of it is hanging out of the bottom of these tiny shorts.

"I thought that was a given."

He pulls me against him and drops his mouth to my ear. "Do you know what I'd like to do now?"

"Fuck Wonder Woman?"

"Exactly."

"You need to try this on so we can make sure it fits." I thrust the costume at Bancroft. He does not look impressed.

He takes it with a skeptical expression. "I thought I was going to be Bruce Wayne."

I may have been a little vague about my plan. "You are Bruce Wayne, as Batman."

His plush lips flatten into a thin line and his eyes

narrow. It's too late to come up with something different. We only have three hours before we have to be at the event and my makeup still needs to be done. Gwendolyn has called Amie four thousand times according to my messages. Murder is a real possibility. Amie will be here in twenty minutes to make my face pretty, and I'm hoping the murder isn't mine.

"I expected to wear a suit."

"It is a suit. It's a superhero suit."

His response is to glare at me. God he's hot when he's annoyed.

I throw him a pout. "I'm going as Catwoman. You have to wear your Batman costume or we won't match."

"I thought you were wearing that." He points to the evening gown hanging from the hook in the bathroom. It's my decoy dress. I copied it from the movie. I'm starting in an evening gown and then changing partway through the night. It's all very well-orchestrated. Sort of like a costume change between acts. I tried to convince Amie to do the same thing, but since she's going as Cinderella the whole rags-to-riches thing wasn't that appealing.

"I will be. Only to start the night. And you'll be in a regular suit. And then you'll change into Batman and I'll change into Catwoman. It'll be fun."

"Why didn't you tell me about this before now?"

"I wanted it to be a surprise."

"What if this costume doesn't fit? Is this Lycra? Where did you even get this?"

"I worked hard on it. Just put it on." The only real work I did was looking online and punching in his credit card number. Although I did tailor it based on his suit measurements and I made a few special alterations.

He sighs, lips still pursed, but strips out of his clothes while I watch.

"Enjoying yourself?" He sticks his hand down the front of his boxer briefs and does some rearranging.

I grin. "Immensely."

He pulls the suit on. I think it's going to look even better than it did on the model who posed in it. Bancroft has amazing legs. Bancroft has an amazing body, period. He's a massive brick wall of a man. Until him, I'd never been into jacked-up guys. His build is often camouflaged under his suits, although the bulges and contours of muscle are still present.

Now all that incredible definition is encased in black Lycra. I press my knees together. Maybe he doesn't even need all the armor stuff that came with it. I also wonder if we have time for a quickie before Amie gets here to do my makeup.

"It's a little tight." Bancroft smoothes a hand down his chest.

"It's supposed to be tight." I start fiddling around with the armor stuff, just to see if I like the costume better with or without it. Bancroft stands with his arms crossed over his chest. He still doesn't look very impressed. But then he hasn't seen himself in the costume yet.

"I'm going to be hot in this."

"Hell yeah, you are."

"I mean I'm going to sweat."

"You'll be fine. And you only have to wear it for like, an hour at most." I fix the cape to his shoulders. All that's missing is the Batman mask and he's perfect. I pull him over to the bed and stand on the mattress so I can get it over his head. Then I take a step back and check him out. He's so hot. It's ridiculous.

I jump down off the bed and grab his hand. "Come look."

He follows me to the full-length mirror by the walk-in

closet, although I'm half dragging him. I cover his eyes with my hand and position him in front of the mirror before I move them. "Ta-da!"

He stares at his reflection for a lot of seconds. "I can see the outline of my cock."

I glance at his crotch. He's right. It's not super obvious, though. "We'll just readjust things." I drop into a crouch, poking him through the shiny fabric. He's half hard, which is likely part of the problem. His low groan draws my gaze up.

His lip is curled in the hint of a smirk. He's not looking at me. He's looking at his reflection in the mirror. "Maybe I don't mind this costume all that much."

I snort and make a small adjustment, but I'm just exacerbating the problem. He's harder now, and more obvious.

"I have a question," he asks.

"Shoot."

"How am I going to use the bathroom when I'm wearing this? Won't I have to take most of it off?"

Now it's my turn to smirk. I took this into consideration when I made some alterations. I slip my hand over the fabric until I find the hidden flap and slide my hand inside. It takes me a few seconds to work my way around his boxer briefs, but I manage to get his mostly erect cock through the opening.

He snort-groans. "You're brilliant."

"Right?"

A wicked grin pulls at the corner of his mouth. "You know what you should do while you're down there?"

I return the smile. How many people can say they've blown Batman?

Nine

Auction

Amie

This dress is so uncomfortable. I can feel the sweat trickling down my spine, as well as down the inside of my thigh. Seriously. I'm disgusting under this thing. Not that it matters. Armstrong had to go out of town on a last-minute business trip this afternoon, leaving me alone as Cinderella in this stupid costume. It was too late to find something else, so here I am, stuck in this poofy dress for the entire night.

Ruby, on the other hand, looks amazing in her form-fitting, sparkly evening gown. It's costume one of two for this evening. She's having way too much fun with this whole event.

I, on the other hand, can't wait for the event to be over so I no longer have to worry about things like the bachelor auction, which Gwendolyn has semi-delegated to me.

Getting out of this dress and escaping Armstrong's mother are two more things I can't wait for. I keep reassuring myself that after the wedding I won't have to spend nearly as much time with her.

Also, there are at least three guys here that I may have fooled around with in college. I may have slept with one or two of them, back in my wild, slightly promiscuous phase. That lasted all through freshman and sophomore year. And half of junior year, as well, and maybe a small blip in senior year, but that was a long time ago. Still, I would really like it if I didn't have to exchange awkward pleasantries with them. At least Armstrong isn't here, so I don't have to worry about explaining any awkwardness to him.

But ex-flings and Armstrong's mother aren't my biggest concern at the moment. It's after nine and Lex has yet to show up. The auction is supposed to begin at ten and I still need to brief everyone. There are six eligible bachelors up for bid tonight and he's one of them. He's last, and expected to fetch the highest bid, but that's not going to happen if he doesn't show. I don't know how reliable he is, and Armstrong seemed to think it was typical for him to flake out. That's my interpretation of his assessment. Armstrong would never use the phrase *flake out*.

Currently I'm hiding in a corner to avoid Gwendolyn, but it's a difficult feat considering the size of this damn dress. I spot her across the room talking with some women dressed in evening gowns. I'm still unsure who she's supposed to be tonight. Maybe some queen? The Queen of Bitches?

Feeling safe, I weave my way through the throng of guests. Some of the costumes are amazing. More than one person decided to be Dracula, or a vampire. There's a couple here who literally look like Barbie and Ken—it's a bit creepy. I pass Alice in Wonderland, a lonely looking zombie—there was a reason I said no to that theme—and Chewbacca, whose date is Princess Leia, which is a bit . . . odd. I have to say *excuse me* every two feet, because my dress is just as puffy as every other woman's in this room. It's like playing dress bumper cars. I also have to duck behind a group of people to avoid one of my past flings. Dear God. I've been to tons of events in the past six months and managed to avoid running into anyone whose bed I've been in. Why does it seem like all my bad choices are here tonight?

I spot Bane. He's a hard man to miss, even if he's dressed in the same suit as the majority of the men here. I should've agreed with Armstrong and had a masquerade party even if it would've taken some of the fun out of this for Ruby. It would've been easier to navigate and I would have had a better chance of hiding from my soon-to-be mother-in-law and the other people I'm not interested in reminiscing with. Or I could've chosen to be a Storm Trooper, I suppose.

I search the area around Bane's massive frame, but I don't see Ruby anywhere. Regardless, he'll have Lex's number, he can contact him and find out when he'll be arriving. I lift my massive skirt and begin the arduous task of crossing the room again.

"Amalie!" Armstrong's father stops me with a hand on my arm. "Come meet some of my associates. I'm so sorry Armstrong couldn't be here tonight to see you in this dress. Has anyone sent him a picture so he knows what he's missing?"

Fredrick's breath is sharp with scotch and I think I might catch a hint of slur in his words. He puts an arm around my shoulder and turns me to the group of men, all holding glasses of amber liquid. He issues introductions, the last names familiar, and I try to be attentive and gracious while I panic internally. I want this evening to go as smoothly as possible to avoid anything negative from Gwendolyn. I need all the help I can get with her. Our missing bachelor is an issue I'd like to rectify, otherwise I need to find someone else to stand in for Lex and that's not going to be easy with less than an hour before the auction begins.

Fredrick's arm is still slung casually over my shoulder. "Isn't she a catch? Armstrong has great taste in women, just like his father, isn't that right?" The question seems to be directed at me.

I'm really not sure what to say to that. Gwendolyn is an insufferable bitch. Although I've seen pictures of her when she was younger and hadn't been subjected to years of Botox and surgery. She was once very pretty. I just nod and smile and blush appropriately before I excuse myself and slip out from under Fredrick's arm.

I finally reach Bane, who's drinking imported beer, chatting with his other brother, Griffin, and someone dressed as a gladiator. His back is to me. I fight an eye roll. Clearly whoever it is wanted a reason to be shirtless. As I get closer I notice he's at least attempted to complete the look with some fake scars. Two thick lines run down his back. His incredibly muscular back. I assume it's supposed to mimic whip or sword marks. He has a shield propped against his leg. Which is also muscular. A helmet, shoulder armor, and an authentic-looking skirt-type thing complete the costume. He can definitely pull the costume off with a back like that. Actually, the whole package is quite nice.

"Bane." I put my hand on his forearm to get his attention. It's loud with the music and the conversation.

"Amie." His white teeth flash in the chandelier light.

"Hey! How's it going? Have you seen my girlfriend? She's been missing for a while."

"I'm actually looking for her. And do you know if Lexington has arrived yet? The bachelor auction starts soon and I haven't seen him. I need to make sure he knows what's going on."

"I'm right here." The deep male voice is close and yet muffled.

I jump and spin around. The voice is coming from under the gladiator helmet.

"Oh! I didn't realize it was you."

I try to keep my eyes above his neck, but they dart down anyway. It's supposed to be the quickest of glimpses. He looks like an airbrushed model. Ridges define each and every contour.

Washboard abs flex and ripple as he raises his arms, thickly corded with muscle, his full-sleeve tattoo on display, and lifts his helmet. His hair is a mess, damp from being contained. He runs a hand through it, sending it into further disarray. Usually it's tamed with a perfect part to the left, making him authentically the businessman he is. But right now he looks very much the part of the untamed gladiator.

"Excellent costume choice, Lexington." I place a hand on his forearm. "You're perfect."

His brow arches. And I blink a few times. Reviewing what I've just said, I rush to complete that thought. "For the auction. You're perfect for the auction."

That panty-dropping smile widens. "Anything for charity, Cinderella. Where's Prince Charming?"

"I'm sorry? What?"

"You're Cinderella, right? Where's my cousin? I assume he's playing at being Charming tonight."

"Oh! Right. He had a business thing to take care of. Very last minute, so he's unable to attend."

"That's unfortunate." He sounds very much like he doesn't mean that in the slightest. He takes my hand and bows, his lips pressing against my knuckle for the briefest moment. It's completely disarming, exactly like it was a year ago when I met him at a Moorehead function. Incidentally, it was the same night I met Armstrong, who warned me off his too-smooth cousin.

I snatch my hand away and laugh, a little disconcerted. "Have you been practicing that move all day? You should definitely do that when you're being auctioned, you'll have women throwing their checkbooks at you. Anyway, once I've found Ruby I'll give you a rundown of how the auction is going to work."

"I've done a bunch of these, so you've got nothing to worry about." He winks.

I turn away from Lexington so I don't succumb to the urge to look at his abs again.

Bane appears annoyed with his brother. I'm not sure why. His costume is genius. He's going to garner lots of attention at the auction.

I glance around the room, searching for Ruby, but it's difficult with the low lighting and all the people. "When was the last time you saw Ruby?" I ask Bane.

"It's been a while. She mentioned changing her costume, but then she went to get a drink and hasn't come back yet. To be honest, it's fine with me if she just stays in that dress so I don't have to change out of this suit."

"Have you seen her in the other costume?" She sent me selfies yesterday. It's amazing how a costume that covers so much skin can still be so scandalously sexy.

"She wanted it to be a surprise. You know how she is."

I give him a sly smile. "I'm pretty sure once you see it you'll feel differently."

Lexington taps me on the shoulder. "Uh. What's Ruby's costume again?"

I maintain actual eye contact this time. "She's supposed to be Catwoman."

"I think she's changed then." He points across the room.

Bane and I follow his finger. I smile as his mouth drops open.

"Sweet fucking Christ."

"It's a really great costume, isn't it?" Ruby is talented with a sewing machine.

The V neckline plunges teasingly low, but stops before it reveals cleavage. Her long hair is pulled up in a ponytail and a simple mask covers her eyes. Her lips are painted a deep, glittery red. The bodysuit clings to her like a second skin, showcasing every curvy inch. Black stilettos complete the look. And of course, a pair of cat ears. She also has a whip. Because why the hell not?

She's grinning as she slips between guests, drawing attention from all sides. "She needs to put that damn dress back on." Bane's hands are in his pockets. I try not to think about what I accidentally got a glimpse of the other day when I was there. Or how Armstrong fails to stack up, even a little.

Ten
Panty Eater

Ruby

Bane looks like he wants to commit several murders as I move through the crowd, which is the exact reason I refused to let him see the costume before this moment. I have a plan for later tonight. And it includes costumes. His and mine. And sex. Hot superhero sex.

Once I'm close enough, I do a little spin and curtsey. "Do you like it?"

Bancroft adjusts his tie, then stuffs his hand back in his pocket, exhaling a low whistle. He clears his throat, but it doesn't help much with the gravel in it. "A little too much."

I bet he has a wicked hard-on right now. I wonder how long I have to wait before I can get my hands on it, or more exciting parts of my body.

"Banny!" A collective group-cringe accompanies the shrill sound.

I know that voice. I know it well. It's Brittany Thorton. I call her Brittany Whore-ton. Because it's fitting and sometimes I'm juvenile. She also wants to sink her claws into my man. She uses the fact that she's known him her entire life as an excuse to hug him every time she sees him. Two broken arms would make that rather difficult.

Back before Bancroft and I were dating, he went out with her once. It was the same night we met.

As expected, she ignores me and throws her arms around his neck like she does every single time. God, I hate her so much. "You have got to be kidding me. Who the hell invited her?" I mutter.

Amie shrugs and Lex watches the interaction with amusement.

I have no idea what her costume is supposed to be. Her dress barely covers her ass, which is typical based on what I've seen her wear at other events. She shows up everywhere we are. It's one of the pitfalls of being connected to all these people with money. They invite each other to everything.

I glare at Bancroft, who's smart enough not to hug her back with the same level of enthusiasm. In fact, he barely pats her back. He touches her. That's enough to make me consider using my whip to strangle her.

When she finally lets go of him her nose crinkles. "Who're you supposed to be?"

She sucks a lollipop into her mouth. Pushing it to the side, she creates a bulge in her cheek.

"Bruce Wayne."

"Oh." She tilts her head as if she doesn't understand. Shrugging, she pulls the lollipop out with a suctiony sound. I want to shove that damn thing up her left nostril. "Are you in the auction again? I brought my checkbook!"

"I'm not a bachelor this year." Bane looks like he's trying to keep his smile under control. He knows how much I loathe Brittany, especially when she ignores me on purpose and gets all touchy-feely with him. He thinks it's funny when I get worked up about it. Probably because the sex afterward is extra feisty. He often comes away with scratches post–Brittany encounters, and then struts around without a shirt on so I can see the damage I've done.

"Oh, right. I forgot. You have a girlfriend."

Lex coughs to cover his laughter. He knows just as well as Bancroft how much Brittany's continued interest in Bane irritates me.

I push my way between them, wrap one arm around his back and slide one under the lapel of his suit. If it wouldn't cause a huge scene I'd stick my tongue right down his throat just to make a point, or grab his crotch, but that would be pushing the line a lot. "Hi, Brittany, it's so great to see you again!" I put on my best fake friendly smile.

"Oh! Hi, Rosemary! I didn't even see you there."

I don't correct her on my name. She purposely gets it wrong every single time. Or she's just too dim to remember.

"Did you know Lexington is up for auction tonight?"

Lex shoots daggers at me, but flashes a smile when Brittany turns her grin on him.

"Oh my God! Lexy!" She launches herself at him. He catches her, wrapping one arm around her waist as she clings to his neck. I unfurl my whip and make like I'm going to strangle her. Lex's white-toothed grin widens, but changes to a cringe when he gets hit in the face with her hair.

Bancroft's chest presses against my back and his mouth is suddenly at my ear. "Don't be catty."

I elbow him in the ribs. "Such a bad joke."

When Brittany finally lets go of "Lexy" she drags her hands down his bare chest. "Oh wow! I love your costume. What're you?"

"A gladiator."

"Of course." Her nose crinkles and she touches the sword holster at his waist, running her finger down the length. "So like, is this similar to a highlander? You know, the whole kilt, no underwear thing?"

Seriously. I detest this chick so much.

Lex smirks. If flirting were a profession, he'd be the CEO of the company. He leans in and says something none of us can hear.

Her giggle tells me he's in full-on flirt mode. "I'll be sure to bid on you. Daddy said I could spend as much as I want this year." She winks exaggeratedly and licks her lollipop.

His eyebrows lift. "Lucky me."

Judging from her smile, she entirely misses the sarcasm. It's amazing that he's able to flirt so shamelessly when even he's admitted his disdain for her.

He settles his hands on her hips and moves back a step so she's not in his personal space anymore and looks her over. "What's your costume?"

"I'm the lollipop girl."

"Right. Of course you are."

After a few beats of silence and a muffled cough from Bancroft, she bounces on her toes, her boobs nearly popping out of her dress. "Okay! Well, I'm going to say hi to some more people. See you all later!" And off she goes.

"Wow." Lex blows out a breath.

I turn to say something to Amie and notice, first, that

she's watching Brittany sashay across the room with the same level of absolute loathing as I usually do. She's such a great best friend. It's why I put up with Armstrong. That and I really have no other choice. It's actually quite nice that he couldn't make it tonight. As I observe Brittany interacting with another group of debutantes, I note a very familiar-looking man headed straight for Amie, dressed as Peter Pan, jaunty cap perched on his head and everything.

It takes me a moment to place him. He's one of Amie's exes. "Oh shit." I grab her arm. "Three o'clock. The panty eater." Of all of Amie's exes, he's one I never would've considered inviting to an event, because I'm pretty sure he's certifiable. I did however slip an invite to a couple of the ones who aren't crazy, but who were definitely enamored of her, likely because she wasn't interested in whatever they were offering for more than a date or two.

Amie's eyes go wide and she glances over. It's too late to escape. He's only fifteen feet away and closing in fast. "Who invited him?" she hisses.

"I have no idea." It's the truth, too. As bad as I feel for Amie right now, I almost wish Armstrong was here to witness this, because I'm pretty sure it's going to be epic. He also needs to understand just how fully obsessed some of Amie's exes are with her.

His smile is almost manic as he closes the gap. "Amie. It's so good to see you."

Before she has a chance to respond at all, he wraps his arms around her and buries his face in her neck, turning his head so his nose is pretty much in her hair. Her hands are frozen in the air, fingers spread wide as if she's being electrocuted. I can't see her face, but I imagine it's filled with horror.

Bancroft's mouth is at my ear. "Who the hell is that?"

"I'll tell you later. It's a great story," I promise.

Prior to meeting Armstrong, Amie had decided to give online dating a chance. She thought it might help weed out some of the undesirables she was prone to going after. Some huge bigwig corporate mogul started messaging her, along with about six hundred other men. As was typical for Amie. She has absolutely no need to use online dating services, apart from being curious. She got asked out standing in lines at the grocery store, at least until Armstrong put a rock on her finger. I'm not sure even that has been much of a deterrent.

Deacon, the man currently hugging her, certainly wasn't her usual type, but he was hot, and she was desperate to break her bad-boy pattern, so she went out with him.

Fast-forward three dates later and she ended up back at his place. Apparently this guy had a thing for dining at the pussy buffet while her panties were still on. Which can be sexy in a teasing kind of way. Except he chewed an actual hole in her panties. And of course he kept them, because what man doesn't need a pair of crotchless panties from a woman he's fucked? We laughed about it.

The sex was insane, though, based on her reports, so she went back for more.

The panty chewing continued. He seemed to be making it his mission to turn all of her panties into crotchless ones.

Anyway, after three panty destructions, she ended things. But in true Amie fashion, she'd managed to secure herself a stage-five clinger. He continued to message her for weeks after she said she wasn't really interested in a relationship. It took a while for the message to sink in; the threat of a restraining order helped.

She shut down her account after that. Unfortunately

the bar scene produced even less favorable dating options. The next guy she went out with was worse than the online ones—and almost landed her in prison.

Deacon embraces her far longer than is appropriate. During that time I shift a little, so I'm able to see her face. Everyone in our small group has stopped talking to watch this interaction.

He finally releases her but holds on to her shoulders as he leans back enough to see her face. His thumbs sweep along her collarbones. "I'd hoped you'd be here."

"Deacon, it's so . . . I didn't . . . How are you?" Her voice is shrill, disarmed.

Lex gives me a questioning look. His fingers curl around the hilt of his sword, as if he's considering using it.

Amie wraps her delicate hands around Deacon's wrists and takes a step back. He moves forward with her. This is getting awkward. Especially when he grips her wrists in return, as if he's unwilling, or possibly unable, to let them go.

Lex moves in, but I hold up a hand. She's had years of self-defense classes, hot yoga, Pilates, and some crazy boxing thing she does to keep her fit and safe. Also, I really want to see how this plays out. It's too bad Armstrong isn't here to witness this. I search the room, hoping to spot him, but I can't find him anywhere. I do, however, spot Brittany flirting with some suits.

It would've made my night if Armstrong happened to get punched out by one of Amie's exes. Well, that and Bancroft fucking me while I'm Catwoman and he's Batman.

Deacon holds Amie's hands together in his and takes another step toward her. "You look so beautiful. It's just so good to smell you again."

And there it is. The weirdness I'm talking about.

Lex makes a face, as if he's unsure he heard that correctly.

"See you again. I mean. So good." He bows his head and brings her knuckles to his lips. I'm pretty sure he licks her, right before he notices the giant rock on her finger.

He snaps up, back ramrod straight. "What is *that*?"

Amie wipes her hand on her dress. "I'm engaged." Her voice still has that reedy quality to it.

He blinks rapidly. Disbelieving.

"Do I need to manage this guy?" Bancroft asks me.

Lex steps up beside Amie before Bancroft can make a move, though, and throws his arm around her shoulder, pulling her into his side. She stumbles a bit and has to brace herself with a hand on his chest. Which is bare since he's dressed as a gladiator. He turns his charming smile on Deacon and holds out his hand. "Hello, I'm Lex, Amalie's fiancé."

Amie looks up at him, her expression reflecting both confusion and shock. He bends down and puts his mouth to her ear, whispering something that makes her eyebrows lift even higher, but she gives him the tiniest of nods. What the hell is happening here?

Deacon looks from Amie to Lex and back again. "Her fiancé?"

"Yes. In just a few months she'll be mine forever." He turns to Amie, smiling down on her with a convincingly loving gaze, and takes her chin between his finger and his thumb. For a second I think he's actually going to kiss her. Instead he dips his head and brushes the end of his nose across the tip of hers. Amie's eyes are wide. Her hand is wrapped around his wrist. The one that's holding her chin.

It occurs to me, as I watch this go down, that those two

would actually look incredible together. It's really too bad she's set on Armstrong.

Deacon's expression has gone from confused to angry. "You're getting married in a few months?"

"I'm sorry, how do you know Amalie?" Lex asks, giving him a full once-over.

"We dated," Deacon snaps.

"Briefly," Amie adds.

"It wasn't that brief." He strokes the square of cloth peeking out of the pouch of his little man satchel. He really committed to the Peter Pan bit. He's even wearing tights. The square of cloth seems out of place, though, since it's lace and satin. "How long have you been engaged?"

"That's irrelevant." Amie's hand flutters to her throat.

Deacon's still stroking the fabric; the satchel is right over his crotch, so it looks a little obscene. "I thought you said you weren't interested in getting serious with anyone."

"At the time I wasn't."

Deacon scoffs. "So it was just about my cock then."

Oh my God. Who the hell says that in public? In front of someone's fiancé, of all people. Even if Lex isn't really Amie's fiancé, Deacon doesn't know that. I'm about to speak up when Lex wraps his gloved hand around the back of Deacon's neck, wearing a jovial smile. From an outsider's perspective, it could look very much like a normal conversation apart from Deacon's angry expression and the way Lex's fingers dig into his skin.

"Listen, buddy, that was fucking rude. You're making a scene and you're embarrassing yourself and Amalie. Now would be a good time to walk away, unless you're interested in a bigger scene and some broken bones."

Deacon closes his eyes, his expression pinched. He inhales and exhales deeply before his livid gaze finally falls on Amie. "I apologize."

I breathe a sigh of relief.

Lex loosens his grip on Deacon's neck and gives him a heavy pat on the shoulder. "Smart move."

Deacon's lip twitches. "I'm sure you'll be very happy together."

Lex forces a tight smile and puts an arm around her shoulder again, giving her an affectionate squeeze. "I'm positive we will. She's too lovely not to be."

Deacon's smile grows viciously wider. "She certainly is lovely. Especially that sweet, tasty pussy of hers."

I choke on a cough. Well, this just got X-rated.

"Motherfucker," Bane steps around me, possibly to take part in what is likely going to be a very public throw down. Poor Amie. She's too hot for her own good.

Lex has already slapped his palm around the back of the panty-chewing, pussy-loving pervert's neck again. "You just couldn't keep your mouth shut, had to have the last word." He cocks a fist and punches Deacon square in the chest while still holding him by the neck. If Deacon could stumble back, he would. But Lex is keeping him firmly in place.

Amie covers her mouth with a palm, eyes wide with horror.

As entertaining as this is, it's definitely not the kind of scene we need. This community loves their scandals, and Amie certainly doesn't need one with her wedding coming up and her fiancé not even present tonight.

Amie glances around to see how many people have noticed. We're tucked away in a corner, and there's a huge table with a chocolate fountain blocking most of the view, thank God.

"Lex," Bane snaps.

Lex must realize that he's making the problem worse, instead of better. He throws his arm around Deacon and slaps him on the chest a couple of times, laughing, as if he's told some hilarious joke.

Any attention we've drawn abates as the men close the circle, obstructing Lex and Deacon further from view.

"You should apologize to my fiancée, that was disrespectful." Lex releases Deacon and steps away, raising his hands slightly as he regards Bancroft with an *I-did-nothing-wrong* look, then turns to Amie. "Why don't you give me the rundown before the auction starts, sweetheart?"

She still looks a little shocked by the whole thing.

Snapping out of her daze she straightens. "Yes. Yes, that would be a good idea."

Lex takes a step toward her, kicking something on the floor. He snatches it up, frowning as he inspects it. I recognize it as the little fabric square that had been peeking out of Deacon's man satchel.

Except it's not a pocket square. It's a pair of panties.

Eleven
Dear Lord

Amie

Deacon makes a grab for the fabric square in Lex's hand. A square I recognize as a pair of panties he gnawed the crotch out of and subsequently stole. He's the creepiest of creepy.

I snatch the scrap of fabric from Lex before Deacon can. I'm sure he already knows what they are. Undoubtedly he's seen many pairs of lacy, satin panties up close and personal. At least those are the rumors.

"Those are mine!" Deacon shouts.

I get right up in Deacon's face. "These are mine, you creepy, perverted bastard. I didn't want to date you because you do bizarre things like carry around pairs of old, chewed-up panties." I whirl around, hike up my giant, stupid skirt, and grab Lex by the elbow before he can punch my ex in the face. "Come on, Lex. Let's go sell you to the highest bidder."

"You have interesting taste in guys."

"He was one of the better ones, if you can believe it," I mutter.

Lex barks out a laugh. "You're just full of fun surprises, aren't you, Cinderella."

"You don't know the half of it." It's actually probably a blessing that Armstrong isn't here, otherwise I'd have to explain this insanity.

Ruby rushes to catch up. She slips her arm through mine. "Are you okay?"

"I don't know." I'm scanning the room as we go. "God, how mortifying was that? I shouldn't have said anything about the damn panties. I made a scene. What if people noticed? What if it gets back to Gwendolyn?"

"No one noticed. You're fine. It's fine. Bane is going to make sure he leaves right now," she reassures me as we pass through the curtains that lead backstage.

Why the hell did Deacon, of all my short-term hookups, have to show up here? This is the exact reason I've generally avoided dating people who run in the same circles as I do—they all know each other. And they all gossip like thirteen-year-old girls at a sleepover.

"What if Deacon says something to someone? What if he does something else to embarrass me—" I spin around, ready to go back, but I slam right into a bare chest. Lex's bare chest. He grabs my arms to steady me.

"Bane's got it. You're good. He's not going to make another scene."

"I don't understand why the hell he was here in the first place!" I throw my hands up and lose my grip on the panties. They fly into the air and Lex manages to nab them before I can.

They were a great pair of panties once, before the crotch went missing. Pale blue with navy lace accents; sexy, classy, a little naughty. With the matching bra and garters I looked pretty damn fantastic.

He raises a brow as he fingers the material. "Nice."

I can feel my face going red. "Thanks. I'll take those back now, since they're mine and all."

"There's a hole in them." He slides two fingers through the tear.

Oh my God. This is not happening. My best friend's boyfriend's brother is not sticking his fingers through a hole in a pair of my old panties. "I'm aware," I barely choke out the words.

"It looks like they've been chewed."

"That's because they have."

His furrow deepens. "Does he have a dog or something?"

"No." Dear lord. This is seriously the worst conversation I've ever had to have. Well, maybe not. That time when I had to explain to my father why I was being held for questioning at the airport in Mexico was worse, and at least I'm not having this conversation with Armstrong. Not that this is much better, mind you. I'm sure I'm making one hell of an impression right now.

"You're a bit of a wild one, aren't you?" Lex's eyebrows lift, a wide smile breaks across his face, and I wait for the next question, because I know it's coming, in three, two, one . . . "Wait, are these *dirty*?"

And there it is. I literally have to fight with my mouth not to smile back at him. "I believe they are, yes."

"You think I should check, just to make sure?" He starts to lift them to his nose.

Ruby jumps in and snatches them from him, but his fingers are still stuck in the hole, which tears more as she yanks them out of his grasp and tosses them to me. She points a finger in his face. "That's just fucking gross. He's probably had those for a year. I bet he jerked off with them."

Lex makes a gagging sound, then turns to me, looking concerned. "Is he a serial killer? Do you need someone to escort you home tonight?"

"I sincerely doubt it. He faints at the sight of blood."

"That guy's a whack job."

"Uh-huh. I sincerely appreciate you posing as my fiancé and punching him."

"Anytime you need me to punch out an ex, or even your current fiancé, you just let me know and I'm there." He winks, but I have a feeling he might be serious about my current fiancé.

"Okay, well," Ruby claps her hands together. "I think you're channeling the spirit of gladiator perfectly tonight, Lex. Keep that up when you're on the stage so we can make some serious money off of you."

Gwendolyn comes rushing backstage, looking as if her head is going to explode. "Amalie! There you are! You won't believe what just happened. Some man dressed as Peter Pan was in the foyer, screaming about having his panties stolen. Can you even believe it? Bancroft is escorting him off the property. I don't even know how he managed to get on the guest list."

Ruby and I give each other a look. Of all the nights for Armstrong to miss a party, this is definitely a good one.

Twelve
Costume Malfunction

Ruby

Gwendolyn has forced Amie to come up onstage with her to help auction off the men. I've been relegated to backstage duty—Gwendolyn thinks my costume is too suggestive. Those weren't her exact words, but her twitchy face and her pinched lips were a significant-enough tell, along with her tone when she called my costume inappropriate.

Amie is not a huge fan of being in front of hundreds of people unless it's associated with presenting in a boardroom. Apparently when there are slides and a presentation it's a lot different. I suppose that makes sense. This is unstructured.

My job is to make sure the guys are prepared, look dapper—or in Lex's case, hot enough to cause women to succumb to the vapors—and make it out onstage for their auction slot. It's pretty easy. So far we've managed to raise more than a hundred and forty thousand dollars and we still have two bachelors to go. One of them is Wentworth Williams. He once flirted with me at a party back when Bancroft and I were yet to be defined and I was only his pet sitter, not his live-in girlfriend.

The first time I met Wentworth, within an hour he intimated that he wanted to get naked with me. He's been well-behaved this evening, perhaps because Lex is right here, and Wentworth is aware that I'm living with Bancroft. He's been ultra-polite.

Lex is looking at his phone when something else catches his attention. He frowns, his stance becoming defensive. Dear God, the panty chewer better not be back. The curtains part and Bancroft comes through, dressed as Batman.

Lex's posture relaxes immediately and he directs his smirk at me. "You have to be responsible for that."

I grin. "Totally."

"You take care of that guy?" Lex asks Bane.

"Oh, yeah. He's gone." Bancroft nods to Wentworth and slips an arm around my waist. It's an intentionally possessive move. Especially when he kisses my temple and pulls me into his side. "That guy's a little obsessed, huh? A bit of a nutbar? Is he from Amie's anarchy days?"

"Anarchy days?" Lex's grin widens.

I wave a hand around, as if it's not important. "She was a bit of a wild child. Anyway, that guy chews holes in panties, and he's a little unhinged. I think that's about as much as you all need to know." It's really not my story to tell, especially in front of Lex. Maybe later, when I'm alone with Bane and we're not having sex, I'll tell him about that brief, weird relationship.

"I'll just leave that one alone, then."

"That's probably for the best." I run my hand over his chest. His broad, Lycra-covered chest. I can't wait until we're up in our room and having superhero sex.

A round of applause makes it difficult to hear Lex's question and a few moments later Wentworth is being called to the stage. I don't adjust his tie like I have for everyone else, because there's no way Bane is going to let go of me to make that happen. Also, his hand is wandering and I can feel his hard-on against my hip.

Once Wentworth disappears through the curtains Lex looks up from his phone. "You two don't need to babysit me, I've done this a bunch of times. I know the drill. Go get a drink." He motions to the curtains leading to the stage. "This'll take a while, anyway."

I'm starting to get hot in this costume. A drink would be great. "Can I get you anything?"

He shakes his empty glass. "Scotch and soda would be good."

I nab it from him. "I'll be back in a few."

"Take your time." He glances at his phone again.

I head for the stairs, but before I get too far, fingers wrap around my wrist and I'm pulled back into a hard wall of muscle. Bancroft's cape flutters around me, caging me in. Picking me up, he takes me in the opposite direction of the bar, and back behind the stage.

"What're you doing?" I whisper hiss.

"This costume is killing me," he mutters.

"Like you're uncomfortable?" I can't see how that's possible; his costume is the softest, stretchiest fabric in the world. Warm maybe, because Lycra isn't known for being super breathable.

I'm dangling about six inches above the floor, my back

pressed to his front. He shifts his hips so I can feel his hard-on. "No. You're making my balls ache. I need to take the edge off."

"But we're supposed to get a drink for Lex."

"Lex can get his own drink. We'll be quick." He heads toward the closest door. Pushing it open, he hits the light. It's a supply closet. "This'll have to do."

It closes behind us and he sets me down, flipping the lock before he pushes me up against the wall and crushes his mouth to mine. Well, I guess I know how he feels about the Catwoman costume. Grinding against me, he strips off his gloves and runs his hands over my shiny black cat suit, groping my breasts, sliding them over my hips, and cupping them between my legs. Tearing his mouth away he exhales a harsh breath. "Fuck, you're so hot. Why is this so hot? Motherfucker."

He groans when I palm him through his Batman suit, then slip my hand into the secret pocket and wrestle him free. He wasn't kidding about this costume driving him nuts; he's rock solid. His cock kicks in my hand as I run my thumb over the head. My nails are painted red.

He takes my face in his hands, tilts my head back and his mouth is on mine again, tongue forcing its way past my lips, each stroke hot and aggressive. Exactly the way he's pumping into my hand.

"I want inside you." His hands move down my sides and he grabs my ass, the other coming around to slip between my thighs. "How do I get into this?"

I have to push on his chest with some real force to get him to back up. "I'll show you."

He closes his hand around mine when I try to let go of his erection.

I give him a devious smile. "I can't show you if you're fucking my hand, can I?"

He's quick to let me go. Arching my back, I reach behind me and find the zipper. When I get halfway I have to move to the front to unzip it the rest of the way. I installed a hidden zipper that starts at my tailbone and ends at my navel in preparation for this exact event.

I turn around and bend over, showing him my bare ass. I'm without panties—otherwise, what would be the point?

"You're a goddamn genius." Bane spins me around, grabs me by the ass and lifts me. I wrap my legs around his waist and his thick head slides over my clit. "I'll love you better later," he promises, and then he slips low and pushes inside.

It's a fast, frantic fuck. I bite his shoulder so I don't make too much noise. I doubt anyone will be able to hear us with the auction going on, but just in case, I want to limit my pleasure sounds. I know when he's getting close because he tugs on my ponytail. I lift my head and his palm slips under my chin, holding my face while he drills me into the door, eyes on mine.

He's wearing the Batman mask. It's so sexy. I think I may have a costume fetish. Thankfully, Bane seems to share it.

He slips his thumb between my lips. "That's gonna be my cock as soon as we get to the room."

I come, groaning his name because I love his dirty mouth, and he's right, that's exactly what's going to happen. I'm so glad we're staying at the hotel tonight and that Bane has booked us into one of the lavish presidential suites. We have all night to get our freaky sex on. It's going to be amazing. A few more thrusts and he follows right after me, declaring his love of *fucking Catwoman*.

After a few long moments of just breathing, he steps back from the door and I unwrap my legs from his waist.

As he starts to set me down there's a horrible ripping sound. We freeze, eyes on each other.

"I really hope that wasn't anything important," he says with a nervous chuckle.

Together, we look down. It's impossible to see what the issue is with the black-on-black material. He bends at the knee and I lower my legs carefully to the ground, but when he tries to pull away another tear reverberates loudly through the room.

My carefully sewed secret front pocket in his Batman leotard is ripped wide open. But that's not the worst part. The zipper on my catsuit has torn as well, leaving a huge hole at my crotch. The two seem to have gotten caught on each other with all the thrusting.

"Oh shit. That's not good."

"No, no, it's not." I try to separate us, but all I manage to do is make the hole in my costume bigger. "I have to be back out there soon. Gwendolyn is going to give some huge speech and make me go out there and thank everyone for coming. I can't do that with my vagina hanging out!" I gesture wildly to my crotch. Panic is setting in. This is an epic wardrobe malfunction.

"Fuck. Shit." Bane tries to run his hand through his hair, except he's wearing the mask, so he runs it over that instead. He takes a deep breath and goes into problem-solving mode. "Where's your dress?"

"In our room."

"Fuck. So we have to get to the elevators."

I bite my lip. "And up to the twenty-third floor without being seen."

He exhales a breath, nods once, grabs my ass, and hoists me back up.

I grab his shoulders. "What're you doing?"

"Taking you to your dress." He wraps his cape around us, holding it closed with one hand.

"Right. Okay." I throw the lock.

Bane peeks his head out into the hallway. The coast is clear so far. He creeps down the hall, as much as a six-three, two-hundred-plus-pound man can creep anywhere with a woman attached to the front of his body. If I wasn't so worried about having to be back onstage, I might think this whole situation was hilarious. I don't even know how long we were in the supply closet. I don't think I'll get over the panic until I'm back in my dress.

We manage to get to the doors leading to the hallway without being seen, which is a miracle since we have to pass Lexington, who's still waiting for his turn to go up onstage. Wow, I didn't expect Wentworth to be such a hit with the ladies, or maybe we were a lot faster than I thought.

Just when I think we're in the clear I peek my head out into the foyer and note several guests milling around there. Goddammit. Why aren't they in the ballroom, taking part in the auction, or at least watching it go down like they're supposed to?

I push him back before anyone sees me. "Shit. What are we going to do?"

Bancroft gives his head a shake. "I'm an idiot."

"No you're not. You were horny, and that's totally okay, but I need to figure out a way to get my dress back on my body so not everyone gets to see my used cooch."

He tries to set me down, but I cling to him. "Let go, babe." He pries my fingers free. "You stay here, I'll get the dress and bring it back down as fast as I can. I'll take the stairs if I have to."

"Why didn't we think of this in the first place?"

"Panic is good for making people dumb. I'll meet you back in the supply room." He kisses me quickly and then he rushes out the door, leaving me in the hallway with a very drafty crotch.

I tug at the zipper, but it's bent and pulled free from the teeth. I'll have to replace it entirely to fix it. With my hands over my crotch and my back against the wall I shimmy my way through the dimly lit hallway, back to the supply closet to wait.

I'm not quite so lucky this time around with going unnoticed. As I'm passing backstage, my black outfit against the cream wallpaper must catch Lex's attention. He glances over and spots me before I can duck out of sight. Not that there's anywhere to duck into. The supply closet is still a good twenty feet away and I'm not free to move quickly unless I want to flash him.

I'm sure my smile is more of a grimace. He leaves his post and saunters over to me, looking suspicious. "What's going on, Ruby? Where's Bane?"

"Oh nothing, he's just gone back to the room for a minute. He'll be right back."

He tilts his head to the side, eyes narrowed a little. "I thought you were getting drinks."

"I was. I am. I just, we uh . . ." Shit. If he finds out what happened he's never going to let either one of us live it down.

"Why are you standing like that?"

"I had a bit of a costume mishap." I can give him a smidgen of truth.

He comes a little closer. "What kind of mishap?"

"My zipper broke." Okay, maybe more of the truth is okay. He doesn't need to know *how* it happened.

That signature smirk pulls at the corner of his mouth. "Oh, yeah? What were you two doing to break a zipper?"

"It just, I just—" God. I lie professionally for a living—I fake being another human being, living another life five nights a week and I can't even come up with a plausible lie to tell my boyfriend's smirking brother.

Suddenly, Lexington's name is called from the other side of the curtain. The crowd erupts in applause, along with the sound of female whistles.

"You have to go." I cross my legs and try to shoo him toward the stage. When he doesn't move right away, I hiss, "Go! You can't keep Amie waiting like that, do you know how much stress this whole thing is causing her?"

"I seriously don't understand why she's marrying my dickbag cousin." He turns and heads toward the stage.

"That makes two of us," I mutter.

I must not have been quiet enough, because he glances over his shoulder, looking like he wants to say something.

"Can you do me a favor?" I don't wait for him to say yes. "Make it take a while, please. I can't go out there until I'm back in my dress."

Lex winks and bows, then steps through the curtains and the crowd screams. God, he really thrives on the attention. And at this moment, I love him for it.

It's another five minutes before Bancroft returns with my dress and his suit in hand. He's sweaty, but at least he's here and I won't have to embarrass myself or anyone else with indecent exposure.

"Did you run into anyone on the way?" I rush to change back into it while Bane does the same. It's the night of missing crotches, it seems.

"Brittany was getting off the elevator when I was getting on, but it was uneventful otherwise."

Bane helps me fix my hair. My lipstick is worn off completely, but there's nothing I can really do about that. I turn around. "I'm good?"

He gives my ass a little squeeze. "You're phenomenal."

"That could've been an absolute disaster." I push up on my toes. "I need to get back out there."

"I'm right behind you."

He opens the supply closet door and peeks out. The coast seems clear. I pretend like I didn't just have sex in a supply closet, where I ripped the crotch out of my costume—thank God I had the good sense to have two—and make my way back to the stage, where I hear a cacophony of screaming women. What the hell is going on out there?

I rush to the curtains and peek through them. Lex is strutting around onstage and there are about fifty hands in the air. Amie's eyes are saucer wide and her hand is at her throat. Gwendolyn is fanning herself with a piece of paper. Bids are being shouted rapid-fire. He's already at a hundred thousand dollars. He's been out there for all of ten minutes and the ladies are going wild.

It takes another ten minutes and fifty thousand dollars before the auction finally ends. Lexington has been purchased by someone other than Brittany. I'm sure he's relieved.

I'm summoned to the stage to celebrate the nearly four hundred thousand dollars we've raised through the bachelor auction. Once we're done thanking the guests, I thread my arm through Amie's and lead her to the bar because I sure as hell need a drink and she looks like she needs about seven.

"What happened with Lex?" I ask after I've placed an order for two glasses of champagne. He's already been claimed by his purchaser. I wonder if she thinks the date starts immediately.

Amie grabs hers almost before the bartender is finished pouring, chugs it, and signals him to refill it. "Lex flipped up his skirt thing." At my confused expression she fills in the blank. "He wasn't wearing underwear."

"Oh!" As that news sets in I ask what I assume I already know, based on the reaction of the women in the audience. "I assume that means he's . . . ample."

"Well." Amie gulps half of her second glass of champagne in one swallow. "I sincerely hope he's a shower and not a grower, otherwise we should consider renaming him Vlad the Vagina Impaler."

I snort. "You're exaggerating."

"Oh no, I am not. He could destroy someone with that thing." Her cheeks flush, whether from the champagne or the memory of being flashed, I can't be sure. Possibly both considering she's finished her second glass and is going for her third.

She motions to me. "What happened to your Catwoman suit?"

I smooth my hand over my stomach. "There was a bit of a problem with the zipper."

"What kind of problem?"

"It broke." I sip my champagne and avoid her gaze.

"And how did that happen?"

"Oh, you know, the usual, quickie in the supply closet."

Amie nearly spit-sprays her champagne all over me. "When did that happen?"

"About twenty minutes ago, give or take."

"During the auction?" She pinches my arm. "You're a jerk. I can't believe you were getting your rocks off while I had to manage this." She gestures to the empty stage.

"You should be thanking me, not pinching me."

"Thanking you for what?"

"You got to see a huge penis, didn't you?"

Bane slips an arm around my waist from behind. "Talking about me again?"

I scoff. "This time we're talking about your brother. Apparently he flashed the entire party."

"It's the night of indecent exposure, isn't it?" His hand is on my hip, but it's low, close to my butt without actually being an ass grab. "You ready to go up to the room soon?"

"In a bit. Amie needs help getting over being exposed to the Millses' genetic monstrosity."

Less than an hour later we're in the elevator on the way up to the penthouse floor. Amie is three sheets to the wind, stumbling down the hall to her room. I'm in better form than she is, but not by much. I use Bancroft's chest as a place to rest my head while he swipes the keycard and lets us into our room.

Once the door is open, he scoops me up and carries me inside. It makes me think about things like getting married. It's a long way off, a hint of an idea, but if things continue the way they are, I imagine that it will be an eventuality. It makes me happy.

"What are you smiling about?" Bancroft kisses my neck, dropping down on the massive king-size poster bed.

"We're lucky Lex and Amie are the only people who know what happened tonight."

Bane lifts his head, his expression dark. "What do you mean Lex knows?"

"He caught me sneaking back to the supply closet."

Bane's eyes go wide and his grip on my hips tightens.

"Calm down, baby, he didn't see anything. His ball flashing probably saved me from other people finding out, so we'll just have to deal with the razzing."

"With his antics tonight, I don't think he has much of a right to razz. My father is not pleased." He kicks off his shoes, pushes back on the mattress, and pulls me on top of him. "Enough talk, I want to put that mouth to good use tonight, bring it here." My dress rides up as I straddle his waist. He slides one wide palm along the side of my neck and pulls my mouth down, the other hand moving up the outside of my bare thigh. I brace myself on his chest and bend to kiss his chin, moving slowly to his lips.

"I'm guessing it's going to take some work to fix your costume," he says. Well, mostly it's a groan.

I push back and run my fingers through his hair. "Probably. Are you disappointed?"

He shrugs. "I'm sure I'll get over it."

"Tomorrow night I could be Wonder Woman again, but tonight you'll just have to take me as I am."

He skims the contours of my lip, grinning. "I'm pretty sure I can handle that."

Before he can monopolize my mouth with his tongue, I say, "I think we should start planning next year's costumes early."

His right eyebrow arches. "You want to throw another party after this shit show?"

"Maybe a private one. In our bedroom. You and me."

"I like private." He grabs my hips and pulls me closer. "And I vote no zippers."

My wheels are already spinning as he pulls my mouth down to his. And then all my thoughts turn to vapor when he kisses me.

My Batman, my Bruce Wayne, my filthy-mouthed Prince Charming.

The Pumpkin
Was Stuffed

Tara Sivec

One

Everyone Loves Clowns

Noel

"It was a dark and stormy night . . ." I whisper in a sinister voice, staring with wide eyes at the scene in front of me.

"No it's not. It's actually a very lovely fall evening. Not a cloud in sight."

I turn to face my husband, Sam, crossing my arms over my chest and above my giant pregnant stomach, which seems to have grown ten times larger in the last week. I'm thirty-five years old, with long, dark-red hair and green eyes. I used to think I was quite pretty, until I turned into a beached whale with swollen ankles. Standing next to my husband, who is a year older than I am—with his gorgeous blue-gray eyes; short, dark-brown hair; and fantastic muscular build, thanks to the Marines—it's hard to remember that I was once skinny and hot and looked like a perfect match for my sexy husband.

"Work with me here. I'm trying to set the tone for when I tell our child this story. If I don't inject the right amount of scary details, he or she will never truly understand the horror of what we're looking at right now."

Sam cocks his head to the side, studying the yard we're currently standing at the edge of while I study his profile. I still can't believe he's my husband, even though we've been married almost a year and a half. He's too hot for his own good, and I'm a hot mess with an ass covered in stretch marks.

"It's not *that* bad," he mutters.

I shake my head at him and then, adding *sociopathic mood swings* to my mental list of pregnancy-related problems, fantasize about jamming a knife into his skull and carving it like a pumpkin.

"Not that bad?!" I argue, my voice rising a few octaves as I fling one arm out, gesturing around my parents' front yard. "My father decorated his yard with hundreds of clowns. CLOWNS, Sam. Scary, creepy, makeup-wearing, red-nosed, big-shoed CLOWNS. This is the stuff nightmares are made of."

I shudder, wrapping my arms around myself, wishing I could unsee this shit. There are clowns cut out of wood and painted; mannequins dressed as clowns; stuffed clowns; blow-up-doll clowns . . . every size you can imagine, from one foot tall to ten feet tall. They're scattered all around the yard. My dad is slightly obsessed with decorating for every holiday, which makes sense, I guess, since our last name is, literally, Holiday. When I brought Sam home for Christmas the year we met, he thought we were pulling up to an airport runway, with all the bright, flashing lights all over the yard. My father's Valentine's Day decorations cover every inch of the yard; all the red hearts make it look like the house is bleeding onto the grass.

The entire state of Ohio went through a flag shortage the year he bought all the American flags that hang from the siding and porch railing on the Fourth of July.

But he has taken this year's neighborhood Halloween decorating contest to a horrifying level. One I'll never be able to erase from my mind; I'll see it every time I close my eyes.

"It's about time you got here!"

I turn to watch my dad jog down the front porch steps—which are littered with giant red clown shoes and jack-o'-lanterns—and hurry across the lawn toward us, dodging all the . . . *clowns*.

Jesus. I can't even THINK that word without getting the chills.

Dad is practically bouncing with excitement by the time he gets to us, his feet crunching through the fallen leaves as he stands next to me and nods at the two of us with a huge smile on his face. At fifty-seven, my dad is a pretty handsome man, standing at just about my husband's six foot stature, with a full head of salt-and-pepper hair.

"Hello, darling Noel, hello, Asshole-Who-Defiled-My-Daughter . . . so, what do you think of the yard?"

I let out a sigh and shake my head at him.

"Dad, for the hundredth time, Sam is my husband and did not defile me. Can't you just be happy about being a grandfather again, like a normal human being?" My brother and his wife already had a baby, a girl named Holly, and neither one of them had to suffer through this kind of sarcastic abuse from my father. My poor husband deserves a medal.

He wraps his arm around my shoulder and kisses the side of my head.

"Of course I'm happy about becoming a grandfather again. But you're my baby girl. And I'd prefer to think of this as an immaculate conception. Otherwise I will have a heart attack and die, picturing how it actually happened. Do you want me to die, Noel?" he demands in his usual, dramatic fashion. "Do you?!"

"Speaking of heart attacks," I mutter, changing the subject before my dad really does kill himself thinking about how I got pregnant. "Why, for the love of God, did you decorate the yard with clowns? No one likes clowns, Dad. No one. You're lucky your neighbors haven't burned your house down in protest."

Dad scoffs and rolls his eyes at me.

"Don't be silly. Clowns are fun. Everyone loves clowns."

A loud, bloodcurdling scream, followed by the most miserable-sounding wails, makes all three of us turn around to find a woman and a little boy standing a few feet away, on the sidewalk. The boy has his face pressed into the woman's side as he continues crying, and they rush past my parents' house.

"Clowns, Reggie? Really? You should be ashamed of yourself," the woman mutters, hurrying down the sidewalk with her distraught child.

"YOU'RE JUST JEALOUS BECAUSE YOUR FRONT YARD LOOKS LIKE A MONKEY TOOK A SHIT ON IT, SUSAN!" my dad yells after her. "EVERYONE LOVES CLOWNS, AND I'M GOING TO PROVE IT WHEN I WIN THIS CONTEST FOR THE TENTH YEAR IN A ROW!"

I should probably be embarrassed that my dad is screaming at one of his poor neighbors, but I was raised by this man. It's not the first time I've seen him turn into a raging lunatic in public, and it certainly won't be the last. He takes every holiday decorating contest very seriously. He starts coming up with ideas and building things for his Halloween display in February. With all of the children on the street, he doesn't like doing anything scary, and usually goes with something fun. One year it was a carnival theme, with a ticket booth and fun carnival games for kids. Another year it was a Charlie Brown theme. Last year, he went with a Mickey Mouse/Disney theme. All sweet and innocent fun. But clowns are anything but sweet and innocent, and clearly he's lost his mind.

"I don't know, Reggie. That house across the street might be giving you a run for your money," Sam states.

My dad starts grumbling and cursing under his breath as I look over at the house Sam is talking about. I can't help the dreamy sigh that escapes me. They've decorated in a *Nightmare Before Christmas* theme. It's one of my absolute favorite movies, and the display is amazing.

There's a huge Jack Skellington and Sally right in the middle of the yard, with a giant light-up moon behind them, and smaller wooden figurines of every other character are scattered all around the grass, from Doctor Finkelstein and the mayor of Halloween Town, to Oogie Boogie and the ghost dog, Zero. There are orange and white spotlights on every wooden character, and at least a hundred carved pumpkins distributed around the entire display.

My dreamy sigh doesn't only have to do with the decorations, though. It also has to do with the house itself. I've loved that house since I was a little girl. It's just a typical, two-story colonial, but the wraparound front porch, professional landscaping, and huge, fenced-in backyard made it my dream house. I always imagined that someday I'd get married, buy that house, and raise my family there.

"That yard looks like horseshit," my father mutters in irritation. "They didn't even put any work into it. They just went out to the closest Halloween store and bought everything they could find. I put my blood, sweat, and tears into *my* display."

"Clearly. The blood when all those creepy-ass clowns come to life and stab you in your sleep, the sweat when you're trying to outrun them, and the tears when they murder your entire family," I inform him.

My dad ignores me and continues to glare at the yard across the street.

"Did you know that house sold in less than two weeks? I haven't even met the new owners yet, and they've been there for a month. What kind of people move into a neighborhood, try to end my reign as Halloween Decorator King, and don't even come over and introduce themselves? Monsters, that's who," Dad complains.

I can't help the wave of sadness that washes over me when I think about how my dream house went on the market and sold before I even knew it was available. When Sam and I got engaged, we moved into his house, since I was unemployed and living with my parents at the time. Don't get me wrong, we have a really great house. It's a ranch, with a big yard. And Sam let me do whatever I wanted with it when I moved in. I do love where we live, out in the middle of nowhere—but it's thirty minutes away from my family. One would think, as crazy as my family is, that I'd be perfectly fine living far enough away from them that they can't come over every five minutes and bring their crazy right to my front door. My over-protective father, who still hasn't adjusted to me being a grown woman with a husband and a baby on the way; my overbearing mother, who talks about sex more than any mother should; and my Aunt Bobbie, who used to be my Uncle Robert, and never leaves home without wearing a sparkling evening gown, a full face of makeup, and a wig, are entirely too much crazy for one family to handle. At least my older brother, Nicholas, and his wife, Casey, help to balance out the normal.

And while a year ago it might have been true that I'd want to be as far away from them as possible, now that Sam and I are about to have a baby, thirty minutes away seems like thirty hours. What if Sam's at work and there's an emergency? And he's a Marine—what if he gets deployed again? I'll be a half hour away from my support system.

"Maybe the new neighbors like to keep to themselves. I'm sure they're very nice people. They just moved in and they're already participating in the decorating contest. That's got to say something," Sam tells my dad, pulling me out of my thoughts.

"Yeah, it says they want a war with the official Halloween Decorator King."

"Dad, that's not a real title," I remind him.

"It's a real title if I say it's a real title!" he argues. "Obviously I need to up my game and prove to those yahoos that they can't beat me. Sam, make yourself useful. Go find me as many clown costumes as you can."

"Where, exactly, am I supposed to find clown costumes?" Sam asks as my father starts walking toward the garage, his current command center for all things Halloween decorations.

"YOU'RE A CLOWN WHO DEFILED MY DAUGHTER! GO LOOK IN YOUR OWN CLOSET!" Dad shouts back to him, over his shoulder.

With one last look at the house across the street, Sam grabs my hand and laces his fingers through mine. Staring straight ahead to avoid eye contact with any of the creepy, lifelike clowns, we make our way through the yard and up the porch steps, pausing in front of the door.

Sam lets go of my hand, rests his palms on my huge stomach, and smiles down at me.

"What are the odds our child will grow up to be completely normal and not at all batshit crazy?" he asks.

"Slim to none," I immediately reply, placing my hands on top of his, our smiles broadening when we feel a little kick from inside my belly.

"At least you're honest," Sam laughs.

"I'm always honest about the craziness of my family. Just remember, you signed up for this shit. You agreed to take me for better or for worse, in sickness and in health, and to protect me from clowns for the rest of your life."

"I don't remember the clown part of our vows," Sam muses.

"It's a recent addendum. So get your ass moving and get me the hell away from these things or I'll take you with me when I get on the bus to crazy town."

Two

Babies Do Not Go in Ovens

Sam

"Everyone, pay attention! I'm bringing this meeting to order, so shut the hell up!"

"Ch-ch-ch-ch-ch-ch, ah-ah-ah-ah-ah-ah." Noel is chanting the creepy theme music from *Friday the 13th* under her breath when her best friend, Scheva Oliver, yells at everyone.

Scheva and Noel were best friends in high school, but lost touch when Noel moved away from Ohio to live in Seattle. As soon as Noel moved back home, the Christmas she and I met, her friendship with Scheva picked up right where it left off, and the two became inseparable again. We introduced Scheva to my best friend, Alex Rose, last Valentine's Day, and what started off as a fling quickly turned into something more. After Scheva announced at Easter that she would be marrying Alex, Noel started humming "Here Comes the Bride" whenever Scheva entered the room. Now, as my wife has become increasingly more miserable and cranky during the last trimester of her pregnancy, and Scheva has turned into a bridezilla on crack, it's safer for everyone involved if Noel lets out her frustrations by channeling Michael Myers.

You know, singing his theme song instead of going on a murderous rampage.

I love my wife more than anything else in this world, but she's been scaring the shit out of me lately with her mood swings. No one will be happier than me when she finally gives birth. Don't tell her I said that, though, or she'll probably stab me in the throat while I sleep.

"I've called everyone here tonight so we can discuss, and make any final changes to, the outfits you'll be wearing next weekend. At my wedding. The moment I officially become a bride. The one day where everyone will be paying attention to me. And the last perfect, amazing day I'll ever have for the rest of my life," Scheva announces, tossing her long blond hair over one shoulder.

"Um, hello? Married to *this* guy for the rest of your life," Alex reminds her, pointing both his thumbs to his chest.

Noel likes to call Alex and me the yin and yang of hot guys. We're pretty much the same height and have the same muscular build thanks to the military, but where I have short dark hair, Alex's is short and blond. I still think I'm better looking than he is, and make sure to tell him that on a regular basis. Alex and I had similar childhoods. We both lost our parents at a young age and were tossed around the system until we turned eighteen, when we joined the Marines. Our similar lives forged a bond that I

can't break, no matter how much he irritates me sometimes. When I introduced Alex to Noel's family, they immediately welcomed him into the fold and made him one
of their own, much like they'd done with Scheva.

Even though Scheva's parents are alive, they've never
really given a shit about her. As soon as she turned eighteen and moved out, they started traveling the world and
forgot they had a daughter. Noel's family may be crazy,
but they've taken in all of us orphans and made us a part
of their family without a second thought.

"Yeah, yeah, whatever," Scheva sighs with a wave of
her hand. "Happily ever after and all that shit. But I've
been dreaming about being a bride all my life, and it's
almost over. I'll never have anything to look forward to
ever again."

"Boy, marriage is going to be fun!" Alex replies sarcastically, which earns him a glare from his bride-to-be.

"Marriage is hard work," Bev, Noel's mother, announces from the other side of the room, where she is busily rearranging the orange pumpkin lights hanging across
the fireplace mantel. "I hope your ups and downs are only
in the bedroom."

"Ew, gross," Noel whispers, her lips curling in disgust.

"Get it? Ups and downs in the bedroom? Because
when you're having sex your bodies move—"

"Oh my God, Mom, we get it. Stop. Don't make me
throw up my dinner," Noel complains.

"There's nothing wrong with a healthy sex life, Noel.
How many times do we need to have this discussion? If
your father weren't such a tiger in bed, I would have
divorced him a long time ago. And he found this new
website called Tumbles where he's gotten a lot of new
moves. Have you heard of this Tumbles thing?" Bev

lights a votive candle and walks over to the coffee table in front of us, sticking it inside a small, carved pumpkin in the middle of the table. "You should try it."

"Bev, my love, it's called Tumblr, not Tumbles. And now you just ruined my favorite website, picturing you and Reggie looking at porn before you get your nasty on." Noel's Aunt Bobbie tosses back her third martini, the short blond wig she's wearing going all askew when she whips her head back to finish the drink. "Sam, come over here and comfort me," she continues. "Let me fondle your pumpkins."

Noel's Aunt Bobbie was her Uncle Robert until his wife left him when she caught him trying on her clothes, and he realized he was much happier being a woman. When I first met Aunt Bobbie, she reached out and grabbed my dick instead of shaking my hand. She toned down her flirting and sexual innuendos with me when Noel and I got married, but obviously this wedding is stressing everyone out lately.

"I'm not wearing what you picked out for me," Noel suddenly says to Scheva with a huff, crossing her arms and pouting.

"What are you doing? Do you want to get us all killed?!" Alex whispers, staring at her with wide eyes.

"It's a Halloween wedding, and you're wearing a costume," Scheva growls.

"You said this was a meeting to discuss any final changes to the outfits. Well, I'm making a final change. I'm NOT wearing the costume you picked out for me," Noel argues.

"You will wear it and you will like it!"

"You made me a cardboard box you expect me to wear, painted like an oven, with a picture of a baby inside that

rests right over my stomach. YOU'RE COOKING A
BABY!" Noel screams.

"IT'S A BUN IN THE OVEN, AND IT'S CUTE!"

"IT'S NOT A BUN IN THE OVEN. IT'S AN ACTUAL
BABY IN THE OVEN. BABIES DO NOT GO IN OV-
ENS!"

"DON'T PISS ME OFF OR I'LL MAKE YOU WEAR
THAT FLUORESCENT-GREEN TAFFETA MATER-
NITY PROM DRESS WITH THE GIANT PUFFY
SLEEVES I FOUND AT GOODWILL!"

"You wouldn't!" Noel fires back, attempting to push
herself up from the couch, her belly getting in the way
and making her fall back to the cushions five times. I sit
next to her and do nothing but watch.

I could be a gentleman and help her up from the couch,
but then I'd just be convicted of aiding and abetting when
Noel finally gets to her feet, charges Scheva, and chokes
her to death.

Noel finally manages to push herself up from the couch
and waddles over to Scheva, getting right in her face.

"I'm NOT dressing up as an oven."

"Yes, you are. I already bought Sam's chef costume so
you two match, and it's too late to change the entire theme
of your matching costumes," Scheva argues.

"I'm dressing up as a slutty witch, or a slutty kitten,
or a slutty devil, just like I do every year, and you're not
going to stop me!"

"This is so hot," Alex whispers as he watches our
women scream at each other from his spot next to me,
perched on the edge of the couch.

"That's my pregnant *wife* you're talking about."

Alex shrugs. "Yeah, so? Pregnant porn is hot. Don't
tell me you've never watched it."

"You're disgusting."

"Thank you," he replies with a smile.

"ALL RIGHT! THAT'S ENOUGH!" Reggie bellows, walking into the living room and handing a fresh martini to Aunt Bobbie before cracking open the can of beer in his other hand. "Noel has already ruined our family name by not decorating for the holidays over the last year, I don't need the neighbors gossiping more about us because they can hear you two screaming about cooking babies and slutty kittens."

He turns his angry look in my direction, and I cower back into the seat cushions. Reggie blames me for Noel's refusal to decorate the outside of our house for any holidays since last Halloween. No one in this neighborhood would even know or care that we haven't decorated, since we live thirty minutes away, but that doesn't matter to Reggie. Noel became a little superstitious when every holiday we spent together after we first met turned disastrous.

We met in an airport bar a few days before Christmas, and she convinced me to come home with her and pretend to be the boyfriend she'd recently broken up with after he proposed to her. But I got shot with a BB gun when we toured the house from *A Christmas Story*, and Aunt Bobbie was so high on drugs, she was convinced she saw a squirrel wearing a sweater.

Then you have our first Valentine's Day, when Bev brought home a stripper named Pinky to live with them, and everyone thought Pinky swallowed Noel's engagement ring and they'd have to wait for her to shit it out to get it back. Not to mention Aunt Bobbie accidentally giving Noel Ecstasy instead of Xanax before a big job interview, which resulted in Noel attempting to strip and dance in the office of her interviewer.

And there was our first Fourth of July, our wedding

day, where we were stalked by a half-dead, pissed-off zombie cat named Turd Ferguson, a few stray fireworks almost burnt my dick off, and Noel's wedding dress went up in flames like a barn full of dry hay.

To say we've had some very eventful holidays is putting it mildly. Noel decided, starting last Halloween, that we would do whatever we could to ignore the holidays in the hopes that this would eventually bring us good luck. It seemed to work, too, until this past Easter, when Noel found out she was pregnant and tried to surprise me with notes hidden in Easter eggs. But her drunk Aunt Bobbie and even drunker best friend, Scheva, found the notes and switched them, and her sweet way of announcing the news turned into the most awkward conversation about anal sex that anyone has ever had.

"Dad, I told you why I haven't decorated for the holidays, give it a rest," Noel says with a sigh.

"And look what happened! You got knocked up and now you have to dress up like an oven," Reggie grumbles.

"Pretty sure that's not what caused my pregnancy."

"IT WAS AN IMMACULATE CONCEPTION!" Reggie shouts.

"Can we please bring this back around to the wedding? MY wedding? The happiest day of my life, and the day all of you people will do exactly as you're told and wear exactly what I've picked out for you?" Scheva interrupts. "Sam will be dressing as a chef, Noel will be dressing as a goddamn oven and will not bitch about it one more time, Aunt Bobbie will be dressing as Barbra Streisand—"

"I get to sing at the reception, right?" Aunt Bobbie interrupts. "I've been practicing 'You Don't Bring Me Flowers,' and the ladies from Drag Queen Bingo will be disappointed if I don't sing it."

Scheva continues without acknowledging Aunt Bobbie. "And Reggie and Bev will be dressed as a priest and a nun."

"How many fucks given? NUN!" Alex cheers with his fist in the air.

"Now, we only have a week left until the wedding. We have treat bags to make, pumpkins to carve, orange lights to string, and all of those god-awful clowns to remove from the front yard," Scheva tells us.

Just like Noel and me, Scheva and Alex have decided to have a small, intimate wedding in Bev and Reggie's backyard. Here's hoping *their* wedding doesn't end with a trip to the emergency room in the back of an ambulance and third-degree burns on anyone's junk.

"THOSE CLOWNS STAY!" Reggie yells. "I've already got a plan ready for the wedding day. As soon as you asked if you could have the wedding here, I started collecting used wedding dresses. All of the clowns will be dressed for the festivities, and my display will remain intact for the judging ceremony."

Yes, because nothing says "happy wedding day" like clowns dressed up as brides.

Noel stomps back over to the couch and flops down next to me. I wrap my arm around her shoulders and pull her against my side.

"You're going to be the sexiest oven anyone has ever seen," I whisper in her ear.

"Forget about cooking a baby. I'm going to chop off your balls and cook those instead."

Did I mention how happy I'll be when this Halloween wedding is over and our baby is finally out of my wife's body?

Three

Apple-Butter Lube

Noel

"I can't believe you're just now telling me this. Also, you're a dumbass."

I pause from grabbing a small pumpkin out of the bin in front of me to glare at Scheva.

"I'm not a dumbass. And I didn't want to bother you with it. You've got a lot going on right now," I explain, putting the pumpkin into the wagon next to me.

Scheva decided late last night that she didn't have enough small pumpkins for the table centerpieces at the wedding, and she sent out an S.O.S. text at midnight that we were all to meet her at our local pumpkin farm to stock up, first thing this morning.

While my mom and dad are busy in the field, picking out a few extra-large pumpkins for their front yard, and Alex and Sam are occupied in one of the old fields a few acres away, watching the pumpkin launcher shoot pumpkins, Scheva and I finally have some alone time in front of the main building, at the bins of small pie pumpkins.

"You can't possibly think Sam is cheating on you. Again. Didn't we already go through this before? And besides, he fears your father too much to ever cheat on you," Scheva reassures me.

"Fine, I don't think he's cheating on me, but he's definitely keeping something from me. He's been acting weird lately. And you know all that overtime he's been working? I went up to the base the other night to take him dinner, and the guard at the gate told me he left hours earlier." I grab another pumpkin from the bin and put it into the wagon, on top of the pile we've already accumulated.

"Aunt Bobbie has been acting weird lately too. Well, weirder than usual. Maybe she finally convinced him to start going to Drag Queen Bingo with her. I bet Sam makes a very lovely woman," Scheva says with a laugh.

She walks over to the wagon, picks up the handle, and starts pulling it toward the cashier at the side of the building. I follow along, walking next to her.

"It's probably just my hormones making me crazy, right? I mean, maybe the guard was wrong and Sam really was there."

"Did you ask Sam if the guard was wrong and he really was there?" Scheva asks, stopping by the cashier and pulling her wallet out of her purse.

"Of course I didn't ask Sam, are you insane?! I'm much happier thinking the worst so that when the truth finally does come out, I can be pleasantly surprised that all my fears were wrong, like a normal human being," I tell her.

"You mean like a neurotic human being."

"Same difference," I shrug.

"All right, someone needs to back up one of their vehicles to the front of the building and help me load my haul," Aunt Bobbie states, coming over to stand next to Scheva and me.

Aunt Bobbie disappeared as soon as we arrived to browse inside the pumpkin farm's store. They sell all sorts of homemade goodies, like apple and pumpkin pies, apple cider, and freshly made pumpkin donuts from their bakery.

Aunt Bobbie pulls a mason jar out of the purse hanging from her shoulder and holds it up for the cashier to see. It's got a pink label wrapped around the glass that says *Steph's Apple Butter.*

"What's the cinnamon content in this?" she asks.

"A very small amount. Just a dash, really. Enough for flavor," the woman replies with a smile.

"Excellent. Cinnamon burns. I know that from experience. A dash should be just fine. I'll take seventy-five jars," Aunt Bobbie informs her before shoving the jar back inside her purse.

The woman's mouth drops open in surprise.

"Aunt Bobbie, what in the hell do you need seventy-five jars of apple butter for?" Scheva asks, her nose scrunched up in confusion.

Aunt Bobbie laughs.

"You're right. What was I thinking? That's just crazy!"

The cashier's face relaxes until Aunt Bobbie continues.

"Make it a hundred. You can never have too much apple-butter lube."

Scheva quickly throws a wad of cash on the counter and thanks the cashier, both of us grabbing Aunt Bobbie's arm and pulling her away before the cashier passes out and our family gets kicked out of yet another public place.

"Hceeeey! I need to pay for my apple-butter lube!"

Aunt Bobbie protests loudly, causing a bunch of pumpkin-farm patrons to look in our direction.

"Oh, don't look at me like that, Suzie Stick-Up-Her-Ass!" she yells at a woman who has stopped in the middle of the walkway to gawk at us. "I bet your husband knows what's up with apple-butter lube."

The man standing next to the woman blushes and quickly looks away from us.

"Yeah, that's right. You've slathered some apple butter on your nether region before, admit it!"

Mom and Dad come walking up to us, each carrying a large pumpkin in their arms, as Scheva and I do our best to shush Aunt Bobbie and smile apologetically at the people watching this horrific scene unfold.

"Why is everyone staring at us?" Mom asks as she sets her pumpkin down by my feet.

"Oh, no big deal. Aunt Bobbie is just making sure we're never allowed to come within a hundred yards of this place," I mutter.

"Dammit, Bobbie! We're already not allowed to go to Target and Starbucks anymore. And we've been banned from two Home Depots because of that incident with the leaf blower," my dad complains.

"It's not my fault the worker didn't understand the sucking power of a machine he sells in his own store, Reggie. And it's also not my fault he allowed me to demonstrate using the crotch of his pants. How was I supposed to know there was an emergency kill switch that would have prevented his penis from being covered in so many popped blood vessels that the thing looked like a bloody nightmare? He should have known his product better," Aunt Bobbie protests.

"Taking a picture of it with your cell phone when the

ambulance arrived was also probably a bad idea," I remind her.

"I needed proof of the dangers of leaf blowers to send to corporate!" she says with a stomp of her foot.

"All right, as fun as all of this has been, we need to get these pumpkins home so the guys can start carving them," Scheva announces.

"I'm not leaving without my apple-butter lube," Aunt Bobbie pouts, crossing her arms over her chest.

"Ooooooh, you can use apple butter as lube? Reggie, maybe we should get a few cases," my mom muses, smiling at my father, who has moved a few feet away, looking anywhere but at our small group, pretending like he doesn't know us.

Scheva starts to drag her wagon of pumpkins toward the parking lot. Aunt Bobbie stomps away with her, and my mother continues trying to convince my dad they should stock up on apple butter. I send a quick text to Sam that we're getting ready to leave, and he replies immediately, telling me he loves me, and that he and Alex will meet us out by the cars.

Like always, I feel like an idiot for the thoughts I've been having about my husband. I'm sure he's just been acting more out of sorts than usual lately because he's anxious about the fact that we're about to become parents. My family provides enough insanity in our daily lives; I don't need to add to it by making up issues that aren't even there. I really do have the best husband in the world. If we weren't still getting dirty looks from half of the staff right now, I'd run inside and pick up a few jars of Steph's Apple Butter myself, for us. Maybe by the time Halloween rolls around next year, it will be safe to come back.

Four

It's So Tingly

Sam

A wad of pumpkin guts smacks me in the face, and I glare at Alex as he sets down his drill and stares at the pumpkin in front of him.

"Is it really necessary for you to use a power tool to carve these pumpkins?" I ask, swiping the globby mess off my cheek and flicking it onto my newspaper-covered kitchen table.

"I've already carved seventeen pumpkins, and you're only on your third. I'd say having a power tool is a necessity," he answers, standing back to look at his work.

"All you've done is drill a giant hole in the center of each one. At least I'm putting effort into mine and giving them faces," I reply, holding up the gap-toothed jack-o'-lantern I just finished.

"It's not a giant hole. It's a glory hole. I'm making

these pumpkins multifunctional for the male guests, since going to a wedding for a dude is hell on earth. They can enjoy the soft glow of the candle inside of it during dinner, or they can take one to the bathroom and have a little in-and-out fun. People will thank me."

Shaking my head at him, I walk over to the sink and start washing some of the goo off my hands.

"I'm pretty sure your bride-to-be will not be thanking you when you explain what you've done."

Alex tosses me a towel when I turn around, and I begin drying my hands as he starts loading the carved pumpkins into a few large plastic containers that we can pack into my truck and take over to Reggie and Bev's later.

"Speaking of thanking me, you didn't even give me any gratitude for the gift I brought you today," he complains.

"These pumpkins look dumb and ugly."

We both turn to look at Tia, the six-year-old girl sitting at my table, who stares with annoyance at the pumpkins Alex puts into the container.

"I'm supposed to thank you for volunteering us to babysit your neighbor's kid?" I whisper to Alex as I come up next to him.

"Children are a delight—especially you, Tia, isn't that right?" Alex asks her with a huge smile on his face.

Tia jumps down from my chair, walks up to Alex, and kicks him right in the shin.

"SON OF A FUCKING BITCH!" he shouts, bending at the waist and grabbing his leg.

"You said a bad word. I'm telling my mommy!" Tia scolds before storming out of the kitchen, her blond pigtails swishing back and forth as she goes.

"I SAID TWO BAD WORDS! AT LEAST I CAN COUNT!" Alex shouts after her.

"Real mature," I mutter with a shake of my head.

"Fine, not *all* children are a delight, but you should still be thanking me. Scheva told me that Noel thinks you've been acting weird lately, and that it might be because you're scared about your impending fatherhood," Alex explains as we start cleaning up the mess covering my kitchen table. "You can't tell me this wasn't a brilliant idea. It will give you a little practice on how to handle kids before the big day arrives, so you don't fuck everything up."

"Gee, thanks for the vote of confidence. And I'm not nervous about becoming a father. You know exactly why I've been acting weird lately, so babysitting duty wasn't necessary."

Alex is the only one who knows about the surprise I've been planning for Noel, and that I've been busting my ass to get it finished before she has the baby. I'm honestly surprised he hasn't let the cat out of the bag, considering this guy usually can't keep a secret to save his life.

"You do realize that once a certain someone finds out what you've done, you're probably going to have to change your name and enter the witness-protection program, right?" Alex asks as he rolls up the pumpkin-guts-filled newspaper and tosses it in the trash.

"It's not going to be that bad," I tell him, even though I know it is.

It's going to be bad. Horribly bad. I'm just hoping I'll be forgiven and they'll see how good this will be for everyone. Eventually. Like, maybe by the time our child goes to college.

"Where's Tia?" I ask suddenly, peeking out of the kitchen doorway and not seeing her in the living room.

"Probably running with scissors, watching porn on YouTube, and lighting things on fire. She'll be fine."

With a sigh, I leave Alex to finish cleaning up my

kitchen while I go in search of the little girl. I might not know a lot about kids, but I do know you should never leave them unattended for long periods of time, and that silence never equals anything good.

Luckily, my house isn't that big, and I find her in the master bathroom, right off my and Noel's bedroom.

"Oh, no," I mutter as soon as I walk in the room.

Tia looks up at me from where she's perched on the edge of the tub, and her eyes immediately fill with tears. I rush to her side and squat down next to her.

"I mean, oh no, I can't believe you're having fun without me!" I lie.

She smiles up at me and finishes squirting the last of an entire bottle of shampoo into the tub before standing up and pointing at it.

"Get in."

I stare at her in confusion.

"Um, what?"

She sighs heavily.

"I said, get in. Take a bath."

Glancing down into the tub, I wince at the mountain of goop that she's dumped into the Jacuzzi tub, several sections of it starting to bubble and hiss. I've never seen shampoo do something like this, and it makes me a little nervous thinking about everything she could have dumped in there along with the hair-cleaning product.

"I don't think—"

"GET IN THE TUB RIGHT NOW!" she screams, with a stomp of her foot.

"Okay, okay, I'm going!" I quickly reply, hopping over the edge of the tub, my feet sinking into the mess, which squeezes between my toes. The feeling makes me want to throw up in my mouth a little. "See? Look at me in the tub! Wheeeeee, this is fun!"

I stomp around a little as she watches me. When I start to climb back out, she blocks my way, her hands on her hips.

"Sit down. Take a *real* bath or I'll tell Mommy you said bad words."

"I didn't say bad words, your neighbor Alex said bad words!" I complain, throwing him under the bus and cursing him under my breath for putting me in this situation.

Her eyes start to fill with tears again, and this time, her lower lip starts to quiver.

Fucking lip quiver. How am I supposed to ignore a lip quiver?

With a sigh, I slowly sink down into the tub, regretting the action as soon as my ass gets swallowed up by the mess.

"Doesn't it feel good?" Tia asks with a smile.

"Yep! It feels great! Really tingly. What exactly did you put in my bath, sweetheart?" I ask as nicely as possible, clenching my teeth to stop myself from screaming.

Tia walks over to the cabinet under the sink and starts pulling out empty bottles and tossing them onto the floor next to the tub. Shampoo, conditioner, shaving cream, bleach, peroxide . . . *well, that explains the tingling.*

She continues throwing out bottles and I quickly realize that maybe I *do* need a crash course in parenting. Obviously children shouldn't have access to any of these products. And obviously I'm paying for my mistake, because the tingling has now turned to full-on burning, which means it's definitely time to panic.

"Tia, honey, I need you to call nine-one-one," I tell her as calmly as possible while my balls feel like they are being lit on fire.

"NINE-ONE-ONE!" Tia screams at the top of her lungs.

"NOT OUT LOUD, ON THE PHONE!" I scream back, forgetting all about how I shouldn't freak out in front of her and scare her, even though my balls feel like they are melting right from my body.

"MOMMY SAYS I'M NOT ALLOWED TO USE THE PHONE, DUMMY!" Tia argues, rolling her eyes at me like I'm an idiot.

"What is all the screaming about?" Alex asks, poking his head in the bathroom door. "Dude, are you bathing in front of my neighbor? I think that's rule number one for Things You Shouldn't Do in Front of Kids. And you thought you didn't need to learn how to be a parent."

Alex moves into the bathroom and scoops Tia up in his arms.

"How about we go into the living room and I put on *It's the Great Pumpkin, Charlie Brown* so Sam can finish whatever kinky thing he's doing on his own?"

"What's kinky mean?" Tia asks him as he carries her out of the room.

"I'll get back to you on that when you're eighteen."

As soon as they're gone, I quickly stand up, pull the plug, and turn on the shower, not even bothering to remove my clothes as I scrub the toxic shit off of me.

It takes thirty minutes and three showers for my balls to finally stop burning, but at least that gives me something to worry about other than the surprise I've been planning for Noel.

Five

The Baby Knows

Noel

Have you ever been in the middle of having sex with someone and found you can't stop your mind from wandering?

Did I remember to pay the electric bill?

Are we almost out of milk?

Did I call my mother back when she left me a voice mail?

Is Sam not making any noise because I've crushed him with my giant belly?

Not that I'm doing any of those things right now, seated on top of my husband in our bed while he thrusts his hips up. My husband is gorgeous, and he's the best sex I've ever had, but I'm too big and irritable and scatterbrained to even pretend I'm enjoying it.

"All right, spit it out," Sam says softly when he stops

moving, sliding his hands up my bare thighs and resting them on my hips.

"That's not what you said last night," I joke, trying to lighten the mood instead of bringing it down with my insecurities and crazy brain.

"Ha ha," he deadpans. "Come on, I know something is bothering you. Do we need to have another intervention, where I tell you all the ways your pregnant body is beautiful and how I still think you're sexy?"

He helps me lift myself up and off of him, and I lay down on my back next to him, staring up at the ceiling. Sam turns on his side, propping himself on one elbow and supporting his head in one hand while the other rests on my stomach. He stares down at me.

"No, I don't need another pregnancy intervention. I'm sorry, my head is just all over the place right now."

"The baby cannot see my penis coming toward its face, we already Googled that shit and found out it isn't true," Sam reminds me.

"It's not that either. But did you know the baby can feel my orgasm? It's like a sense of euphoria for them. That's weird. Our baby is having orgasms in the womb. Our baby is having orgasms before it can walk or talk. Isn't that weird? Doesn't that creep you out?"

This is not at all the thought that was running through my head, but I don't want my husband to know I feel gross and ugly, because he'll just think I'm being silly.

"It didn't five seconds ago, but thanks for giving me *that* image right before I go to sleep," Sam complains.

"I'm sorry," I apologize again, turning on my side and resting my hand on his chest. "I think I'm just feeling a little off because it's almost Halloween and we don't have one decoration up. I know, I know, it was all my idea last year, but this is my favorite holiday. And we don't have one pumpkin or any corn stalks on the front porch. And it still kind of sucks that we don't get any trick-or-treaters living way out here in the boonies."

"Honey, we can do whatever you want. If you want to make Halloween throw up all over this house, we'll do it. And we always go to your parents' house for trick-or-treaters anyway, so it doesn't even matter that we don't get any kids here," Sam reminds me.

He's right, and I don't know why I'm being all emo about this all of a sudden. My parents' street, aside from having a Halloween decorating contest, goes all out on Halloween night. Everyone sets up tables and chairs and fire pits in their driveways, and the neighbors spend the night going from house to house, voting on which house has the best decorations, sharing food and drinks everyone has set out, and having a fun time hanging out in between passing out candy to all the kids.

It's probably because of that stupid house across the street from my parents. Knowing someone else is living there and will get to enjoy the fun that is Halloween night right in their own front yard is depressing. But Sam's right. We go there every year, and this year will be no different, even though it will be the day after Alex and Scheva's wedding, and a week before I'm due to give birth.

I stare at Sam's face and for the first time see just how exhausted he looks. He's been working a ton of overtime lately, leaving the house before the sun comes up and coming home long after it's gone down most nights. I feel bad that I'm making *him* feel bad about where we live. This is a great house to raise a baby, and I'm just going to have to deal with the fact that we're thirty minutes away from my family and I'll always have to go there if I want to enjoy the fun of trick-or-treat night.

"First thing tomorrow, I'll go out and get us a bunch of

pumpkins to carve and corn stalks to put on the front porch. And before I leave, I'll bring all of your boxes full of Halloween decorations down from the attic so you can go crazy around this place. Sound good?" Sam asks.

Giving him a smile, I push myself up, and with a few grunts and sighs and a lot of effort, I climb back onto his lap and rock my hips against him until I feel him start to grow hard again between my thighs.

"Have I told you lately how much I love you?" I ask, lifting my body a few inches so Sam can reach between us and line himself up.

I sink down on him and we both groan.

"Yes, but I don't mind you telling me again," Sam mutters, his eyes fluttering closed as I swivel my hips and he jerks his up to meet me. "Oh, shit. Do that again."

I do as he asks, wishing my huge belly weren't in the way so I could look down and see him moving inside me.

Right when my mind finally clears of all the nonsense and I can feel my release start to creep up on me, the baby kicks, and my body jerks to a halt.

"What's wrong? What happened? Are you okay?" Sam asks, his eyes flying open as he looks up at me with worry.

"The baby kicked," I whisper.

"Um, okay?"

"The baby knows I was almost ready to have an orgasm," I whisper again.

"The baby does *not* know you were almost ready to have an orgasm," Sam says with a sigh.

"The baby knows. I can't be responsible for my baby learning about orgasms when it can't even speak to tell me to stop talking about orgasms," I complain.

"It's like you want me to throw up in my mouth right now," Sam mutters.

"I'm sorry. I'll make it up to you. When this baby is out of me and is nowhere near my orgasms, everything will be fine."

"You can make it up to me right now. Let me do that thing," he demands.

Sam gently lifts me off his body again, moving out from under me and sitting up in bed next to me as I grunt and huff and position myself until my back is leaning up against the headboard.

"No. Absolutely not. I told you to never ask me if you could do that again. That was NOT fun for me, nor was it a pleasurable experience," I remind him, crossing my arms in front of me and resting them on my huge belly.

"I'll go slower this time. I promise you'll like it."

"You said that last time, and it ended in me crying and having to take five showers," I argue.

His mouth turns into a pout, and he bats his eyelashes at me.

"Please, Noel? Pretty please? I promise I'll never ask you to do this again. I know it's more fun for me than it is for you, but I'll be quick. It will be over before you know it," he begs.

Considering I just ruined his evening, I have no choice but to give in.

Sam lets out a whoop of excitement and scrambles off the bed to grab all of the necessary supplies.

True to his word, he's quick and it's over before I know it. There are no screams of protest or crying from me this time, just a look of complete annoyance that I don't even bother hiding from my husband.

"Okay, all finished. Shit, baby. You're so cute. I don't know why you won't let me take a picture. Your mother would love this."

Lifting my head from the pillows where I scooted down to let him do his thing, I stare at my huge belly, now completely covered in orange paint, with a jack-o'-lantern face drawn on with black paint.

"Stop giving me that look. You're adorable. This is what happens when you're going to have a baby right after Halloween, so deal with it. This is all I have to live for right now. Don't ruin it," Sam scolds, unable to keep the stern look on his face, his dimples popping out as he stares at the masterpiece he just painted on my stomach.

I know I should probably think this is cute, but it just makes me feel even more unattractive, knowing my stomach resembles a giant, plump pumpkin.

"Fuck it. I'm taking a picture," Sam mutters, reaching over to grab his cell phone from his nightstand.

"I will shove that thing up your ass if you take a picture of my stomach right now," I threaten.

"Too late," Sam says with a smile, pressing a couple of buttons on his phone until I hear a *whoosh* sound, letting me know he just sent the damn thing to God knows how many people.

Instead of throwing a fit, I get up out of bed and head to the shower, quietly plotting his death as I turn on the water and let it warm up.

"Ch-ch-ch-ch-ch-ch, ah-ah-ah-ah-ah-ah," I start chanting.

"I HEARD THAT!" Sam shouts from the other side of the door. "STOP DOING THAT. IT'S FREAKING ME THE FUCK OUT!"

With a laugh, I get into the shower and start scrubbing the damn pumpkin off my stomach, looking forward to getting into the Halloween spirit tomorrow and forgetting all about my stupid superstition. Alex and Scheva are going to have a fun, awesome wedding, we're going to hang out at my parents' house for trick-or-treat and have an amazing time, and Sam and I will celebrate another holiday without any mishaps. I can feel it.

Six

Phteven

Sam

"Sorry! I know I'm late, just give me two seconds to wash up really quick and then we can go," I tell Noel as I rush into the kitchen where she's seated at the table with her laptop in front of her.

She tips her head up and smiles at me as I lean down and give her a quick kiss on the lips.

"It's fine. I'm just trying to finish up some work."

I pause for a minute to stare at her as she fiddles around on her computer. She looks exhausted, and I feel like the biggest ass in the world for being away from her so much lately and for keeping a secret from her. I hate that she thinks I've been working all this overtime lately and feels bad for me whenever I tell her I'm tired. I'm deceiving my wife, and right now, it doesn't make me feel good.

"Is that a beaver?" I ask, leaning down closer to look at her laptop screen.

"It's a wombat. And yes, I Photoshopped a wombat, the ShamWow guy, and the Virgin Mary into our family's Christmas picture from last year. Don't judge me. I'm trying to get my creative juices flowing so I can get as much work done as I can before I go on maternity leave," she tells me.

Noel got a job working for Seduction and Snacks two years ago on Valentine's Day. It's a huge company with chains all over the U.S. One side sells sex toys, and the other side is a bakery. They hired Noel to design inappropriate greeting cards for their stores. The popularity of Noel's cards grew so quickly, the owners made her a partner last Easter, changed the name of the store to Seduction and Snacks and Salutations, and let her add whatever she wanted to the line, like T-shirts, pens, notepads, and a bunch of other shit, all with inappropriate sayings on them.

"What is all that stuff?" Noel asks, looking away from her laptop and noticing the two huge duffel bags I brought home from work.

"Don't ask. Your dad called me earlier in a panic, asking me to bring a bunch of stuff home for him. He's taking this Halloween-decorating contest to an extreme level," I tell her.

"If he doesn't win that thing this year, we're all going to suffer, Sam."

I swallow past the lump in my throat and let out a nervous, high-pitched laugh.

"Why wouldn't he win? He's totally going to win. Everyone knows he's going to win. He wins every year. Why would this year be any different? He's going to win. Should we update our passports just in case? I've heard Belize is a nice place to live," I ramble.

Noel stares at me, her brow furrowed questioningly.

"Are you okay? If you don't want to go to my parents' house to help put together the treat bags, I can call my mom and make something up."

I laugh again, all weird and girly, wondering why in the hell I can't just laugh like a fucking man when I'm nervous and hiding something from my wife.

"I'm fine! Excellent. Everything is good. Give me five minutes to jump in the shower and then we can go."

Giving Noel a kiss on the top of her head, I leave her to her wombats and ShamWow guy and head to the bathroom, hoping she's not getting suspicious and that my surprise will still be a surprise, even though now I'm starting to worry that once everyone finds out what I've done, this family will go a hell of a lot more insane.

"Get your shit together, Sam! I thought you said you'd done this before. Stop acting like a pansy-ass little girl!" Reggie whisper-yells as our feet crunch through the leaves and we gingerly step over pumpkins and extension cords.

"I HAVE done this before. IN A FUCKING WAR ZONE, not for breaking and entering!" I whisper back angrily.

When Reggie called me at work earlier and told me to bring over night-vision goggles, tactical vests, camo face-paint sticks, a Ka-Bar knife, and combat helmets, I thought he needed these items for another asinine decorating idea for his front yard. I had no idea, when Noel and I got here for dinner and to help put together candy bags for wedding favors and trick-or-treat, that Reggie would drag me out to the garage, make me suit up, and threaten to cut off my balls if I didn't do exactly as he said.

"I still can't believe you didn't bring the rifles. The ONE thing I told you was most important, and you conveniently forgot them," he complains. I let out a groan when he kicks a jack-o'-lantern out of the way, caving in the front of the intricately carved thing.

"That took someone over two hours to carve, and you just ruined it!" I complain. "And I may be an idiot, but I'm not dumb enough to give you a loaded weapon."

Reggie crouches down behind a shrub, grabs my arm, and yanks me down next to him. Since the sun set over an hour ago, the neighborhood is shrouded in darkness, making me feel like I'm in the middle of a scary movie gone wrong, and that a deranged killer will any minute jump out from behind a nearby tree and try to kill us.

"You have no idea how long that ugly-ass thing took to carve. It looked stupid and I put it out of its misery."

"It was an exact replica of the DVD cover of *The Nightmare Before Christmas*. It was artistic and genius," I mutter like a petulant child.

"Do you need Midol? Are you on your man period? Quit your bitching and get your head in the game. We're here to see what kind of lowlife scum moved into this house and is trying to take my title away from me."

I can't believe this is what my life has become. I used to be a strong, badass Marine. Now I'm wearing tactical gear, my face is covered in camo paint, and I'm lurking in shrubbery with my insane father-in-law, hoping none of the neighbors catch us and call the cops.

"Obviously these people aren't lowlife scum. Lowlife scum wouldn't decorate for Halloween with such attention to detail and fantastically lifelike figurines."

Reggie glares at me over his shoulder before shuffling away from me in a crouched position.

"What are you doing?! Get back here!" I whisper

loudly as Reggie walks right through the landscaping on the side of the house and up to one of the windows.

I have no choice but to follow him, studying my surroundings as I look for neighbors out on evening walks, or cops driving by to make sure a crazy man wearing a tactical vest over his wife's pink, frilly bathrobe isn't attempting to break into a house.

When I make it up to Reggie, the orange glow of the lights strung around the frame of the window highlights his face, giving his profile a creepy look. He cups his hands around his eyes and leans forward, pressing them against the window.

"There isn't even any furniture in there. They've owned this house for a month and there's no furniture. I bet they're serial killers and they're using this house to dismember the bodies in the basement," Reggie mutters.

"Yes, because serial killers always get into the Halloween-decorating spirit," I reply sarcastically.

"I bet they roofie their victims at a local bar; put them in the back of a white, nondescript van with dirty windows that someone wrote the word *penis* on; pull into the garage and close the door; drag the unconscious body inside and down into the basement; and put it onto a metal hospital table. Then they put on white butchering aprons and, using a knife from Paula Deen's Walmart collection, chop up the body, starting with the fingers and finishing with the ears. Then they store everything in Halloween-themed Ziploc bags in seven chest freezers," Reggie says.

"That was strangely specific . . . and horrifying."

"I've had a lot of time to think about this," he replies.

"Clearly. Can we go back across the street now? I'd much rather watch Aunt Bobbie get drunk and try to put pot cookies into the kids' treat bags than have to explain to the police that you're not a sociopath who dreams about how his neighbors chop up people and put them in baggies with pumpkins and ghosts on them."

Reggie sighs and finally pulls his face away from the window.

"Fine. We'll go home for now, but this isn't over," Reggie complains as we sneak back through the obstacle course of the front yard, dodging pumpkins and other decorations as we go. "These people have declared war. If a war is what they want, a war is what they'll get. Everyone on this street loves me and my Halloween decorations. I'm not going to let some serial killers ruin my life's work."

"You mean everyone but Susan, who called Bev today and told her that her son had a clown nightmare last night," I remind him.

Noel called me at work right after Bev called *her* to tell her about Susan, because Noel likes to bring me down to her level of misery whenever she has to deal with either one of her parents.

"I can't help it if her son is a sissy. He'll have a lot more to cry about when he finds out he's living down the street from people who will kidnap him and cut off his fingers."

"Jesus Christ," I mutter as we cross the street and make our way up to the porch. "Never, ever say that out loud again. I don't have enough money saved for your bail or to hire a reputable defense attorney."

As soon as we walk in the front door, Noel comes into the front hallway from the living room, stopping in her tracks when she sees her father and me.

"Do I even want to ask?"

I shake my head. "Definitely not."

"You married a dipshit, Noel. He wouldn't even let me carry a rifle," Reggie complains.

"Noel, we need more Snickers for the—"

Bev joins us in the hall and stops next to my wife, her words cutting off as soon as she looks up.

"It's not what it looks like," I tell her.

I have no idea why I said that. It's exactly what it looks like. It looks like we just put on tactical gear and face paint and went creeping through the neighbor's yard.

"Oh, Sam, you don't have to be embarrassed. It's about time Reggie told you how he likes to dress up as G.I. Joe when we role play." She smiles at me before turning toward her husband. "Honey, did you tell him about how you make me pretend to be your commanding officer and I get to yell at you and give you orders?"

Reggie groans, Noel grimaces, and I try my hardest not to run screaming back out the front door.

"He likes it when I make him bark," Bev whispers conspiratorially, giving me a wink.

"Jesus, Beverly! Is nothing sacred in this house?" Reggie complains.

Just then, the front door opens behind us, and we all turn to see Aunt Bobbie stumble in with an ungodly amount of makeup smudged all over her face and wiped off in random places on the sparkly black dress she's wearing. It's only eight o'clock and she already looks like she's been on an all-night bender.

"Bobbie, what in the world happened to you?" Bev asks, rushing to her side to help her stand.

"It was a rough night at Drag Queen Bingo. I don't remember much about what happened after the fifteenth round," she tells us.

"The fifteenth round of bingo or of drinks?" Noel questions.

"Bacon!" Aunt Bobbie answers.

"Reggie, go make Bobbie some coffee. Sweetie, are

you going to feel up to helping with the treat bags tonight?" Bev asks her softly.

"PHTEVEN!" Aunt Bobbie shouts as Bev wraps her arm around her waist and helps her walk down the hall and into the living room, moving around the shit-tons of Kit Kats, Reese's Peanut Butter Cups, Twix bars, Heath bars, bubble gum, and Blow Pops. She deposits Aunt Bobbie onto the couch.

"What's a phteven? Aunt Bobbie, are you having a brain aneurysm? Do you need medical attention?" Bev asks, bending down to stare into Aunt Bobbie's glassy, unfocused eyes.

"It's Steven with a PH! BACON!" Aunt Bobbie shouts.

"Sweet Jesus, she looks like a clown that just woke up after a gang bang," Scheva states, looking up from her spot on the floor, where she's already started assembling bags.

"In local news tonight, there have been several recent sightings of an individual dressed up as a clown, wandering neighborhoods and frightening people. The police have yet to ascertain if this person is just having some good old Halloween fun or is a genuine threat to the community. Please stay vigilant, and if you see anyone dressed up as a clown, call the local police. Back to you, Richard."

We're all staring at the television in the corner of the room with our mouths wide open when Reggie walks in with a steaming mug of coffee in his hand.

"See, Dad? I told you clowns were evil!" Noel reminds him.

"Are you talking about that stupid news report they've been running all night? Poppycock. Bunch of horseshit, if you ask me. People getting scared over clowns . . . Clowns bring joy and laughter into people's lives. What is this world coming to when people are afraid of something like that? It's going to hell in a handbasket, that's what's happening," Reggie complains.

He hands Aunt Bobbie the coffee, pushing it up to her mouth and forcing her to drink it as the rest of us stare out the front window, wondering how the hell we'll be able to tell a real killer clown from the clowns all over the damn front yard.

Seven
Smell These Pills

Noel

I'm setting a small, carved pumpkin in the middle of a table when a Braxton Hicks contraction hits me. I grab my stomach and focus on my breathing.

"You okay?"

I nod at Scheva as she walks over, taking a few deep breaths until the tightness in my belly finally goes away.

"I'm fine. Just getting these stupid things more and more lately," I tell her, glancing around the yard and changing the subject. "This place looks amazing. We did a pretty awesome job."

Scheva smiles in agreement as we take in the transformation of my parents' backyard. Since Scheva's parents suck and couldn't be bothered to come home from their vacation in Barbados for the wedding, naturally my parents immediately agreed to have the wedding here.

Scheva and Alex rented the same giant white tent that Sam and I used for our wedding. Underneath it is a bunch of round tables with dark brown tablecloths. In the center of each tablecloth is a cluster of fake leaves in every fall color, and nestled on those are jack-o'-lanterns containing candles we'll light right before the guests arrive, in two days. We decided to set everything up today, instead of tomorrow, so we won't be exhausted rushing around the day before the wedding, scrambling to get everything ready.

My dad, Alex, and Sam strung orange lights all around the ceiling of the tent, and bows made from orange and brown plaid fabric are tied around the backs of all the chairs. My mom and Aunt Bobbie are currently sticking black wrought-iron stakes into the ground all around the outer edge of the tent. The stakes are topped with small orange-glass pumpkins, which will also hold lit candles.

It's beautiful and not over-the-top crazy with decorations, like I initially imagined it would be when Scheva announced she wanted a Halloween wedding.

"Honey, are you okay? You look a little pale," my mom states as she walks up next to us with a box of treat bags for us to start putting at every place setting.

"Just some Braxton Hicks contractions, I'm fine."

I'm exhausted is what I am. Sam, true to his word, brought out all of my Halloween decorations the other day, and I immediately went to work putting out pumpkins and ghosts, hanging leaf garlands from every doorway, and stringing orange and purple lights wherever I could find room. And now I've been here all day, helping Scheva get ready for her wedding when what I really want to do is take a nap with a giant container of cookie-dough ice cream.

Mom sets the box down on the table in front of us and gives me a stern look.

"You should be taking it easy. Didn't you learn anything in that *What to Expect When You're Expecting* book I gave you at the start of your pregnancy?"

"Yes. I learned not to jump on a trampoline, smoke meth, or handle a firearm while pregnant," I deadpan.

"All excellent suggestions," Scheva muses.

"Did you read the chapter about having more sex to induce labor? Are you and Sam having enough sex? Your father and I did it at least three times a day when I was pregnant with you. This one time he even used a spatula to—"

I hold up my hand to stop her from talking, her eyes— the same bright green shade as mine—blinking in confusion when I cut her off. With her long red hair pulled back into a low bun that she doesn't even need to touch up with color to hide the grays, we could easily pass for sisters. The thought that my child will be blessed with good genes makes me smile to myself, before I realize I was getting ready to scold my mother and now is not the time for distractions.

"Mom, how many times do I have to tell you to stop telling me about your and Dad's sex life? A daughter does not need to know these things about her mother. Ever."

"Will you tell *your* daughter about these things?" she asks with an excited smile.

"Nice try. Not falling for it. We're not telling you what we're having because *we* don't even know what we're having," I remind her.

My mom has not been pleased that we haven't found out the sex of the baby. She insists we've been lying to her this whole time and really do know what we're having. I know it's unusual in this day and age not to find out, but there aren't that many surprises in life. Sam and I want to enjoy every minute of the day our child is born, including the moment when the doctor tells us what's been growing inside of me for the last nine months, wreaking havoc on my body and making me feel more psychotic than usual.

"Regardless, I think you should just have more sex with Sam. It will put some color back into your cheeks and remove that permanent scowl from your face," Mom informs me.

"It's called a resting bitch face, Bev," Scheva adds with a smile.

"Kiss my ass, fuck truck," I mutter, giving her the finger. "You try carrying around an extra thirty pounds of weight and feeling like you're sweating from every inch of your body. My thighs are sweating, my back is sweating, my pits are sweating, my vagina is sweating. . . . I'm sweating from places I didn't even know *could* sweat."

Scheva scrunches up her face in disgust.

"No thank you. You couldn't pay me enough to push a human out of my body and ruin my vagina forever. How does that thing even go back to normal after something like that? You know how? It doesn't. *Ever.* It's just a bunch of loose, flappy skin that gets in the way and scares penises," Scheva says, though she immediately clamps her mouth shut when she sees the look of horror on my face. "I mean, for other women," she continues. "Not you, obviously. You'll have the perfect birth, and the perfect vagina, and your life will be awesome!"

She holds up her palm for me to give her a high five, dropping it after a few seconds when I refuse to smack my hand with hers.

"Bobbie! What did you do to these treat bags?" Mom

suddenly yells as she busily paws through the box on the table.

Scheva and I move closer, peering into the box as Mom brings out one of the bags, digs around inside, and pulls out a handful of pills.

"Are these Xanax, Ecstasy, or pot pills? Noel, smell these and tell me what they are," she orders, sticking her hand up to my nose.

"That's not how you know the difference between pills, Mom. And how in the hell would I know the difference anyway?"

"Do you really want me to bring up the day you tried to take off your clothes during a job interview?" she asks.

"I WAS ROOFIED! THAT WASN'T MY FAULT!" I scream.

"And the time you ate a pot cookie and peed standing up?" she adds.

"I was using a she-funnel, and it was convenient and time-saving," I inform her. "Besides, that was the night I was drunk. The night I ate a pot cookie, Sam and I had sex on your washing machine, he found a pair of crotchless panties that were yours, and we both almost curled up in the fetal position and never had sex again."

My mom wipes an imaginary tear from her eye and smiles at me.

"You had sex on a washing machine? You really *are* my daughter. I was so proud, up until the crotchless panties part. They're very sexy and freeing. I'll buy you a pair." She drops the handful of pills into the box and grabs her phone from the table.

"Do *not* buy me a pair."

"I'm buying you a pair. I bet they have them on Amazon.

They have everything on Amazon. I got your dad assless chaps with two-day free shipping," she states.

"What's all the yelling about? You're killing my buzz," Aunt Bobbie complains, coming up next to us with a full martini glass in her hand.

"Bobbie, did you put pot pills in the treat bags for the guests?" Mom asks, setting down her phone and forgetting all about buying me crotchless panties, thank God.

"What the hell are pot pills? And no, I most certainly did not put anything like that into the treat bags," Bobbie replies, taking a sip of her drink.

Mom reaches back into the box and grabs the pills, holding them out for Aunt Bobbie to see.

"Oh, okay, yeah. I totally put those in there."

She leans down and sniffs the pills in the palm of my mom's hand.

"Yep, those are Ecstasy," Aunt Bobbie confirms.

"See! I knew you could smell the difference, Noel!" Mom scolds me.

"Seriously? *That's* what you're worried about right now? Aunt Bobbie tried to roofie an entire wedding!"

"And possibly the neighborhood. We might want to check on the treat bags we put aside for the kids. Also, I can't find the pot brownies I had in a Tupperware container in the fridge," Aunt Bobbie adds.

We all stare at her for a few seconds, none of us able to come up with anything to say that will make the situation any better.

"What?" she asks. "So a few kids get a little high. There are worse things that could happen, like a killer clown on the loose. Look at it this way: If he creeps in their bedroom window, they won't even care!"

With a groan, we all make our way up to the house,

each of us grabbing boxes of treat bags set aside for the guests. We now have to go through them all, as well as the more than three hundred trick-or-treat bags inside the house.

I take back everything I said about wanting to live closer to my parents. Whoever bought the house across the street can have it, along with my sympathies.

Eight
Butthole Meat

Sam

"That's it. The wedding is cancelled!" Alex announces, walking into the living room and throwing himself dramatically onto the couch as he stares at the cell phone in his hand.

Everyone stops picking pills, pot brownies, loose pennies, random pieces of Aunt Bobbie's makeup, and travel-sized bars of soap and shampoo out of the treat bags we have strewn all over the living room, and looks at Alex.

"The wedding is in two days. What are you talking about?" Scheva asks, pushing herself up from the floor, walking over to the couch, and snatching the phone out of his hand.

"If the wedding is cancelled, can I still keep the wedding dresses on all the clowns in the front yard? I even added veils to half of them. That was a lot of work and I'm not ruining it now," Reggie asks Bev.

"I can't possibly get married. My life has lost all meaning. My dreams have died," Alex complains, resting his elbows on his knees and dropping his head into his hands.

"Are you upset just because of this silly email?" Scheva asks, still staring at his phone.

Alex looks up and glares at her.

"It's not just ANY email. It's an email from Urban Dictionary. THE Urban Dictionary. The ruler of all things awesome on the internet. They killed my hopes and dreams, Scheva. Do you not understand the severity of this situation? How can I possibly be a good husband when I can't even be a good Urban Dictionary-er?" Alex asks.

"Is that even a word?"

"DON'T YOU JUDGE ME, SAM! DON'T JUDGE ME UNTIL YOU'VE WALKED A MILE IN MY SHOES OR RECEIVED A REJECTION EMAIL THAT HAS BROKEN YOUR HEART!" Alex shouts.

"So they rejected a word definition from you. It's not the end of the world," Noel informs him.

"I . . . you . . . how . . . SHITBALLS!" Alex yells, pointing his finger at her, unable to speak in any kind of coherent way.

"What is this Urban Dictionary thing? Is it filled with street slang? I've been trying to use the word *thug* more often in a sentence. I really think it's making a difference in my life," Bev tells us.

"It's the Holy Grail of everything, Beverly!" Alex states, throwing his hands in the air in frustration. "And they've denied me entry!"

"Oh my God," Scheva groans. "You seriously tried to submit the phrase *butthole meat* to them?"

"It's another word for poop, Scheva, and it's genius! Don't shit on my butthole meat!" Alex argues.

Noel and I both laugh, quickly hiding our amusement when Alex looks at us angrily.

"I even provided them with a definition and very well-thought-out sentence, just like they asked. *'Beth was mad when Chris left his butthole meat in the toilet.'* It was perfect and informative, and they denied my word!"

Scheva tosses Alex's phone onto the couch cushions next to him and walks back over to the rest of us, taking back her spot on the floor to resume combing through treat bags.

"You have exactly five minutes to mourn the loss of your exclusion from Urban Dictionary, and then you need to get your ass back to work. There are still pumpkins to carve and illegal narcotics to remove from treat bags," Scheva announces.

Alex gets up from the couch and stomps out of the room toward the kitchen, where a pile of pumpkins is waiting, along with stacks of newspapers to catch all the guts.

We all work quietly until someone rings the doorbell. Bev gets up to answer it, and a few minutes later walks in with Todd, one of the neighbors.

"Hi, everyone, sorry to interrupt," Todd tells us with a smile.

"Well, hello there, *Todd*," Reggie says, speaking the name with contempt as he stares at the man standing in the doorway of the living room.

I look at Reggie questioningly, and he leans closer to whisper in my ear.

"Todd lives on the other side of the serial killers. I asked him the other day if he'd seen anyone coming and going, maybe with a white van, but he claimed he hasn't seen anything. I know he's lying. I can see it in his eyes. They're all squirrely and shifty. Stupid Todd with the shifty eyes."

I look away from Reggie and the idiotic words coming out of his mouth to listen to Todd when he starts speaking.

"Just wanted to tell you folks that my wife saw that clown lurking around our house last night, the one they've been talking about on the news. I was at the store and she got spooked and called the cops. Thought I'd give you guys a heads-up in case they come over here and ask any questions. Damn things scare the hell out of me. Why anyone thinks clowns are funny is beyond me," Todd states.

"There is nothing wrong with red noses, polka-dot clothing, and big red shoes, *Todd*!" Reggie informs him angrily.

"Okay, well, thank you for letting us know," Bev interrupts, grabbing Todd's arm and pulling him out of the room. "We'll be sure to keep an eye out. Tell Linda to give me a call. Poor dear must be just beside herself."

"SISSY!" Reggie screams, just as Bev gets Todd to the door and practically shoves him out of it.

When Bev comes back into the room, Reggie is already up from the floor and stalking past her.

"Where are you going? We still have about a hundred more bags to go through." Bev asks him.

"I've got a twelve-foot-tall Ronald McDonald sculpture to finish painting. Then, I'm going to walk over to Todd and Linda's house and piss on their front lawn," Reggie informs her as he stomps down the hallway to the kitchen and the door leading out to the garage.

"My wedding is going to be ruined!" Scheva wails, burying her face in Noel's shoulder.

"Nonsense. Your wedding is not going to be ruined. There might be a clown burned in effigy on our front lawn, but your wedding will be fine," Bev reassures her. "If Sam and Noel can survive the disaster of their wedding day and live to tell the tale, you can survive clowns and Reggie angering all the neighbors. We'll just hire extra security. And maybe uninvite a few of the neighbors, just to be safe."

Scheva starts crying harder, and Noel pats her back soothingly.

"It's all fun and games until you buzzkills make me remove all the good stuff from the treat bags," Aunt Bobbie complains, sticking her hand into one of the bags and pulling something out. "Ooooooh, that's where my purple butt plug went! Sam, check the bags over by you. I'm still missing twenty Percocets, a sparkly necklace that says *whore* on it, and three sets of anal beads that glow in the dark. I don't want some kid to mistake those things for glow-stick necklaces. Talk about awkward."

I immediately drop the bag in my hand and push myself away from the bags all around my legs. Nothing says Halloween like getting three Snickers bars, a Kit Kat, and a set of used anal beads to wear around your neck.

Nine
Hung Stocking

Noel

"It's from the enemy and they're trying to get in our heads . . . weaken our defenses," my dad grumbles as we all get out of our cars and walk in small groups toward the festivities.

Instead of a typical rehearsal dinner, Scheva and Alex decided we should just spend the night before the wedding at our town's Halloween festival. It takes place at a local Metro Park, and there are food vendors, pumpkin-carving contests, face painting for the kids, and scary movies projected on a huge screen, with hay bales to sit on. The walking trail through the woods is all decked out for Halloween, with candlelit jack-o'-lanterns lighting the path and different scary movie displays throughout.

"Dad, you were *BOO-zed*. It's a Halloween tradition in a lot of neighborhoods. It's fun and it's sweet that your neighbors decided to start something like that this year. It's not some imaginary enemy trying to screw with you," I tell him with a sigh.

Earlier today, my mom found a basket on the front porch filled with bottles of vodka, tequila, whiskey, Fireball, two mason jars of homemade apple-pie moonshine, and four shot glasses with pumpkins painted on them. The basket included a note that read:

> *You've been BOO-ZED!*
> *The ghosts and goblins love to spy,*
> *They noticed your liquor cabinet has run dry!*
> *Enjoy these spirits just for you!*
> *Nothing says Halloween like a Witch's Brew!*
> *Make a copy of this and spread the good cheer soon,*
> *Within two nights in the light of the moon!*
> *Booze to you!*

Ever since my mom brought the basket into the house, my dad has been acting even crazier than normal. He checked the entire house for bugs, closed all the blinds and curtains, and wouldn't let anyone near the windows. He unplugged their landline house phone and made everyone stop talking and write what they needed to say on pads of paper.

"Noel, it says they've been spying on us! They admitted they're out to get me. Why would they do that? It's like some sort of reverse psychology, I know it. They want me scared. They want me off my game, but it's not going to work," Dad states as Sam comes up next to me and laces his fingers through mine.

"Are you still talking about that basket of booze?" Sam asks. "The apple-pie moonshine was the best I've ever had."

Dad glances over at Sam with wide eyes.

"They've gotten to you, haven't they? They've brought you over to the dark side. I always knew you'd betray this family."

"For the love of God, Dad . . ." I mutter with a roll of my eyes.

"Okay, fine. Maybe he didn't betray us. Maybe they poisoned him with that apple-pie moonshine crap. How are you feeling, Sam? A little woozy? Lightheaded? How many fingers am I holding up?" Dad asks, holding up three fingers.

Tugging Sam's hand, I lead him away from my dad before he can answer, walking us over to the booth that sells tickets for the hayride. With a quick head count, I tell the woman behind the counter how many we need, and Sam pulls out his wallet to pay.

By the time we make it across the parking lot to the tractor parked at the edge of the woods, climb aboard the wagon hitched to it, and take seats on hay bales, my dad has run out of steam and finally stopped bitching about Sam being poisoned and how he's going to take "the enemy" down.

One of the workers starts up the tractor, and we take off slowly, moving into another area of the woods, separate from the walking trail. This one is more kids-oriented and has nothing that will scare them. The tractor takes us through a five-acre pumpkin patch, filled with every light-up, blow-up Halloween decoration there is: pumpkins, ghosts, black cats, Frankensteins, and witches popping out of cauldrons. We count at least a hundred, and I can't help but smile at the excitement on the face of my two-year-old niece, Holly, as she points at every one of them with wide eyes and a squeal of happiness.

Placing my hands on my stomach, I give it a little rub,

imagining how much fun it's going to be when Sam and I have our own child, finally here with us, in our arms, to carry on these types of traditions.

"So, have you guys picked out names yet for your little bundle of joy?" Alex asks as we all hold on to the railing at our backs when the tractor takes a sharp turn.

"We've been tossing a few around, but we're not going to pick one until we meet the baby and see which one fits," Sam tells him.

"Obviously you're going to keep with the family tradition and pick a name that embraces your last name, right?" my mom asks.

Sam and I share a look, knowing we most certainly are NOT going to saddle our child with a dumb name like the ones my brother and I have. The main reason I hated Christmas until I met Sam was because my name was Noel Holiday, and it was definitely fate when I met Sam Stocking that day in the airport bar. He also despised the Christmas season because of his name. My brother, Nicholas, never shared my hatred, and when he was growing up, he thought it was the coolest thing ever when people referred to him as Saint Nick Holiday. Which is why he and Casey had no trouble naming their daughter Holly Holiday.

Luckily, having the last name of Stocking now, there isn't too much damage we could do picking out a name for our child, unless we named the baby something like Stinky Stocking.

Or Silk Stocking, Fishnet Stocking, Holey Stocking . . . shit. I guess there *is* a lot of damage we could do. Note to self: Don't let Sam make any name decisions when he's drunk and hanging out with my family.

"I'm partial to the name Hung. Hung Stocking has a nice ring to it. Perfect for a boy or a girl," Alex tells us.

"We're not naming our baby Hung," I reply with a heavy sigh.

"Fine. But you should at least pick something with a Halloween theme."

My mother nods, and everyone else silently agrees, including Scheva. The traitor. And then they all start throwing out ideas, each one more horrifying than the next, until no one is paying attention to the hayride or the Halloween decorations that we drive by.

"If it's a boy, you could name him Jack, middle name O'-Lantern."

"Noel's favorite movie is *The Nightmare Before Christmas*. If they're going to use Jack, his middle name obviously needs to be Skellington."

"Pumpkin is an adorable name for a girl. It should definitely be Pumpkin."

"What about Cock Goblin Stocking?"

"No, it should definitely be Blumpkin. Blumpkin Stocking," Alex adds.

"What in the world is a Blumpkin?" my mom questions.

"Blumpkin is the act of performing fellatio while the recipient is taking a dump," Alex informs us.

"That's the most disgusting thing I've ever heard," Scheva complains.

"That's Urban Dictionary, baby. Do you see the kind of amazingness I was denied? I was meant for that website. Born to be an Urban Dictionary king, and I've been denied my rightful place on the throne," he complains.

The hayride comes to an end with all the other families who were unfortunate enough to be on this thing with my family, giving us strange looks as they continue throwing out name ideas. As we get off the wagon and head over to check out the pumpkin-carving contest entries, I've finally had enough and hold up both of my hands.

"All right, that's enough. And while we're on this subject, can we also discuss how everyone needs to start toning down their language? This baby is due in a little over a week, and you all need to start learning how to not swear in front of it. And don't any of you say one word about how I've never mentioned this before. I'm pregnant and crabby and I can do what I want, including make spur-of-the-moment decisions about my child's future well-being," I tell them. "No more f-bombs, no more taking the Lord's name in vain, none of it."

"Why would we do that? That's dumb," Alex grumbles.

"Because you can't swear in front of the forking baby! This bullshirt stops now," I argue.

"We didn't have to do that when Holly was born, did we, sweetie?" my dad says, ruffling the hair on top of Holly's head as she walks next to him, holding my brother's hand.

"Where da fuck punkins go?" Holly asks, looking up at him with her sweet, innocent face.

"Okay, I see your point," Dad concedes, smiling down at his granddaughter. "Holly, we don't say that word. It's a bad word."

"Da fuck, da fuck, da fuck!" she chants excitedly, jumping up and down.

Dad bends down and scoops Holly up into his arms, walking away from us to try and explain to her again about words she can't use.

Sam stands behind me, sliding his arms around my waist and placing them on top of my belly as he pulls me back against him. He rests his chin on top of my head as we watch everyone slowly make their way down the rows of tables covered with carved pumpkins, filling out voting cards to choose their favorite ones.

"Are you sure you don't want to keep with your family's tradition and pick a holiday-themed name for our baby?" he asks quietly.

"Cock Goblin Stocking is growing on you, isn't it?" I joke.

I feel the rumble of Sam's laughter against my back, and I rest my hands on top of his over my belly.

"Not exactly, but I don't really want your family to disown me. They're certifiably insane, but I kind of like them."

Closing my eyes, I rest my head back against Sam's chest, wondering how in the hell I got so lucky to find a man like him. It takes a strong man to deal with my family and actually love them. I've never felt more lucky than I do right now that I convinced him to come home with me and pretend to be my boyfriend that Christmas almost three years ago.

I have a feeling this is going to be the best Halloween ever, and I can't wait to kick things off with Alex and Scheva's wedding tomorrow.

Ten

I'm in Mother-Forking Labor!

Sam

As we stand under the tent in Reggie and Bev's backyard, I smile to myself when Noel squeezes the life out of my hand for the hundredth time in the last fifteen minutes as we watch Alex and Scheva pledge their lives to each other. The bride and groom are standing under a wooden lattice arch completely covered in orange, red, and yellow mums. Noel and I stand off to their right, Noel unhappily wearing a giant cardboard box painted to look like an oven with a magazine photo cut-out of an actual baby cooking, visible through a window in the oven door. I'm in a chef's hat and apron. Of course, the happy couple is dressed as a bride and groom, while the rest of us look like we fell off the back of a Halloween costume truck. But since it's their day, I won't complain.

The weather couldn't be more perfect. The sun is

shining brightly, the temperature is in the low seventies, and all of the trees surrounding the backyard are filled with fall-colored leaves that haven't dropped to the ground yet, making the perfect backdrop for the Halloween-themed ceremony. Reggie and Bev sit in the front row, dressed as a priest and a nun, as they were instructed. And surprisingly, every single guest in attendance showed up wearing a costume. As I look out at the rows of chairs on either side of the aisle, I see everything from doctors and nurses to a guy in a red-and-white striped shirt and matching hat, dressed as Waldo (I'm pretty proud of myself for finding him immediately in the sea of people, I kick ass at *Where's Waldo*)—and even a giant plastic Mr. Peanut.

"It's so sweet you're getting emotional over their vows," I whisper out of the corner of my mouth, as we stand a few feet away from the happy couple. I shoot Noel a smile when she gives my hand another death-grip squeeze.

"I'm not emotional," she says in a low voice through clenched teeth. "How could anyone possibly be emotional with what they're saying?"

"I promise to never tell you I have a headache when you want sex, and I vow to always love you, even when you suggest we need to spice things up with a threesome."

Alex wipes a tear from his eye when Scheva finishes her vows. They quickly exchange rings, and the minister declares them husband and wife. Everyone seated stands up and starts to clap as Alex and Scheva lean in for a kiss, and I silently thank God they made it through their own wedding ceremony without any mishaps.

As soon as their lips touch, a shrill scream pierces the air and all eyes under the tent turn to see Aunt Bobbie racing up the center aisle. She's wearing a white, floor-length sparkly dress covered with red, yellow, green, and blue felt circles. The dress is skintight, making her run look more like a waddle. A short, curly, bright-red wig is askew on top of her head, and her normally pristine makeup is horrifying. Her red lipstick is way outside the lines and looks like she just drew a giant red circle around her mouth, and she covered every inch of her face with cakey white makeup that is half sweated off, half smeared, leaving some of her natural skin tone peeking through the white mess.

"What in the actual fork?" Noel mutters.

"Is she dressed like a drag clown? She was supposed to be Barbra Streisand!" Scheva complains.

"Oh my God. There are people chasing her," I mutter with a shake of my head when a large mob of angry people comes bursting into the tent, shouting and racing after Aunt Bobbie.

The assembled guests start tipping over chairs as they make a hasty exit out of the tent and away from whatever the hell is happening right now.

Aunt Bobbie flies the rest of the way down the aisle and takes cover behind us, ducking down and clinging to the back of my shirt.

The angry group of people comes to a stop right in front of Alex, Scheva, Noel, and me. Putting my hands up in the air in a sign of peace, I take a step forward to talk to them, with Aunt Bobbie still holding tight to me.

"This is private property, and we're in the middle of a wedding ceremony. I'm going to have to ask you people to kindly leave," I inform them.

"Um, Sam?" Noel whispers.

I start to look over at my wife when one of the men in front of the pack points behind me.

"We caught her red handed! She was doing it in broad daylight!" he shouts angrily.

"My daughter has been crying for three solid nights because of her!" someone else yells.

"Sam . . ." Noel says my name again, but I'm too busy trying to figure out what these people are doing here and how to stop any other disaster from ruining Alex and Scheva's wedding.

"What the hell are they talking about?" I ask Aunt Bobbie, turning my head to look back at her.

"So, it turns out, I'm the clown from the news. I wondered why I kept waking up every morning with white, cakey makeup all over my face and pillows. I should probably stop doing drugs," she whispers.

"See?! I told you clowns weren't bad! It's just Bobbie with a couple of screws loose," Reggie pipes up as he walks away from his chair in the front row to join us.

Noel's hand latches on to my arm and squeezes hard.

"Sam."

I figure she's probably just upset about the fact that her Aunt Bobbie has caused a riot with her stupidity, so I take another step forward to try and defuse the situation and get everyone to calm down.

"Will you guys go home and forget this ever happened if Bobbie apologizes and promises to never do anything like this again?" I ask the crowd.

There are a bunch of murmurs from the people as they talk amongst themselves. After a few minutes, one of the women speaks up.

"We will, but only if she apologizes *and* you take down that hideous display in the front yard. It's scaring small children, and we've had to start taking detours so we don't drive by the house. It's very inconvenient."

"HORSESHIT!" Reggie shouts. "That display is not coming down until the votes are tallied tomorrow night after trick-or-treat. I've got a title to defend!"

The group chuckles softly, and the woman with the demands speaks again.

"Reggie, have you even looked at the display across the street? It's the best one we've ever seen!"

Oh, no. Please, God, no.

"Such attention to detail. Did you see the jack-o'-lanterns? Those must have taken hours to carve."

"And the giant Jack Skellington? That was hand-painted. Best one I've ever seen."

"And the little dog, Zero! Did you guys see that his tail wags? I don't know how they did it, but it's adorable."

"Have you seen the projector in the front windows? It plays the movie against the glass. That's high-tech and awesome."

I watch silently as Reggie's face turns the color of a tomato, and I hope to God someone here has a nitroglycerin pill, because he's about two seconds away from having a full-blown heart attack.

Right when Reggie opens his mouth to let hellfire and brimstone rain down on everyone, Noel lets out her own bloodcurdling scream.

"SAAAAAAAAAAAAAAAAAAAM!"

Everyone turns in her direction, and my heart starts beating out of my chest when I see how flushed her face is.

"Honey? What's wrong?"

She mumbles something under her breath as she squeezes her eyes closed, and I notice beads of sweat popping out on her forehead.

"You're going to have to speak up. And just so you know, I can't take anything you say seriously right now when you're dressed like a kitchen appliance," Alex laughs.

"I'M IN MOTHER FORKING LABOR AND MY GOSH DINGED WATER JUST BROKE!" Noel screams at the top of her lungs.

"See? It sounds dumb when you're not using real swear words. I told you this was a stupid idea," Alex mutters.

My eyes widen in shock and my jaw drops when I look down at Noel's feet to see a small puddle of water.

In all the baby books I've read, they tell you not to panic. You should remain calm, have a plan, and follow it. But our plan wasn't supposed to go into effect for another week and OH MY FUCKING GOD MY WIFE IS IN LABOR!

"What do you need me to do?" I ask her when she bends at the waist and smacks her hand against the oven door of her costume, where a happy baby is lying on its back, looking out at everyone with a gummy smile.

"GET THIS STUPID SPORKING COSTUME OFF ME! I'M NOT GIVING BIRTH DRESSED LIKE AN OVEN WITH A BABY COOKING AT 450 DEGREES!" she screams through clenched teeth as she winces in pain with another contraction.

Everyone moves at once, helping me rip the cardboard box around Noel into a hundred pieces until she's standing next to me in a tank top and yoga pants, both of her hands flying to her stomach as she yells out in pain.

"I NEED A DOCTOR! SOMEONE GET ME A DOCTOR!" I scream at the top of my lungs.

No less than fifteen men and women in scrubs come running up to us, pushing people out of the way as they go. I roll my eyes as they hover around us.

"I meant *real* doctors," I complain, wondering why in the hell so many people decided to dress up as medical personnel for this wedding.

"We *are* real doctors!" they shout in unison.

I point at the guy standing closest to me.

"No, you aren't. Especially *you*, Greg. Alex and I work with you."

Greg from work moves closer to me and lowers his voice, looking back over his shoulder at Scheva.

"Scheva told us we had to stay in character today or she'd chop off our balls. But I saw a cow birth on TV once. I can totally do this. Have your wife take off her pants and get on all fours."

Before I can punch Greg in the face, Scheva comes rushing over to us and wraps her arms around Noel.

"I just called nine-one-one. Ambulance should be here any second now. Oh my God. You're going to have a baby today!" she tells Noel.

"Why in the hell would you call nine-one-one? My car is right out front," I remind Scheva.

"Um, because I don't have anyone wearing an EMS worker costume at my wedding, Sam. How will the pictures look if I don't have an EMS worker in the mix? Jesus, get your shit together, Sam," Scheva mutters with a roll of her eyes.

"I ruined your wedding," Noel sobs to her best friend.

Moving to stand in front of Noel, I take her face in my hands and wipe the tears from her cheeks as Scheva gives her a gentle squeeze.

"You didn't ruin anything. Your bun is coming out of the oven. It's perfect!" Scheva reassures her as we hear the wail of the ambulance siren out front.

Bending down, I scoop Noel up into my arms, and Alex and Scheva move in front of us, clearing a path and telling people to get out of the way. The paramedics meet us on the side of the house with a gurney, and they help me get Noel situated and buckled in. I grab her hand and give it a kiss as I run beside her, then help them load her into the back of the ambulance.

"Honey, we'll be right behind you! Make sure they save me a pair of scrubs for the delivery room!" Bev shouts to Noel with a wave as we both stare out at them through the ambulance doors.

"Make sure they save me the afterbirth! I hear it's high in protein!" Alex adds with a thumbs up.

The doors close with a slam and I sit down on the bench next to the gurney, one hand still holding tightly to Noel's as I use to other one to smooth sweaty strands of hair off her forehead and cheeks.

"We're going to have a baby," I whisper to her with a smile, my eyes filling with tears.

"We're going to have a baby," she whispers back as the paramedic starts an IV line in her other arm. "Please don't let any of those crazy people in the delivery room to stare at my vagina."

I chuckle softly before leaning down and kissing the top of her head. Noel squeezes my hand harder and starts taking chanting breaths through a contraction.

"I will guard the delivery room and your vagina with my life," I reassure her as the ambulance sails through intersections and stop signs and gets us to the hospital in record time.

Eleven
Stupid Man

Noel

"Honey, wake up. We're here."

The sound of Sam's voice stirs me awake, and I rub my eyes and sit up higher in the front seat of the car.

"Sorry I fell asleep," I tell him with a yawn as he unbuckles his seat belt.

"Noel, you just gave birth last night. You're allowed to sleep whenever you want," he tells me with a smile.

We both turn around and stare at the car seat in the back, our baby nestled in it, fast asleep.

"I can't even stand how beautiful she is," I whisper.

"Of course she's beautiful, have you seen her mother?"

Looking away from our daughter, I smile at my husband and lean over the center console to kiss him. Sam brings both of his hands up to cup my cheeks as I pull back, and stares into my eyes.

"Thank you for making me a father," he tells me softly, emotion filling his voice.

"Thank you for not wanting to divorce me when I saw her face and knew immediately what her name should be." I laugh softly.

Christmas Holiday Stocking, Christy for short, was born at exactly 12:01 a.m., making her the first official Halloween baby in our small town.

I know, I know. I refused to ever saddle my child with an insane name and carry on the tradition my family started, but I couldn't help it. I took one look at her perfect tiny pink lips, perfect pink cheeks, perfect pudgy little fingers, looked over at my family—who Sam was unable to keep out of the delivery room, all with tears falling down their cheeks, including my father—and knew I had no other choice.

As insane as my family is, they're still my family. I love them unconditionally, and I'm proud to be a part of them. I never want Christy to feel like she should be ashamed or embarrassed about being in this family, even though I'm sure everyone will give her plenty of reasons to feel that way. And on top of that, her father and I met at Christmas. Bringing him home from the airport bar was the best decision I ever made. I wouldn't have her if I never took that leap. And even though she's only been mine for sixteen hours, I can't imagine my life without her in it.

Tilting my head to the side and out of Sam's hands, I look over his shoulder and out the driver's side window in confusion.

"Wait, why are we parked across the street from my parents' house? I thought we were going home and everyone was coming over for an early dinner before trick-or-treating?" I ask.

Even though Halloween is my favorite night of the

year, I couldn't possibly be sad about missing it this year, when I'd be spending the evening staring at my daughter.

Sam doesn't say a word as he gets out of the car. I watch as he walks around the front of the vehicle, opening the backseat door behind me and carefully unbuckling Christy from her car seat. He gently lifts her out and tucks her against his chest before opening my door and holding out his hand for me.

He pulls me out of the front seat and closes the door behind me, wrapping his arm around my waist and turning the three of us away from the car, which is parked along the curb across from my parents' house.

"We are home," Sam tells me with a nervous smile.

He nods at the house we're standing in front of, the one across the street from my parents' house, and I stare up at him, my heart beating faster.

"What are you talking about?" I whisper.

Leaning down, he kisses the top of my head.

"Welcome home, baby."

My mouth opens and closes wordlessly as I look back and forth between my husband and the house of my dreams.

"No, you didn't . . ." I mutter, wondering if I'm still back at the hospital. Maybe I haven't really been discharged yet, and I'm still asleep in my hospital bed, having the best dream ever.

"I did. And, full disclosure, I haven't been working any overtime the last month. I've been busy getting these decorations built and set up."

I think someone needs to pinch me. Or throw a bucket of cold water on my face. My eyes quickly fill with tears, and the *Nightmare Before Christmas* yard decorations become one big blur.

"I can't believe you did this. You really bought me my

dream house? You really spent all this time decorating the front yard with things from my favorite movie?" I ask, the tears falling fast and hard down my face.

"Of course I did. As soon as the house went on the market, your mom called me and told me about it and how you'd always loved this house. I know you've been worried about being so far away from your family once Christy arrived, and I didn't want you to worry about anything. I want to make all your dreams come true, Noel, just like you've done for me."

Turning to face him, I wrap my arms around his waist, careful not to squish our sleeping daughter between us.

"But Alex is the only one who knew I actually bought the house and have been decorating it. I wanted to wait to tell everyone else until after I told you," he says with a smile, reaching up with his free hand to wipe the tears off my cheeks.

"How in the hell did you even manage to do all this without anyone seeing you?"

Sam gives me another heart-stopping smile.

"Are you forgetting I'm a Marine? I've trained for years for shit like this. I spent months canvassing the neighborhood at different times of the day throughout the week, so I knew when the neighbors wouldn't be home and I could unload all of my decorations and supplies into the garage. Then I'd get up in the middle of the night, while everyone was sleeping, don my camo gear, and creep around the yard in the dark, setting everything up."

The smile on my face immediately falls, and my happiness suddenly turns to worry.

"You bought me my dream house and spent all this time decorating the front yard," I say again, in a soft, nervous voice.

Sam laughs, looking down at me quizzically.

"Pretty sure we already established that."

I shake my head at him, trying to make him understand without screaming.

"You. Decorated. It."

Sam still isn't getting what I'm trying to say, and right when I open my mouth to spell it out, there's a loud commotion from across the street.

"SORRY, GUYS! I HAD TO SPILL THE BEANS!" Alex shouts from my parents' front porch as my dad shoves him out of the way and comes racing down the steps in our direction.

"Oh, shit. I decorated it," Sam mutters, finally understanding the gravity of the situation.

"I'LL KILL YOU, YOU LITTLE SHIT!" Dad screams as he trips over one of his clowns, quickly righting himself to continue charging across the yard toward us.

Sam hastily passes Christy over to me and gives me a kiss on the cheek. With one last look at the two of us, he glances over at my dad running full speed across the street and takes off running down the sidewalk.

"IF I DON'T SURVIVE THIS, TELL OUR DAUGHTER I LOVE HER AND I WAS ONCE A BRAVE MAN!" Sam shouts over his shoulder to me.

"DON'T YOU MEAN A STUPID MAN?" I yell back.

"THAT TOO!" Sam replies before he disappears around the corner of the block.

My dad makes it over to me and runs right by without a word, his sights set on my husband and how much bodily harm he can do if he manages to catch him.

"DAD! DON'T YOU DARE KILL MY HUSBAND!" I shout.

He ignores me and continues running, and I shake my head as Alex, Scheva, my mom, and Aunt Bobbie join me on the curb in front of my dream home.

My mom immediately takes Christy from my arms and starts cooing at her, running the palm of her hand gently over her soft, red hair.

"That blur who just ran past was your grandfather, Christy, and he's insane. Yes, he is. He's a crazy man!" my mom tells her in a lilting baby voice.

"Good news: I called the pumpkin farm and disguised my voice. They're delivering four cases of apple butter by tomorrow," Aunt Bobbie announces.

"And your Aunt Bobbie likes to do kinky things with apple butter," Scheva informs my daughter, bending down and kissing one of her pudgy little cheeks.

"Can we please hold off on teaching my child what kinky means?" I ask, watching everyone crowd around my mom and stare down at Christy with smiles on their faces.

"How long are we going to give those two idiots before someone goes after them?" Alex asks, staring off into the distance where Sam and my dad disappeared.

Scheva pulls her phone out of the pocket of her jeans and checks the time.

"We've got two hours before trick-or-treating starts. Let's go set up the fire pit in the driveway and the table of food and candy. If they're not back by the time we're finished, I'll go look for them," she tells us.

We all cross the street to my parents' house to get things ready, and I pause in the middle of the street, taking a moment to look back at the house Sam bought for me.

Who would have thought that almost three years ago, when I was unemployed, homeless, and alone, that I'd find the man of my dreams, fall in love, and have a baby, and that all of my dreams would come true?

Definitely not me, and yet, here I am. I don't know how life could get much better than this.

I join my family and friends in my parents' driveway. Alex has set up tables for us, and we set out all the treat bags, which no longer include illegal narcotics or sex toys; light the candles in all the jack-o'-lanterns spread around the front lawn and the white luminary bags lining the driveway; and start bringing out trays of food and coolers of drinks to share with the rest of the neighborhood.

Sam and my dad make it back to the house just as the first group of trick-or-treaters walks up the driveway, both of them calling a truce until the festivities are over. With Christy in her car seat on top of the table, sleeping through everything, I enjoy a few glasses of apple-pie moonshine with my husband, since I'm not nursing Christy; I decided to formula feed her for the sake of my own sanity. I daydream about all of the Halloweens we'll get to celebrate with my family, in the house across the street, with our very own trick-or-treaters and table full of goodies.

"Happy Halloween," I tell Sam with a smile as I wrap my arm around his waist and look up at him.

"Happy Halloween," he replies, leaning down to kiss the tip of my nose. "Don't worry, your dad won't kill me as long as I don't win the decorating contest. I already spoke with a bunch of the neighbors and told them not to vote for me this year, since technically we haven't been living in the house. But just be prepared. Next year, it's war."

I laugh and shake my head at him, knowing I'll never be able to believe my luck that I was able to find a man who fits in with this family so perfectly.

Tijan is the *New York Times* bestselling author of the Carter Reed series, the Fallen Crest series, and the Broken and Screwed series, among others. She lives in northern Minnesota.

J. Daniels is the *New York Times* and *USA Today* best-selling author of the Sweet Addiction series, the Alabama Summer series, and the Dirty Deeds series. J. grew up in Baltimore and resides in Maryland with her family.

New York Times and *USA Today* bestselling author of the Pucked series, **Helena Hunting** lives on the outskirts of Toronto with her incredibly tolerant family and two moderately intolerant cats. She writes contemporary romance ranging from new adult angst to romantic comedy.

Tara Sivec is a *USA Today* bestselling author and the Best Indie Author in the Indie Romance Convention Reader's Choice Awards in 2014. She lives in Ohio with her husband and two children.